MAN IN THE RING

A HISTORICAL FICTION NOVEL

By

Terry Williamson

Illustrated by Norman Johnson

ISBN-13: 979-8-9879789-0-0
ISBN: 979-8-9879789-1-7

In Memory of

Terry Lane Williamson
1946-2022

Terry
#60, Snyder High School Football
1963

Table of Contents

List of Illustrations
by Norman Johnson

Introduction

MAN IN THE RING

"It is not the critic who counts; not the man who points out how the strong man stumbles, or where the doer of deeds could have done them better. The credit belongs to the man who is actually in the arena, whose face is marred by dust and sweat and blood; who strives valiantly; who errs, who comes short again and again, because there is no effort without error and shortcoming; but who does actually strive to do the deeds; who knows great enthusiasms, the great devotions; who spends himself in a worthy cause; who at the best knows in the end the triumph of high achievement, and who at the worst, if he fails, at least fails while daring greatly, so that his place shall never be with those cold and timid souls who neither know victory nor defeat."

-Theodore Roosevelt
The Man in the Arena

Man in the Ring, for Terry Williamson, was a labor of love for over 10 years. Terry worked as a journalist and editor for the Midland Reporter-Telegram for 41 years and always dreamed of having his own published novel. Within Man in the Ring, you will find a historical fiction novel that includes Terry's actual 7th grade football schedule in Snyder, Texas and a small glimpse into his Vietnam career. While he continuously reminded his family that this, indeed, is a fiction story, there are many nods to Terry and the life experiences he lived. What is true and what is fiction, only Terry fully knows. He finished his manuscript just a few months before he passed away on April 29, 2022. One of his very last requests before meeting his Jesus, was to please get his book published. This copy is a dream realized and a legacy left for Terry's family and friends. We hope you enjoy The Man in the Ring.

MAY, 1970
Chui Lai, South Vietnam

Private First Class Noah "Cue Ball" Brantley walked with purpose down Chu Lai's sand-blown airstrip, looking for Spec. 4 Cody Joe Carter. Brantley continuously looked to his left and right, beginning to think he might fail in his mission. Where could Cody Joe be?

B Company of the 1/52nd Infantry was preparing to return to the bush for an extended mission in Happy Valley after a brief three-day re-fit in Chu Lai. Food, beverage and entertainment had flowed all three days as grunts got a rare break from the demands placed on them from the jungle.

But now, members of Bravo Company were lined up in two rows on opposite sides of the airstrip runway, waiting for eight helicopters to come for the pickup and a trip back to the jungle. The soldiers were matched in fours on each side of the airstrip, deployed perfectly for rapid boarding once the Hueys were safely on the ground.

Most of the Bravo Company members had been through this routine several times before. The choppers were still 20 to 30 minutes out, so there was time to work on equipment, talk or even sleep. Sleep was a bit tricky since the temperature hovered right around 110 degrees on the hot tarmac. Most were used to the heat from above, but not from the heat also radiating back from the bottom up. It was a nice recipe for getting a two-way burn.

Cody Joe, no stranger to the pickup procedure, knew the "hurry up and wait" routine as well as most. Carter even figured the choppers wouldn't be here for another 45 minutes tops. So, he found a tin structure about 25 yards from the runway that cast a long shadow from east to west. It was here that Carter was waiting for his ride while thinking about better times and how he longed to be home in more innocent days.

He thought about the great meals he could have sitting at Rue Carter's table. He thought of his days when he played baseball and football. Old friends and old girlfriends also crossed his mind. He even admitted that being back in school would be better than this. Heck, just about anything would be better than this.

It's a good bet that a majority of this 64-person contingent felt much like Cody Joe Carter. Depression was commonly associated with troops returning to the bush after some well-deserved time off. The depression would wear off in two or three days when the mundane work of soldiering found its way back into the lifestyle dedicated to the bush country.

With his eyes closed, Carter was deep in thought about better days when he was startled by Brantley's screaming voice, "Cody Joe, why are you way over here? Don't you know those choppers are going to land way over there?"

"Settle down, Cue," Carter said in a tone of chastisement. "Do you hear the rotors yet? They won't be here for some time. Meanwhile, I'm going to enjoy this shade. Sit down, join me and quit worrying about those choppers. By the way, where have you been?"

"Well, last night I got in this pool game over at the officer's club," Cue stated matter of factly. "I beat about four or five of them officers, but they wouldn't pay up. I beat them fair and square even if I wasn't supposed to be playing in their club. Those officers are more dishonest than any of us enlisted guys."

Carter let out a small giggle and offered, "So, you're takin' on the big dogs now? That cue stick is going to get you in deep trouble."

Cue answered, "Yeah, I know. I'm probably the only one in the whole unit that will be glad to get out of here. I heard a guy say this morning that some of the officers had reported me to the military police. They said the MPs were going to send a couple of guys over to the refit area to pick me up. I hope those choppers aren't too late because I just might not be going with you."

Brantley carried his cue stick with him everywhere, including the jungle. It was encased in a special water-proof case that was won by Cue during an all-night pool hall tournament in Leesville, La., on a weekend pass from basic training at Fort Polk. That was just one of many "tournaments" Cue had barely escaped with his life.

Cody Joe Carter and Noah "Cue Ball" Brantley were an odd set of friends cast together in an odd set of circumstances. Relationships between whites and blacks were only beginning to find a path of acceptance in 1970. In fact, neither Cody Joe nor Cue had even had a real conversation with a member of the opposite race until Vietnam.

Somehow, Vietnam had stripped the color from the skin. Cody Joe didn't even think of Cue as a black man. Instead, Carter only thought of Cue Ball as being much younger. Cody Joe was 24 and Cue was only 20. Still, they had become close by walking point, searching enemy caves and tunnels and sharing C-rations together. They had each other's back -- except for pool where Cue was on his own. Cue's infamous forays into the pool halls of Chu Lai were more adventurous than Cody Joe bargained for, even in Vietnam.

Cue liked the fact that Carter was never condescending. He could talk to Cody Joe like he was a brother and Cue never had a brother, only seven sisters. He always knew that Cody Joe appreciated him for what he could give to the platoon.

Cue was the best man in the platoon for walking point. No telling how many lives he had saved by discovering booby traps. He had even saved the life of a dog by discovering a thin trip wire across a jungle path. It was the dog that had been trained to find booby traps. Cue had proved his worth over and over. Besides, Cody Joe just liked Cue.

The two friends never even talked about race or what it was like growing up. That was probably because both possessed pent up fears that the relationship they now enjoyed would be endangered by harping on the past. Therefore, all talk between them centered on the present. The past extended only as far back as when the two first met almost three months ago. On that basis alone, they were equals and that's where they wanted this playing field centered.

Cody Joe rose up on one elbow when he thought he heard the whipping sound of a helicopter rotor blade. Sure enough, through a series of rising heat waves, Cody Joe could see the first of eight choppers moving in from the far side of the runway. Soon you could see all eight Hueys coming in to form a long line and each sitting down in their proper landing location almost simultaneously.

Carter and Brantley were already in place by the time the choppers landed and boarded the seventh helicopter in line. Each chopper had four soldiers sitting on opposite sides. There were no seat belts in place, only nature's centrifugal force to keep them from falling out.

Helicopter pilots always took a sharp turn at the beginning of the flight just to make sure all first time flyers got the true feeling of pending death. It's an experience none of them will ever forget. Cody Joe loved hanging over the edge while Cue Ball would rather face Charlie in the bush than fly in a helicopter without a seat belt. There was no question that Brantley was a black man, but he was doing his best imitation of turning purple. With ample grins on their faces, you can bet both pilots noticed.

After a flight of about 20 minutes, the eight choppers unloaded the cargo in much the same manner as they had loaded it. The choppers all hovered to within three feet of the ground as the troops disembarked with a short jump. It proved to be a clean landing with no injuries – and no incoming fire. That alone helped to calm the mindset of Bravo Company. Landing without a welcoming committee is the best news an infantry company can receive in the bush.

Next, marching orders came to proceed to a predetermined spot to set up base camp for the night. The march took a little over an hour at which time the troops made busy the tasks of digging foxholes, getting something to eat and getting bed rolls unpacked. Claymore mines were also deposited in advance of the large circle, ensuring that any military threat would have to penetrate two rings of firepower to obtain entry into the base ring.

"Can't you dig a little faster, Cue?" asked Carter. "You haven't even gotten deep enough to get past the worms."

Cue responded, "I can dig faster than you ever could, Cody Joe, but I'm still not feeling too well after that copter ride. There was a time there that I was wishing the MPs had caught up with me."

Carter said, "Forget the MPs and get to digging. They really don't want to take anyone down that's willing to return to the bush. You're home now, so act like it."

Cody Joe drew the first guard shift that would last until midnight. He would wake up Cue when his shift ended and Cue would wake up the next on the list at 2 a.m. It was at this lonely time that Cody Joe once again felt depression descending upon his soul.

He tried to find a more comfortable position on top of his foxhole, but didn't have much luck. That seemed to fit his mood. It would be asking too much to take the edge off the depression while being more comfortable at the same time. That was Nam for you.

Still, Cody Joe began to think of the better days of his youth. He wondered if that time had forever passed him or if he would ever return to experience some of those carefree moments again. He hoped so.

Chapter 1

SUNDAYS

Snyder, Texas, 1958

In Cody Joe Carter's way of thinking, Sunday mornings were made for the Baptist, Methodist and the Church of Christ. Even 12-year-old Cody Joe knew this was nothing more than a convenient theology, but it fit his lifestyle close enough for him to slide past all the other religious denominations.

After all, this was the "Big Three" on the religious front of Snyder, a small West Texas community nestled right in the middle of oil, cattle and cotton country. It has been said that the only other real religion in town was Friday night football and it unanimously held sway over the hearts of all 12-year-old boys, who dreamed of one day playing in Tiger Stadium. Cody Joe was no exception.

And while football was never far from the thoughts of those who made a living in this land of contrasts, Sundays were left for church. If you lived in Jack Carter's house, your behind owned a spot on a pew at Colonial Hill Baptist Church on Sunday morning. Cody Joe never questioned the pre-ordained status of Sunday morning because he had never experienced anything else. If he wasn't on his deathbed, vacation or offered a rare divine intervention, Cody Joe was sitting on the second row from the back on Sunday at Colonial Hill, trying not to catch the attention of the pastor or his parents.

As far as the other denominations were concerned, the

Carter family often passed the First Christian Church on 37th Street, which was on the way to Colonial Hill, but Cody Joe easily dismissed this church because he never knew anyone who went there. There was a Catholic church on the east side of town, but Cody Joe had never even seen it. He was pretty sure a Mexican kid in his school went there because Cody Joe had seen him make the sign of the cross one day on the playground at school. Cody Joe also knew that other Catholics were in town because he didn't think they would serve fish in all the schools on Friday if there weren't more than one Mexican kid who was a Catholic.

Yes, Cody Joe was well aware of a diverse religiosity in the community, but the fact was that he just didn't know many of them, or they simply kept it to themselves. His friends were all members of the "Big Three." James "Pug" Preston, Cody Joe's best friend in the whole world, was a Methodist. Rick Tracks, known only as "Tracks" in the neighborhood, attended the Church of Christ, and, of course, Cody Joe was a Southern Baptist. Once again the "Big Three" of Cody Joe's gang also attended the "Big Three" denominations. It wasn't exactly a Holy Trinity, but it was enough for Cody Joe to put a firm stamp on his teetering theology. After all, he was just 12 years old.

And even though Cody Joe accepted his "Big Three" on near equal terms, he was observant enough to recognize that there was a certain amount of contention even among the threesome of frontrunners. Cody Joe had seen some rather heated "arguments" over religion between his dad, Jack, and his aunt, Wanda Carter, a devout member of the Church of Christ. Wanda was Jack's sister-in-law and it was not a rare occurrence to find them locked in heated debate over a particular scripture from the Bible.

Cody Joe asked his Dad more than once what he and

Aunt Wanda were fighting about. Jack always had the same answer, "Oh, son, we aren't fighting. We're just having a little discussion over the meaning of a scripture. Your aunt and I never fight."

Somewhere in the middle of that explanation was a semblance of truth. Aunt Wanda and Jack rarely agreed over the meaning of scripture, but their disputes never seemed to interfere with the workings of the extended family. In fact, Aunt Wanda and Jack actually seemed to care for each other, extending the proverbial olive branch more often than not.

* * *

Also, in Cody Joe's way of thinking, if Sunday mornings were made for church, then Sunday afternoons were made for baseball. For Carter, this simple summer activity on each and every summer Sunday afternoon was a matter of sacred honor and binding tradition. It was right up there with church on the priority list, so it was a bit tough for the youngster to last through the last "Amen" of the church service, the final signal that it was now time to play baseball. On this particular Sunday, Cody Joe was most anxious to get to Towle Memorial Park where this second Sunday rite would be performed.

As soon as the church service had dismissed, about 10 minutes late according to Cody Joe's calculations, he headed straight for the car, hoping that his mad dash would signal to other family members an urgency to get home for lunch. The ploy didn't work at all. It was three or four minutes before younger brother Chip slid into the back seat with Cody Joe. Sister Kate, the middle of the Carter siblings, showed up in another four or five minutes as Cody Joe steamed.

Jack and Rue Carter were left glad-handing friends and church acquaintances as they moved slowly toward the car. Cody Joe silently wondered if his Mom and Dad were going to shake hands with every member of the church before leaving. His greatest fear was that the two would then simply turn and talk to each other after the parking lot had cleared.

It was a good 15 minutes after the final "Amen" before the Carter family was headed home. As usual, Rue would have a pot roast in the oven ready to go. She would whip up some luscious mashed potatoes to go with a variety of corn, green beans and brown gravy. It was the standard Sunday fare, a menu that only changed if the family ever ate out or were visitors in another home, both rare occasions.

Rue always got a meal on the table quickly, but it wasn't quick enough for Cody Joe on this special day. Chip, four years younger than Cody Joe, had no Sunday afternoon agenda and took his time about eating. He also ate a lot. Cody Joe kept taking food away from him. Kate, two years younger than Cody Joe, got up during the middle of the meal to change out of a gravy-stained blouse.

"What's wrong with these people?" Cody Joe wondered. "Nobody seems to care that this is baseball Sunday."

Finally, after what seemed like agonizing hours, the family meal ended and Rue Carter dismissed the troops for the afternoon. Jack headed for his lounge chair to catch his usual 20-minute nap. Rue started washing the dishes, but a nap was also in her immediate future while Kate went to her room to do whatever fifth-grade girls do on Sunday afternoon. Cody Joe had no clue on this front. Chip also retired to the room he shared with Cody Joe. It was here that Chip pelted a barrage of questions at Cody Joe about where he was going. Cody Joe remained vague as usual. He didn't want Chip showing up to ruin this unique day. Cody Joe just knew that Chip would end up in the middle of his stuff before the afternoon was over, but he couldn't concern himself with that prospect right now.

Cody Joe put on some well-worn tennis shoes and some

Levi jeans. He then picked up his glove, hat, bat and two balls. Cody Joe somehow packed all his gear onto his Schwinn English racer and without another moment of hesitation, he was off to the park for a landmark afternoon.

This was the last Sunday of the summer season. There would be no more Sunday afternoon baseball, and as far as Cody Joe knew, this could be the final baseball outing of his life because he would be entering Snyder Junior High School as a seventh-grader in just over a week. Starting Monday morning, Cody Joe was to begin football two-a-days. This was the start of his new life. He had only this afternoon to finish his old life. He had never seen any seventh-graders playing baseball on Sunday afternoons, so he naturally wondered if this truly was the end of baseball as he knew it. Cody Joe wanted this last day of baseball to be special – and it would help if he wasn't late for the sacred occasion.

Chapter 2

THE DAY BASEBALL SHUT DOWN

Cody Joe's racer zoomed past Snyder High School on Austin Ave. and down toward the entrance of Towle Memorial Park. Carter then hung a quick right in back of the baseball practice facility and in front of the SHS football practice fields and flew onward toward a more western park entryway. This time he hung a left and powered his way into the park at blazing speed toward the National Guard Armory. From here, it was a hard uphill sprint that led to the city's Little League complex. First was Little League's main field, but no one was allowed to play on this field even after the season. But it was from there that Cody Joe first saw eight figures gathered at the B League diamond where today's last baseball rites would take shape.

"Cody Joe, where you been, man?" screamed a disgusted James "Pug" Preston. "We've all had a turn at bat already. If you're going to play, you'll already be behind in points. That's just the way it goes. You're late."

This was news Cody Joe had feared. The pastor had preached too long, Jack and Rue had talked too much, Kate tried to be a fashion model and that pesky Chip tried to set a world record eating pot roast. His worst fear on the last day of baseball had finally become a reality. He was officially late and Pug was first to let him know it.

Still, Cody Joe's arrival was enough to stop the game. Everyone ran to the gate to greet the late entry. No one really doubted that Cody Joe would be late without a good reason.

"C.J., you plannin' on playin' today," teased Kevin Tumbler. "We could put this whole thing off until around 3 p.m. if you ain't ready to play. We don't want to interfere with your schedule."

"Shut up, Tumbler." Cody Joe snapped. "Let's play some ball."

"Oh, we've been playing, Carter. You've been the holdup," chimed in Stacy Trout, who had arrived only moments before Cody Joe. "Pug's right though. You missed your bat and everyone scored at least two points, so we go into the second round with you way behind."

Also on hand was John "Butch" Cassidy, a rotund, but powerful kid who could easily run through a wall without damaging his pea-sized brain. In fact, Cody Joe had theorized that when God made Butch, he spent too much time putting together the big arms and big legs and not enough time on the intelligence factor. But make no mistake, Butch could play sports with the best of them and offer no apologies.

Joining Butch was Rick Tracks, one of Cody Joe's best friends, and the threesome of Wayne Lock, Henry Styles and John Clint. The weekly Sunday game was really open to anyone and guys from all over town participated from time to time. The last three were not really regulars to the Sunday event, but they were here today and more than welcome.

Cody Joe knew Lock even though they weren't close friends. Styles lived just down the street from Cody Joe and the two had tossed a football back and forth on a few occasions. Clint was the stranger of the group and had never played ball with this group of guys. He was riding his bike through the park when Pug asked him if he wanted to join in. Pug always brought an extra glove for such occasions. Clint had jumped at the opportunity, telling Pug, "I love to play baseball."

So, with Cody Joe now in hand, today's tearful farewell to baseball totaled nine participants. The largest number to ever turn out had been 14, but the average Sunday showing stood around six or seven.

Since there was never a full contingent of 18 to form two complete teams, Sunday afternoon rules were a bit different than regular baseball. Actually, the game played here had little to do with the real game of baseball other than the hitting, throwing and running.

The guys called this game "Move Up." There could be a game with just about any number over four. The idea was to move up from position to position until it was your turn to be the batter. It was while batting you could score points for yourself. You got to bat until you made three outs. Outs were recorded just like in baseball by strikeouts, groundouts and fly outs. The pitcher had the authority to move the defensive guys where he wanted them. The batter scored points when he hit safely; one point for a single, two for a double, three for a triple and four for a homerun. Only three points were awarded for an inside the park homer. You had to hit it over the Little League fence to get all four points. Each player kept his running total of points throughout the day and this usually caused the biggest bone of contention when the day was done. When a batter made three outs, he would go to left field and continue moving up until he was back in the batter's box. This would usually keep the game rolling until around 4:30 p.m. or so.

Tracks inherited the batter's box when play resumed. He nailed a single to start the new rotation, but then quickly made three outs to bring Cassidy to the plate. Cody Joe was close to Tracks, but not as close as he was to Pug. Cody Joe and Pug were just about tied at the hip. Tracks, however, was still a loyal friend to Cody Joe. If there was a problem at all, Pug and Tracks didn't always get along. They, for sure, were not best friends. There was no hatred here, but there may have been a little jealous zeal emanating from each other's friendship with Cody Joe. If that were the case, Cody Joe was completely oblivious to the well-hidden friction.

As usual, Cassidy put on a hitting display, racking up 21 points to go with his towering shot to right field that landed in the outfield of the adjacent A League diamond. Styles had to chase the ball down, which meant meandering his way through two gates. Everyone yielded a sigh of relief when Butch's hitting turn was over. The only way they ever got him out was that the heavy-set Cassidy wore himself out running the bases.

And thus it went throughout the afternoon. Few skirmishes erupted and no ill-feelings were created other than the fact that Lock decided he liked Pug's extra glove better than his own and appropriated it from Clint without even asking. Clint didn't really confront Lock about "stealing" the borrowed glove since the glove really wasn't his in the first place. Clint had found new friends and didn't want to cause a row. Unfortunately, this friendship wasn't going to continue anyway since Clint would only be entering the sixth grade when school started next week while all the rest were headed for the seventh grade and different schools.

Lost in the glorious West Texas afternoon sunshine were the thoughts of this being the last Sunday baseball game – maybe forever. They were having too much fun to think of the heavy and somber repercussions of ending an endless summer of Sunday baseball and walking into a man's world – or, at least, into the world of the seventh grade – when a new day dawned.

The game had ended when Trout fell rounding first base while trying to extend a single into a double. He planted his face in the dirt and sent dust flying in all directions. The dirt was so loose around the first base area from all the day's activity that Trout literally disappeared into oblivion.

"Guys, I can't go anymore," Trout said while climbing out of his dusty haze. "I'm so tired I don't know how I'm even going to get my bike back home."

No one argued. In fact, there seemed to be a rather quick progression toward the third base dugout where the afternoon shadows now extended all the way out to the third base foul line. The Sunday Summer League had officially ended without fanfare or remorse. Everyone was simply too tired to object and all relished the thought of collapsing in the shade.

No one was surprised to learn that Butch led the way with 124 points on the afternoon. Stacy Trout was a distant second at 84 points and was followed by Pug with 75. Surprisingly, the young Clint was fourth with 73. Carter was close behind with 70 and was sure his standing in the game rested squarely on the shoulders of Chip Carter, who ate too much pot roast, costing Cody Joe a whole turn at the plate.

As winner of the game, Butch Cassidy was the first awarded access to the park's water hose and he let it run a few seconds before some cool liquid finally came forth. He then drank like he was intent on emptying Lake J.B. Thomas, the source of Snyder's water supply.

It was several minutes before anyone said a word. Everyone took a turn at getting water from the hose and then returned to the shade with each lying silently on their backs.

Finally, Cody Joe broke the silence, saying, "This is it guys. This could very well be our last chance to play baseball with each other. Starting tomorrow we start football and who knows if we will ever return with this group to ever play baseball again."

"Aren't you turning a little dark on us, Cody Joe?" asked Tumbler. "I'm not even going to play football. I'm going to be in the band. You guys probably won't even talk to me in the hallways after next week."

"We'll always talk to you, Tumbler," said Cassidy. "You'll just be tootin' for us now."

For sure, Cassidy was already in high form for junior high humor and his statement brought out a roar of laughter.

"I'm not going to try out for football either," offered Trout, "but I think we should all make a pack that we will meet here on the first Sunday afternoon after school is out to play baseball. We can do that, can't we?"

Even Styles and Lock agreed to this new bond. The young Clint was quickly beginning to understand that he did not own a long-term place in this new society. He had not even thought about going into junior high school. These guys were out of his league. He suddenly felt small despite his respectable point total in Move Up.

Tracks took the conversation to an even deeper level. "Hey guys, I'm a bit worried about tomorrow. I don't know if I can make the football team or not. I never did make Little League and I had to play in the B League two years. Most of you guys had at least one or two years in Little League."

Tumbler tried to take the edge off for Tracks by saying, "Oh, you'll make it, Tracks. After all, you don't even have to beat me out." However, Tumbler noticed that Tracks never smiled at the joke attempt. Tracks was really worried he wouldn't make the team.

Secretly, Tracks wasn't the only one with fears about tomorrow's football debut. Cody Joe felt the same pangs of anxiety. He, too, had not been selected to play Little League in his first year of eligibility. He still harbored nightmares from that horrendous Sunday he still claims as the worst day of his life. He remembered it clearly as though it was yesterday.

He was in the fourth grade when he was first able to try out for a team. Cody Joe thought things went well in the try-out. He caught two of three fly balls, was perfect on fielding his three grounders and even got one solid hit during his at-bat.

Following the tryout, the team rosters were to be published in the Sunday edition of the Snyder Daily News. Cody Joe fervently searched for his name when the paper came out. He poured over the list, two then three and four times. He simply wasn't listed.

Rue and Jack Carter already knew the verdict. They had gotten to the paper even before Cody Joe. Besides, Jack had heard that the coaches had called all their new players the night before the paper was published and the Carters had been home all night. The simple truth was Cody Joe did not get picked.

Cody Joe was literally sick in the stomach. How could he ever face his friends again? As far as Cody Joe Carter was concerned, life had come to an end. He had already decided he was never going to church or school again. How could he ever face the gang and how would he explain that he wasn't good enough to play Little League? Carter had already seen that both Pug and Butch had been placed on teams. Their names were in the paper. Only Cody Joe and Tracks were omitted, forgotten as worthless meat in a heap of neglected garbage. Cody Joe's ego and confidence had never been the same after that, even though more than three years had since passed.

Rue Carter was furious. She didn't think it was right to publish the names in the paper, leaving only ridicule and disappointment to those not chosen. It was a bit like choosing sides on the playing field, but worse. Even the last one chosen in that format got a chance to play. Nothing is worse than not being chosen at all.

Trout was the first to call it the end of summer, saying, "I guess I better get home. We've laid around here longer than usual."

The group moseyed over to the stand of bikes and one by one started down the hill toward the National Guard Armory and on to the park entry where trails divided and summer ended.

Pug and Cody Joe were the last to leave, as usual. They diligently checked to see if all equipment had been picked up and did find one of Tumbler's lost balls lodged in the backstop's chain link fence.

The two then made their way to the bike stand for the final time before Cody Joe broke the silence, "Pug, to tell you the truth, I'm just as scared as Tracks about not being able to make the football team. It's happened once before, you know."

Pug couldn't believe what he was hearing and said so. "Cody Joe, this is completely different from Little League. First, you're great at football. You made All-Stars in the Boys' Club last fall and you had that big sack in the All-Star game. I'll bet our coaches saw that play. There ain't no coach in football that's going to kick you off the team. You have nothing to worry about, but I am a bit concerned about Tracks. I'm not sure he's got what it takes for football. Shoot, he's better at baseball than football, and he never even made it in baseball. You still got to play in Little League for two years."

Cody Joe replied, "It'll be a bummer if Tracks gets cut. Heck, it'll be a bummer if I get cut. I'm going to give it my best shot and see what happens, but if I get cut, it's going to be like I've died for the second time. I just don't know if I can handle that again."

Chapter 3

DRESSING

Early Monday morning Rue Carter walked in quick step down the hallway toward the bedroom shared by Cody Joe and Chip. When Rue entered the room, she was utterly shocked to find that Cody Joe's bed was empty. It was not made up; otherwise, this unexpected event might have been too much for her heart.

For one thing, Cody Joe rarely got up this early on his own initiative. In fact, Rue could only remember one other time when Cody Joe got up before 6 a.m. without literally being dragged out of bed. That was a year ago when Jack promised to take Cody Joe on a fishing trip. Jack got up at 4 a.m. and Cody Joe was already waiting in the pickup when Jack finally opened the door leading to the garage.

Rue found Cody Joe this time eating a bowl of cereal at the kitchen countertop. It was the only breakfast feast that Cody Joe knew how to make. He didn't like cereal much, but it would do when he was in a hurry. Today, he was in a hurry.

"Hi, Mom," said the cheerful Cody Joe. "I hope it won't take you long to get dressed. We need to get going because we have to pick up Pug and Tracks along the way."

"Cody Joe you must be crazy," said Rue, shaking her head while posing with closed fists stuck to her hips in a stance of admonishment. It's still two hours before you even have to be there. Why are you in such a hurry?"

"Mom, this is the first day of football. We have to be there early. We want to make an impression on the first day," said

Cody Joe, sounding a bit like begging instead of explaining.

"Well, Cody Joe, you can't make an impression if the coaches aren't even there. They won't be there this early," Rue reasoned. "Now, go get ready and I'll make sure all three of you get to the field house on time. No, I promise to get you there early."

Cody Joe felt as if he had at least extracted a promise from his Mother. If she said they would be there early, she would keep her promise. She always did. Cody Joe never doubted that.

It still seemed like a long time before Rue finally gave the signal to leave the house. As soon as she reached for her purse and set off the jingle of car keys, Cody Joe was out the door and sliding into the front seat of the family car, a 1955 green and white Chevy.

Rue picked up Pug first and then Tracks. Both boys were outside sitting on the front porch, waiting for their ride. Rue was beginning to understand the importance of the day at hand. She dearly hoped the boys wouldn't be the last to arrive. She would never have their trust again.

The Carter automobile arrived about 7:40 a.m., a full 20 minutes before reporting time. There were already about 30 boys waiting outside the field house, but fortunately for Rue Carter, the coaches had yet to make an appearance. The door to the field house was still closed with a posted sign that read, "Stay Out." The threesome was in uniform agreement that Rue could leave now since her mission had been performed. "Just pick us up at noon," Cody Joe reminded.

Cody Joe, Pug and Tracks quickly found Butch Cassidy and all four noticed how many people had turned out for the first day. Once again, Cody Joe and Tracks had an anxiety attack. They couldn't possibly keep all these kids.

These unnerving thoughts blew away with the cool morning breeze when the door to the field house suddenly flew open. Out walked three coaches and they stood side-by-side on the porch platform that led into the field house, which was nothing more than an old converted Army barracks.

In the center of the group, there stood Coach Jimmy Lee Heart. He was entering his third year as head coach of the Snyder Junior High School seventh grade Blue Devils. Coach Heart was built like a rock with muscles on top of muscles. He wasn't that tall, but he was in great shape. He was first to blow a whistle.

"OK, guys stand still," Coach Heart opened. "Coach Bear get a head count for me. Let's see what we've got here."

Coach Bear was Bear Hixler. No one, except maybe Robert Tankard, the principal at SJHS, actually knew Bear's real first name. He was short and a bit rotund, but his total loyalty was to Coach Heart. Most kids ended up loving Coach Bear because he was fair and always upbeat. He even liked being around the kids.

"Coach Heart, I've got a count of 81 kids," Bear said when his count was complete.

"Well, guys, this seventh grade class has just set a Blue Devil record for the most players to ever try out for football," Coach Heart said. "We really weren't expecting this many kids, but we're hoping there are some real football players out there. If you are good enough to play, we will find you.

"I have only three rules and they must be followed at all times if you want to be a Blue Devil," Heart added. "First, the coaches are the boss at all times. If you don't understand that, leave now. Second, when a coach blows a whistle, you listen. And third, if a coach tells you to do something, you do it, or die trying. If you follow those rules, we will get along. If you don't, well, you won't be a part of this team anyway."

This no-nonsense approach left this particular crowd with

a bunch of wide eyes and lowered expectations of ever becoming a football player.

The other coach was Tom Nix. It was probably by design that Nix said nothing during this quick introduction. It had been said that Coach Nix had a bit of a mean streak in him. Most kids feared the path he walked because he had a booming voice and he wasn't afraid to use it while in your face. He could make a point better than most and he really never cared much about making lifetime friends. The kids would meet him up close and personal in due time.

"Here's what is going to happen today," Coach Heart continued. "This morning will be devoted to two objectives. We hope to equip all of you with football gear. That may be impossible since we have far more kids here than we expected, but I promise all of you that we will get the right equipment for you in time.

"Second, we have two doctors coming here this morning and all 81 of you will have to pass a physical before being allowed to play. At some point, you will be asked to stand in a line to go through this procedure and we expect you to be quiet and follow simple instructions.

"The doctors are not here yet, so let's start by issuing equipment. Each of you will get a football helmet, fitted by one of us three coaches. We have three eighth grade managers that will aid us in passing out jerseys, football pants, knee pads, thigh pads, jockey strap, hip pads, T-shirt, socks and shoulder pads. When you get all of this, we will work together on getting you your first set of shoes with football cleats. OK, line up at the door."

It was going to be a major problem fitting uniforms for 81 kids, so Heart sent two of his managers over to the eighth grade complex at the other end of the field to gather up any leftover equipment the eighth grade coaches weren't planning on using. All in all, they could take care of most of the boys. There weren't enough helmets or knee pads, but they could get by for a day or two by sharing. Heart knew by experience some of these kids would be dropping out sooner than later.

There was some major jostling for line position in the equipment room with the thinking that the ones in front of the line had a better chance of getting equipment that fit. Of course, that brought on a whistle from Coach Nix, who bellowed out, "I better see this line straighten up now or I'm coming down there to do it myself."

The unruly crowd suddenly became the Sunday choir. They filed into the field house in perfect harmony under the watchful eye of Coach Nix. He pulled one rowdy boy aside and kept his hand on the boy's shoulder until the end of the line. He then let him go in. And the first day of football had begun.

* * *

The process wasn't what one would call a well-oiled machine, but considering the circumstances, it could at least be considered controlled chaos. First of all, the boys went through the equipment line. The equipment was a load even for the larger boys to carry. Some of the smaller hopefuls had to have help getting their equipment to their lockers.

Coach Heart told the youngsters that they could pick any locker space they wanted when they got through the equipment line. Cody Joe, Pug, Tracks and Cassidy had stayed together the whole time despite their first encounter with Coach Nix. Still, they had to go to the back of the field house to find four lockers together. Cody Joe picked a locker on the very corner of the room. The locker next to his on the wall going down the other side of the room had a busted bench and some clothes hooks missing. Cody Joe reasoned no one would want that locker, so he could use it for extra space.

Naturally, Tracks couldn't carry all his equipment to his locker, so Cassidy went back to help him. When the task was accomplished, Tracks admitted, "I'm already tired and we don't even have practice until this afternoon."

Cassidy replied, "I think you will know what tired really means when this afternoon is over. This ain't nothin', boy."

Cody Joe was the first of his group to get in line for a helmet. All four boys were eager to get a set of low cut spikes, but all four got a pair of old-fashioned high tops with old rubber cleats. Not only did they look terrible, but there were rumors in the field house that the high tops caused severe blisters until your feet adjusted.

The coaches already had an idea who could play and who couldn't. They had already talked to many of the men that worked with this age group in the Boy's Club youth football league. All the speed guys and known running backs got the low cuts. The fearsome foursome was quickly learning that there was a definite caste system even in football. The best got the best and the rest got the rest.

Cody Joe was philosophical about the whole thing, saying, "At this point, I'm just glad to have a uniform. I'm going to show them I can play even if I have to dress in my sister's tutu."

Cody Joe fared better with his helmet. It fit snug against the head and the chin strap, and when buckled, held the helmet firm and in place. Tracks could nearly turn around in his helmet while Cassidy and Pug knew there were better helmet fits out there, but when they really cinched down the chin strap, everything seemed to be just fine. It was a well-known fact that seventh graders were at the bottom of the football food chain and got a lot of equipment that was passed down from one year to the next.

When everyone had their gear, Coach Heart issued an order for everyone to put it on and form four lines outside. "Do it now and do it fast," Coach Heart said. "And be sure to pay close attention to those thigh pads. If you put them in the wrong way, you will be singing two octaves higher come tomorrow morning. They can crush your valuables. It'll take only one time for you to learn how to get those pads in right."

Again, teamwork proved valuable to Cody Joe's group. Pug finished first and he helped Cody Joe finish out. Cassidy had a hard time figuring out the pads, but Tracks was finally able to help him. Everyone needed help getting the jersey over the shoulder pads. A lot of kids without close friends had trouble getting the full uniform on. Everyone in Carter's group was good about aiding others around them.

Not all were so helpful. Two big guys, Dirk Bolger and Mac Cone, had lockers in the middle aisle right across from Tracks and Cassidy. Next to them was Kirby Tanner, a small but fast kid, who obviously had never been around a lock-er room. He had the misfortune of asking Bolger and Cone what he was supposed to do with the jock strap.

Bolger quickly explained, "Oh, Kirby, that's a nose guard. That middle webbing goes over your nose and then you stretch those straps over your head. Your helmet will keep it all in place when you get it on."

Cone took up on the joke, adding, "That's right, Tanner. Just like that. Remember most people in here don't know what that thing is for, so you may be one of the few to have it on right when you get outside. We'll really impress the coach if we are the only ones to put it on correctly.

With that, the fully dressed Kirby Tanner proudly marched outside with his "nose guard" firmly in place. He was highly pleased when he got outside and no one had their "nose guard" on in the proper position.

Cody Joe and Pug failed in an attempt to keep from laughing out loud, but the joke also bothered them a great deal. Tanner was going to be humiliated in front of everyone. Cody Joe knew in his heart that the jockstrap incident would be big news all over school next week. He couldn't imagine what it would be like to be known as the kid who wore his jockey strap over his nose. Still, Cody Joe let the prank run its course.

Coach Bear was the first to notice even before the official uniform inspection, saying, "Oh my gosh son, that's not where your jockstrap goes. This goes around your crotch to protect the valuables. Who told you how to put this on?"

"Well, Coach, Bolger and Cone showed me. It didn't seem right, but they said they were going to do it," answered Tanner.

About that time Bolger and Cone came outside for the inspection with no jock strap hanging from their noses. Coach Bear called, "Bolger and Cone come over here. Did you guys tell Tanner to put his jock strap over his nose?"

They both meekly answered in unison, "Yes, sir."

"Then strip down right out here on the grass and put on

your jockstraps just like you told Tanner. Then get dressed again and start running laps around that track over there until I tell you to stop. Let's just see if you gave out proper instructions to a teammate on the function of a jockstrap. You should know by the end of a few laps."

There was no laughter at this point. The seventh grade Blue Devils were already learning that teammates should be taking care of each other.

* * *

The equipment inspection was relatively smooth. Four players had put their thigh pads in backwards and all four were well aware that some bodily furniture needed moving down below. The pressure from the thigh pads for Hank Cline was so severe, he was about to turn green. Even though everyone was laughing at him, he was more than grateful that there was an actual solution for the problem.

The coaches decided to change out a few helmets, there were some equipment issues and some of the kids couldn't wear the shoes they had been given. All in all, everything was fixable, and for Coach Heart, that was great news for what he considered the very worst part of the season. He thought this was about as good as it gets for a record 81 kids.

Bolger and Cone had missed the inspection. They were still running laps while breathing through a briefly used jockstrap. Coach Bear finally called them in as Coach Heart gave orders for the rest to return to the field house, undress down to their underwear and form two lines in front of the training room for the physicals. The doctors had arrived in almost perfect timing.

Coach Bear stopped Bolger and Cone. He gave them a brief equipment inspection, and if there was anything wrong, neither Bolger nor Cone was going to point it out. They were dead tired and did not want to spark the ire of Coach Bear ever again.

"Did you guys learn how to properly wear a jockstrap on your little run today?" Coach Bear asked.

"Yes sir," both answered in an unsurprising response.

Coach Bear then firmly stated, "I hope you two jokers will be better teammates this afternoon. You both owe Tanner an apology and I expect each of you to man up and do it. I personally hope he beats both of you in practice this afternoon.

"And by the way, you both can now go get in line for your physical, but just keep your famous nose guard in place so everyone else on the team can see an example of what pulling pranks can get you with the Blue Devils. Oh, and make sure you are at the end of the line."

Cody Joe was the first to undress. No one had taken the locker next to him as he expected, so he put some of his equipment over in that locker and invited others of his group to do the same. Once again the four friends stayed together and got in line for their physicals.

When everyone was in line, Coach Heart gave a toot on his whistle and said, "The doctors are going to check you out and you do exactly as he asks."

Joey Taylor, a stout kid, was first in line. The doctor said, "Pull down your shorts, it's time for a little physical exam."

Taylor was shocked and that was before the doctor poked his forefinger into the corner of the family jewels. The doctor said, "Now, turn your head and cough."

There were giggles all through the two lines, leading Coach Heart to say, "What's so hard about turning your head and coughing. Just do it."

The doctors made note and then moved on listening to the heartbeat, testing blood pressure, etc. So it went on down the line. No matter how many times it was seen, it was always a surprise when the doctor went for the valuables and there were some awfully strained coughs along the way.

The physicals concluded the morning session and Coach Heart reminded them that the afternoon practice would begin sharply at 4 p.m. The kids were asked to be dressed and ready to go by starting time.

Rue Carter had been waiting only five minutes when Cody Joe, Pug and Tracks came through the gate headed for the car. Rue was anxious to hear about the day and asked, "What did you boys do this morning?"

Cody Joe answered, "Oh, Mom, not much. We learned how to put on a jockstrap and how to turn our head and cough."

Of course, there was laughter all around and Rue Carter was well aware that she had been the target for some well-placed junior high humor. She just let it go as all three boys continued with a bout of uncontrollable laughter.

Chapter 4

FIRST PRACTICE

The best way to cross town to get to the practice field was to go down 30th Street until you ran into the field house at Ave. M. That was a straight shot. Everyone who lived in Snyder considered everything east of Big Spring Street the eastern part of town, but if the truth be known, Snyder Junior High School was more in the central part of the community.

As streets go, Ave. M was about as diverse as there was in Snyder. SJHS was at the corner of 26th Street and Ave. M and the campus covered about two blocks. On the south side of the school grounds set the old high school gymnasium. SJHS was once the site of Snyder High School. That school had suffered a terrible fire three decades before and was rebuilt and eventually turned into the junior high when Snyder built a new high school on the west part of the city, near where Cody Joe now lived. The gym was a survivor from the old high school days. It was two blocks further south where the football field and two field houses were located. Another two blocks on Ave. M placed you right in the middle of "colored town."

This is where most of Snyder's black community resided. You could travel all the way across Snyder from east to west by taking 37th Street. You could turn north onto Ave. M from 37th Street to gain access to the practice field and SJHS, but few of the white folks choose that route just to avoid going through "colored town."

It was this dynamic that pretty much kept blacks and whites separated in this era and one of the contributing factors that had kept Cody Joe Carter from ever talking to a black, save the shoe shine man that owned a subterranean shop just off the square, the hub of downtown Snyder.

There was even a high school, Lincoln, in "colored town" that served as the black community school since Snyder was still very much a segregated population. And even though the seventh and eighth grade practice facilities were only two blocks from "colored town," there were no blacks on the football teams.

That is not to say the "coloreds" didn't play football because Lincoln had a very competitive team that played its home games on Saturday nights on the junior high field. Cody Joe had gone with his uncle to several "colored" games and it was a happening event. Cody Joe loved the halftime performances where dancing was in vogue and the game itself was full of double reverses and other razzle-dazzle plays. It presented a different atmosphere than what he saw on Friday nights at Tiger Stadium. But as far as Cody Joe was concerned, life in "colored town" was the same as being on another planet. He didn't condemn it nor embrace it. He simply ignored it for the most part, just like most everyone else in Snyder.

So it was that Rue Carter once again took the 30th Street route to reach the practice facility this time arriving precisely at 3 p.m. because Cody Joe wanted plenty of time to get his uniform on before the 4 p.m. deadline set by Coach Heart.

Rue couldn't help but think that she was going to get real cozy with this cross-town trip before the next two school years ended. But it wasn't going to be too bad this week because Rue would carry the boys on Monday and Friday while Tracks' mom would take Tuesday and Thursday. Pug's mom drew the short stick and would be responsible for Wednesday.

When school started, the boys could ride the bus from West Elementary. Cassidy always rode with his Dad since they lived outside the city limits and Mr. Cassidy always liked to watch a little practice while he was there. Rue was still concerned about picking up Cody Joe after practice once school started. She wasn't exactly thrilled with the prospect of her son waiting on a ride to come after dark in this part of town. But that was a concern for another day. For now, everything was covered for two-a-days.

* * *

Cody Joe, Pug and Tracks started dressing immediately upon arrival to the field house even though Cassidy hadn't arrived. Butch had a hard time convincing his dad that he needed to be there a full hour early, especially since Ernest Cassidy wanted to stick around and see how the first practice started out. He wasn't going to wait there forever.

Tracks had just finished pulling on Cody Joe's jersey over his shoulder pads when Butch came storming in. "You guys better hang around and help me with my stuff because my Dad didn't want to come early."

"You've got plenty of time," Cody Joe said. "I think I'm about the only one already dressed and we still have 40 minutes before practice."

That made Butch feel much better, but he was still in high speed as he was close to ripping his clothes off. Pug cinched up the belt to his football pants after a helping hand with the jersey from Cody Joe, once again leaving Tracks and Cassidy the last to finish dressing. Cody Joe and Pug walked outside of the field house and down the platform steps only to find five or six guys already dressed.

One in full equipment without his "nose guard" was Kirby

Tanner. He was standing all alone for two reasons. First, he had just moved to Snyder and really didn't have any friends and now he was a bit shy of taking the lead in talking to people since the nose guard incident earlier that morning. Cody Joe and Pug headed Tanner's way but before they covered the distance, Mac Cone intercepted Kirby and said, "Tanner I'm sorry about the joke. We just thought it would be funny. I apologize just like Coach told me to."

"I didn't think it was very funny," Tanner countered honestly. "I trusted you guys and you took advantage of me. You two are a lot bigger than me, so you don't really have to resort to belittling me in front of the other guys. That was a cheap shot if you ask me."

"Well, I'm trying to do the right thing here," said Mac. "You can take it any way you want to." With that, Cone walked away.

Cody Joe approached Kirby and said, "Hi, I'm Cody Joe Carter. I couldn't help but hear that you put Mac down pretty hard. I'm not saying he didn't deserve it, but you know as well as I do that Cone and Bolger are going to be two of the better players on this team. Whether you like it or not, I think you are going to have to learn to get along with them."

"Yeah, I think you are probably right, but I couldn't walk away and let them think I'm scared of them. Besides, I don't think they are ever going to try anything with me here at practice because they are much more afraid of Coach Bear than me. For now, I just hope I don't run into them on the street somewhere. They might kill me."

"Well, no one told me to apologize, but I want to say I'm sorry," Cody Joe confessed. "I saw the whole thing and I did nothing to stop it. That bothered me all afternoon and I just had to tell you."

"Thanks Cody Joe," Tanner said. "You know, we're going

to be playing real football soon, and we both may have a lot of growing up to do. I think it's already started."

Cody Joe agreed, saying, "Well, let's make it a new start and consider me a friend. I won't let you down the next time – unless I'm the one pulling off the joke."

It was about that time that Dirk Bolger emerged from the field house. He sauntered over to Mac Cone and paid no attention to Tanner and Carter. Bolger was not ready to even attempt making amends with Tanner. He was still seething from the morning's events that turned sour and painful. He was still tired from running laps. He planned to get even – and he had no intention of apologizing.

Slowly, all 79 kids filed out of the field house ready for the first practice. Two kids had failed the physical and were dismissed in the morning session. When the field house was empty of the players at 3:49 p.m., out walked the three coaches. This was a rebirth for all involved because life was about to begin anew for about half of these kids. They were about to enter the world of West Texas football and no dream was greater or filled with more peril.

* * *

The eighth grade team worked out on the south end of the field while the seventh grade worked out on the north end as generations had done before them. The seventh grade was the first to hit the field running on orders from Coach Jimmy Lee Heart.

Calisthenics were the first order of business and coaches spent the entire session on correcting form and admonishing poor effort. Calisthenics were followed by 25-yard sprints. This served two purposes. First, it would get the boys used to wearing their hand-me-down shoes and would allow the coaches to evaluate the speed merchants on the team.

After all, the coaches wanted to identify as many of the skill people as possible. They wanted to start picking out their running backs and defensive backs as soon as possible. It came as little surprise that Hank Cline was the fastest guy on the team. He beat all comers in this drill time and again. Cline won the elementary school Olympics in the 100-yard dash two years running and was considered the best running back in the Boys' Club youth football league. He had star status written all over him even before practice ever started.

Tanner was in the top third of this group, but coaches still didn't know much about him, being new to town. They didn't know how tough he was and he was awfully small. Lester Jarvis was not only fast, but also had decent size. Coaches wanted to watch his progress because Jarvis didn't play Boys' Club ball. Jack King, Nate Carrillo and Jay Coy all showed decent speed and already had a documented presence in town.

Naturally, Cody Joe's crew all had just average speed, except for poor Tracks, who proved once again to be one of the slowest players on the team. Tracks was well aware of his status already feeling that his demise as a football player was near. He just felt like he didn't belong.

Coach Heart was taking copious notes with his clipboard in hand while Bear and Nix would point out the flaws and virtues of every player they had an eye on. When they were satisfied, they moved to the next drill.

This was a tackling drill, and would be the first full contact of the season for the boys. The coaches gave each boy a chance to tackle a ball carrier, who had to run between two blocking dummies. After a turn at tackling, a player would then take his turn at running back.

Naturally, this drill didn't go as smoothly as the running drill. There were some awful tackling efforts, including Tracks, who just got run over by Stoney Wall, a big hulk of a kid. Cody Joe, however, came up with one of the session's better efforts by nailing prospective quarterback Joseph Moore right at the line of scrimmage.

But the best effort of the day came from Butch Cassidy, who demolished Joey Taylor like he had been playing defense forever. When the pop of shoulder pads had ended, the whole team let out a collective, "Ohhhhhhh!" Cassidy was now on the coaches' radar and Ernest was getting hand shakes from some of the fathers watching practice on the sidelines. Ernest was a proud father on this day and not one game had yet been played.

But there was one more interesting incident to take place in the first practice that captured the whole attention of the youthful Blue Devils and the coaching staff. Just by chance, Dirk Bolger lined up for his tackling turn only to see the fleet-footed Kirby Tanner holding the football for his time to run. A formal hush came over the entire group with the anticipation that something big was about to happen. No one knew exactly what "big" would entail, but whatever happened would be talked about after practice and beyond.

Bolger had fire in his eyes. He knew this was a chance to get back at Tanner and he was looking forward to squashing this peanut. Tanner, on the other hand, knew that Coach Bear couldn't protect him here. This was football and to the victor goes the spoils. Tanner knew his reputation was once again on the line and this would be a defining moment for his young football career.

The coaches, too, looked at each other and shook their heads. Coach Heart almost pulled the plug on the whole thing, but decided that he couldn't solve problems by ignoring them. This was a problem that had to work itself out. He blew his whistle for the drill to begin.

Tanner took off for the corner of the practice dummy on his right. Bolger countered by heading to the impact point at full speed intent on delivering the hardest blow he could muster. Just as the two reached the collision point, Tanner gave a quick swivel of his hips to the left while Bolger launched a full force attack at where he thought Tanner would be. Dust flew everywhere, but no contact was heard by the captivated audience.

Bolger had come up completely empty on the tackle attempt, landing squarely face down in the dirt. In fact, when the embarrassed Bolger stood up, he had dirt in his mouth. Tanner was skipping along untouched well past the dummies.

A cheer went up from the entire team, but everyone quickly realized that this feud was only beginning. But today, Tanner had won for the second time.

Coach Bear couldn't help but turn the knife a bit. He said, "Bolger is that you with your face in the dirt? Maybe you did have the right idea about that nose guard of yours. If you had worn that this afternoon, you might not have a mouth full of mud."

Bolger bounced his helmet about 10 yards away, but Coach Bear put an end to the incident by grabbing Bolger by the shoulder pads, marching him over to collect his helmet.

Then Coach Bear once again began coaching, "Bolger, here's what you did wrong, which was about everything. You have to always stay under control. Never leave your feet and stick that headgear right here in the chest. Always watch the runner's hips and not his eyes. You have to square him up. You have a lot of potential, son, but you have to stay in control."

Bolger was given another chance, but not against Tanner. Coach Heart thought the entire team had had enough excitement for one day. This time Bolger drilled Eric Blade, drawing another collective "Ohhhh" from his teammates. In the end, both Tanner and Bolger came away with their pride intact. But that only meant that the status quo had been preserved and capped for another day.

Practice ended on a rather dull note as Coach Bear and Coach Nix took the majority of the team to work on technique matters like getting into a proper offensive and defensive stance. Those drawing Coach Nix were the first to learn the perfection this young coach demanded. He accepted no excuses. It was his way or you didn't exist. In fact, he was the only coach to have players running laps on the first practice. Cody Joe and Pug were both under Coach Nix and both thought their biggest success of the day was surviving Coach Nix' technique drills without running laps. It was quickly learned to be thankful for the small things when it came to Coach Nix. He was demanding and decidedly unapologetic about it.

Coach Heart took quarterback prospects Joseph Moore and Lee Line aside along with Adam Quay and Mac Cone. Coach Heart thought Quay and Cone might make good receivers because they were both rather tall. He hoped they could both catch the football. Coach Heart put them through some passing drills and was more than a little encouraged when all was said and done.

With that, the first practice ended and Coach Heart looked at his two assistants and said, "All in all, I think we had a pretty good day. But, Coach Bear, I want this Tanner-Bolger episode put on the back burner. We don't need the kids choosing sides and we don't need the distractions that come with it."

Coach Bear responded, "Coach, I really believe that everything will work itself out the further we go along. These aren't bad kids. They both want to play football just like most of the kids out here."

Chapter 5

TWO-A-DAYS

When Cody Joe went to bed on Monday night, he had no idea that Tuesday was going to be the worst day of his life. He had no inkling of the excruciating pain he would experience when he tried to move any part of his body when he woke up.

His first taste of what it meant to be a football player came at 6:30 a.m. when Rue Carter called, "Cody Joe, it's time to get up. Get a move on, boy. You have practice again this morning."

Carter was anxious to get going and snapped to an upright position before yelping with uncontrollable surrender. Every muscle in his body rebelled at every act of movement. Pain was in every part of his body. Any attempt to move was greeted by a hellish pain that seemed to permeate every fiber in his being. Even his eyelids seem to hurt. He had never felt anything like it.

Carter quickly decided that no movement was worth the pain and he was quite content to just sit there and let the world pass him by. Playing football again wasn't all that appealing as it had been only yesterday.

Chip Carter heard Cody Joe's woeful yelping and said, "What's wrong Cody Joe? You hurt or something? Can I help?"

"Chip, if you so much as touch me, you'll be sitting on Mars this time tomorrow," Cody Joe growled. "I mean it; don't touch me."

It was all Chip wanted to hear. He immediately knew it was time for fun. "C'mon, Cody Joe, let me give you a hand."

With that, Chip grabbed the arm of Cody Joe and gave a hearty yank, sending waves of pain through his older brother's body. Cody Joe made an instinctive effort to grab Chip and settle this matter quickly, but his body wouldn't respond. He just sat there. Chip ran out of the room intent on causing further disruption to Cody Joe's morning.

"Mom, Cody Joe can't get out of bed," Chip said. "I think he's hurt or something. Anyway, he won't let me help him get out of bed."

Rue walked to the bedroom and asked, "Cody Joe are you OK? Chip says you can't get out of bed."

"Mom, I hurt all over. It hurts to move anything. I think my fingernails even hurt," explained Cody Joe.

Rue had no more sympathy for Cody Joe than did Chip. She exclaimed, "You're the one that wanted to play football, so play football or quit. I'm going to fix breakfast and by the time you come to eat, you let me know if you are going to play football or not."

That's when Cody Joe overcame the pain. He couldn't give in and let Chip and his Mother win this game. He'd never live it down. Cody Joe got dressed and made it to the breakfast table without the aid of another human being. That didn't mean it was easy as his muscles continued to rebel and scream at him. Every movement was still a nightmare.

* * *

Mrs. Tracks delivered the hurting threesome to the field house this morning. Tracks, Pug and Cody Joe were all in extreme pain. Few words were exchanged on the trip across town down 30th Street.

Rick Tracks was even worse off than Cody Joe, saying, "I'll never fear death again because I think dying would be highly preferable to this state of grief."

Pug countered, "But what if dying is worse than this? Just in case, I'm going to live forever."

When the boys reached the football practice facility, they joined a long line of friends that were limping toward the field house porch. All were moaning and disheartened. This would easily pass for a funeral march.

It hurt to put the shoulder pads on. The practice gear carried a stink that would chase buzzards away. And the field house had transformed overnight into a noxious haven of smells that could have killed the dinosaurs.

All in all, it was a dismal sight to behold and one not unexpected for the coaching staff. They had seen it and experienced it many times before. There was only one way to rid the gloom of the second day of practice and that was to work through it. And work they would.

About 10 minutes before practice, the players began to notice that a lot of guys hadn't shown up. There seemed to be a lot of lockers without bodies in front of them. Cody Joe didn't know what to make of it until the coaches made an announcement before the start of practice.

Coach Heart said, "Take a look around you. There are fewer of you today than yesterday. Coach Bear says 15 guys quit the team last night, so we only have 64 players left after only one practice. We never said it would be easy.

"If you want to be on this team, you will have to learn to endure pain, heartache, mistakes and the coaches. The ones we have left at the end of this week will be the best of the best in your age group in Snyder. Then we will see how you stack up with the best of the best in other West Texas towns.

"If you still want to be a Blue Devil, get on that practice

field now."

It wasn't exactly a speedy garrison to storm the practice field, but those wanting to play did the best they could heading for another round of calisthenics. But muscles still ached.

The coaches put the kids through another set of intensive drills and everyone noticed that the soreness began to wane as practice progressed. Most were beginning to think they were actually going to live. The second practice had little of the drama that unfolded on Monday afternoon. The face guard feud already seemed years ago. But then again, there was always the afternoon.

* * *

Cody Joe was racked by pain once again before the afternoon practice session. It didn't take long for the muscles to tighten up from the morning practice. He wondered if the cycle of pain and relief would ever end. It was a hard existence and Carter couldn't help but wonder if he could survive this daily grind.

But his day was about to get even worse upon his arrival to the field house. When Cody Joe walked into the field house, he quickly noticed that all the extra equipment and extra clothes he, Pug, Tracks and Butch had placed in the extra locker had been tossed out in the middle of the floor.

An angry Cody Joe called out, "Who dumped all our stuff out on the floor? There's no call for this. Who did this?"

It was then that a new boy came walking toward Cody Joe with both arms full of football equipment. He unceremoniously dumped the equipment in Cody Joe's now vacant extra locker.

Then he stood nose-to-nose against Carter and said, "I did, you want to do something about it?"

Cody Joe replied, "You didn't have to dump our stuff on the floor. That was uncalled for."

"Didn't know whose stuff it was and didn't care. Coach said I could have any locker I wanted and I could tell this was an extra. So, I got it. If you want to make me move, you're welcome to try."

"Listen, I'm not trying to cause trouble and we're all glad you are joining the team, but I want to show you that the bench in front of the locker you chose is broken. And there's only one hanging hook. That's why we are using the locker," Cody Joe explained. "I don't think you really want that locker."

"Don't tell me what I want and don't want you sorry excuse for a scum bag. If you give me any problems, I'll cut out your tongue," the new boy said as he reached into his crowded locker and pulled out a switchblade that looked more like a Bowie knife in the eyes of Cody Joe.

The new guy smiled as he got the desired result. All the boys witnessing this audacious display of intimidation drew back into a silent shell, yielding not one round of protest. No one wanted to be the first to give blood to the switchblade of the new tyrant on the block. Some secretly wondered if this social misfit was as good at playing football as he was putting people down with his mouth. If he was, they all dreaded facing him on the field of play.

When Pug and Cody Joe left the field house, Pug asked, "Who is that guy? I've seen some bad guys in the movies, but this one takes the cake."

Cody Joe said, "Right before we left, he put a tape on his locker with the name Nate Christian on it."

Pug laughed, "Well, that beats all. I don't think Christian is exactly the word I'd use to describe him. And Blue Devil seems to be a bit mild. Yep, I think he's the real thing without the horns. He probably had them sawed off so he could get his football helmet on. I'm just glad you are sitting beside him instead of me. I don't like that guy."

"That makes two of us," Cody Joe lamented. "Somehow I don't see us being best of friends."

* * *

Tuesday afternoon's practice produced less suspense than one would think, but one significant thing took place that would change the football life of Butch Cassidy forever.

Coach Heart held another tackling drill, but made the game a bit more challenging by placing two blockers on two defenders with a running back behind them. The object was for the defenders to shed the blockers and make the tackle, hopefully at the line of scrimmage. This drill let some of the offensive linemen get more opportunity to work on blocking technique while hardening them up at the same time.

Coach Bear picked the Quay brothers, Adam and Thomas, to be on defense. The Quay boys were twins. They were not of the identical twin variety, but wherever you saw one, you usually saw the other. They were extremely close. Thomas Quay simply went by the name "T-Quay" while Adam carried no nickname at all.

Coach Nix picked Robert Liberman and Eric Blade as the two blockers. Liberman was a potential center while Blade was a big kid with promise in either the offensive or defensive line. It promised to be a good matchup. Just to make it more interesting Coach Heart placed the hefty Cassidy at the fullback slot, ensuring that everyone on the field carried a good amount of beef. The coaches knew this matchup would probably feature five guys on the team that would be major contributors. The coaches knew, however, that the Quay boys had an advantage over Liberman and Blade because not much work had been done yet on blocking. In fact, the youthful Blue Devils had spent more time on getting into a proper offensive stance than they had on actual blocking.

When Coach Heart blew his whistle, Adam and T-Quay pretty much demolished their opponents, shoving Liberman and Blade to the side while nicely filling the hole that Cassidy was to enter. T-Quay was the first to meet Butch head on. The crack of the pads could be heard even down in the eighth grade camp. Adam wasn't far behind, delivering another big blow on Cassidy. But when the dust had cleared, Cassidy was still on his feet, driving straight through the Quay boys like a bowling ball going through bowling pins. Butch finally broke Adam's final grip and raced onward in triumph. All the Blue Devils erupted into a frenzy of yelling and wonderment.

"Gol darn, Coach Heart," screamed Coach Bear. "I think we've found our fullback. I've never seen anything like that in my life."

Ernest Cassidy was once again on the sideline and he couldn't believe his eyes either. He always thought his boy would be an outstanding offensive lineman or a linebacker, but he never dreamed his powerful son would be in the back-field. Now, that was a real possibility.

Coach Heart was already intrigued with Cassidy because he had not identified a true fullback as of yet. If Butch was the answer, he would fill another key puzzle piece in his lineup.

Cassidy walked away from that drill with new found respect and Cody Joe was the first to let him know.

"Hey, Butch, how did you stay up when T-Quay clocked you on that first hit?"

"What hit are you talking about, Cody Joe? I don't remember a thing. I just put my head down, closed my eyes and rolled on. I was just wondering why no one was blocking those two Quay freaks."

"You truly are amazing, Butch," said Cody Joe. "You're kickin' butt and takin' names. Way to go."

Nate Christian was not much of a factor in the afternoon since the coaches did not call his name for any of the individual drills. Still, the guys could tell he was going to be a factor in the days to come because he was coordinated and moved well in all the team drills. He could also deliver a punch, a fact that surprised no one. His reputation had already achieved team recognition even before he busted anyone in the chops. Christian talked to no one during this practice, but he carried an outward attitude that he was ready to take on whoever had the guts to face him – whether it was in the field house or on the football field.

* * *

In the locker room, Christian continued to shock his new teammates. First, the boys noticed that Nate didn't wear his jockey strap. He just wore his regular underwear. And when he got all his football gear off, he simply put on his regular clothes. He didn't even shower.

Cody Joe looked at Pug in amazement, privately saying, "Is he for real? He's filthy."

Pug said, "He's probably got a hot date tonight."

Carter countered, "Can you imagine what a girl would look like if she would date him?"

"Bet she doesn't have a nose," Pug replied. Both giggled.

Carter wasn't quite sure if Christian had heard a part of that conversation, but Christian said out of the blue, "There's a bunch of wimps on this team and I can't wait to get my hands on a couple of them. Cody Joe, you're one of them and you're going to pay. You mark my words."

With that, Nate Christian walked out of the locker room, marking even another new era for Cody Joe Carter. And this new era didn't seem nearly as promising as his first taste of seventh grade football. Cody Joe felt as if he had seen real evil for the first time in his life.

Cody Joe thought about telling his Dad about Nate Christian because he was more than a little concerned with the way the afternoon had gone. Christian's menacing eyes were enough to scare the bejeebers out of him, but when you add in that sparkling switchblade, that goes far out of the realm of expected saneness.

However, Cody Joe didn't want to look as if he couldn't take care of himself. His father might be disappointed in him. If he told the coaches about the knife, Christian would know who turned him in. Nobody liked a snitch. It was with this set of circumstances that Carter decided to ride it out and see how things worked out. Cody Joe knew one thing; he wasn't going to quit this team or give up his chances to play football for anyone – not even a guy with a switchblade.

* * *

Cody Joe's soreness didn't improve much from Tuesday to Wednesday. He was almost paralyzed from the top of his hair to the tip of his toenail from the end of practice until the next practice. It was this blissful curse that actually made him look forward to practice every day. It was a painful routine, but it was the only way to escape his torment even for an hour or so.

Pug's mom picked up Cody Joe for the Wednesday morning practice, but Rick Tracks was not sitting on his porch when Mrs. Preston arrived at the Tracks residence. Pug quickly volunteered to go get him, but no one was home. Pug rang the doorbell three times before walking to the family garage. He found out by looking in a side window that Mrs. Tracks' car was gone.

"Nobody's home, Mom," revealed Pug when he got back to the car. "I don't know where they are, but we can't be late for practice. I guess we'll have to go on without him."

Cody Joe and Pug arrived to the foul locker room smells in plenty of time. Cody Joe was happy to see that Nate Christian hadn't arrived. But thoughts of Christian quickly dissipated when Cody Joe noticed that Rick Tracks' locker was empty.

"What's going on here?" Cody Joe asked Pug. "Where's Tracks' stuff? I wonder if Christian is playing another of his jokes. Maybe he's trying to intimidate Tracks."

"Oh, I don't know Cody Joe," answered Pug. "I think something's going on. Tracks wasn't at home and now this."

Before either could speculate, Rick Tracks walked in and simply said, "Hi guys."

"Where you been?" Cody Joe demanded. "We thought you left town or something."

Tracks lowered his head and said, "I just quit the team.

59

I just now told the coaches and turned in my gear. I can't do this anymore. I was getting killed out there. I can't think of one positive thing I've done on that field since we started.

"The coaches even agreed. Coach Heart said that he was afraid I was going to get hurt. He said he thought it was the best for everyone concerned. He thanked me for trying out. Coach Bear said he could tell that I gave it all I had, but that I might not be right for this sport.

"Then Coach Bear said that I could still be a big part of the team if I would become a team manager. He said two or three other guys in my same boat had already agreed to do that. I took him up on it and now I'm a manager. I still get to go to all the games and I'll still be at all the practices."

"That's great, Tracks," Pug said. "I'm glad you will still be with us. I think you probably made the right decision."

"It's still a little sad," Cody Joe said. "I just expected us three to be together on the team."

"I am on the team," Tracks said. "Coach Heart says I'll get a letter sweater just like the football players if I stay the whole season. I'm happy with the decision and we can still ride with each other on all the road trips. I'm just happy that the football thing is over for me."

Christian walked in as Tracks was talking. He couldn't let the moment pass, saying, "I figured you were a wimp, Tracks. Now we know it. I say good riddance, but I'm kind of sad that leaves me two less ears to cut off."

Tracks stared hard into those black eyes of Christian and then walked off thinking, "I know how I can get even with him."

Tracks may not have had the physical stature to play football, but he may have been harder to intimidate than Cody Joe, Pug and even Butch.

It was a bland practice on Wednesday morning since most of the team was sore and tired. There wasn't much pep left in the young legs. The coaches responded with a lot of one-on-one drills and a lot of running.

However, Wednesday afternoon brought a renewed vigor. The coaches helped inspire the kids by asking the question, "Who wants to be a Blue Devil?" The challenge permeated the practice.

In one drill, Joey Taylor, who had played pretty well in the first five practices, missed a tackle and Coach Nix lit into him, "Taylor, you couldn't tackle my grandmother and she's 85 years old. Man that stinks. You may be able to get a job cleaning cowpens one day, but you aren't a Blue Devil."

Taylor was furious. He jumped up and screamed, "Coach, let me have another chance."

Nix said, "OK, get after it, but you'll probably only enforce what I said."

Taylor was intent on proving the coach was wrong and that proved to be unfortunate for the fleet-footed, but small Kirby Tanner. Taylor literally drove Tanner into the dirt with a perfect form tackle. Tanner's feet left the ground and his helmet was the first to make contact with the ground. The whole team ignited with hand clapping and yelling. Taylor had just upped the stakes in this practice. Coach Nix couldn't help but smile.

This was also the first practice that Carter and Christian were matched up in a one-on-one blocking drill. It was no team secret that there was no love lost between these two. It was an eagerly anticipated moment; one everyone knew was coming sooner or later.

Christian couldn't wait for this opportunity. He knew this

could establish him as one to fear on this football team. For Christian, football had nothing to do with team play or camaraderie. It was all about intimidation while feeding his self-image.

Cody Joe, on the other hand, had mixed emotions. A part of him did fear Nate Christian, but there was another part that wanted to get this meeting over with and see where things really stand. Cody Joe predetermined that he was going to give this drill his best effort.

The idea of the drill was to simply block each other with no tackling involved. The first one to block the other out of the way of the marking dummies was the winner.

Both took a stance and Christian gave a wicked smile at Cody Joe. Carter bowed his neck and waited for the whistle. Coach Nix didn't disappoint, sending a long shriek into the late afternoon air.

Cody Joe was first off the line of scrimmage and got his shoulders up under the fast charging Christian. Christian would have easily been bowled over by Carter's fundamentally sound block, but Nate's strength overcame his bad technique and began to push Carter backwards. Both kids battled move for move until both rolled over the left dummy spent from the effort. No one had won this fight, but it sure caught the eye of everyone who witnessed the drill. Nearly all took comfort in the fact that Christian didn't win the battle outright. Cody Joe thought he had held his own and that was good enough for him. He at least knew that he could hold his own against one of the great thorns in his side.

And for Nate Christian, he slid away behind everyone with a huge scowl on his face. Cody Joe would have to pay for this. This was not the victory Christian had hoped for.

* * *

By the end of the week, Coach Heart could see some improvement in the team. It was already beginning to come together. They were even ready to run plays by Thursday afternoon and held a brief team scrimmage on Friday afternoon. This scrimmage was simply to let everyone play so the coaches could evaluate position players. There would be a future scrimmage where coaches would make some determinations on who would carry the load for the Blue Devils.

Butch Cassidy was running with authority at fullback and getting better every day, even though he had never been a running back before. Cody Joe had become a staple at right guard on offense and Pug had been installed as a left tackle. Both also played on defense, Cody Joe at inside linebacker and Pug at nose guard. Cody Joe was constantly joking with Pug to wear the designated team "nose guard." Kirby Tanner said he would even offer Pug his famous "nose guard."

By Friday, the daily soreness was much less severe. The lack of soreness both helped the team energy level and the team morale. The guys were beginning to get the feel of what it meant to be a team. And school hadn't even started.

Coach Heart ended two-a-days on Friday afternoon with just 45 kids left from the original 81. The heat, the soreness, the contact and the realization that football was not meant for everyone had all taken a toll on the numbers. It was nothing unexpected. Coach Heart had gone into a season before with only 24 players.

School was scheduled to start on Tuesday, the day after Labor Day. Since Monday was a holiday, Coach Heart had decided that the team would work out only on Monday morning and then come together for the regular practice schedule on Tuesday afternoon after school.

"I think you guys have come a long way this week," said Coach Heart following the Friday sessions. "All of you here made it through two-a-days, so you are now officially Blue Devils. We expect a few more to leave, but this is the best we have in town. You should be proud of yourselves. I'm proud of you.

"We still have a long way to go, but we are a lot closer to being where we want to be than we were last week. You now know how to work and how to get along. You learned some big lessons this week. Have a good weekend and we'll see you at 8 a.m. on Monday morning."

Chapter 6

LABOR DAY WEEKEND

It was 9:06 a.m. before Cody Joe moved an eyebrow on Saturday morning. He had been playing football for only five days, but in Cody Joe Carter's way of thinking, it was more like a lifetime.

He was still sore in spots and he was nursing all kinds of new scrapes and bruises, but Cody Joe was no longer racked with the pain that had paralyzed his body Tuesday through Thursday. Now he had been allowed to sleep in as long as he wanted. Rue Carter had bestowed mercy on her eldest son after cracking the sunrise whip on him all during this week of two-a-days.

Carter continued to lie in bed as he contemplated the events of the past week. He couldn't believe how many things happened that had an impact on his life. And he was now a part of a new team that promised a lot more experiences down the road.

The events of the week rolled past Carter like a wave of distant memories. The week seemed like it lasted years. For sure, Carter thought more had happened in one week than all the things that made up his life before football.

He was still embarrassed that he let Kirby Tanner go through the "nose guard" joke. He was still sad that Tracks had quit the team. He was especially upset that Nate Christian had entered his life. He was elated, however, that he had made the team and he was now thinking that he had a realistic chance of actually being a two-way starter for the Snyder Junior High School Blue Devils. Carter was also proud of Pug and Butch. Both had done well. So far, Butch was the highlight of the team and had earned the fullback position right out of the blue. Cody Joe still remembered Cassidy breaking through the attempted tackles by the Quay brothers. Pug could also be a two-way starter. Cody Joe still laughed whenever he thought about Dirk Bolger and Mac Cone running laps with a jock strap attached to their faces. Cody Joe thought about his blocking duel with Christian and was satisfied that he had nothing to be ashamed of. He held his own in that encounter.

Yes, it had been quite a week, but he was glad to take a break and he wondered what the long weekend would bring. It didn't take long for Cody Joe to find out as Rue Carter walked into the room, while folding a pair of pants, saying, "Isn't it about time for you to get up. Chip and Kate are antsy for you to get up. We need to go and get school supplies. This is the only day we have left before school starts on Tuesday."

Cody Joe hated shopping with the family. In fact, he just plain and simple hated shopping. He thought it was a total waste of time and was convinced that shopping before school started was a losing cause. He knew every teacher would want something special for their class and that meant that he would have to go shopping twice instead of once. But Cody Joe could be realistic on occasion. He knew his schedule was tight these days and there wouldn't be much extra time to get things done if he didn't use this break to take care of business. Even seventh grade football players had to take care of business.

This was a big day for Chip. He was moving from the big pencils and the Big Chief notepads to regular pencils and notebooks. He got a 48-count Crayola box that contained every color imaginable. After all, a third grader needed to be prepared for the hard stuff. Everything Kate picked out just happened to be pink with flowers. Cody Joe wondered if the fifth grade required pink flowers on all assignments. Chip and Kate both got new clothes. Chip got new tennis shoes and Kate, well, she got a bunch of pink dresses.

Cody Joe hated trying on clothes, but he hated it even worse when Rue would pull and tug and look over every pair of jeans he tried on. She would always say, "They'll shrink when I wash them. That will make them fit perfectly."

The day was saved for Cody Joe when he ran across a terrific notebook that was covered with a black and gold plastic covering. On the front was a snarling Tiger with the word "Snyder" over the Tigers' head and the word "Tigers" below the paws. It was the most awesome notebook Cody Joe had ever seen, but the price was an unbelievable two dollars more than a regular notebook binder. Cody Joe thought his mother would never go for that. But Rue relented when she was bombarded by a very reasonable argument that it was made better and might last him until high school. Also, Cody Joe's pleading puppy-dog eyes might have had something to do with the purchase.

At last, the shopping spree was over and Cody Joe had the rest of the day off. He had planned to go over to Pug's house to spend the afternoon, but before he went, he wanted to ask his mom if he could ask Pug to go to the big family barbeque over at Grandpa Taggert's house on Monday. The Taggerts always held a big Labor Day cookout with Grandpa cooking all the meat while all the aunts, uncles and cousins brought all the trimmings. There would be steak, hamburgers, hot dogs and all the homemade ice cream one could eat. It was one of the best holidays of the year as far as Cody Joe was concerned.

Rue thought it would be fine because her dad never knew when to stop cooking anyway. The annual Labor Day bash drew anywhere from 20 to 40 people because the Taggert family was widely entrenched in Snyder. There would be plenty of food.

After lunch, he rode his bike over to Pug's house and they decided to go into the back yard and shoot some baskets. They ended up just lying on the grass, both too tired from the week's workouts to put out the effort. They ended up talking about the week. Mostly they rehashed the week's events that Cody Joe had already thought about in bed that morning.

Somewhere in the afternoon's conversation, Cody Joe told Pug that his family was going to have a big barbeque on Labor Day. He asked Pug if he wanted to go. The two never turned down an opportunity to be together, so naturally, Pug quickly agreed.

"Then you need to tell your mom that you need to come home with me after practice on Monday," Cody Joe instructed. "The feed is Monday evening, but we will be going over to my grandpa's house pretty early in the afternoon. Tell your mother that my mom has already agreed."

* * *

Cody Joe found himself in his regular church pew on Sunday morning. There was never any sleeping in on Sundays in Jack Carter's house. Cody Joe wondered why churches didn't hold a holiday every once in a while so the whole congregation could sleep in. In Cody Joe's way of thinking, it didn't make much sense for the congregation to never get a day off from church. In his opinion, church goers were forced to commit a grievous sin by staying at home in order to get some rest on occasion. If the church had a few holidays, nobody would have to sin for skipping church. This made perfect sense to him, but after all, he was just a 12-year-old boy.

Carter found it much more bearable to concentrate on this particular service than it had been last week when he was anxiously awaiting dismissal of church for the last summer Sunday session of baseball. It actually seemed like the church service went quick. In fact, Carter was more than a little miffed when the service ended and the whole family actually beat him to the car. Where were they last weekend?

As usual, the Carter's enjoyed another meal of Rue's pot roast, but in Cody Joe's mind, the meal went much different than a week ago. Kate hardly ate anything and left the table quickly. Chip didn't even act like he was hungry and retired to the bedroom in record time. Even Jack Carter finished his meal before his son. Cody Joe was almost furious as he pushed down another round of mashed potatoes. He was certain there was a family conspiracy against him.

Rue Carter, of course, viewed the entire situation in an entirely different light. She noticed that Cody Joe was like a ravenous wolf at the dinner table as of late. He was eating everything in sight. She was convinced that if Cody Joe kept playing football, Jack would have to get another job just to feed his oldest son.

Cody Joe finally got up from the table and decided to retire to his room. Chip immediately asked Cody Joe if he could play some of his records. Cody Joe seemed to be too tired to resist and gave Chipper permission to play the music. Cody Joe remembered little else and didn't wake up again until nightfall.

* * *

Cody Joe swore that the weekend was the shortest on record when Rue Carter brought the glad tidings that it was time to get up for another practice session. Cody Joe thought it was probably illegal to enjoy time off that much. But all good things really do come to an end and even 12-year-old Cody Joe Carter understood that life had many demands placed on it.

However, it was still a mystery to Cody Joe why there was so much work demanded by life and so little fun allowed. For instance, Cody Joe thought there should be much more Sunday afternoon baseball and more football games than football practices. That combination would probably come close to creating the perfect world.

Mrs. Preston drew the honors this Labor Day morning to haul the boys to practice. Rue Carter would pick them up after practice since Pug was going home with Cody Joe.

Unfortunately for Cody Joe and Pug, Nate Christian was already at the field house and was in the process of pulling his football pants over his soiled underwear. Cody Joe couldn't help but be disgusted every time he laid eyes on the creep.

"Well, the two sissies decided to show up," Christian taunted. "I don't know why you two even want to play football. You would do a lot better with dolls."

Cody Joe was in no mood to spar with Nate today. He surprised even himself by shooting back, "Don't go there, Nate. You don't have to like us, but I'm tired of your mouth. Why don't you quit the team and make us all happy?"

Cody Joe wasn't sure where he got the courage to speak up like that, but his ability to play on even terms with him on the football field last week seemed to have leveled the playing field quite a bit. Besides, Carter was tired of listening to the garbage coming out of Nate's mouth.

It was also somewhat surprising that Nate did not offer a vocal comeback to Cody Joe's outbreak. He just sat there with that menacing smile on his face while he reached down to pick up his switchblade. The spring-loaded blade flashed bright as it sprang into the extended position. Nate smiled and began to trim his nails, saying nothing.

After Nate left the field house, Tracks came to meet his friends with a somewhat wicked smile on his face.

"I told Nate I'd get him back for that outburst last week," Tracks said. "I put a liberal amount of that hot sports balm in his workout pants. He'll be on fire in the groin area before practice is over."

It turned out to be a fun practice for most of the Blue Devils on this hot and steamy morning, but Christian started squirming even before the team completed callecintics. Pug and Cody Joe were watching him closely and began to giggle the more Christian started scratching and pulling at his pants. Christian never said a word about his condition, but it wasn't long before he had a brief talk with Coach Bear and quickly left the field. Pug and Cody Joe gave a mock wave at the departing Christian, but Nate didn't notice as he had urgent business to take care of in the field house.

"It looks like Tracks got him good," Pug said with a big grin on his face. "I wonder if this will make him take a shower more often."

Tracks, however, probably wouldn't even be considered as the culprit by Christian, but it was certain that he would turn this event back on Cody Joe Carter.

* * *

Coach Jimmy Lee Heart had decided to hold a team scrimmage and would alternate some of the kids from offense to defense in order to get a look at the depth issue. Coach Heart was a bit concerned that a lot of kids would have to play both ways. Cody Joe and Pug were two he was looking at. On the negative side, it was looking like Butch Cassidy

71

would not play much defense. Coach Heart wanted him to keep his legs fresh for his new foray at fullback. Cassidy was a big kid and Coach Heart didn't think Butch could take on going two ways. That was a shame because Cassidy had probably been the best defensive player in the entire Boys Club youth league. Some of his tackles had become legendary in the sixth grade. But Coach Heart knew that he had Cassidy to use whenever the need came.

Carter made a couple of tackles right at the line of scrimmage from his inside linebacker post that brought a couple of "attaboys" from Coach Nix. Carter took that as a real compliment since Coach Nix rarely said anything positive. Pug plugged up a sweep by breaking into the backfield, dropping the runner for a 10-yard loss. That brought cheers from all the players not on the field and from the seven or eight parents watching the workout.

Cody Joe also got a stint at right guard and once mashed T-Quay into the ground on a double team block. Even though no one really noticed that play, it was the most pleasing of the day for Carter because T-Quay was much larger than Cody Joe. Coach Bear immediately jumped on T-Quay, "You're going in there too high, son. You got your clocked cleaned, didn't you? Maybe you'll listen to me next time when I tell you something. If you think you can stand straight up in there, then your clock is going to be the cleanest in town."

T-Quay was almost foaming at the mouth, but said nothing. But he was thinking, "Carter will have to pay for that. I'm not about to take a dressing down because of him." Soon, however, T-Quay's anger subsided after he nailed running back Lester Jarvis with a good tackle and that brought a positive reaction from Coach Bear.

Practice ended with Coach Heart once again explaining that the next practice would be after the first school day on

Tuesday.

"All of you have athletics for the last period, so at 2:30 you get down to the field house as quickly as possible. It's just a two-block walk and practice will begin at 3:15 p.m. sharp. If you are late, you will run gassers. We don't tolerate guys being late. If you are late because of a teacher, bring a note. If you are late because of a girlfriend, bring a note and we'll post it on the wall for all to see. But you will still run laps because you are wrong either way."

* * *

Cody Joe and Pug now had the whole afternoon off and it felt like another vacation. Even football practice had been fun this morning. Rue Carter was waiting to pick up the boys as soon as they left the field house. Lunch was already on the table with the full fixings for sandwiches. It came as no surprise that the two boys ate as if they had never had a meal before. It was a good thing that Jack, Kate and Chip had already gotten a head start on the pair that could pass as vacuum cleaners.

Sated from Rue's lunch spread, Cody Joe and Pug each picked a couch in the Carter den. Neither planned to sleep, but most of the afternoon had passed before Jack woke the boys up, telling them it was time to go to the barbeque. It was around 3:45 p.m. before the Carter family and Pug were headed for the Taggert home place that resided just outside the city limits in a stand of pecan trees. Grandpa Taggert swore that his homestead was once a major highway intersection for the old buffalo herds.

Everyone in Snyder knew the story of when J. Wright Mooar killed a rare white buffalo in 1876 along the banks of Deep Creek, a waterway that still meandered through downtown Snyder and on just west of "colored" town. In fact, that white buffalo tale was known far and wide, giving Snyder its best claim to fame outside of the oil boom. The white hide was shown from time to time at community events, but was usually kept well hidden by Mooar's relatives that still resided in Snyder. But Grandpa Taggert had another spin on the story. He claimed that his great granddad also killed a white buffalo not two miles from this very house down by the dry creek bed somewhere around 1874 or 1875. He said the old buffalo hunters just wanted the hides and didn't think much about placing a white hide in with the brown ones. Grandpa Taggert would say, "One hide sold was as good as another back in them days. So, we got no proof that our family shot a white buffalo. Mooar got all the fame, but we were the first to take down a white buffalo."

It was somewhere around 1878 when Pete Snyder opened a trading post on the banks of Deep Creek, and that humble beginning provided supplies for the buffalo hunters and the humble creation of Snyder, Texas, the community.

Cody Joe always doubted Grandpa's buffalo story, but he loved listening to it anyway. Grandpa could tell a yarn and make you believe it. Jack Carter said he thought Grandpa had told that story so many times, he now believed it. Jack always held the opinion that the event never happened even though Grandpa Taggert had a couple of old buffalo rifles to prove that the family toiled in the buffalo trade at one time. But there was one thing for sure – no one in the family was ever going to contest Grandpa's story face-to-face. He was still very much the patriarch of the family. And he still very much liked the family barbeque – even if it was only good American-bred beef and not buffalo meat.

When Pug arrived, he was an instant hit with Carter's cousins. There were three girls in the family close to the age of Cody Joe. Emily Taggert was the professed leader of the group and would be entering the eighth grade. Alexi Taggert would be joining Cody Joe and Pug in the seventh grade and Cindy Taggert would be in the sixth grade. The three stair steps were the daughters of Rue's three brothers.

"Hey, James, come over here and sit with us," Emily said in her sweetest voice.

Pug didn't delay in making a decision because he had long had his eye on Alexi and he was looking forward to going to school with her this year. Alexi went to a different elementary school than Pug and Cody Joe. Pug saw this as an opportunity to get to know Alexi better. She seemed more than willing to cooperate in that endeavor, going by the smile she threw toward Pug as he walked toward the table where the girls were sitting. Pug, however, was a little intimidated by the older Emily even though Emily was the one doing most of the talking.

Cody Joe was a bit disappointed since he had lost his best friend two minutes into the party. He ended up sitting with Alexi's brother, Stacey, who was two years older than Cody Joe. Stacey was headed for high school and Cody Joe thought he was full of himself. Still, there was little else to choose from unless he chose to sit with the cousin's closer to the age of Chip and Kate. Cody Joe decided Stacey wasn't all that bad after all.

It wasn't long before Emily dropped over by the bench where Cody Joe and Stacey were sitting. She told Cody Joe, "James doesn't know anyone else exists except Alexi. I think he's got it bad for her, and I have to say I think Alexi likes him too. I wouldn't be surprised if they end up getting together."

Cody Joe answered, "I've seen it myself. He asks a lot of questions about her ever since he sat by her at the movies at the Palace a few weeks back. I think he'd be tickled to death to go out with her. But don't tell him I said anything. He gets really jumpy when we start talking about things like that. And don't call him James. He doesn't like that."

"I swear you boys need a sledge hammer put to your head before you recognize the obvious. It's not like you are keeping a good secret around here. Cody Joe, I bet your mom can even translate this scene. This is a prime example why us girls have the dickens getting a boyfriend. You guys are just frustrating and you can tell Pug that, too."

Finally the dinner bell rang. Pug rejoined Cody Joe for the eats. Both picked hamburgers while most of the adults went for the steaks. There wasn't really a bad choice. Everything was delicious.

Grandpa Taggert walked all around his domain under the pecan trees to see if his guests were happy. He stopped at the table of Cody Joe, Pug and Stacey. He said, "I noticed you boys are eating hamburgers without my famous chow-chow. Personally, I don't think barbeque is proper without chow-chow. Cody Joe, you want some?"

Cody Joe never disagreed or went against the grain when it came to his Grandpa. "Well, Grandpa, if you think the chow-chow will make it better, sure, I'll try some."

Pug jumped in, "Mr. Taggert, I'll try some of that chow-chow myself. That sounds good."

Stacey couldn't be outdone by these youngsters and also agreed to try the chow-chow.

Grandpa's chow-chow was a staple and few ever refused to try it – until the second offering. It was so hot no one on the planet could survive a mouthful of it, including Grandpa, a fact he always hid from other family members. When Grandpa tried it in his youth, it made sweat break out under his nose and on the top of his head. Still, he made chow-chow from his pepper crop every year and had preserved jars of it hidden all over the house.

Cody Joe and Stacey had never had their Grandpa's chow-chow. That was because Grandpa always picked just the right moment to unveil his greatest invention. He only foisted this trial upon the boys of the family because Grandma thought it was too cruel to pull this on the girls. In fact, Grandma came close to actually hitting Grandpa with a frying pan when he enticed her into trying his chow-chow in the early years of their marriage. Since then, this rite of passage was left for the boys.

Jack Carter, who had also experienced chow-chow as his baptism into the family, got a better seat without drawing any attention. He wanted to see this. Rue joined him, giving Jack a sly smile. She had never tried the chow-chow, but knew the results.

Grandpa returned with his self-proclaimed world famous chow-chow and liberally spread his concoction on all three burgers. Pug was the first to go, but Stacey and Cody Joe were right behind in taking huge bites of their burgers. Almost instantly the yelping started. You could almost see the steam rising out of their ears and nostrils. Welcome to Grandpa's chow-chow, maybe the hottest creation ever made by mankind.

Cody Joe guzzled a big tankard of ice tea, but it didn't help. He burned from the top of his head to the depths of his stomach. His eyes watered and they began to burn as he tried to wash away the tears with contaminated hands. Pug was helpless. He couldn't even talk. He was waving his hand up and down by his mouth, but there was no breeze in the world strong enough to put out this fire. Stacey pleaded for more water, but it was as if no one was listening. He decided he was going to die from the fire in his throat and stomach. There was no relief.

"See you boys like my chow-chow," Grandpa said before releasing a cackle of laughter. "Be sure to finish those burgers. There's plenty more where that came from."

It was only a few moments, but it seemed like days before the threesome recovered enough that they were able to talk again in complete sentences without gasping for air. Grandpa had pulled off his chow-chow gig one more time and the threesome would never forget it.

The one positive of the Labor Day barbeque was that the homemade ice cream now seemed to be made by the angels in heaven. Cody Joe delighted in the banana nut recipe of his Aunt Gerdie while Pug's choice was Rue's special strawberry ice cream. It was a great way to see the sun set over the western pasture, ending another family barbeque.

As was the case recently, Cody Joe and Pug were on the threshold of officially entering junior high school and another life changing event. After a rugged introduction to football, that prospect didn't seem as ominous as a week ago. They were now hardened veterans and chow-chow tested.

Chapter 7

SCHOOL DAYS

This was new territory for Cody Joe Carter. He was actually excited about going to school; his very first day in junior high school. He couldn't wait. It was the first time in his life he wanted to go to school. Even in the first grade he cried most of the first day when Rue Carter had unceremoniously dropped him off in Mrs. White's class and then had the audacity to turn and go home.

But today was much different. This was a different world, full of excitement, change and importance. First, Cody Joe would get to ride the bus to school for the first time. He had always walked the short distance to West Elementary from his home. Now he would catch the bus at West and enjoy the ride across town down 30th Street. He was already acquainted with that route because of football practice. He now had no fear of junior high because he already had a week of football under his belt and Cody Joe figured if he could handle that, he could handle anything that school had to offer. For the first time in a long while, Carter was brimming with confidence.

Also, junior high was going to be completely different. He was going to have a schedule that had six separate classes with a one hour time period. He would also have a 30-minute homeroom period to begin the day. His class schedule would be in this order: Homeroom, Science, Texas History, Arts and Crafts, Lunch, English, Math and Athletics.

Cody Joe did not know where any of his classes were, but his mother said they would explain everything at school.

She said the only thing he needed to know before arriving at school was to meet in room 104 for homeroom. Elmer Perry, who would also be Carter's math teacher, would oversee the homeroom period. Carter also had a card with all seven periods listed on it and the room numbers. For athletics, the card read "field house," and he knew where that was located.

Carter walked to West Elementary to begin his first day, covering the five blocks in less than 15 minutes. He was not one to set time records on the football field or walking to school. When he arrived at the bus circle, he noticed Pug getting out of his mother's car. Pug had a greater distance to walk than Cody Joe, so Mrs. Preston planned on driving Pug to the bus stop each morning and probably would end up taking him to school about as often as not.

Cody Joe could also see Rick Tracks waiting under the awning for the bus and Tracks was the first person Cody Joe spoke to.

"I haven't seen you much in the last few days," said Cody Joe.

"Being a manager takes up more time than I thought it would. We go to practice before you guys and leave after," Tracks noted. "It's a pretty hard job, but I like it and there are some really good guys with me. I'm actually enjoying it. It's better than getting beat up every day. How are you and Christian getting along?"

"Don't bring him up," Cody Joe pleaded. "Everything's fine except for him. I'm just hoping I don't have any classes with him."

About that time Kevin Tumbler and Stacy Trout joined in. Cody Joe hadn't seen them since that last Sunday of baseball. That seemed like years ago.

Tumbler looked at Cody Joe and asked, "How's football going, Carter?"

"Well, it seems like we've been at it a lot longer than a week and I nearly died from the soreness, but I think the worst is over. We started with 81 kids and we are down to 45 after one week."

"Sounds like a tough week," chimed in Trout. "You guys should have stuck to baseball."

"Oh, I did," said Tracks. "I'm now a team manager. Football's not for me. At least, you don't have to die every day in baseball."

Cody Joe sat with Pug on the trip across town while Tumbler and Trout sat across the aisle. Tracks sat with Kirby Tanner, the new kid on the block, so most of the trip to school was consumed with everyone introducing Tanner to Trout and Tumbler. Tanner was not looking forward to his first day at school because he didn't know anyone except those he had met on the football field, and at this point, he didn't really know if he was friends with many of those. He had nightmares of big Dirk Bolger being at the bus stop. He had certainly been glad to see Tracks, Carter and Preston on this ride to school. Now all he had to avoid was any mention of his famous "nose guard." But he was realistic enough to know that something that juicy would be all over school before long.

The bus stop at the junior high ran parallel to the shop and arts and crafts centers. This building also housed the choir and band rooms. The complex was separate from the main school building. One more building completed the campus and that was the gymnasium on the southern end. Off to the west of the campus was a beautiful stand of pecan and oak trees, sitting on the sloped banks of an old creek bed. Water seldom ran through the creek anymore, but was at one time a major tributary off Deep Creek, which still served Snyder well as a city runoff drain during times of heavy rains. In the fact or fiction department, one of these trees is said to have hosted a hanging before the turn of the century. Cody Joe had heard the legend of the Snyder hanging tree, but never knew the real story behind it. People just like saying the area was cursed and still visited by the man that once swung from the branches of one of these trees. It was in this stand of trees where the famous wooden snack bar resided, giving students options for lunch. Lunch fare included the likes of Frito pie, chili-cheese sandwiches, hamburgers, ham sandwiches and all kinds of candy and dessert items. Students had to purchase all items separately, but the ghosts of the past that supposedly haunted this creek bed are said to tell their stories for free.

In Cody Joe's way of thinking, the snack bar was a campus necessity providing the essential requirements of the four food groups. In the vernacular, this was the equivalent to dying and going to heaven.

All six boys got off the bus and walked quickly toward the main school building, a massive structure that rose two stories into the air. The school basically had four wings. The front two wings, facing 26th Street, were separated by a large auditorium. Cody Joe would be entering the school from the back side of the building where there were covered walkways separating the band and choir areas from the main building. Room numbers with arrows showed students which way to go. Tumbler, Tanner and Tracks had to go around the side of the building to a side entrance. Pug had to go to the other side of the building, then upstairs to find his homeroom. Cody Joe and Trout were in the same homeroom just off the back corridor and in the far corner of the wing. Elmer Perry was there to greet them.

"Come in boys. My name is Mr. Perry. Find a seat to your liking and we'll get started when everyone arrives."

It didn't take long for Cody Joe to notice that Mandy Mayor was in his homeroom class. He specifically took a seat right across the aisle from her while Trout climbed in a desk just behind Carter. Cody Joe knew Mayor at West Elementary and he has had a crush on her for the past two years. Of course, just about every boy in Snyder, of Cody Joe's age, had some sort of crush on Mandy Mayor.

Cody Joe mostly lived his life in the realm of realism, so he knew that he would never stand a chance at landing a Mandy Mayor, but he couldn't help getting as close to her as possible. It was like an ugly bug being drawn to the light of a fire. Cody Joe knew he would end up getting burned, but he didn't care.

Mayor didn't even give Cody Joe the time of day when he sat down since she was in deep conversation with two girls on the other side of her. It was good that Cody Joe had no greater expectations.

A moment later, Jennifer Axel took a seat in front of Carter. He had never seen her before in his life, thinking she lived in a part of town he was unfamiliar with. Actually, he only knew kids that came out of West Elementary, so he was pretty sure he was going to meet a lot of new people. He had already found that to be true on the football team. But it hadn't really sunk in that a bunch of those new people just might be girls. Jennifer Axel was the first to drive that point home for Cody Joe. This school year just got more interesting.

Unlike Mandy Mayor, Jennifer was eager to strike up a conversation with a boy she didn't know.

"Hi, my name is Jennifer, what's yours?" Axel said to Carter.

"My name is Cody Joe. How ya' doin'?"

"Cody Joe, that's a swell name. I don't know anyone here, so I'm kind of nervous," Jennifer confessed.

"Guess we all are a bit nervous today. It'll take all of us a while before we get used to the surroundings," Cody Joe said. "The guy in back of me is Stacy Trout. He's a good friend of mine, but I don't see him much these days because he's in the band and I'm in football. The girl right across from me is Mandy Mayor. She went to West last year with me, but you could never tell. She doesn't even act like she knows me, and she probably doesn't. We've never officially been in an actual class with each other."

"You play football?" Jennifer asked without expecting an answer. "That's really neat. I've never known a boy on a football team."

At that point, the day's first class bell rang and Mr. Perry walked to the front of the class and said, "Welcome to Snyder Junior High School. I know many of you are a bit nervous on this first day, but we're going to make it very easy for you. Each of you will find a packet on my desk with your name on it. The packet contains your class schedule, the time of your class and the room number of your class. Some of you may already have this class schedule because it was mailed out. However, if you don't, the packet will provide your schedule. There is also a map of the SJHS campus to help you find your way around. Also, in the packet is a locker number. There are individual lockers on the lower floors only. Your map should indicate what wing contains your locker number. Sometime today try to find your locker. You will be responsible for buying a lock for that locker. The school is not responsible for any stolen items. So, it's a good idea to keep that locker locked at all times."

Everyone in the room had a packet, so the first day of homeroom went amazingly smooth.

The bell rang after another 15 minutes and Carter was on his way to the next class. He bid farewell to Trout and headed to science just down the hall. Pug had already hit a homerun in his first class. Alexi Taggert had been in his homeroom class and she had asked Pug to eat with her at lunch in the cafeteria. He wasn't about to turn her down. He was walking on a cloud the rest of the morning.

Cody Joe made it to the lunch break without a problem, but he had not found his locker. He wanted to drop off some of the stuff he was carrying before lunch. Today, however, he was going to have to carry everything with him and go to his locker the first thing after lunch.

Cody Joe was in Arts and Crafts when the lunch bell rang. He bounded out of the classroom, down the steps above the creek bank and into a long line for the snack bar. Cody Joe was worried he wouldn't have time to eat with the long line, but it moved fast. He got a soft drink, a chili cheese sandwich and a bag of chips before moving outside where he found Trout, Tracks, Tanner and Tumbler sitting together at an outside picnic table. Butch Cassidy had also joined the group. In fact, the whole gang was present except Pug Preston. Cody Joe wondered what happened to him. But Pug never showed up for his first lunch out with the boys.

Pug didn't miss his friends at all. It was just like being on a date by being with Alexi Taggert. He never expected her to be in one of his classes and he found out at lunch that he was in the same class as Alexi for Texas History right after lunch. He could walk her to class and was one of the first guys to be carrying a girl's books down the hall. In his mind, he had hit it big and already felt like a big man on campus.

It was obvious that the pert Alexi was greatly enamored with Pug. She relished the attention Pug poured on her. But the most obvious thing was that everyone seemed to think they already belonged to each other or it was quickly heading that way. Carter knew nothing of this new liaison between Pug and Alexi, so he didn't know that he was also losing part of his best friend at the same time as he was looking for his lost locker.

Carter finally found his locker in the middle of a long hallway. He was thinking that this locker was a long way away from most of his classes, but soon felt better when he discovered that Jennifer Axel's locker was right next to his. She already had a lock for her locker and told Cody Joe that he could get one at Perry Brother's on the Snyder square downtown for 50 cents.

But Carter got another bonus for this chance meeting when another new girl walked up to join Cody Joe and Jennifer.

"Cody Joe, this is Veronica Slade, my best friend," said Jennifer by the way of introduction.

Carter was caught a bit off guard and literally fumbled his response. All he could get out was a weak, "Hello."

Jennifer saved him by saying, "Cody Joe is on the football team and we sat together today in homeroom. Cody Joe, Veronica and I went to East Elementary and we've been best friends since the first grade. We do everything together."

Carter liked just about everything about Veronica Slade. She had dark, shoulder-length hair that had a reddish tint and an infectious smile that seemed to stun Carter every time she flashed it. In Cody Joe's way of thinking, Veronica Slade could give Mandy Mayor a run for her money.

Veronica was quick on the uptake as Carter acted as if he had lost his voice, asking, "Cody Joe, when do you play your first game? I'd love to see that. I really like football and my dad told me we would have our own seventh grade team in junior high. You are the first person Jennifer and I have met that's on the football team."

"We play on Thursdays, starting next week, but I don't know a schedule yet. Coach Heart is supposed to announce that at practice today," Carter explained.

He was sure glad the conversation turned to football because it seemed like that was the only thing he could talk about without embarrassing himself. He was at a loss as to why he was so nervous around Veronica Slade.

The bell sounded for the next class and that meant he had five minutes to make it to John Grimes' English class. He said goodbye to his two new acquaintances and headed out for his next first day adventure.

As it turned out, Cody Joe had faced enough excitement for one day and the rest of the afternoon went without undue stress. Cody Joe met no more girls and was sad that he didn't have Pug in a single class. He already knew that since he had seen Pug's schedule, but they had always planned to eat together at lunch. Even that didn't happen today and it kept Carter off balance all day. "What in the world has happened to Pug?" wondered Cody Joe.

Carter did have Kirby Tanner, Butch Cassidy and Thomas Quay in Mr. Perry's math class, so that helped Cody Joe end the day on a high note. They could all walk to practice together every day.

All in all, Cody Joe felt as if the day had gone well. He thought there were great looking girls in every class except Arts and Crafts, which had all boys. He had also met two new girls in Jennifer Axel and Veronica Slade. He wouldn't overtly admit it, but he was already smitten by the lovely Veronica. She had rung his bell and he couldn't wait to run into her again. But before that happens, he better study up on what to say to her when they do meet again. These were pressures he had never considered when he went off to his first day in junior high school this very morning. It seemed like his life was changing with every rising of the sun. He never knew what a new day would bring – and that made his new life challenging and interesting in a myriad of ways.

* * *

Just as Elmer Perry was finishing up his fifth period math class, the classroom bell rang sharply at 2:30 p.m. The eighth grade and seventh grade Blue Devils all began their trek to the field houses. For the seventh graders, this was their first walk down Ave. M. It was about a three block walk by the time you cleared campus. Since school wasn't officially out for another hour, there was never any serious traffic on Ave. M this time of day, so the boys leisurely strolled down the middle of the street, moving out of the way only for a rare vehicle.

Cody Joe and Tanner started out together, but Butch Cassidy and T-Quay caught up with them before they even cleared the back end of the school campus after a brief trip to their lockers. Everyone was still wondering what could have happened to Pug.

A grateful Tanner turned to Cody Joe and said, "I can't tell you how relieved I am. No one brought up the nose guard incident. I just knew it was going to be all over the school and I just knew I was going to be ridiculed all day. But it didn't happen. This is the first day I'm glad my parents moved to Snyder."

"Well, don't get too comfortable just yet," reasoned Cody Joe. "That story may still get some legs before all is said and done. But I really think most of the guys on the team really like you and you gained a lot of respect when you put Bolger's face in the dirt. Team things tend to stick with the team. Maybe this will too."

"I don't even care anymore because you have helped me meet some other guys and I now have people around me I consider as friends," said Tanner.

Butch jumped in, "Kirby, if anyone gives you trouble about the nose guard thing, come see me. I'll put a stop to it. We're all in this together now."

"Thanks Butch, but I just might take you up on that offer," Tanner said.

The foursome then heard a loud, "Wait up guys." It was Pug.

"Where have you been all day, Pug?" Cody Joe said with an air of disappointment. "You were supposed to meet us for lunch. Where were you?"

"Well, you'll never believe who was in my homeroom period," began Pug. "Your cousin, Alexi, was in there and she asked me to eat with her in the cafeteria. You know, Cody Joe, that I couldn't turn her down. She's swell. I even walked her to class after lunch because we had Texas History together.

"What do you think if I ask her to go steady?" Pug asked. "I think I could have a girlfriend on the first day of school."

Cody Joe was so dumbfounded he didn't know what to say. First, he thought the term was trading disks. He had done that a few times in elementary school with a girl, but he had never gone steady. He guessed Pug had already put a lot of attention into this for him to know how it was done in junior high. Cody Joe felt out of place and behind the times. That made it hard to focus on Pug's direct question.

In fact, it was T-Quay, who was mere steps behind the Carter gang that answered Pug, saying, "Pug, you talkin' about that Alexi Taggert gal? Now, that's some real stuff there. Isn't she a little out of your league?"

Pug said, "That's what I was thinking, T-Quay, but she's the one that asked me to eat with her and I really think she likes me."

"Then go for it," T-Quay snapped. "What's she gonna do anyway, cut your head off? The worst thing she can do is tell you no and then you are no worse off than you are now."

"Oh, I'll be worse off. I don't think I could take it if she turned me down. I'd rather her cut my head off," Pug theorized. "If she turned me down, I'd never talk to another girl."

"All I'm sayin' is you better learn to take some rejection from girls or you'll end up a hermit," T-Quay said in delivering his succinct sermon of prophecy.

"Just how many girlfriends do you have, T-Quay?" asked Pug.

"None right now," he said. "But I plan on having one before football is over. I guarantee you that. I might even have more than one before the school year is out."

The boys arrived at the field house in plenty of time to dress and be on the field by 3:15 p.m. as Coach Heart had directed. Unfortunately, Nate Christian was already in his stall by Cody Joe's dressing area.

Christian greeted Cody Joe with, "I'm glad we didn't have any classes together, Cody Joe. I'd probably have to cut your nose off before the proper time."

That was the first time all day that Carter had even

90

thought about Nate Christian. It was so sublime to not have him around that he had totally put him out of his mind. Well, football always seemed to have a knack for bringing back the real world.

Coach Heart greeted the boys back by saying, "Hope all of you had a good first day at school. I want to remind you that school is the most important thing you do. If you don't make your grades, you don't play football. That's the simple fact of it. So start now and keep up with your work. The teachers will let me know if you aren't doing your work and we will give you some additional motivation, if you know what I mean.

"Also, I got our schedule for the year. The managers will give you cards that have the seventh and eighth grade schedules written on them. It will show the day of the game, the game time and where that game will be. Our first game will be Sept. 11, a week from Thursday on this very field at 4 p.m. against Big Spring Goliad. We have no idea whether they will be good or bad, but Goliad is a bigger school than Snyder, so we expect a tough game.

"Make sure you will be ready for that game by giving everything you have in practice. Being prepared is how you win games. If you are not willing to be prepared, you are not willing to be a member of this team and we will get rid of you. Now get out there and prove to me you can play some football."

With that a loud cheer was offered up in unison and the seventh grade Blue Devils went back to work – but this time with an actual opponent in sight.

Chapter 8

JITTERS

Before Carter took off for his walk to school on Wednesday morning, he had twisted a promise out of his mother to make sure she would purchase a lock for his locker. He told her about the one that Jennifer Axel had, a combination lock that cost 50 cents at Perry Brother's on the square in downtown Snyder.

Rue Carter was one to not ask many questions from her son unless he was willing to divulge the information willingly, but she was pretty good at recognizing key clues that went beyond words. In this case, her intuition told her that this Jennifer Axel must be a special girl because he was so insistent on getting a lock just like hers. Usually, Cody Joe was only this insistent if Pug had suggested something like this. Rue had never heard of the Axel girl before Tuesday night in connection to the combination lock and was sure that she was a new entry into the life of her eldest son. Actually, Mrs. Carter was glad that Cody Joe was making new friends and she knew in her heart that some of those friends were going to be girls. She just didn't know if she was ready for that transition. That was a whole other world. What she didn't know, or even have a clue about, was that Veronica Slade had been the one Cody Joe dreamed about on Tuesday night. Rue had good intuition, but her son was racing way ahead of her these days.

Cody Joe arrived at the bus circle about the same time as Kevin Tumbler. Tumbler told Carter all about his first day of band. Cody Joe really didn't relate and wondered if Tumbler felt the same way when he talked about football. He also wondered if this would eventually lead them even further apart.

Junior high school was changing his life literally overnight and it was all happening so fast that he hadn't had time to absorb the good and the bad of it all. Right now, all he knew was his world had exploded. It was exciting, depressing, adventurous, confusing, enchanting and uncertain all at the same time. But there was no doubt that Carter was more confident than a week ago and eager to take on this new challenge. Maybe Carter felt that this was his opportunity to remake himself, forgetting the days of doubt created by the untimely snub from Little League.

Pug's mom had decided to take him all the way to school on this morning, and that left Cody Joe feeling a bit empty once again. He did possess that added confidence, but it didn't take all that much to give it a shake. Facing life's challenges without Pug was one of those confidence shakers. Carter took it for granted that he would not see Pug again until football practice. He liked his cousin Alexi, but why did she have to make waves now when everything was changing so rapidly? Pug had always been a calming force for Cody Joe. They always worked through the problems of life together. It would be putting it mildly, but Carter was perturbed with one Pug Preston. Cody Joe was thinking one should never place that much faith in a Methodist.

To make matters worse, Pug wasn't missing Cody Joe at all. In fact, he found Alexi Taggert sitting on a bench by the trees near the snack bar when he got to school as had been prearranged the day before at lunch. He happily joined her and the two did not move until the opening bell rang for school. Pug was plain and simple enjoying his new Baptist friend.

Cody Joe saw Pug and Alexi down by the creek bed when he got off the bus. He just shrugged his shoulders and walked toward his homeroom class with Stacy Trout. He passed Butch Cassidy along the way and stopped for a few words. It was becoming clear to Cody Joe that life was going to be a series of changes. Unlike elementary school, every day would see changes by the hour instead of the semester. If you survive in this new world, you will have to do it on the fly with different teachers, different friends, different days and different circumstances. If this was growing up, it was a challenging rollercoaster of emotions and events rolled into each and every day.

* * *

Before Jennifer Axel ever sat down in homeroom, she asked Cody Joe, "Did you get your football schedule from your coach?"

"Yeah, we're playing Big Spring Goliad on September 11 on our field at 4 p.m.," Cody Joe explained.

"Oh, that's next week," said a surprised Jennifer. "We didn't think it would be that quick, but Veronica and I can walk to the field right after school and be there for the game. My parents aren't crazy about us going to a game at night down there by colored town, but since you play so early, you'll be through before night."

"We will play all our games on Thursday afternoons," Cody Joe related. "I can't wait for the season to start."

It was clear that Mandy Mayor had heard part of that conversation because she turned and gave Cody Joe a wide smile. "Well, Cody Joe, I didn't know that you played football. We try out for cheerleader today and I hope to make the squad."

Cody Joe thought she would have no trouble making the cheerleading squad. She was one of the prettiest girls in school and she would be the boys' choice hands down.

"I bet you get it," fired back Cody Joe. "I didn't even know we were going to have cheerleaders. This is a bigger deal than I ever thought."

"You mean you didn't know about the big pep rally we're going to have on the morning of the game in the gym?" Mayor asked. "The new cheerleaders will have to come up with some routines for the pep rally. I can't wait. The whole school will be asked to show up 30 minutes early and the pep rally will run through the homeroom period."

"No one has said anything about a pep rally to the football team, but then again, nobody seems to tell us anything until we need to know," Carter reasoned. "I don't think coaches spend much time thinking about things in the future. They mostly tell us stuff that's happening today."

Mayor giggled like she was really interested, and she really was now that she knew Cody Joe was on the football team. She winked at Cody Joe and said, "I'll be looking for you at the pep rally."

Elmer Perry called the class to order, after the tardy bell, and told the class it was time to elect a homeroom representative for the student council. It came as no surprise that Mandy Mayor got 75 percent of the vote. Cody Joe even got three votes and Stacy Trout got two. Mandy played her best "I'm surprised" card, leaving Cody Joe to think that Mandy had the cheerleading thing locked up in the bank. If there was one thing that Mandy knew about, it was playing the game of politics.

He told Jennifer, "She'll have so many awards before school is out, she could really be a mayor."

Jennifer gave a disapproving affirmative nod, knowing that she would never be a great friend of Mandy Mayor. And she didn't like the way Cody Joe fawned over the cheerleader in waiting and newly elected student council member. She secretly thought, "Why do the same people always get everything?"

* * *

Once again Cody Joe went through lunch without Pug at his side. He couldn't help but feel lonely even though he had the T-Gang – Trout, Tanner, Tracks and Tumbler – with him. Cassidy was also with the lunch bunch. They even got in a little touch football game under the shade of the trees on the creek bank. Tanner brought a small rubber football to school that was perfect for a tag game at lunch.

Pug went to the cafeteria with Alexi Taggert and this was promising to be a regular routine. At least, Pug was hoping it would turn into a permanent lunch date. He didn't seem to miss the guys at all. In fact, all he could think about was Alexi.

Pug did join Cody Joe, T-Quay, Tanner and Cassidy for the trek to the field house after school, but he even proved to be a downer for the whole group as he talked only of Alexi Taggert. Cody Joe thought Pug Preston was a lost cause to the feminine wiles of the weaker sex. He hated this about Pug and resented the fact that Pug didn't seem to care that he had forgotten his real friends.

Cody Joe patiently listened to the day's events that transpired between Pug and Alexi while strolling down a deserted Ave. M, but when he finally had enough, he said "Pug, you've been run over by a truck and don't even know it."

* * *

It was brutally hot on this particular Wednesday as Mother Nature threw one last and unforgiving heat wave at West Texas. The temperature hovered around 100 degrees and made the practice session almost unbearable. To make matters worse, Coach Heart had prepared one of the toughest workouts of the year. He knew the team didn't have much longer to prepare for the first game with Goliad and he, at least, wanted the team to be in shape when they played. Coach Heart also knew that the West Texas weather rarely cooperated with the time schedule of any coach.

The practice was the second worst of the year for Cody Joe. It could have easily been the worst, but in Cody Joe's way of thinking, nothing could top that first day of soreness. But he wasn't much into quibbling about the ranking of worst days. He was miserable from the heat and wasn't interested in taking part in the ranking process. Suffering was suffering no matter how you ranked it. The heat, combined with a high level of humidity, had the whole team dragging. It was rare for the temperature to climb over 100 degrees in September, but certainly not unheard of in Texas. No one in Snyder ever lifted an eyebrow when triple-digit temperatures were mentioned. It was part of life in this part of the world, except most of those living in this world were not playing football.

The heat radiating from under Cody Joe's helmet was almost unbearable. He took his helmet off at every opportunity just so he could breathe properly. His mouth was so dry that his tongue had become swollen and filled his mouth. Carter even thought for a brief minute that he was willing to give up football for just one long, cool drink of water.

Coach Heart was violently opposed to letting his players drink water during a practice. He thought it would make them sick. Besides, they needed to toughen up and learn how to play even when they are uncomfortable. He gave no water breaks and continued practice as if it were 70 degrees outside. After all, this was football practice.

Ominous clouds were building up in the northwest as practice continued, but the heat held its brutal grip on the immediate area. Several players, including Jay Coy and Henry Styles, had to be taken out of some drills because of the heat. No one ever mentioned the possibility of heat stroke. Everyone was equally suffering and most were wondering if the unrelenting heat would ever loosen its grip or if practice would ever come to an end.

Then a miracle happened. Just as Cody Joe was about to go down on his knees from the heat, a cool breeze hit him square in the face. It was like a jolt of new life. The breeze quickly swept through the whole team like a life giving ghost out of the blue. It quickly revitalized the team. The heat was suddenly gone and only a soothing coolness remained. A cool front had moved through the area, chasing away the 100-degree threat for the rest of the season. Now it was time to play football.

The rest of the practice went as Coach Heart had envisioned as the players responded with a new vigor and eagerness. Chants of "Beat Goliad" hung over the field and the team truly began to look forward to a real game. Practice was becoming tiresome, but now a new carrot had been dangled in front of their collective noses and they were now practicing, maybe for the first time, with a real purpose in mind other than mere survival. They were finally having fun.

When the coaches called for the gassers at the end of practice, the clouds opened up and delivered a downpour. The players ran harder, laughed louder and slid in the mud. Even though many of these kids might never even remember this event, they would never be the same again. The team had discovered the joy of being a team. And this was something not being taught in most of the classrooms two blocks down the street. A new light had been turned on. Those who survive together develop a bond that mere mortals can never break.

* * *

Rue Carter bought Cody Joe a combination lock at Perry Brother's just as he had ordered. She gave it to him during supper as Cody Joe devoured a whole pan of tacos that had been made just for him. Everyone else in the family had already eaten. The Carter family was used to eating early in the evening, around 5:30 p.m., and didn't like waiting for Cody Joe to get home. An athletic bus took some players to West Elementary where Carter then walked home. He usually was home a little before 7 p.m., but it was almost 7:30 p.m. on this night because all the players had to clean mud off their uniforms and turn them in for a cleaning because of the rain. Cody Joe wondered what that meant for Tracks. He might be at the field house all night.

Cody Joe spent the rest of the night locking and unlocking his combination lock. He could work that lock blindfolded if he had to. He was confident that he would never forget the combination.

While Cody Joe was fumbling with the lock sequence, Kate Carter asked her brother a rare question, "Cody Joe, do you think you will ever have a girlfriend in junior high school? My friend, Amy, told me today that her brother had a girlfriend in the seventh grade. Are you the only boy in school without a girlfriend?"

"Kate," Cody Joe lied, "I don't spend much time thinking about things like that. I guess if it happens, it happens. If it doesn't, it doesn't. Do you have a boyfriend?"

"Of course not, I'm just in the fifth grade, Cody Joe," Kate said as her face reddened. "But I do like Tom Henderson a lot. He never pays any attention to me. Why don't you boys pay attention when we want you to?"

"Why don't you girls pay attention when we want you to?" asked Cody Joe. "Kate, I guess that's the whole secret to getting a boyfriend or girlfriend. You need two people to pay attention at the same time."

* * *

The next morning Cody Joe specifically sought out Rick Tracks, asking, "How late did you have to stay last night?"

Tracks said, "I was there until 9 o'clock. I hope we don't have too much more rain this year. At least, you guys will have some nice, clean uniforms to wear at practice today. We still don't have them in the lockers yet, but we get to miss homeroom today to get that done."

"Well, I was wondering how it went. The field house was a mess when I left," related Cody Joe.

"It still is a mess, but Coach Bear says you guys will have to clean up your own mess today. You're going to love getting down on your knees with Christian to clean your area," Tracks informed.

"Oh, I can't wait," Cody Joe whined. "He'll probably be wearing that same old stinky pair of underwear he was wearing yesterday. That rain is the first shower he has had this season."

Thursday went much like the other days of the week. Pug was literally a no-show. And Mandy Mayor had her way again after being named to the cheerleading squad. The only surprising outcome on that front was the fact that Molly Gathers was named head cheerleader. Cody Joe was certain that Mandy was distraught over that outcome, but it seems that there was an even more popular girl in Snyder than Mandy. That was sure to be a huge blight on Mandy's reputation and a huge upswing for the new Queen Gathers. Molly Gathers was from North Elementary and Mandy remained under the conviction that nothing good could possibly come out of North Elementary.

Cody Joe tried valiantly to cheer up Mandy in homeroom when the cheerleading results were announced over the homeroom loudspeaker much to the dismay of Jennifer Axel, who was almost gagging over the whole episode.

"Mandy, I'm thinking the judges made a huge mistake in picking the Gathers girl as head cheerleader," said Carter, who was hoping to build up a few brownie points with the now second most popular girl in school. "I haven't met Molly Gathers, but she can't be half as talented as you are."

"Oh, Cody Joe, they say Molly went to a cheerleading school in Dallas over the summer. I didn't even know there was such a thing. She already had her routine down to a tee. The rest of us looked like a bunch of bumpkins from Snyder, Texas," said the distraught Mandy.

Jennifer said to Cody Joe, "Don't lay it on too thick. It may be the only thing Mandy gets outsmarted on this whole year. I guarantee you that a new war has started at SJHS."

Cody Joe didn't really care one way or the other who the head cheerleader was. He only knew this opened the door for him to walk through and if Mandy needed some comforting, he was glad to oblige. And now he was officially going to have a member of the cheerleaders looking for him next week at the pep rally.

* * *

Sure enough, Tracks was right. Coach Bear brought cleaning equipment to the field house and said the place had to be clean before practice. If it wasn't cleaned, there would be extra gassers before and after practice.

Nate Christian, as usual, was a thorn in the side of the team, refusing to do any of the work. It actually made Cody Joe's job easier because he didn't have to deal with Christian. And as usual, Nate got away with it since no one turned him in for refusing to help. Christian still held an amazing sway over all the team members, who were more than a little afraid to challenge that shiny switchblade that seemed to slide out of Christian's pocket the moment Christian ever needed to make a firm statement.

But on the practice side, football was never so much fun. There was a feeling in the air that something special was close at hand. They were getting ready to play a real game. This would be the first game. They were actually going to represent Snyder as a team. None of them had been a part of anything like that except Henry Styles and Hank Cline, who were both on the Snyder Little League championship team that went to the regional tournament in Abilene before being eliminated. Those playoff games had been broadcast over KSNY radio in Snyder.

"I'm already getting a bit nervous and it's still a week before we play," confessed Tanner to Butch Cassidy.

"Kirby, I've got you topped on the nervous chart," Cassidy confessed back to Tanner. "I've never even carried a football in a game and now I'm starting at fullback. I always thought I'd be playing linebacker on defense. The only thing I've got going for me is I know I'll be running scared, running for my life."

Cody Joe jumped in, "Don't worry; we'll open holes so wide for you that you won't even see a player from the other team. Even as slow as you are, you'll be able to walk into the end zone."

But everyone was beginning to understand that this wasn't

Boys' Club football anymore. This was the best. This wasn't a recreational league. This is where the road began for becoming a Snyder Tiger. The whole community followed the high school Tigers. They were the heroes of the town. The spirit of the city revolved around how the Snyder Tigers did on Friday night. The seventh grade Blue Devils were simply walking a path carved out by many before them. It was a rocky road, but the lure of playing on Friday night was a strong pull just like the moon on the tide. It was part of the life cycle in West Texas.

* * *

By Friday, the kids in school were beginning to learn about the existence of the football team. The Snyder Tigers were to open their season today at Tiger Stadium, just west of the high school campus. The Snyder Daily News was running daily features on the team and the community was gearing up for some serious Friday night football.

The fallout trickled down to the seventh and eighth grade Blue Devils. Being a football player in Snyder carried some weight. Cody Joe was finding that out every time he mentioned he was on the football team, people began to take notice of what he was saying. Playing football set him apart from the crowd.

At 12 years old, however, Cody Joe had not figured how to sustain this favored status once he got past the "I play football" introduction. His conversation mode always quickly broke down after a fair start, especially with girls. If he actually liked the girl, he went numb all over.

The only girl he could really talk to was Jennifer Axel, but that was because Jennifer did enough talking for both of them. She was free and easy and talked to Cody Joe like he was her best friend. In fact, that's the exact category in which Cody Joe placed Jennifer Axel. They were good friends. But when Cody Joe was with Jennifer and her best friend, Veronica Slade, his mouth turned into mush. He just couldn't get the words out. Veronica was beautiful, but it worked against her when she was with Cody Joe. She had instantly taken a liking to him, but he was so quiet. Jennifer keeps telling Veronica that Carter is actually easy to talk to. She takes all these signals as meaning Cody Joe isn't interested in her.

After lunch on Friday, Cody Joe places his new lock on his locker after depositing some books he has carried around all morning. Jennifer and Veronica also make a trip to their lockers.

"Hey, Cody Joe, how's it going?" says Jennifer. "Veronica and I have choir together next period. Are you going that way?"

"I guess not," answered Cody Joe. "I've got English upstairs."

He glances at Veronica, but can't quite force himself to look her square in the eyes. He then turns to Jennifer and says, "Have a good weekend." He then walks away.

Cody Joe is now totally angry with himself. He could have taken time to walk with them to their next class. There was still an extra three minutes left before the first bell. But he couldn't think of anything to say. Why did Veronica Slade always make him feel this way? It was the question that haunted Cody Joe. No matter what he did, he would just fall apart when he was around Veronica. He wanted desperately to get to know Veronica much better, but he knew he was only serving to drive her away.

Cody Joe felt he was much more comfortable even with Mandy Mayor than Veronica. He was now talking to Mandy on a daily basis. The secret here, however, should have been obvious, even to Cody Joe. Carter realized up front that he really didn't have a chance of landing a Mandy Mayor. He still held out hope that anything was possible with Veronica Slade.

Cody Joe thought it a bit ironic that he was getting ready to play his first football game, yet the only real jitters he felt was over a girl he barely knew.

Chapter 9

GOLIAD

By Saturday morning, the whole town was feeling the effects that linger after the Snyder Tigers have won a football game. It seems that everyone walks with a quicker gait and the greetings on the street come with a much grander smile. Snyder 14, Borger 6.

Cody Joe got to sit in the junior high section for the first time on Friday night, and he had never had so much fun. They taunted the Borger team, yelled for the Tigers and generally acted like junior high school students. Butch Cassidy even treated the crowd to his bare belly routine by taking off his shirt, exposing his amply painted black and gold stomach. It didn't do too much for the girls in the crowd, but the Blue Devils loved it, especially when he rolled his barrel belly to his best imitation of a Hawaiian hula dance.

Most of the seventh grade Blue Devils sat together, forming a formidable fraternity that definitely established their status as team members. After all, they were the next generation of Tigers. Cody Joe naturally sat with Cassidy, Tracks, Styles and Tanner. His band friends, Stacy Trout and Kevin Tumbler, didn't think it was proper to sit with their best friends because the band and the football players obviously didn't mix except when the lazy, hazy days of summer yielded to the game of "Move Up" on Sunday afternoons or at school lunch for some tag football.

Segregation comes in many forms in Snyder and it was not missing even in the environs of Tiger Stadium. Still, this tribal practice did serve a purpose, intended or otherwise. The seventh grade Blue Devils were becoming a team. They were learning to depend on each other and learning their place in this new society that has so quickly left elementary school in the fading dust of time.

But not all the Blue Devils were present and accounted for. Pug Preston was sitting about 10 rows in front of his football team with none other than Alexi Taggert. A whole gaggle of Alexi's friends had gathered around her to meet her new beau. Pug was right in the middle of eight girls and getting a lot of attention.

T-Quay was continually throwing barbs at Pug. "Kiss her, Pug." "Hold her hand, Pug." "Are you driving her home tonight, Pug?" It was a never ending barrage and Preston didn't even seem to notice. He was actually glad to see all the guys watching. He knew they all were jealous of his great fortune.

Cody Joe acted as if he didn't even notice, but he was upset with Pug on so many levels that ignoring him seemed like the best thing to do. First, he thought Pug should be with the team. This was a special night, the opening of football season, and Pug was off chasing a girl. Pug simply had his priorities mixed up in Cody Joe's way of thinking. Also, Cody Joe had noticed Jennifer Axel and Veronica Slade sitting with some of the band kids. That group also had its share of boys in it. Secretly Cody Joe wished he could go and sit with Jennifer and Veronica, but he would never have the real guts to do that. What if they told him he couldn't sit there because the seats were promised to someone else? What if they didn't really want him to sit with them? And what would he ever talk to them about for a whole game? Well, Pug didn't seem to be having a problem with the girls and that steamed Cody Joe even more.

Every other week Cody Joe made a trek to the barber shop to get his flattop rejuvenated. The Saturday talk during football season was always about the Tiger performance the night before.

A rascally codger with a heavy beard proclaimed, "The Tigers are a better football team than they were a year ago."

He had plenty on hand willing to rebut the statement. Another older gentleman, who was in a suit and tie, even though it was Saturday, chimed in, "But they still can't throw the football a lick. I'd feel better about their chances if they could throw the ball. They threw only four times in the whole game and completed only one of them."

Another said, "They didn't need to throw the ball. They had nearly 300 yards rushing. And besides, this was only a non-conference game, so you don't want to show all the eggs in your basket."

The barber working on Cody Joe's neat flattop asked, "Cody Joe, aren't you playing junior high football this year?"

"Yes sir," Carter proudly stated. "We start Thursday against Big Spring Goliad."

"Have we got some good kids over there on the creek that can play for Snyder High in a few years? I sure hope so."

"Well, we haven't even played a game, but I think we're pretty good. We've been working hard and we're all anxious to play a game and see what we've got," Cody Joe said.

The barber added, "I've never seen a junior high game in my whole life, but I need to take a break one Thursday and come watch you play. After all, you're one of my best customers."

* * *

Watching the Tigers play on Friday night made the seventh grade Blue Devils antsy to play a game. The guys were beginning to feel some butterflies in the pit of their stomachs.

Events at school didn't help either. In homeroom, on Monday, Robert "Moose" Tankard, SJHS principal, delivered an announcement over the P.A. system about the upcoming pep rally on Thursday morning. The ex-football coach said the football teams would be present and that the pep rally would start 30 minutes before the start of school and he urged the student body to come early and take part, "because our boys need your support." He also said that the pep rally would last less than an hour and all students would briefly report to their homeroom class when it was over.

During homeroom period each day, the cheerleaders were allowed to go from class to class while yelling things like "Go Blue Devils" and "Beat Goliad." That's when Elmer Perry's homeroom class was given its first introduction to the new queen of the school, Molly Gathers, head cheerleader extraordinaire.

Cody Joe had to admit that Molly was stunning and very confident of herself, despite the disparaging remarks he kept hearing from Mandy Mayor every day. He could certainly see why Molly was such a threat to Mandy.

Molly said in her sweet sing-song style, "I want to invite all of you to the pep rally on Thursday in the gym 30 minutes before the start of school. Our Blue Devils will play their first game at 4 o'clock Thursday afternoon against Big Spring Goliad. We also want everyone to make plans to attend that game. All students of SJHS will be able to get into the game free, so we want everyone to come. This is really important because this is the first game in history for the boys in our grade. Let's give them our support. I'll be there and I hope you are. Go Blue Devils."

After seeing Molly for the first time, Cody Joe had a feeling that if he had had a vote to name a head cheerleader, he might even vote for the Gathers girl himself.

With the weather turning a little cooler, practice seemed to perk up a bit. Also, the Blue Devils were getting better day by day as the coaches pushed to get them game ready. The coaches were still running practice as if they had just started. They had not eased up on any drills at all.

There were no major injuries to speak of, but just about everyone was nursing some type of bump, scrape or bruise. Center Robert Lieberman had a slightly turned ankle and cornerback Marc Sanchez had a severely bruised knee. Several team members were having problems with their feet whether it was from blisters or athlete's foot. None of this was going to keep anyone from practicing or from the game.

On the team front, it looked like Lee Line had won the quarterback's race over Joseph Moore and he was now getting the most snaps in the practice sessions. Hank Cline and the fleet Lester Jarvis would be the two halfbacks, joining newly appointed fullback Butch Cassidy in the backfield.

Both Cody Joe and Pug would have the distinction of being two-way starters. Cody Joe would be at right guard on offense and at the strong side linebacker post on defense. Joey Taylor would be the weak side linebacker. Pug would be an offensive tackle and the nose guard in the Blue Devils' 5-2 defense. Other two-way starters would be Adam Quay (wide receiver and defensive end), Dirk Bolger (offensive tackle and defensive end) and Robert Lieberman (center and defensive tackle).

Other starters named by Coach Heart included Mac Cone at tight end and T-Quay at left guard on offense. Other defensive starters were Nate Christian at left tackle, Stoney Wall at right tackle, Marc Sanchez at the right corner slot, Jay Coy at safety and Tony Carrillo at safety.

The coaches still thought Kirby Tanner could contribute to the team at halfback, but he was considered a cut below Jarvis and Cline. Even though Tanner was too short, Coach Heart was also thinking about playing Tanner behind Adam Quay at wide receiver since Adam was going to be playing on offense and defense.

The coaches were in a pickle when it came to the hefty Cassidy. Butch was probably the best defensive player on the entire team, yet Coach Heart was reluctant to use him on defense since he needed his fresh legs at fullback. Besides, Cassidy tended to tire quickly since he was such a big kid. So the decision was made to start Taylor at linebacker on defense. Cassidy could still be Coach Heart's secret weapon in key situations during a game and the coaches wouldn't hesitate to bring Cassidy in on defense when they needed to make something happen.

T-Quay was another player who could play on defense at tackle without losing much at all. Eric Blade was also not a starter, but he could play in both the offensive or defensive line without losing much quality. Jack King could probably sub as a defensive back and nearly won the job at safety before being edged out by Carrillo. Henry Styles probably wouldn't play much, but the coaches had discovered he could kick the ball and spent most of practice working on his kicking skills. As of yet, the team had worked on kicking extra points only once.

Everyone on the team had been trained for two positions. The coaches did not cut one player. Every kid that wanted to be on the team was given a game uniform on Tuesday. Tracks counted the uniforms as they were passed out and there were now 39 Blue Devils battle tested and qualified to wear a blue number on the front and back of a solid white jersey. The pants and helmets were also solid white. The players were given new game socks. Each and every player earned new status by putting on this uniform. For many on the team, this was actually the first time it dawned on them that they were really on the team. All the work, the soreness, the heat, the grueling practices, the thirst, the aches and pains had all been worth it. They had beaten the odds and were the 39 best Snyder had to offer.

* * *

The fanatic adulation shown to football players is not necessarily unique to Texas, but there is an atmosphere created within the framework that allows the art of personal homage to be carried to greater heights in the Lone Star State. Football players are stars in Texas and Snyder surely wasn't bucking the trend. The pep rallies before each and every game helped enhance the overall attitude that football was the lifeblood of the school and community. School spirit simply made things run smoother at school and gave the students something to pull for together. The thinking was that unity in the school system must never be underestimated or undervalued. In the meantime, the status of the players rose to new heights, something none of them ever experienced in elementary school.

The band students had learned just enough spirit songs to get by. They wouldn't actually march until the last game of the season when the Blue Devils took on hated rival Sweetwater, but they would perform at the pep rallies.

The gym quickly filled to near capacity by 8 a.m. on Thursday. Many parents and relatives of the football team had come as well as parents and relatives of band members. The football boys had gathered on the south side of the gym as ordered by Coach Heart. The eighth grade team would enter first and then the seventh grade.

The pep rally began when the band played a slowed down and squeaky version of the rousing march tune "Cotton King March" as the gym doors opened for the entrance of the 1958 edition of the SJHS Blue Devils. Molly Gathers accentuated the entrance with a tumbling run of amazing hand-over-hand flips that covered the entire basketball floor. The two teams stood across the court from the west side bleachers.

The cheerleaders opened the day's event with a series of cheers, teaching the student body how to participate as they went along. It didn't take long to work the crowd into a wild frenzy and even raised the sound barrier with some healthy competition between the students in the seventh and eighth grades. It got even louder when it was announced that the winner of the grade yelling competition would get to go to lunch 15 minutes early. The seventh grade won the competition, but lost a few voices in the process.

Cody Joe felt important standing with the football team. He could see Rue and Jack Carter sitting across the way. He could tell they were proud and were gamely taking in the whole show. Carter also found Jennifer Axel and Veronica Slade sitting in the far right corner near the top of the bleachers. They were clapping their hands and appeared to be immersed in every activity. Cody Joe was now beginning to get the message that what they did on the field really mattered. This was a big deal. It was more than just playing football.

The cheerleaders then turned and faced the football teams. The seventh grade cheerleaders positioned themselves in front of the seventh grade team and likewise for the eighth graders. The seventh grade cheerleaders then did a yell just for the seventh grade team. Cody Joe was standing in the front line of the boys and was directly facing Mandy Mayor. She gave him a little wink before diving into the routine. That made Cody

Joe's day. He knew Pug and Tanner saw it and he was pretty sure it was obvious enough that several others noticed. It just proved that Mandy might now be the No. 2 lady on campus, but she still knew how to cause a stir among the boys. For now, Cody Joe was the first hero of the day.

When the cheerleaders finally gave way, the school's eight twirlers took the stage and dazzled with a glitzy routine. Cody Joe didn't even know there was going to be twirlers and he only knew one girl on the squad. Kathy Bunt was at West Elementary last year. Only two of the eight girls were in the seventh grade. Cody Joe knew none of the eighth grade twirlers.

Coach Heart was the first to say a few words to the crowd, saying, "I think this group of seventh graders is going to represent this school well in the coming weeks. They have worked awfully hard the last three weeks and I think they are ready to take on Goliad this afternoon."

The crowd roared its approval and the band broke out into a brief rendition of the fight song. When a tentative quiet gripped the gym, Coach Heart said, "It is now with great pleasure to announce our season's first team captains for the game against Goliad. They are Lee Line for the offense and Adam Quay for the defense."

Another roar erupted as Coach Heart made them come forward and say something on behalf of the team. Line, obviously a team leader from the quarterback position, had little trouble in handling this task, saying, "I hope all you guys will come out and support us today because we are going to beat Goliad."

The crowd once again approved of the message, releasing another wave of sound. Adam Quay was still stunned at even being picked for team captain by Coach Heart. He offered a meek, "Beat Goliad." and walked back behind his teammates.

However, not even his weak attempt with this puny rally speech was enough to keep from setting off this lusty crowd once again. The football season was now officially opened with a good old Texas pep rally baptism. It ended with the students singing the school alma mater. Well, in reality, it ended with the eighth graders singing the school alma mater because this was the first time for the seventh graders to have ever heard it.

Cody Joe's last thought, before leaving the gym for his first pep rally, was that it was going to be an eternity before 4 p.m.

* * *

On what seemed like the longest day of the year, Cody Joe's stomach was rolling long before the 2:30 p.m. bell. He was even questioning whether or not he could play. He was sick to his stomach.

The slow and frivolous walk to practice was replaced on game day with a serious, quick-step march to the field house. No one said much at all. There was a nervousness that permeated the seventh grade Blue Devils.

When Cody Joe reached the field house, he went to the restroom and promptly lost his chili-cheese sandwich. He wasn't the only kid who lost his lunch as the realization began to set in that the Blue Devils were going to be playing their first game and a lot of people were actually going to be interested in the outcome. They were now representing an entire community. And if it was going to be like this every week, Cody Joe had decided he was going to change his Thursday diet by eating in the cafeteria. Chili-cheese sandwiches were a bit much for game day.

Cody Joe felt much better after losing the battle with his

stomach, but he took great care in dressing into his new uniform and proudly looked at the number "60" on the front and back of his blue and white jersey. Pug wore number "55" and Butch Cassidy was labeled with the number "40." The three had requested those numbers through manager Rick Tracks and Tracks had come through for all three of them. The Blue Devils of SJHS were every bit as snazzy as their college counterparts at Duke University. The younger version wore identical uniforms as Duke, but the SJHS Blue Devils hoped to win more football games this year.

Not even Nate Christian mouthed off on this day. He seemed to be as nervous as everyone else. Cody Joe thought it sure would be nice if Nate acted like this on a daily basis instead of just on game day. But then again, with Nate, you take about anything you can get.

Coach Heart sent the team out for the warm-up drills without much fanfare. The kids quickly noticed that the field didn't even look the same. New bright, white lines marked the field, a transition that quickly said, "There's a game here today."

Also, the stands had people in them. In fact, a lot of people were on hand in Cody Joe's way of thinking. The student body was there in force. Carter immediately found Jennifer Axel and Veronica Slade sitting on the top row of the bleachers with Blue Devil pennants waving as the team trotted onto the field.

Cody Joe also saw Jack and Rue Carter in the stands, but was somewhat shocked to also find Grandpa and Grandma Taggert sitting beside the Carters. Cody Joe didn't know his grandparents had even planned to come. This would be the first game they would see Cody Joe play in. The Taggerts did come to see a Little League game two years ago, but Cody Joe never actually got into that game.

The warm-up process went agonizingly slow and the Blue Devils were relieved when they got the whistle to return to the field house. Coach Heart gathered the whole team around him. The time had come to unleash his Blue Devils.

"Guys, this is what we have worked so hard for," Coach Heart started. "This is the moment we get tested. Today, you will show us your heart.

"You either have it or you don't. Take pride in what you are and what you have become. Don't cheat yourself on that playing field," he said pointing outside. "Make every block. Make every tackle. Don't quit playing the game until the final whistle. We are the Blue Devils and Goliad better know it when this game is over. Now go out there and win this ball game."

A stampede of screaming Blue Devils reached the door's entrance almost simultaneously, causing a severe logjam. But the onslaught didn't slow down. Several players were literally knocked off the field house platform and down the wooden stairs. No one was hurt, but the debut of the Blue Devils was more Keystone Cops than vanquishing heroes.

Coach Heart quietly thought, "Maybe we need to work a bit more on our game entrance. I think they have the enthusiasm thing down pat."

* * *

When Cody Joe took to the field for the opening kickoff, time slowed to a crawl. It felt like the officials were talking in slow motion. He felt awkward and his feet seemed extremely heavy. He was in a time warp until he finally heard the screeching sounds of the season's first whistle. Cody Joe was finally playing football.

He sprinted to the south end of the field and he had the Goliad return man square in his sights. But when Carter was just about to nail the unsuspecting runner, Cody Joe was blind-sided with a ferocious block that sent him crashing to the earth. He had been hit so hard his teeth hurt. Jack King had saved the day by dragging the Goliad runner down at the 30-yard line.

"I wonder if Nate Christian has a cousin on the Goliad team," Cody Joe thought as he climbed to his feet after the jarring block. "I just hope he doesn't have a switchblade on him."

Cody Joe got a speck of revenge on the next play when he nicely filled a hole and dropped the Big Spring halfback for a mere two-yard gain. Pug busted up an inside counter play on second down while Stoney Wall clogged the middle for little gain on third down. Goliad three and out.

After a Goliad punt, it was time for the Blue Devils' turn to establish some offensive dominance, and it didn't take long. Halfback Lester Jarvis ripped off left guard for 20 yards on great blocks from Pug and T-Quay. Then Lee Line gave Butch

Cassidy the opportunity to carry for the first time in his young career. It was a beautiful and brutal thing to watch.

Cassidy quickly got into the secondary when Cody Joe flattened the linebacker. The lumbering bowling ball then lowered his head and demolished the safety. Cassidy was then in the clear, but he was not exactly outrunning the field. A Goliad defender caught Cassidy at about the 15-yard line and grabbed hold of this steaming locomotive. Cassidy just wouldn't go down and he carried his unwilling rider right into the end zone. Snyder 6, Goliad 0 on just two plays.

Goliad's players were in a state of shock and showed it the rest of the half. Goliad had only three first downs in the entire half. Snyder got another touchdown in the second quarter when Jarvis broke a 45-yard sweep for a score and Hank Cline scored a two-point conversion on a flare route that Line threw to perfection. Blue Devils 14, Goliad 0.

Cody Joe's biggest moment in the game came near the start of the second half when he met a Goliad runner right on the sideline and rolled him out of bounds all the way in front of the cheerleader corps. When he got up, he was staring at none other than Mandy Mayor square in the face.

As he returned to the field, he heard her say, "Did you see that? That was Cody Joe Carter. He's in my homeroom class. I've never seen anybody hit somebody that hard right in front of me like that."

It was the second time in one day that he had received special attention from one of the most popular girls in school. After that, Cody Joe's day was pretty much complete. In fact, he played only sparingly the rest of the game as Eric Blade got a chance to show his wares. But you couldn't take the smile off Cody Joe's face.

Pug, of course, was being watched on every play by Alexi Taggert and her band of girlfriends. They would discuss his merits or lack thereof after each play. In truth, he could do no wrong in their eyes. This was complete fan worship for the star of their day.

Even Kirby Tanner came full circle against Goliad. He got a huge chunk of playing time in the second half and scored the first touchdown of his life on a 37-yard scamper in the fourth quarter. Cassidy converted the two-point conversion right up the middle for a 22-0 lead.

But something much more significant happened on Tanner's TD. At the end of his run, Tanner dove for the end zone to avoid being tackled near the one-yard line, but the Goliad player still launched his body with full force into a prone and defenseless Tanner. Dirk Bolger, who had earlier thrown a clearing block for Tanner, followed the play all the way to the goal line. When he saw the player maliciously hit Tanner in the square of the back, he rushed to Tanner's aid. He literally picked up the offending player and tossed him aside like a matchstick.

Tanner looked at Bolger in the face and both started laughing. It was like the chains of the past had been cut in half. The air had once again been cleared and a new era had begun.

"Thanks, Dirk, that guy was beginning to get on my nerves," Tanner joked.

Bolger answered, "If you would run a little faster, I wouldn't have to pull your tail out of the fire so often."

The two walked off the field together and stood on the sideline side by side. Coach Bear noticed and made a point to drop by and say, "Nice going guys. Now that's teamwork."

Bolger and Tanner smiled and the legend of the nose guard jockey strap was laid to rest forever. Tanner really was a member of the team now and Bolger had been freed of his revenge-minded quest. The two might never be best friends, but they could now play together and no one was going to take out a teammate and get away with it against the Blue Devils.

First Game: Snyder 22, Goliad 0. Now, if the Blue Devils could only learn to make a simple game entrance.

Chapter 10

FIRST ROAD TRIP

Both the seventh and eighth grade Blue Devils won their football openers on Thursday and both teams were the talk of the school on Friday. It was good to be a football player on the day after a victory.

Cody Joe was greeted time and again in the hallway by well-wishers. It seemed like everyone in school had been at the game. After Thursday morning's pep rally, students quickly were able to recognize all the football players because they had stood across from the student body during the kickoff rally.

Life was good on Friday, but it ended rather abruptly with the arrival of the weekend break. The Snyder Tigers were off for the first road trip of the year to Andrews, robbing the youthful Blue Devils of a chance to publicly proclaim their victory and sit together as the conquering heroes. The Tigers continued the hot start with a 34-12 upset over the highly regarded Mustangs.

Otherwise, it was a rather dull weekend. Grandpa Taggert called to offer his congratulations and to say he had enjoyed the game. He also mentioned the fact that he still had some chow-chow left if Cody Joe ever wanted to spice up his life a little. Chip had a friend over to spend the weekend, so Cody Joe spent most of Saturday just trying to stay hidden from the two scavenging inmates of the Carter household. It seemed like Kate practiced her piano all day, making Cody Joe think that his Dad should build Kate a practice shed in the back of the house so the family wouldn't have to endure the contentious butchered plunking of the piano keys. At home, Cody Joe didn't feel much like a hero. He was more the forgotten lamb in a big flock of sheep.

After church on Sunday, Cody Joe escaped his mundane home life by walking over to Pug Preston's house. This was becoming a Sunday routine since baseball had ceased. The fact was that the boys were now so tired from the rest of the week, there was no energy left to play football or basketball with the gang on Sunday. They just hung around in Pug's backyard, mostly lying under a huge elm shade tree until time to call it an afternoon.

Sunday was now the only time of the week that the two really spent any time together. Neither one would admit it, but they missed each other's company and daily talks. The pair had been a part of each other's world since the first grade, but now that line of brotherhood had been somewhat blurred by football and girls, specifically Alexi Taggert. Still, through it all, Sunday afternoons had saved the relationship, and without even knowing it, both were eternally grateful. Neither Cody Joe nor Pug would ever put it in meaningful words, and maybe they never even fully realized it, but they needed each other.

Just as Cody Joe was getting up from under the tree, Pug said, "On October 18, my Dad and I are going to Lubbock to visit my grandmother. She lives just two blocks from the Texas Tech campus. I'm planning to walk from there to the football stadium and watch Tech play TCU. You want to go with me that weekend?"

"I'd love to go, Pug, but I'll have to clear it with my parents. I don't think they will object to this since your Dad will be taking us up there."

"That's great. Let me know. I can't wait because that will

be so much fun. My dad won't mind a bit, and tell your parents that my grandmother has plenty of bedrooms."

* * *

Cody Joe was glad to get back in school on Monday morning. It had been a long weekend, but it didn't take long before Cody Joe would have to deal with an unexpected turn of events. The storm came right off the bat in Mr. Perry's homeroom class.

Cody Joe took his seat right behind Jennifer Axel as usual, but he was first greeted on his left by the stunning Mandy Mayor.

"Hi, Cody Joe," Mandy offered with those bright and blinking eyes of hers. "I saw you in the game on Thursday. My goodness, I thought you were going to run right over me. I didn't know you were that strong. You really put that Goliad player on the ground. That's the hardest hit I've ever seen up close like that."

"Well thanks, Mandy," Cody Joe said with a full blush visible in his cheeks. "I think we played pretty good. We're going to Colorado City on Thursday. Are the cheerleaders going to that one?"

"Yes we are. We have two moms that are going to take the eight of us. They plan to take us to all the games. We are so excited about that.

"But, Cody Joe, I want to ask you a question."

"Go ahead, ask."

"Do you know Lee Line, the quarterback on your team?" Mandy asked.

"Sure, I know him. I don't know him well because he didn't go to West with us last year, but I've gotten to know him in football," Cody Joe answered.

This is when Cody Joe gets the bombshell dropped on him as Mandy says in a whiny voice, "Well, could you introduce Lee to me. I'd like to meet him sometime. He's so cute and he's the quarterback."

Cody Joe immediately feels like he has been kicked in the stomach. Mandy Mayor is only interested in Cody Joe Carter if he can be used to get her in with Lee Line. He now feels like Mayor's stooge, but he can't tell her no because he'll lose the chance to talk to her forever.

"I guess I could do that," Cody Joe says without conviction. "But it's up to him on whether or not he'll agree."

Cody Joe was thinking that was a horrible response. What boy in school would ever turn down a chance to meet Mandy Mayor, especially when she asks for the meeting? Cody Joe is sure Lee Line will jump at the opportunity unless the "quarterback of the team" already has a Molly Gathers under his wing. Once again the world is not fair. Cody Joe has quickly learned the basic fact of the junior high food chain: There are linemen and then there is the quarterback. And to the quarterback ultimately go the victory and the spoils.

Jennifer didn't help much. She turned to face Cody Joe eye-to-eye and whispered, "Well, Cody Joe, mama's got a job for you; you better get crackin'. You're now Mandy Mayor's go-to guy. Do you need any sugar with those marching orders?"

"Oh, Jennifer, leave me alone," Cody Joe admonished. "This ain't nothin'. She doesn't own me."

* * *

When fifth period ended, Cody Joe raced from Perry's math class to catch Lee Line. Line always was ahead of Cody Joe's group because he left school from the arts and crafts building, giving him a daily head start on the football parade down Ave. M. On this day, Cody Joe found Line walking to the field house with safety Jay Coy.

"Lee, wait up a minute," called out Cody Joe when he got within earshot of Line. "I want to talk with you for a minute."

Line was a little surprised when he turned to see Cody Joe Carter making the plea. He barely knew Cody Joe and he couldn't ever remember ever having a real conversation with him. Still, he had no reason to dislike Carter and he yielded to Cody Joe's call.

"What do you want, Cody Joe? Is everything OK?" Line asked, expecting some bad news for some odd reason. The only reason he could think of for Cody Joe to approach him like this was because bad news was involved.

"I really don't know how to say this because I don't know you very well, so I'll just start from the top," Cody Joe began. "Do you know Mandy Mayor?"

"Yeah, I know who she is. Who in school doesn't know her? She's that good looking cheerleader. But I sure would like to get to know her better."

That was the answer Cody Joe expected and that response was going to make his job easier. Still, it rankled him that Line was going to get exactly what he wanted. Deep down he was hoping Line would show no interest in Mandy, leaving Cody Joe as maybe next in line. At least, he would get to console her.

"Then this is your lucky day," said Cody Joe. "Mandy wants to meet you. I can set it up if you are interested. I don't think she's one to ask twice."

"And I'm not one you have to ask twice. You set it up and I'm there," Line beamed.

Jay Coy couldn't believe his ears, saying, "Line, you are always the luckiest guy in the world. We're talking about

Mandy Mayor here and she wants to meet you. Why don't you just be a no-show and I'll take your place any day of the week."

Cody Joe offered, "Line, I see you eating lunch at the snack shack every day. Be there tomorrow and I'll either have Mandy there or I'll have the details worked out. How's that?"

"Thanks Cody Joe, you've made my day. Why didn't you just save her for yourself?" Line joked.

"Believe me. I'd rather it be me than you, but you're the quarterback, and she wants the quarterback. Mandy Mayor gets just about everything she wants, except maybe head cheerleader. I'd say you are pretty much already a trophy on her wall unless Joseph Moore takes your job away from you."

"You can bet that's not happening," Line confidently stated. "And I'll take my chances with Mandy. Who wouldn't, including you Cody Joe?"

* * *

Cody Joe arrived before Mandy Mayor to homeroom on Tuesday morning and Jennifer Axel teased by rapidly blinking her eyelids, "Dear Cody Joe did you do your job? Did you get me a date with Lee Line?"

"Cut it out Jennifer," Cody Joe pleaded. "He wants to meet her worse than she wants to meet him."

"Oh, I bet you are right about that," Jennifer said. "She walks in a room and you can sit back and watch all the boys' tongues fall out."

At that point, Mayor's entourage entered the room and took their usual seats. Mandy had not forgotten about her request. She quickly asked Cody Joe with her honey sweet voice, "Did you talk to Lee Line about me?"

"I did and he would like to meet you. I asked him to be

down by the snack shack at lunch today and I would introduce you to him. I told him you might change your mind and not come, but I'd try to get you there."

"You're swell, Cody Joe," Mandy said. "This is the best day of my life and I owe it all to you. I'll meet you there for lunch."

With that, she leaned across the aisle and planted a big kiss right on Cody Joe's cheek. Cody Joe's embarrassment doubled when Elmer Perry walked into the room and stated, "That'll be quite enough from you two. We'll have no making out sessions in this room today or any other day."

Mandy Mayor coyly sat facing forward with a big grin on her face while Cody Joe was still trying to recover from what had just happened. He had been kissed by Mandy Mayor and had not been prepared for it. In fact, he was so stunned he was still trying to figure out if it had happened at all. Jennifer reinforced the incident in a way that left Cody Joe cold.

"You better enjoy that kiss. It's the only one you'll ever get from her. She's Line's girl now."

At lunch, Cody Joe began to look for Mandy Mayor because she never ate at the snack shack. She always ate in the cafeteria with her horde of followers. She would be lost out here in the netherworld without her customary gaggle of friends. But one thing was for sure, she wasn't hard to find because she lit up the day when she walked by.

Several onlookers were a bit surprised to see Cody Joe walk up to her, and more surprised when she fell into step with him. They headed to the snack shack and Cody Joe showed her the menu and told her how to order. Cody Joe got a cheeseburger while Mandy ordered something healthy like a chicken salad sandwich. It wasn't cafeteria fare, but sacrifices had to be made to meet the quarterback of the team.

When they got outside, Cody Joe quickly found Line and

halfback Lester Jarvis sitting at one of the picnic tables. Jarvis gulped, "Man, you weren't kidding. That's Mandy Mayor and she's coming right for this table. Good luck Line. I'm leaving."

When Cody Joe and Mandy arrived at the table, Cody Joe said, "Lee, this is Mandy Mayor and she wants to meet you."

Lee Line never even acknowledged the presence of Cody Joe. He stared Mandy straight in the eye and offered, "And I want to meet her. How are you Mandy? You look great and it would be an honor for you to share this table with me."

"I saw you play Thursday and I thought you were terrific out there," Mandy explained. "I've been wanting to meet you ever since I saw you on the sideline."

The two were acting as if Cody Joe wasn't even there. They didn't even notice when he left. Mandy didn't even acknowledge his help or bid him farewell. Cody Joe recognized sparks when he saw them and he was abandoning ship before things got even more awkward. Love was once again in natural bloom at SJHS.

* * *

As the Blue Devils were dressing for Wednesday afternoon's final practice of the week, Cody Joe borrowed a bottle of glue from manager Rick Tracks. He wanted to attach a new name plate over his locker that was given to him by his father. Jack Carter had ordered a name plate for his insurance office downtown, so he thought he would also get one for Cody Joe. He was a bit disappointed that it had not arrived before Cody Joe's first game, but there were still nine games left in the season.

Carter set the bottle of glue down on the corner of the locker bench where part of the bottle was sitting on Cody

Joe's side and part on Nate Christian's side. When Cody Joe stood on the locker bench to reach where he was going to attach his name, he knocked over the open bottle of glue. The contents slowly dribbled its way under Christian's switchblade and then down the side of Nate's jeans that had been laid across the bench.

Christian came back into the room just in time to see the ugly mess while Carter was oblivious to what had happened altogether. Christian was furious and started yelling profanities at Carter. Carter was taken aback by the verbal attack and quickly turned around on his bench perch just as Christian crashed into him about waist level. Carter was sent spiraling into his locker cutout and one of the locker hooks made a gash just to the left of Carter's right shoulder blade.

The injury wasn't all that serious, but it was a bleeder, making this brief fight look like a vicious attack. Pug noticed the blood right away. Without even thinking, he tore into Christian with every ounce of energy he could muster. Pug was intimidated by Christian just as much as Cody Joe, but when he realized that his best friend was under serious attack, he joined in the fray without reservation. It was time to sink or swim.

What Cody Joe and Pug didn't know was that help was on the way. Dirk Bolger, Mac Cone and Butch Cassidy also jumped in to help rescue Cody Joe. It was only a matter of seconds that there was more blood on the field house floor, but this time it was coming from the nose of Nate Christian. Finally, Cassidy gave Christian a push back across the aisle. Christian stared at each of the boys as if to leave a message.

"This isn't over," Christian warned. "You won't always be together and I'll get you. I'm especially going to get you Cody Joe."

Coach Tom Nix came storming into the room after hearing the commotion from the coach's office. He didn't think it was necessary to ask what had happened. He just took Christian and moved him to an empty locker that had been vacated by a player that had quit the team. He told Christian not to go back into that far corner until after practice. Coach Nix then got the rest of Christian's equipment and took it to him.

"Now, Nate, get dressed and get out to the practice field. Let's see if you can focus all this negative energy into something positive."

Cody Joe thanked all the guys for coming to his aid. Coach Nix came back over to inspect Carter's back wound and called Tracks to come in and place a first aid bandage over Cody Joe's injury. Both Coach Nix and Carter didn't think the wound was serious enough to miss practice.

After Coach Nix left the scene, Bolger was the first to speak, "Christian is a jerk. He probably had a right to be mad, but he had no right to attack Cody Joe like that."

"I think he might have tried to hurt Cody Joe if we hadn't jumped in to help," added Pug. "He can't stand up against all of us, but all of us better keep an eye out for him around town. There's no telling what he might do if he gets one of us alone."

Cassidy noticed that Nate's switchblade was still sitting on the bench where Christian had left it. The glue was now hardening at a rapid rate. Cody Joe was desperately trying to clean up the mess, but the guys urged him to leave the knife alone. It would be fun to see if Christian could even pry it free after practice.

"That knife may be a permanent part of this old field house," reasoned Cassidy.

* * *

The guys never saw how Nate Christian freed his glued switchblade from the locker bench because Christian was taken to Coach Heart's office immediately after practice. He was still there when Cody Joe and Kirby Tanner got on the bus for the trip back to West Elementary.

Cody Joe told the story of the incident to his parents at the supper table and he showed them the ugly scrape on his back. Now that practice was over, the injured area was extremely sore and angry looking. When Rue Carter saw the wound, she became almost hysterical, quickly jumping up from the table in a frantic search for medicine that she might use to treat this unexpected calamity.

Jack Carter wanted to know if Nate Christian had been kicked off the team. Cody Joe noted that Nate was allowed to practice, but that he was still in the coach's office when Cody Joe left the field house.

"Well, that's unacceptable as far as I'm concerned," Jack said. "Nate should be gone. That's just not any way to handle a dispute. He's already threatened you and we can't keep worrying about this every day. I think it's time I had a talk with the coach."

"But Dad," Cody Joe pleaded. "I was the one who spilled the glue. We do have to take that into account and you would only make it worse. Everyone on the team will think I sent my dad to fix my problems. I can handle this."

"I know you think you can, son, but this has gone too far. I'll meet with Coach Heart at school and no one will know. At least you won't have to worry about that."

Jack Carter knew Coach Heart had no homeroom in the mornings because of an information sheet he had sent to prospective football players concerning the season. Coach Heart had asked parents to visit him during that time if the need ever came up.

So, on the day of the team's first road trip, Jack Carter walked right into the Coach Heart's math class where the coach was making his list of things that had to be done and things to be taken on the bus trip to Colorado City.

"Ah, Mr. Carter," said Coach Heart. "I've been half-way expecting you. I know you are probably concerned about the incident at the field house yesterday."

"Yes I am Coach Heart," Jack opened without pulling any punches. "I want to know if Nate Christian is off the team. He's been threatening my son and now he's taken to physical violence. I'm not putting up with anymore of this nonsense. I want the kid gone."

Coach Heart paused before answering, and then calmly stated, "You have every right to be angry, Mr. Carter. I'm concerned about Nate, too. You see, I'm the one who brought him into this program. We need to save this kid. Football might help pull him up by the bootstraps. I want you to give me a little more time with him. I've taken every precaution to keep him separated from Cody Joe, but I need this time right now. It's critical. If we drop him now, there's no telling where he will end up or who he will hurt really bad."

"I'm really not interested in your projects if it's at the expense of my son," Jack responded. "My son is just too important to us for his safety to be compromised. I'm on record here that Nate Christian needs to be off this team. But if you are not willing to do that, I hold you responsible for any other incidents where my son comes home with any non-football related injury inflicted by Nate. That's as far as I can go and as fair as I can be."

When Jack Carter left the meeting, Coach Heart sat back in his chair immersed in deep thought, thinking, "I see the potential in Nate. I think he could make it in this world if he could just shake his anger issues. But just how far can I go to help him when the safety of others comes into play? I see Jack Carter's point of view, but I've got to give Nate a little more time to come around. I'm confident the team would accept him, if he would only give them a chance. I hope that point sunk in to Nate yesterday when we talked for over an hour. It's now up to him to try because I've done just about all that I can."

* * *

The seventh grade Blue Devils got to miss all of fifth period in order to pack for the first road trip of the season. Calling the 20-mile trip to Colorado City a road trip was pushing it a bit since it was about a 20 to 30 minute trip tops.

But there is something about a road trip that placed a special mark on the event. It felt like an important game because someone was willing to send you to another town to play a game. That made it exciting.

For this trip, the Blue Devils were asked to dress in the field house, then place the shoulder pads in the game jerseys and carry them in their laps as they made the quick trip to C-City. They were told they could shower when they got back to the field house after the game.

Of course, Cody Joe sat with Pug on the trip while Kirby Tanner and Butch Cassidy chose to be seat mates. Fortunately, Nate Christian sat alone in a seat right behind the coaching staff as instructed. With 39 players and four managers on the squad, someone had to sit alone and virtually everyone thought it should be Christian.

Others were also choosing traveling partners. Rue Carter decided, only on Wednesday, that she was going to the game. She was concerned about her son. She couldn't believe Nate Christian was going to be allowed to make the trip and she just couldn't stay at home. Jack Carter was happy to have her come along. He had planned to make the trip long before the season. Jack had looked at the schedule and he thought he could make every game except when the team traveled to Lamesa on Oct. 30. He and Ernest Cassidy had decided to make the road trips together. Butch had lost his mom two years ago in a freak automobile accident, so Ernest was without a travelling partner. He gladly jumped at the opportunity to travel with the Carters. He was still desperately trying to make a new life after his loss and he wanted to support Butch in any way he could. That's why he went to most of Butch's practices and games and why he drove Butch every day to school. He had lost his wife, but he was desperately trying to see that his son didn't miss the attention he would have received from his departed mother.

* * *

It was hardly a trip at all. Cody Joe thought the bus got to the C-City stadium faster than it took his bus to go to West Elementary before school and after practice. But it was time to play another game. Time to put it all on the line once again.

During calisthenics, Cody Joe noticed that the Snyder crowd was mostly parents of team members except for the cheerleading squad, which had arrived in full force. The voices of Molly Gathers and Mandy Mayor were in full bloom and could clearly be heard from one side of the junior high field to the other.

The Blue Devils controlled the contest from beginning to end. They scored on the afternoon's first possession, going 75 yards in 10 plays while eating up most of the first quarter clock. Cassidy dominated most of the drive with simple four-yard bursts. He carried the ball on seven of the 10 plays, but

Lester Jarvis got the touchdown on a two-yard dive between T-Quay and Pug on the left side. Henry Styles was lucky on the extra point when he bounced the ball through the goal posts after hitting the left upright. Blue Devils 7, C-City 0.

The Wolf Pups of Colorado City simply had a hard time moving the football. They couldn't throw the ball, so the defensive front of the Blue Devils had their way with the small running backs of the opponents. Much to the displeasure of Rue Carter in the stands, Nate Christian had a virtual field day, making tackle after tackle while dominating play for the entire first half.

Cody Joe's play was sketchy at best. He missed a tackle on a C-City running back, allowing the largest gain of the day, a 14-yard first down. It was the only first down of the first half for Colorado City.

Blue Devil running back Hank Cline scored on a 54-yard sweep in the second period on a great downfield block by end Adam Quay. Styles wasn't as lucky on this extra point attempt as he nailed Cody Joe right square in the buttocks with his kick attempt. Styles' extra point kicking game was still very much a work in progress.

The team sat in the shade of the bus at the half. The coaches weren't overly pleased with the overall effort. The Blue Devils were controlling the game, but there seemed to be no real passion on the field except the performance coming from Nate Christian. Coach Heart wondered if he could inspire his squad by giving each of his team members a two-hour grilling before the game as he had done to Nate on Wednesday. Coach Heart felt somewhat helpless in this moment of discovery. There simply weren't enough hours in a day to coach a football team.

The second half was more of the same. Cassidy got himself a touchdown right over Cody Joe to end the third quarter.

The biggest celebration of the day came when Henry Styles kicked the extra point right down the middle of the goal posts. The Blue Devils at least looked like a football team on that drive.

Coach Heart emptied his bench in the fourth quarter, giving Kirby Tanner a lot of playing time. He also got six carries for 35 yards, but the subs didn't put any points on the board. In the end, it was: Blue Devils 20, Colorado City 0. The Blue Devils were now 2-0 on the season and still undefeated after a home game and a road trip.

Coach Heart somehow didn't feel undefeated. There were still problems to work out on the field and off the field.

There were a bunch of sweaty bodies on the bus back to Snyder, and even with the bus windows down all the way back, the bus carried a rank odor. The bus driver, Thomas Mann, was sure he was going to have to fumigate his bus to get rid of the smell. Nevertheless, it was the smell of victory – regardless of the many negatives that quickly came to mind.

Chapter 11

ANOTHER CONFRONTATION

The Blue Devils once again had favored seats in the junior high student section as the Snyder Tigers hosted the Big Spring Steers at Tiger Stadium on Friday night. And once again, Pug Preston had favored status at the side of Alexi Taggert. Quarterback Lee Line was not learning quarterback techniques from the hometown quarterback; he was immersed in the cheerleading aspects of one Mandy Mayor just two rows above Pug and Alexi. Mandy had Line mesmerized, casting flirty glances at Line at every break of the conversation. It was pretty much Friday night business as usual for the seventh grade class of 1958-59.

Cody Joe Carter loved going to the high school games, but he couldn't help feeling left out even though Butch Cassidy, Kirby Tanner, Henry Styles, Mac Cone, Dirk Bolger and the Quay brothers were all becoming close friends.

Lee Line, Hank Cline, Lester Jarvis, Jay Coy and Joseph Moore formed another team group and they weren't so thrilled that team leader Lee Line had deserted them for Mandy, but not one of them could find fault with his decision. Any one of them would have been at Mandy's side with even the vaguest invitation.

There were also more groups within the team and groups within the groups. It was all normal, and none of it mattered very much when they hit the practice field. In fact, most everyone got along extremely well even if they weren't best of friends. Nate Christian didn't fit within any group, and as usual, he was not present on this Friday night. Some of the guys joked that Christian was flashing his open switchblade at the ghosts that occupied the downtown square when a high school football game was being played in Snyder. It did seem that Snyder rolled up its sidewalks at dark on game days. Christian was in a very lonely group of Snyderites that did not attend the game.

Friday night football in Snyder was most certainly one of the great social events of the community and it was not unusual to find the women of the town wearing their best finery and high heels to the games. The football games offered the town a place to step out. Not only was it important to see the game, but it was important to be seen at the game. It was simply good for business.

Cody Joe scanned the students below his team perch and quickly noticed that Jennifer Axel and Veronica Slade were sitting together again. He certainly had no reason to question the people they chose to sit with. He had never asked either one to sit with him, yet he felt somehow uncomfortable that Jennifer and Veronica were sitting with a group of boys in the band. He remained comforted in the thought that none of the boys were Kevin Tumbler or Stacy Trout, his baseball buddies.

It wasn't long before Cody Joe gave in to his unwarranted jealousy. He got up and entered the row below where Jennifer and Veronica were sitting. He walked down the row and then looked surprised that he had found Jennifer sitting in the next row.

"Hi, Cody Joe," Jennifer said in a tone that was neither overly inviting nor necessarily dismissive. "I thought you were sitting with the football guys. Are you just slumming around with the poor folks now?"

Cody Joe hated it when Jennifer teased him like that. She had this annoying ability to cut your feet right out from under you. But at least she was real and Cody Joe always felt like he could talk to her and he always knew up front where he stood with her. Those were two traits that endeared Jennifer Axel to Carter even though she could be caustic around the edges.

"Good to see you, too, Jennifer," Cody Joe shot back. "I came to say hello and you jump all over me. That's not a very good welcome."

"Oh, he's pouting again," Jennifer joked. "C'mon sit with us, Cody Joe."

Jennifer scooted to her left, making room for Cody Joe between her and Veronica. This did not sit well with the boys to the left of Jennifer or to the right of Veronica. They didn't say anything, but Cody Joe could visibly see the scowl on their faces. They didn't embrace this interloper with open arms. In fact, to a man, they wanted this football meddler to find his own girl. They felt as if he was trying to cash in on both girls. In truth, they were absolutely right. Cody Joe was hoping all these guys would somehow disappear.

Cody Joe turned and looked Veronica Slade right in the eye and shyly said, "Hello, Veronica."

But as soon as he made eye contact, he completely froze up because she was looking right back at him and he was sure she was interested. This threw Cody Joe completely off his game. He panicked and did the only thing he knew how to do and that was to start talking to Jennifer Axel. He didn't stutter when he talked with Jennifer. He could make complete sentences. When he tried to talk to Veronica, he felt like his lips were glued to each other. He simply couldn't talk to Veronica without proving he was an idiot. He really didn't care if he was an idiot with Jennifer or not.

Cody Joe tried two or three times to make small talk with Veronica, but every time Cody Joe somehow found a way to stall out the conversation. He could never think of anything to say around Veronica, but he could talk to Jennifer all day – about anything or about nothing.

Cody Joe became so frustrated with the situation that he made some excuse to get him back with the football team. He desperately wanted to stay and he frantically needed to leave.

"I don't know what's wrong with that boy," Jennifer told Veronica as Cody Joe departed. "I think he really likes you, but you seem to make him go all crazy or something."

"Don't put it off on me, Jennifer. I didn't do anything. We didn't even say three words to each other. If he likes me, he's got a funny way of showing it. You're like his best friend. I think he likes you."

Jennifer said, "Well, I probably could go for him, but then I would just lose a good friend. I don't make him go goofy like you do. I'm sure you are the one he likes. He thinks he likes Mandy Mayor, but even he knows she's not good for him. He's never going to fit in there."

"And if he does like me, it's really going to be awkward because he's never, ever going to talk to me," said Veronica, ending the private discussion as the band boys began to demand some attention.

The Tigers, at least, got it right. Snyder 25, Big Spring 20.

* * *

Cody Joe was quick to pick up on the fact that when the Blue Devils played out of town, few students even knew how the game came out. Instead of congratulations, Carter was getting questions like, "Did you guys win on Thursday?" or worse, "Did you play a game on Thursday?"

Not many students traveled to see the seventh or eighth grade Blue Devils play football. The away crowd consisted mostly of parents, grandparents and a few cheerleaders. When the team played at home, there was always a large number of students on hand because the game was right after school and just a short walk down Ave. M for the game.

Cody Joe couldn't help but remember how the students reacted the week before when they won a home game. Everyone seemed excited about the win. This week no one even seems to care if there was a game or not.

That was the topic of conversation as the seventh grade Blue Devils walked down Ave. M for its Monday practice session. Most were dreading practice since Monday and Tuesday's sessions were hard workouts, so the talk usually centered on things other than the upcoming practice.

The entire group may have felt a little less important this week since few even knew they had won a game, but they were going to feel a lot less important after this particular practice.

Coach Heart felt it was time to tighten the screws a bit on his team. He was not pleased with the overall effort against Colorado City. He wanted his kids to play with more passion, more urgency and more enthusiasm. He felt like that was the only way to play football. Winning without enthusiasm is a dead victory. These kids should be enjoying what they are doing. They didn't seem like it on Thursday; they were simply going through the motions.

He greeted his team with, "I thought this group was going to have a bunch of football players. But you just wasted a whole game against Colorado City. It was as if none of you cared. I graded the film over the weekend and Christian is the only player that graded out above average. I'm really disappointed in this team, so we are going to go back to work and start all over again."

Coach Heart was true to his word. The team went back to the basic fundamentals with one-on-one blocking and tackling drills for almost a full practice. By the end of the session, some nerves had been frayed and practically the entire squad had new scrapes and bruises to tend. Manager Rick Tracks would have to stay an extra 30 minutes after practice to make sure all the players were treated.

But this practice wasn't over. It would be dark before the Blue Devils quit. A lot of waiting moms were understandably upset, but few even brought the subject up because they didn't want their sons to bear the backlash that might come from the coaches.

Coach Heart ended the practice with a semi-controlled scrimmage, saying, "We'll quit when I see some fire and hustle out here and when I see a team that wants to play football."

It was a spirited end to the day. There was a lot of team chatter and a lot of enthusiasm until the last play of the day. The offense ran a simple dive with Cassidy up the middle. With the kids ramped up on the enthusiasm scale, there was a massive pile-up at the line of scrimmage as every player headed to the ball.

It was here that Nate Christian saw an opportunity to get at Cody Joe Carter. At the bottom of the pile, Christian stuck his fingers under Cody Joe's face mask and began digging at his eyes. Cody Joe didn't know who was gouging him in the face, but he instinctively fought back with all he could muster.

The pile emptied slowly as one player after another climbed off the pile. As the pile decreased in thickness, Cody Joe came roaring through the remaining bodies and tore into his assailant. Christian started fighting back immediately and the coaches had an all-out fight on their hands.

Coach Bear was the first to intervene, but he literally got

knocked down by the two combatants. Pug Preston was next to join the fray, and that of course, ignited action from Cassidy, Bolger and Cone.

Coach Nix finally separated the boys, saying, "OK, that's enough of this. The next one to throw a punch is running till sunup."

Cody Joe was still furious. He didn't much care if the coaches were there or not. He started after Christian once again, but Pug and Cassidy were able to catch him by the shoulder pads and pull him back.

Cody Joe complained to anyone who would listen, "He tried to gouge my eyes out. I'm not taking this anymore. Nate, if you want some of me, come and get me. I'm right here."

Coach Heart yelled, "That's enough. We're through here. This practice is over."

Christian was smiling even when Coach Nix grabbed him by the collar and dragged him toward the field house. Cody Joe was allowed to go on his own, but Pug and Cassidy never left his side. They had never seen Cody Joe this mad and they weren't certain what he might do before the blood settled back to a regular flow. Nate Christian was good at the game of intimidation, but Pug thought that Nate might have been the lucky one, lucky that this happened at practice. He secretly thought Cody Joe just might have taken Nate apart piece by piece if this episode had continued. Cody Joe was madder than a wet hen.

* * *

Cody Joe didn't say one word about practice or the gouging incident at the supper table that night despite repeated tries by Rue and Jack Carter to pry information out of him. Both Rue and Jack remained concerned about Nate Christian.

Cody Joe basically lied to his parents, telling them everything was fine with football. He was afraid that if he told his parents about the fight at practice, his father would make waves again and he didn't want that. And there was a part of him that felt like he should take care of this matter on his own. In fact, he really wanted to put all this behind him. If that meant facing off against Christian one-on-one, so be it. He no longer feared the prospect, except for the knife. He didn't mind slugging it out with Christian, but he always had that knife.

* * *

On Tuesday morning in homeroom, Jennifer Axel asked Carter, "Did you leave us Friday because you were mad at us?"

"No, Jennifer, not at all," Cody Joe said while hanging his head down to avoid looking directly into Jennifer's eyes. "The truth is I can't talk to Veronica. I can't think of anything to say when I'm around her. She's really a nice girl and I would love to get to know her better, but I feel like a dunce when I'm around her."

"I knew it. I just knew it," Jennifer proclaimed. "Cody Joe, you do like Veronica Slade. I told her that after you left us the other night."

Cody Joe then looked Jennifer Axel straight in the eye and commanded, "Jennifer, you can't tell anyone what I told you. This is just between us. Do you understand that? If you tell anyone, I'll never talk to you again."

"Oh, OK," Jennifer reluctantly agreed, "but I swear I don't know how you two will ever get together if you don't let me help. Cody Joe, you aren't ever going to tell her. You're just going to sit in this class and run errands for Mandy Mayor in hopes that she'll give you a peck on the cheek every once in a while. You're pathetic, Cody Joe."

The rest of the week was really tough on Jennifer Axel. She wasn't good at keeping secrets and this was the best secret ever – and she couldn't say a word because she had promised Cody Joe.

First, she could not foresee how this was ever going to work out since Cody Joe had taken her out of the game by placing her on the bench. Second, how could she ever survive on Cody Joe's timetable? She might be 40 years old before he tries to make a move. She couldn't bear to hold this secret for that long. Holding secrets simply wasn't in her job description as best friend to one Veronica Slade. And third, she thought, this wasn't fair to Jennifer Axel. This was too much information to hide. Cody Joe surely doesn't expect this information to just be buried out behind the snack shack and forget that it ever happened.

However, Jennifer was true to her word and never mentioned even a hint of Cody Joe's confession to anyone, including Veronica Slade. She had no clue how long she could carry on this charade because she was absolutely the most miserable student in the halls of SJHS. She now wished that Cody Joe Carter had kept his mouth shut.

* * *

There had been no more incidents at practice involving Cody Joe and Nate, but defensive backs Jack King and Jay Coy had a brief spat during Wednesday's practice session over a late hit. No one ever really knew how it started, but it ended with both of the squabblers running two laps around the field together.

Coach Heart felt his team was better prepared for this

game with Lamesa than it had been against Colorado City despite the chippy attitude that reared its ugly head during the week. The team responded to his challenge and was "enthusiastic" all week. Coach Heart liked the spirited atmosphere even though you could sometimes stir it with a stick.

The school held its second pep rally in the school gym on Thursday morning. It was a raucous affair with the eighth graders winning the extended lunch period on the yell-off. The players were somewhat stunned when Nate Christian was named team captain for the game by Coach Heart.

Furtive glances were exchanged between team members when the announcement was made. Each team member was trying to figure out why Coach Heart made this decision. Coach Heart had told the team that Nate played the best game of anyone on the team against Goliad. But he had also caused a lot of trouble on this team.

As far as the team was concerned, the message was bright and clear. Playing well and hard is cherished above everything else. Perform or be forgotten. If the seventh grade Blue Devils weren't ready to play before this announcement, they sure were afterwards. They were not going to let Nate Christian stand out like that again. Bring on the Whirlwinds!

Jack Carter, in the crowd for the pep rally, wasn't amused by Coach Heart's selection of game captain. He got up and left the rally for his downtown office and he was glad Rue wasn't with him for this rally. She would have blown a gasket.

After the pep rally, members of the student council sold spirit ribbons that had all the names of the seventh grade Blue Devils written on one side and all the names of the eighth grade players on the other side. Cody Joe purchased his ribbon for a quarter from Mandy Mayor. She blinked her eyes at Cody Joe after the purchase. It didn't take much to make Cody Joe's day.

* * *

Another good crowd turned out for the Blue Devils that afternoon after school. In fact, Jack Carter was sure the crowd was larger than the one that turned out for the first game. Cody Joe quickly scanned the crowd and saw what he wanted to see. Jennifer Axel and Veronica Slade were in their usual perch on the 40-yard line. Both were wearing spirit ribbons and waving Blue Devil pennants. Cody Joe was praying that Jennifer would be true to her word. At least she hadn't driven Veronica off. That was a good sign, wasn't it?

Cody Joe then found his mother and father in the stands. Ernest Cassidy was sitting with them, but Grandpa Taggert did not make it to this game.

It was a great day for football because it had turned much cooler as a mild September cold front moved through the area. It was 71 degrees at game time and a few sweaters could be seen sprinkled throughout the crowd.

The seventh grade Blue Devils were also a different team, feeling their oats, so to speak. You could see a spring in their step and a stiff determination in their eyes.

"Coach Heart, I think the guys are ready to play today," noted Coach Bear. "I think they would run through a brick wall right now if you asked them."

It didn't take long for Coach Bear's observation to get a confirmation. On the opening kickoff, six Blue Devils arrived at Lamesa's return man at the same time and the cracking of leather reverberated throughout the stadium. Lamesa ran three plays and lost five yards before punting. The offense then cranked up a six-play drive that found, Butch Cassidy, Lester Jarvis and Hank Cline all breaking plays over 10 yards each. Cassidy got the score on a 14-yard bull rush to the goal line. Even Henry Styles nailed the extra point. Blue Devils 7, Lamesa 0.

This is exactly what Coach Heart had wished for. His backs were running with authority and Lee Line was in total charge at quarterback, cajoling his teammates to perform whenever needed. The offensive line was actually knocking people down while the defensive front was giving up nothing.

In fact, that was pretty much the story of the game. The Blue Devils did whatever they wanted, when they wanted. Even the passing game was beginning to click. Line threw a touchdown pass to Adam Quay. It wasn't exactly a thing of beauty, but Quay caught the wobbly pass on the end of his fingertips, going 42 yards for another score. It was only the third completion of the season and the first touchdown passing. Coach Heart accepted this event as a milestone in the team's growth process.

It was a great game from another perspective. Everyone on the team logged a lot of playing time. And everyone performed at a high level. Lamesa never crossed midfield and made only three first downs all day. Meanwhile, sub running back Kirby Tanner had his first 100-yard rushing game and scored two touchdowns off the bench.

That led Cody Joe to say to Tanner, "You better watch out or Mandy Mayor may be asking to meet you one of these days."

Nate Christian played well, but he didn't stand out over the rest of the team in this game. The Blue Devils showed up to play and Lamesa ultimately fell, 46-0. The Blue Devils were now 3-0 on the season and had not given up a single point to their opponents. The seventh graders had put 88 points on the boards in three games without allowing a point against them. And they had found their enthusiasm.

In Cody Joe Carter's way of thinking, it just didn't get any better than this. He was so proud of the team. He now knew what Coach Heart was seeking. You couldn't explain it, but you could feel it when it happened. If this was playing with passion, he liked it.

But Cody Joe's euphoric outlook on football would soon be tested. Darker days were ahead and the Runnels Mavericks of Big Spring were next on the schedule. Coach Heart knew all about Runnels. The test was coming.

After the game, Coach Heart told his team, "Guys, that was a nice win. I'm proud of the way all of you answered the bell today. Now that's the way to play this game. That's what we are looking for in effort.

"But buckle on your chin straps next week when you come to practice because Runnels is next. I guarantee they will be the best team you will meet this year. If you are not up to it, don't even show up next week or they will hand you your head. We will have to play even better than we did today. So, I'm just telling you, get ready."

Coach Heart then walked out of the room, leaving his team to ponder his words of warning. Coach Heart certainly had a way of taking the thrill out of a victory. If you were going to play football in West Texas, you had to learn about carrying the burden of expectations as well as realizing the fact that there was always another team out there that was probably as good as you.

Chapter 12

END OF THE WORLD

It proved to be a long weekend for Cody Joe. The Tigers were out of town, Chip and Kate were asked to spend the night with Grandma and Grandpa Taggert and no one had approached Cody Joe about doing anything.

He spent Saturday morning listening to records and kicked around in the backyard during the afternoon, doing absolutely nothing. The truth was Cody Joe was bored stiff, but he didn't dare tell Rue Carter.

Telling Rue that you were bored was the death knell in the Carter household. Cody Joe could hear her in his mind, "Bored? I'll show you bored. When you get through with the things I have for you to do, you'll never be bored again. That's a promise."

So, Cody Joe never said the words, but he felt the agony of being alone. He got some relief on Sunday by going to church and visiting his grandparents to pick up Chip and Kate on Sunday afternoon. But he never saw Pug or any of his other friends for the whole weekend. He was quite ready for Monday morning to arrive. He'd even rather practice football than go through another lost weekend like this. And adding to the agony was the fact that the high school Tigers had lost their first game of the year, 14-8 to Levelland.

Cody Joe's Monday didn't start out on a good note. Jennifer Axel always had a way of throwing him off course at the start of every week.

As usual, Cody Joe and Kevin Tumbler arrived at

homeroom together prior to the entrance of Jennifer. Cody Joe and Tumbler were engaged in deep conversation when Jennifer rudely burst upon the scene, giving no regard to the meeting of minds between Carter and Tumbler.

She almost screamed out loud enough for the whole class to hear, "Cody Joe, I can't do it any longer. I just can't keep your secret. It's too much to ask of me. You should have never told me that you like Veronica."

Cody Joe was embarrassed and it showed. Mandy Mayor and her three groupies were all giggling at the new news. If Cody Joe wanted to keep this fact a secret, he had now lost that ability as soon as Jennifer had opened her mouth. Jennifer might as well have announced it to the school newspaper. Mandy Mayor would have it all over school by lunch. He couldn't bear for this to get out for public consumption, but he now had no way to avoid the upcoming and agonizing onslaught of being the joke of the campus.

In Cody Joe Carter's way of thinking, Jennifer Axel had let him down. She had played the role of Judas and had left Cody Joe hanging in the wind of ridicule and scorn. He would now be the brunt of every joke in the school. To make matters worse, Veronica Slade would probably be so shocked by the news that she would never have anything to do with him again. Cody Joe wished he could go back and hide in the anonymous safety of his boring weekend.

"Jennifer, you promised," Cody Joe babbled. "I'll never tell you another thing. Why did you say that in front of all these people?"

Jennifer started to cry, sending the episode to a new height. "I'm sorry, Cody Joe, but I couldn't help it. It was too hard for me to know that you liked Veronica and didn't have the guts to tell her yourself. I still think you should tell her, or I will. I'm going to break my promise."

"You might as well go ahead and tell her because she's probably going to know it before you even get a chance to see her," Cody Joe quietly said with a hanging head. He then looked up and stared Jennifer square in the eyes and continued, "Jennifer, I don't know how I will ever trust you again with anything. I thought we were good friends."

"I am your friend," Jennifer said through free-flowing tears. "I just want you and Veronica to be together, but if it's up to you, it's never going to happen. Don't you understand, Cody Joe? I want to help you, not hurt you."

Cody Joe and Jennifer didn't speak again during the homeroom period as Elmer Perry entered the room and started passing out some new school forms that each student had to fill out. When Cody Joe left homeroom for his science class, he carried a heavy heart. He just knew his day was going to get much worse. Mandy Mayor passed him in the hallway like he was standing still as if on an urgent mission. That mission included delivering the hottest news of the day; news that was surely to impact the life of Cody Joe Carter.

* * *

The morning was excruciatingly slow for Carter. He was waiting for the other shoe to drop. He didn't know how it would come, but he expected the laughter, smirks and snickers to come any time he changed classes.

Cody Joe had attacked this problem much like he did most problems in his life. He just ignored it until someone pushed him too far on the issue. Usually, it was Rue Carter that pushed him off dead center, but he was in junior high now and the advice of his Mom wasn't going to help him today. He was going to have to man up and face the coming ridicule on his own.

The other shoe fell later than he expected, but it fell all the same. It happened at lunch when he hit the snack shack alone. First to mention the new-found news was none other than the burly Butch Cassidy.

"Cody Joe, I'm hearing you got yourself a new girlfriend whether you want one or not," Cassidy said with a wide grin on his face. "I have Mandy Mayor in Texas history and she says you're ape over Veronica Slade, but afraid to tell her. You never told me about any of this, so is it true, Cody Joe?"

"Cut it out, Butch," said a squirming Cody Joe as he desperately tried to find a way around his predicament. He now knew that his secret was public knowledge and there was little else to do but face the music. It was his only course left.

"Listen, Butch, I don't really feel like talking about it right now, so just leave me alone."

Cassidy didn't stop, however, offering, "Then it must be true. You're hot for Veronica Slade and you ain't even going to tell your buddies about it. That's a cryin' shame, but I guess that's your business. I don't know why you are keeping it a secret. You'd be lucky to have a girlfriend like Veronica, but I've never even seen you talk to her, much less cozy up to her. I've never been so surprised when I heard this story. I didn't believe it until now. How did Mandy find out about it?"

Cody Joe didn't want to deal with any of this, but as he started to explain the morning's events to Butch, Pug Preston came bursting into the snack shack, frantically searching for Cody Joe. It seems that the news about Veronica Slade and Cody Joe Carter was important enough for Pug to drop his standing lunch date with Alexi Taggert to find his best friend on the fly.

"Cody Joe, is it true? Are you going to ask Veronica Slade to go steady with you?"

"Oh, Pug, I don't know what's going to happen? This whole

thing has gotten out of hand. I made the mistake of telling Jennifer that I liked Veronica and Jennifer went kind of nuts over it. Now, she wants to tell Veronica. Shoot, Pug, Butch here is right. I haven't even said a dozen words to Veronica before and now everyone thinks we should be together. I don't know what's going to happen."

"Well, you don't have to worry about Jennifer telling Veronica. Mandy Mayor, or one of her girlfriends, will make sure of that," Preston said. "I think the whole school already thinks you two will be together at some point, but I don't even know how you or Veronica feel about this whole thing. I think you need to talk to Veronica and find out where you two stand. It seems like everyone in school knows what you two should do except you two."

Cassidy chimed in, "Boy, this is a real mess, isn't it, Cody Joe? I don't know anyone in this whole world that can create a mess like you can. That's what you get when you keep secrets from your friends."

Cody Joe quickly countered, "No, Butch, you've got it all wrong. This is the kind of trouble you get into when you do tell your friends a secret. This is a disaster."

* * *

The remainder of the school day went much the same way. Cody Joe was besieged by friends and acquaintances. He could even feel heads turning as he passed people in the hallways. He wasn't ready to cope with any of this – and above all – he wanted to avoid Veronica Slade at all costs until he figured out how this matter could be handled properly.

Rick Tracks tracked down Cody Joe and wanted to know the real "scoop." Kevin Tumbler had relayed the news to his close friends in the band, so Tumbler actually ended up spreading the word around school more than Mandy Mayor. Of course, he, too, had been an eye witness to the whole affair.

Stacy Trout was astonished at the news from Tumbler. Kirby Tanner found out the news at lunch in the snack shack. And the impending knot-tying had been thoroughly discussed in the cafeteria as Alexi Taggert made the most of her time at lunch without Pug Preston around by delivering the juicy morsels of school gossip.

Veronica Slade handled the news in her own way. She went home after first period.

Jennifer Axel knew she had to tell Veronica before anyone else approached her, so Jennifer raced to Veronica's English class as soon as homeroom was over. Veronica was already sitting in her first period class with three minutes still left before the bell and had her textbook already open, ready for the day's lesson to begin. Jennifer waved to Veronica from the classroom doorway and Veronica quickly identified that something was up. She got up from her desk and went to Jennifer.

"Come with me. We have to talk," Jennifer commanded.

The two went to the nearest ladies' restroom where Jennifer quickly laid out the events that transpired during the homeroom period. She told Veronica how she had been keeping Cody Joe's secret and how miserable it had made her. She told Veronica how she told Cody Joe that she was no longer going to keep that secret and that Mandy Mayor, of all people, had heard the whole thing. She also promised that she would never again keep a secret from Veronica and she blatantly asked for Veronica's forgiveness.

"Veronica, it's going to be all over school in the next hour or so. You can bank that. I wanted you to know before someone else told you. I'm so sorry about this and I don't know what we should do from here."

"Jennifer, I don't think I can face this right now. I'm going to call my Mom to come and get me. I'll tell the people in the office that I have an upset stomach," Veronica said.

"I'll go with you," Jennifer said as the two walked back to the English class where Veronica walked right into Mrs. Proctor's class, picked up her books and walked out, all while the stunned teacher watched her come and go. No words were exchanged either way.

* * *

Ave. M was full of Carter and Slade commentary as the seventh grade Blue Devils headed for practice Monday after school. Carter tucked himself in between Cassidy and Preston as a way to shield himself from the others. It wasn't much of a shield.

The Quay brothers came up from behind and Adam asked first, "C.J., we hear you're locked up on pulling the trigger with the Slade girl. Any truth to that."

"C'mon Adam, things are a bit messed up right now. None of this should be happening. I didn't mean for any of this to take place. I'm disgusted with the whole thing."

"Well, I just plain don't see the problem, Cody Joe," responded T-Quay. "Veronica is a swell looking girl. Any boy in school would be glad to have her on his arm. Even if this didn't come about like you planned it, you should jump on this opportunity. Man, if you don't, I just might take a shot at her myself."

Even Cody Joe had not lost his comedic timing, saying, "Right T-Quay, you wouldn't stand a chance with her because she ain't blind."

Everyone, even T-Quay, enjoyed a laugh and Cody Joe's comment did seem to lighten the air until Lee Line came running up.

"Mandy tells me you got it bad for Veronica Slade. Have you asked her to be your girlfriend yet?" Line asked.

"No, I haven't asked her. She probably will never have anything to do with me after this and I wouldn't blame her."

Line responded, "Well, Mandy wants to help you out. She's offering to talk to Veronica because you got us together. Believe me, there's not many people that can say no to Mandy. She's got a way with people."

Cassidy interrupted, saying, "You mean she's got a way of making you do anything she wants."

Again laughter erupted all around as the marching troop entered the gates leading to the field house and practice field. There wouldn't be much laughter for the rest of the afternoon.

* * *

Coach Jimmy Lee Heart knew about the task at hand. He had learned that Big Spring Runnels was also undefeated, averaging over 30 points per game. They had not allowed a score in three previous games, just like the Blue Devils. This was probably going to be the toughest challenge of the year and he wanted his team to be prepared.

Of course, that meant some tough workouts ahead on Monday and Tuesday. Coach Heart had instructed Coach Nix and Coach Bear to push the troops and the two assistants were awfully good at following instructions.

The seventh graders began to get the idea even in calisthenics. The coaches were grinding on every player.

"Get your legs up, Cassidy," yelled Coach Nix. "You're acting like you're tired or something."

Coach Bear screamed "You're just plain lazy, Liberman. Get all the way down in that squat. Doesn't anyone want to play football today?"

And so it went in drill after drill. As hard as the Blue Devils tried to please the coaches, the more they seemed to fail. It was a miserable practice session and Coach Heart loved every minute of it. He could see they were trying hard and he couldn't really ask more than that. But more than anything, he was seeing players helping each other through the difficult times.

He saw Lee Line take Lester Jarvis aside after Coach Heart criticized him for not hitting the right hole. Line said, "Jarvis, you know that play. Run it right. We're all in this together and we can't win if you don't hit the hole. We can do this."

Linebacker Joey Taylor gave defensive sub Eric Blade a big pat on the back for making a good play, saying, "Christian, you just might lose your job if Blade keeps playing like this."

Christian, taking a breather on the sideline, turned and sent a savage stare at Taylor, who got exactly the rise out of Christian he wanted. The comment made both Christian and Blade play harder the rest of the day.

Ever since Cody Joe's eye-gouging encounter with Christian, more and more members of the team were willing to challenge Nate head-on. For one thing, the Blue Devils were no longer feeling like individuals. They were now team members and there was great strength in that concept. They were now inexorably linked like a chain of DNA. The team persona was literally becoming part of the makeup of each team player in his own way. There was no formula to make this happen, but you knew it when it did happen. It was now happening for the 1958 Blue Devils. Nate Christian's bad boy image suffered at the team level and he was beginning to notice. He didn't like being openly challenged on any level.

As far as Cody Joe Carter was concerned, the intense

practice was a God-given relief. It gave him the opportunity to release a little steam and a diversion from thinking about his "other" problem. There was a part of Cody Joe that never wanted this practice to end and another part that told him he was just too tired to care.

* * *

Cody Joe tried to get through the family supper without divulging the day's critical information. The last thing he wanted was to explain to his father and mother how he had screwed up his life so badly that he was now the talk of the school. This was a mess he had to settle himself and he saw no good reason to have to also live with it at home.

Chip explained in great detail how his best friend, Todd McAfee, was asked by the teacher to take the chalk erasers outside and beat the chalk dust out of them by banging them on the back steps of the school. Instead, McAfee had beat the erasers on the window panes of another classroom while they were at recess, but he got caught by the teacher of the vacant classroom and was sent to the principal's office. That was the end of the story because Chip had not seen Todd since the door of the principal's office closed.

Kate told how piano practice had gone and tried to talk her parents into signing her up for twirling classes. Cody Joe knew it was only a matter of time before Kate was signed up for twirling. Kate usually got anything she wanted in Cody Joe's view.

Rue, as usual, did ask Cody Joe if he had any more problems with Nate Christian, and Cody Joe truthfully said that there had been no more incidents with the boy or the knife. In short, Cody Joe led Jack and Rue to believe that nothing much of interest had happened at school and he would just as soon leave it at that.

Surprisingly, Rue had not heard a word about the incident even though she tried to stay on top of things when it came to her family. Both Chip and Cody Joe were not beyond leaving out a few details on their day. But she usually found out about the important things in their life given enough time with or without their help.

Meanwhile, Veronica Slade had poured out the whole story to her mother, telling every sordid detail. Her mother was attentive like always, but she didn't have a clue as to how she could help her daughter. This was a sticky mess and she was a bit upset at Jennifer Axel for opening this can of worms.

Jennifer called Veronica around 7 p.m., late enough not to interrupt the supper hour. They talked until 10 p.m., kicking this beaten can down the road from start to finish. When the conversation had ended, a plan had been set in motion that could break this dreadful deadlock. At the very worst, it would make Tuesday interesting.

Chapter 13

END OF THE WORLD PART II

On Tuesday, Jennifer Axel once again threw Cody Joe's world into a frenzied state by just walking into Elmer Perry's homeroom class.

"Cody Joe, we have to talk," Jennifer started. "I want you to meet me at the stand of pecan trees down by the snack shack at lunch. I don't want to have to look for you, so go there first before you get your food. This is important."

"Wait a minute, Jennifer," said Cody Joe, breaking in. "What's this all about? Why do we need to meet?"

"I swear, Cody Joe. You're almost impossible to deal with and you are about as dense as they come," Jennifer responded. "You know what this is about. I have a plan to end all the controversy so we can get on with our lives. Don't you think that's important enough to at least hear me out at lunch?"

"OK, OK. I'll listen," Cody Joe conceded. "If you can end this mess, I'm all ears."

Cody Joe couldn't imagine what Jennifer's plan would call for, but he was pretty sure it would involve him doing more than he was willing to do. She always made things more difficult than they should be. He also knew this was going to involve Veronica Slade and that prospect alone made him weak in the knees. He still wasn't ready to meet with Veronica face-to-face. At least, Jennifer hadn't proposed that Veronica be at this meeting. He still had the option of putting a halt to the whole thing.

As much as Cody Joe trembled at the thought of meeting with Jennifer, he thought lunch would never arrive. Jennifer's possible solution was so intriguing to him that he could think of little else. He couldn't imagine what Jennifer had in mind. He also wondered if he really was as thick between the ears as Jennifer claimed. The solution might be right in front of him, but he might be too dense to see it. Oh, he hoped it could be that simple.

While it had been Axel that had asked Cody Joe to appear without delay, it was Carter who arrived first at the stand of pecan trees. Cody Joe knew a lot of students like to eat under the trees, so he raced to the spot so he and Jennifer could be alone. Jennifer quickly appeared and wasted no time in getting to the business at hand.

"I talked with Veronica last night, so she's good with this," Jennifer explained. "I just want you to know this up front.

"This predicament can come to a close one of two ways. You two can get together as a couple and that would end the speculation and make it old news. People might joke about it from time to time, but it would no longer be a hot item around school. That would take the pressure off everything. And, of course, this is the option I prefer. Also, it's the option both of you really want. Admit it, Cody Joe, this is the outcome you really want in your heart.

"The other course of action is to let Veronica turn down an offer to go with you. It would let Veronica off the hook. You would come away as the sad figure in this case, but at least it would end the talk. It's like running into a brick wall to save your own neck, so to speak.

"Well, what do you think?"

"Uh, well, I just don't know," Cody Joe squirmed. "I just knew you were going to make it difficult for me one way or the other. Jennifer, I don't even know if I can face Veronica now or ever again. You've made this whole thing uncomfortable for me just because you couldn't keep your mouth shut. We shouldn't have to be doing this at all."

"That's where you are wrong," Jennifer said as tears once again began to flow down her face. "Don't you see it? You two need to be together. You like her. You admitted it. And she likes you. She's willing to give this a chance and you need to take advantage of this opportunity.

"In my humble opinion, you're getting more out of this than Veronica Slade. She's way too good for you."

"Well, let me think about it and I'll get back to you," Carter said.

"Just don't think too long, Cody Joe. Veronica's going to take this hesitation as a bad sign. She likes you, but she doesn't like being in this situation any better than you do."

"OK, I'll have an answer for you in homeroom tomorrow," Carter ended.

It was Kirby Tanner who watched as Jennifer Axel walked away from the stand of pecan trees. He could visibly see that Jennifer was wiping tears from her eyes. He could also see that Cody Joe was left slowly walking in a circle with his head down and in deep thought. Tanner was certain that this was not the time to talk with Cody Joe. Instead, he turned and scurried away.

* * *

Cody Joe had a miserable Tuesday practice session. He could do nothing right and this wasn't the week to be screwing up in practice. The coaching staff was hell-bent on making this week a focal point of the season. Big Spring Runnels was just two days away and Coach Jimmy Lee Heart was convinced that he would find out all he needed to know about his team after Thursday's game in Big Spring.

Coach Tom Nix relished the thought of tough workouts and he was almost diabolical in his approach to toughness. Cody Joe, who rarely drew the ire of any of the coaches, found himself running laps on this Tuesday as Coach Nix refused to tolerate Carter's lackadaisical approach to practice.

Cody Joe wasn't purposely trying to be obstinate, but his thinking wasn't centered on football. He was more concerned about his limited options with Veronica Slade. As Cody Joe took off on a third punishment lap of the day for failing to follow instructions during a controlled scrimmage session, he was beginning to get the feeling that girls and football don't mix. Or was it that Coach Nix and girls don't mix? Either way it made for a rough day on the old gridiron.

* * *

It was no better at home. Cody Joe could think of nothing else. He slept little and he really didn't know what to tell Jennifer when he finally got out of bed at 6:30 a.m. on Wednesday.

Carter tried to weigh it from every angle possible, but he kept coming to the same conclusion: He really didn't have much of a choice in the matter. He agreed with Jennifer that the snickering and lunchtime gossip would probably end quickly if he and Veronica became boyfriend and girlfriend. He also knew that Jennifer would see to it that Veronica would be protected in the end. All Veronica had to say was that she didn't want to have anything to do with that Carter boy and Cody Joe would end up being the continued joke of the campus. That, too, would pass in time, but it would definitely turn out to be a painful outcome for Cody Joe.

165

Even with all his woes and worries, Cody Joe was intrigued that Jennifer flat out told him that Veronica would readily agree to be his girlfriend. That was all he ever wanted in the first place. He never was astute enough to pick up on that fact and he surely had never been brave enough to act on it. He was now in a corner with no place left to paint. There was really no decision to make. Fate – and Jennifer Axel – had seen to that.

On the way out of the house to catch the school bus at West Elementary, Cody Joe rummaged through the top drawer of his dresser and found his favorite wrist bracelet. The bracelet had been given to him by Rue Carter the previous Christmas and his full name had been inscribed on the front face. Cody Joe only wore it on Sundays and other special occasions. The sparkling memento was one of his prized possessions. He slipped it into his pocket and departed the house and headed west for West.

* * *

Cody Joe went to class early on Wednesday morning and was grateful that Jennifer Axel arrived seconds behind him. This time it was Cody Joe who took the bull by the horns. He grabbed Jennifer's arm and firmly guided her to the rear of the classroom where no one could hear them talking.

"Jennifer, are you sure that Veronica is willing to go through with this?" Cody Joe whispered. "Are you sure she really likes me and isn't doing this just to get out of this mess?"

Jennifer took Carter's lead and whispered back, "Well, you ought to know all this for yourself, but since you can't recognize the signs, I'm here to tell you that she really wants you to ask her to be your steady. She wants the same thing you do. That's why all this is so crazy."

Carter thought a minute before answering and then took the cold plunge, "OK, then. What's the next step?"

"You're really going to do it?" Jennifer said, almost losing her whispering regimen. "This is great. I can't wait to tell Veronica. Meet us at the lockers after lunch on the way to fourth period. You can ask her then when there are only a few people around.

"You're doing the right thing, Cody Joe. And you didn't even have Mandy Mayor tell you what to do."

"Yeah, well, what do I say to Veronica? I have no clue where to go from here."

Jennifer was loving every minute of torture that Cody Joe was experiencing and wasn't about to help him get off the hook, saying, "Oh, Cody Joe, you'll figure it all out before lunch."

Giggling, she added, "I suggest you say something romantic."

With that statement, Cody Joe was ready to forget the whole deal. This was going to be much more difficult than he ever imagined. Still, he had to clear up one other matter.

He reached deep into the right pocket of his jeans and pulled out his bracelet for Jennifer to see. He asked, "Would it be proper to give her this to wear? I know it's a boy's bracelet, but it could be a signal that we are now going together, kind of like the discs we traded in elementary school."

Jennifer took one look at the bracelet and put her hand over her mouth as if she were in a state of shock. She whispered, "Oh, Cody Joe, there may be hope for you after all. That's what I call romantic. Never in a thousand years would I expect something like this coming from you. She's going to love it."

* * *

Cody Joe showed up early at his locker, trying to figure out what to say to Veronica Slade, who would become his girlfriend within the next 15 minutes. He couldn't believe this was happening. He felt he had no control over the events of the day, yet he desperately wanted this to work out. In Cody Joe Carter's way of thinking, he would be the luckiest guy in the entire seventh grade class if Veronica Slade was his girlfriend. Lee Line can have Mandy Mayor – and her short cheerleading outfit.

It was only a few minutes later when Jennifer and Veronica turned the corner at the end of the hallway and began their approach toward Cody Joe. They quickly saw Carter at the midpoint of the hallway. They looked at each other and failed in an attempt to suppress a giggle. That made Cody Joe nervous as they approached, but there was no backing out now – unless he started running for his life.

But Cody Joe was glued to his spot and politely opened the conversation with, "Hello Jennifer and Veronica. I don't know whether to laugh or run, but I'm here like I said I would be."

Then Cody Joe shyly turned his head to Veronica and almost froze in his tracks. Talking openly to Veronica Slade was still very much problematic for Carter. He loved the way she looked, but he was intimidated by her very presence. He reached into his pocket and asked Veronica Slade without looking directly into her eyes, "Will you wear this as a symbol of us being a couple?"

Veronica was quick to answer and she looked full into the face of Cody Joe when she said, "I would be proud to wear your bracelet, Cody Joe."

It was done. It had not gone as Cody Joe had envisioned, but it was at least over and done. Since he could think of nothing else that needed to be accomplished, he turned and left the two girls, who were still admiring the bracelet while trying to figure out the latch in order to place it on Veronica's wrist. By the time the task was accomplished, Cody Joe Carter had disappeared around the corner and back into the safety of his own world.

* * *

Cody Joe was new to being a girl's boyfriend and it showed. By Thursday's pep rally, Carter had not seen or talked to Veronica Slade since he gave her the bracelet. Yes, Cody Joe Carter officially had a girlfriend, but there was no outward evidence of it other than the fact that Veronica Slade was wearing a wrist bracelet that had Cody Joe's full name engraved on it. He had not even told his parents of the momentous occasion, but stranger still, he had not even talked to Pug Preston about the event despite Pug's continuous bombardment of questions about the "predicament" Cody Joe had gotten himself into. Cody Joe did think about calling Veronica on the phone Wednesday night, but the prospect terrified him even more than the bracelet meeting. First, he didn't know her phone number and there were three sets of Slades listed in the phone book. He would have died if Veronica's parents answered the phone instead of her or if he had dialed up the wrong Slade family. No, it was better to do what Cody Joe had a tendency to do in these kinds of situations – just ignore the problem altogether. It was the easiest course of action and this was a prime example of something in which Cody Joe could really excel.

As the team marched into the pep rally arena on Thursday morning, Cody Joe caught his first glance of Veronica since Wednesday. The two made eye contact almost simultaneously. Cody Joe felt proud when Veronica's face lit up like a Christmas light. She held up her right arm to show his bracelet dangling around her wrist. Cody Joe broke out in a wide smile and vigorously waved at her. Veronica nudged Jennifer and pointed to where Cody Joe was walking with the team. Both Jennifer and Veronica waved again and Cody Joe responded with enthusiasm. Cody Joe couldn't help but think that it would be a lot easier to have a girlfriend if communication could be done from long distance. Carter also saw Jack and Rue Carter on the entry and shared a wave with them also.

Following the pep rally skits, cheerleading and twirling performances, SJHS principal Robert "Moose" Tankard made a brief speech. The former football coach had never spoken at the pep rally, so it got the attention of the Blue Devils and the students.

"Many of you may have read in the Snyder Daily News yesterday that our seventh and eighth grade teams are undefeated and will be playing Runnels in Big Spring today at 4 and 7 p.m. Both Runnels teams are undefeated and the paper says this will be the highlight of our football season. Let's show our teams we support them."

A loud yell erupted and the gauntlet had been thrown down. Let the battle for supremacy begin.

The pep rally held one more surprise for Cody Joe. Coach Jimmy Lee Heart made a brief speech on how this was going to be the toughest challenge for his team this year.

"If I'm going into a tough battle, I want to do it with people I can trust and who will give me great effort for every minute of action," Heart said. "That's why I have chosen Cody Joe Carter and Dirk Bolger to be my team captains today."

Cody Joe was stunned by the announcement, especially considering his terrible practice performance on Tuesday. All the team members around him were slapping him on the back. Bolger was getting the same treatment.

Cody Joe approached the microphone and said, "I really don't know what to say about all of this, so let's just go to Big

Spring."

Bolger countered, "I say what he just said. Beat Runnels."

Carter saw that Rue was dabbing her eyes with a lace handkerchief and he saw Veronica and Jennifer hugging each other in the far reaches of the bleachers. If this was Cody Joe's 10 seconds of fame, he was pretty sure he could die happy.

He never got to speak with his parents, but he was happy that Veronica and Jennifer fell in step with him as they exited the gym, heading for first period class. Cody Joe actually walked beside Veronica instead of Jennifer. It was his first big foray into the world of having a steady girlfriend. It excited him and terrified him all at the same time.

* * *

The seventh grade Blue Devils were ordered to leave campus for the field house at 12:30 p.m. That would give all the players time to eat a team meal in the cafeteria. All the players got to go to the front of the line and then join their teammates to get their trays and food. On this day, the cafeteria ladies had prepared fried chicken, mashed potatoes and green beans. In Cody Joe Carter's way of thinking, this was the perfect pregame meal. Then, it was the routine stroll down Ave. M to the field house to begin preparations for the team's second road trip of the year.

This road trip would be a bit different since they would pack all their gear and dress when they got to Runnels game field. The trip to Big Spring, a city of close to 40,000, consisted of a 50-mile bus ride south of Snyder on a well-traveled Highway 350.

In comparison to the 14,000 or so that lived in Snyder, Big Spring was considered a metropolitan area. Snyder was also a very important cog in the overall economy of Big Spring.

Scurry County, of which Snyder served as the county seat, was a dry county left over from the vestiges of Prohibition. Big Spring, on the other hand, was wet and openly sold alcohol as a member of Howard County. That made Highway 350 an important route for many Snyderites and an economic cash flow for the city of Big Spring. It was also a major route for Scurry County's many bootleggers, who would buy alcohol products in Big Spring and sell them in Snyder for inflated prices to those who were gladly willing to pay the price. Cody Joe and Pug were still a bit young to understand all the intricacies of Highway 350, but they were not so young to know where Snyder's booze supply came from. In fact, they were well aware that many in Snyder's white community bought illegal booze from bootleggers in colored town just two blocks from where the Blue Devils were preparing for their own trip down 350.

Each travel bag would hold two uniforms, so players packed in pairs and checked each other to see if they had included all the equipment. This system generally worked well, but it wasn't without its flaws. Invariably, some knucklehead would forget a jockey strap or some other important piece of equipment. That's why manager Rick Tracks would always carry two extra uniforms along just to fill in the gaps left by those who couldn't follow instructions.

Generally, however, the Blue Devils went about their business of packing in a very orderly and quiet manner. The team was anxious to play Runnels and they had their minds tuned in to the task they would face this very afternoon.

There was little noise in the bus on the one-hour drive to Big Spring, but the players and coaches got an unexpected surprise. A cold rain began to fall just as the team bus passed through the small town of Ira, about 10 miles south of Snyder. Rain had not been forecasted and the coaches looked at each other with quizzical glances. Coaches do not like surprises or any events that are beyond their control.

The closer the bus got to Big Spring, the harder it rained. Coach Heart believed that even if the rain stopped now, the field would be a muddy mess. His teams had played at Runnels before and it didn't have a good field of grass. The field was splotchy patches of grass at best and could quickly turn into a swampy quagmire if the rain persisted.

The Blue Devils quickly scampered from the school bus into their dressing quarters. The rain was pounding so hard on the tin roof of the building that the Snyder team could hear little else. So, most of them said nothing at all and started dressing for the game.

Rue and Jack Carter decided to turn around and head back to Snyder. Neither one of them carried any rain gear. Rue wasn't keen on sitting in the rain even if they had rain equipment. Cody Joe would have to play this game without their support. Several cheerleaders showed up, but there would basically be no crowd in the stands. Even the cheerleaders would be back in the safety of their cars before this game was over. Ernest Cassidy was one of the few parents to show up for the game and he roamed the sideline from start to finish, wearing his working boots and an old set of coveralls. He also wore a light jacket that was about as much protection from the rain as a bucket with holes in it.

The Blue Devils were totally drenched from head to foot even before the end of calisthenics. The temperature fell just below the 50-degree mark at game time, making this outing cold and miserable. Just to add to the woe, the rain picked up a notch just as Henry Styles kicked off to Runnels to start the game.

Runnels started on its own 29-yard line, but quickly lost a total of five yards when its running backs slipped in the mud and fell short of the line of scrimmage on successive plays. On third down, Runnels kept it simple by running a simple dive play right over Cody Joe. Carter made a good tackle, but a pile-up quickly resulted. Cody Joe was not new to the eye-gouging experience and he felt another attempt in this pile-up. Cody Joe reacted decisively this time. He just took the finger and bit into it until he drew blood. One of the Runnels players came out of the pile holding his right hand with blood dripping into the muddy ooze at his feet. The player left the game.

That was just the first indication of what this game was going to be like. Neither team could move the ball in the messy conditions that existed nor was the weather improving. Frustrated, the two teams began to throw a few extra punches here and there. It was a physical game and neither team was backing down. The refs were also miserable and were letting the game rules slide a bit in order to keep the clock running.

Halfback Lester Jarvis twisted a knee trying to turn up field on a sweep and was replaced by Kirby Tanner. It was a big break for Tanner, but it hurt the Blue Devils' ability to have a power back in the lineup at a time when the game counted on a power attack. However, even the bull-like Butch Cassidy was having little success with his forays into the Runnels middle. The Snyder line really was no match for the larger Runnels team.

Nevertheless, the Blue Devils caught a break early in the third quarter when they mounted a semi-successful drive to the Runnels 30-yard line before stalling out. Regardless, Styles punted the ball on fourth and six and Runnels allowed it to roll all the way to the one-yard line. On the next play, Pug Preston and Nate Christian surged together past the Runnels offensive front to blow up an off-tackle attempt, landing the Big Spring runner in the end zone for a safety. Blue Devils 2, Runnels 0 with six minutes left in the third period.

The rest of the game had the two teams battling from mid-field. Neither team could mount a drive nor hit a big play. It quickly began to look like Big Spring was going to lose on a safety.

Late in the fourth quarter, quarterback Lee Line fumbled a handoff attempt to fullback Butch Cassidy. Again a huge pile-up resulted as both teams tried to recover the fumble. Cody Joe almost had the slippery pig hide in his grasp before a fist found its way under his jaw. This time Cody Joe came out of the pile bleeding from a chin gash and Runnels had the ball at the Blue Devils' 23-yard line.

On the next play, a Runnels back tip-toed on a sweep to the right. Safety Jay Coy had him lined up in his sights, but slipped right at the point of attack to allow the Runnels back to continue wading down the right sideline. Linebacker Joey Taylor managed to catch the waddling Big Spring runner, but not before he gained the five-yard line with 45 seconds left in the game.

Runnels then gave its powerful fullback the ball on a slant to the left where tackle Christian was blocked and end Kirk Bolger couldn't keep his footing. The big back lumbered into the end zone with just 39 seconds left. Runnels celebrated the touchdown, but missed the meaningless extra point. Runnels 6, Blue Devils 2.

The seventh grade Blue Devils had lost for the first time. The numbing effect of losing set in quickly. No longer was the rain or the mud an issue. The Blue Devils had literally let a victory escape from their grasp and there was no consoling the sheer magnitude of defeat. These kids had never experienced defeat as a team.

Cody Joe trudged alone toward the dressing room with the rain drops hiding his own tears. He was embarrassed and wondered how he could face his teammates in the locker room. He was sure the loss was on his shoulders as captain of the team.

What he didn't know was that everyone on the team was feeling the same pain of self-doubt. While the loss was a new experience for this youthful group, this low point would bring in another new experience into their lives come Monday afternoon.

Chapter 14

COPING WITH THE FIRST LOSS

Jack Carter picked up Cody Joe at the field house on Thursday night and he arrived even before the team bus got there from Big Spring. Jack was almost desperate to find out how the game had turned out.

Jack learned of the loss by just looking at the body language of the kids coming out to the waiting cars, but when he got his first glimpse of his son, his first thought was that Cody Joe had gotten into another fight with Nate Christian. His son had never come home before from a game looking like he had been in a war zone. Cody Joe was sporting a makeshift bandage on his chin and he had a huge strawberry bruise on his right forearm.

Cody Joe had assured his dad it was all from the game, but the fragile youngster was much more concerned about the loss the team had suffered.

"Dad, we lost the game. We just gave it to them," and with that Cody Joe broke down into uncontrollable sobbing for much of the way home. Jack Carter let his son cry without any admonishment or words of wisdom. Jack knew that this was one of those moments where his son had some growing up to do and he had to get past this part on his own. But Jack silently vowed that he would be there when his son needed him the next time.

Rue Carter was stunned when she first saw her eldest son

walk into the door that night. She almost made Jack and Cody Joe turn around and drive straight to the hospital emergency room.

Rick Tracks had placed the bandage on Cody Joe's chin in the bus on the way back from Big Spring. Tracks' heart was in the right place, but his bandage was ill-fitting and loose. It really didn't serve any useful purpose since Cody Joe wasn't bleeding or showing any signs of infection.

What really made Cody Joe's face look so mangled was because Tracks had also applied a liberal dose of mercurochrome to the injury. Cody Joe actually looked like he was bleeding. The bruised arm didn't require any covering, but of the two wounds, the aching in the arm was by far the more painful.

Of course, Rue thought Cody Joe had just come out of some Civil War field hospital ward. She was quick to scurry to the bathroom to find proper bandages and ointments of which she had a ready supply.

The wounded warrior was now home and that helped soften the pain of both physical and mental anguish. Still, Cody Joe despised the thought of going to school Friday morning. He already had endured the torture of kids ragging all week on him about Veronica and now he was the announced captain of a losing football team. He just didn't know if he could face another round of ridicule and embarrassment.

If he had hoped to get a round of sympathy from Rue, he was sadly mistaken.

Cody Joe tossed out an innocent question to test the waters. "Mom, do you think I might need to stay home tomorrow? I'm not feeling very good."

"I don't think these injuries will keep you from going to school. You'll feel much better after you get a good night's sleep," she answered.

"But Mom, since I was the captain, everyone is going to

think the loss was my fault."

"Well, was the loss your fault?"

"I had a lot to do with it. We played really bad and now everyone will think I'm a bad player."

"Cody Joe, you can't let what other people think or do affect the way you live your life. You have to learn that things don't always work out the way you want them to. That's a hard lesson, but you have to face it. You signed up to play football and your father and I agreed that you could play if it didn't hurt your school work. You agreed to that condition, so you aren't going to miss school just because you can't cope with a loss. The games aren't as important as school. You better get that straight in your head right now."

She ended with another terse reminder. "I know you've played a tough game today, but you still have homework to do and it's getting late. You better get to it."

Cody Joe knew his mother was right on all points, but it was a struggle to get the homework done. He fell asleep right in the middle of a math problem. Rue discovered her son lying face down on his desk around 9:45 p.m. and helped guide her exhausted son to his bed. He never really woke up.

* * *

Few in the city of Snyder had even heard about the seventh graders losing to Runnels because this was the week the Snyder Tigers were set to host the Breckenridge Buckaroos at Tiger Stadium. So when Cody Joe woke up on Friday morning, the radio was full of news about the big game.

Breckenridge was a legendary team during the oil boom days of Texas and the green-clad machine was always in the Top 10 rankings in the state.

And 4-0 Breckenridge was coming to Snyder to meet the

3-1 Tigers in what was being hailed as one of the top games in the state. Of course, with greatness in tow, there was always controversy when it came to Breckenridge. The team had been accused more than once of recruiting high school football players by employing the tactic of landing their fathers well-paying jobs in the oil field.

The land around Snyder was also rich in oil, but no one had ever accused the Tigers of recruiting. Even if Snyder was guilty, few would care since the Tigers had no state championships on their resume like Breckenridge.

As the significance of that game began to soak in on Cody Joe, he started to feel somewhat better because he really did have something to look forward to when school was out today.

Cody Joe made it through the day without much mental pain. Jennifer Axel was appalled to see his scratches and bruises. In home room, both Jennifer and Mandy Mayor fawned over him like a little baby that had fallen out of its crib. Cody Joe was uncomfortable with this over the top treatment, but the other boys in the class were wishing they had a few bruises to show off.

Carter didn't even see Veronica Slade during school hours since he chose not to eat with her at lunch. He was afraid his gnarly face and arm might put her off. Anyway, he was sure he would see her at the game because everybody in town would be there in their finest attire.

Cody Joe still hadn't mentioned his new status as boyfriend to his Mom, but Rue had a family visit from the Taggert family on Thursday after the failed trip to Big Spring and Alexi spilled the beans about Veronica. Rue wanted to know every sorted detail and Alexi was more than happy to oblige. Rue placed the new information on her agenda and promised to have a conservation with Cody Joe at the proper time.

* * *

Cody Joe was correct in his assumption that there would be a large crowd on hand to see the Tigers play Breckenridge. Although no one was turned away from the game and no one was denied a seat, it was being called a sellout.

For sure the student section was jammed packed and Cody Joe was having a hard time saving seats for Veronica Slade and Jennifer Axel. He wished they would show up earlier for the games, especially one like this.

It wasn't long, however, when Veronica started climbing her way up the stadium stairs and Cody Joe quickly caught a glimpse of her before he went completely numb. Veronica was stunning in Cody Joe's mind and his world totally shut down at the mere sight of her.

Veronica was decked out in an amazing cowgirl outfit that included black pointed boots, tight jeans topped with an oversized belt buckle, an orange satin blouse that was partially covered by a leather jacket that had leather tassels running up and down the sleeves and along the bottom. There was even a row of tassels on the back of the jacket. The tassels moved with every step she took, commanding attention on every front. Her head was topped by a sophisticated felt cowboy hat that fit her perfectly.

Cody Joe wasn't the only one to notice. Every seventh grade boy in the stands noticed her arrival and there were more than just a few dropped jaws. Carter suddenly became self-conscious of his own appearance with a patch covering his chin and his old pair of boots that looked more like he had walked through a pig pen than the water puddle that stood in front of the stadium.

Rick Tracks, sitting just two rows behind Cody Joe, stepped down and whispered into Cody Joe's ear, "Man you've hit pay dirt with that girl. She's the most beautiful thing I've ever seen."

For Tracks, that was a big statement because he never even talked to or about girls. In fact, some of the guys wondered if Tracks even knew any girls.

Cody Joe knew Tracks was just trying to pay a compliment to Veronica, but it made him even more uncomfortable. While Veronica looked like something out of a West Texas fashion magazine, Cody Joe felt even more pressure. If it was hard to talk to her before, how much harder would it be to even face her on this night? Cody Joe felt he was now playing way out of his league.

He did muster the courage to lift his hand and wave at Veronica. She instantly smiled and quickly worked her way toward him.

Pug Preston, who was sitting by his girlfriend Alexi Taggert and to the left of Cody Joe, asked Carter to tell Veronica how good she looks tonight. Cody Joe shrugged as if to doubt the friendly advice. Pug then jabbed him rather hard with his elbow on Cody Joe's good arm. Carter winced and took a deep breath.

"Veronica, you look great," Cody Joe offered. "I really like your outfit, but please don't look down at my boots tonight. They've got a few miles on them."

"I hoped you would like my new duds," Veronica answered with a huge grin. "I bought these thinking you might like it.

"By the way, I also brought this blanket because the weather report says it might get a little nippy tonight."

About that time, Jennifer arrived to break Cody Joe's concentration just as he was feeling he was on a roll with Veronica. He had actually talked to her in a complete sentence and she had given him two sentences straight back. In Cody Joe's book, they had just had a conversation.

"It's murder trying to get into the stadium," Jennifer said. "My Dad had to drive all around the neighborhood just to find a parking place. I thought I was going to miss the start of the game."

"You're in plenty of time, Jennifer," Veronica said. "Help me with this blanket. I think all three of us can share if we sit really close together."

Jennifer let out a small giggle while Veronica smiled as she covered Cody Joe's lap with one end of the blanket. She then nestled in close to Cody Joe. Carter had his right hand caught between him and Veronica and he tried to move it in a casual manner. Veronica took it that Cody Joe was trying to take hold of her hand, so she took hold of his and rested both hands in her lap.

Cody Joe didn't know what had happened, but he was suddenly holding hands under a blanket with the most beautiful girl in Snyder, Texas, just as Breckenridge took a 7-0 lead on the Tigers. Cody Joe never even noticed.

Veronica did seem concerned about Cody Joe's wounds. His chin, by now, had developed some pretty thick scabs, making his face look much worse than it really was.

"Has a doctor looked at your face?" Veronica asked. "It looks pretty bad."

"Oh, my Mom is better than any doctor," Cody Joe deflected. "It didn't need any stitches. It just needs to be kept clean and Mom is all about keeping things clean."

"Well, what about practice?" Veronica continued. "How are you going to keep it clean while rolling around on the ground? And what about your chin strap on your helmet, won't that hurt when you put it on?"

"Well, I'll cross that bridge on Monday," Cody Joe reasoned. "Since we lost, I can't see the coaches giving me a day off. We're all dreading Monday. It will be our first practice after a loss."

"You'll be fine, I'm sure," Veronica added, "but take care of yourself because this will be a hard time for you."

Cody Joe wished he could talk more to Veronica, but the rest of the game passed without much conversation. Veronica, however, never once let go of Cody Joe's hand. During the halftime, the blanket slipped and several of Cody Joe's friends, including Butch Cassidy, spied the hand holding event.

Cassidy slapped Kirby Tanner on the arm and asked, "Did you see that?" Tanner nodded and passed the news down the row because a couple holding hands in public was big news on the seventh grade front in Snyder, Texas.

While this had been one of the greatest nights in the history of all mankind for Cody Joe Carter, it was a total bust for the Tigers as they lost 34-7 to the state-ranked Buckaroos. Fans were somberly leaving the stadium after the final gun, but Carter was on cloud nine. This was simply the best night of his life and he was only sorry it had ended. The plight of the Tigers was of no concern to him.

What a difference in attitude a day can bring in the life of one who plays the games of men.

* * *

Carter was still in a dream-like state as he left the stadium with Pug Preston, Butch Cassidy, Rick Tracks and Kirby Tanner. Cody Joe was immersed in his own thoughts as they walked toward the car while Carter's four friends were consumed with how the Tigers had choked in the really big game.

"My Dad said this was a great chance to earn some state-wide recognition," Cassidy offered. "And what do they do? They just go out there and blow it for the whole world to see.

Just like we did against Runnels yesterday."

Pug answered, "I guess this town is plain pitiful when it comes to football. And when you are pitiful in football in West Texas, you don't count for much. We've just got to put things back together – and quick."

Cody Joe was trying to listen to the conversation, but he couldn't think about anything else other than holding hands with the lovely Veronica Slade. He had not said a word since the gang had left their seats. Veronica had squeezed Cody Joe's hand one last time before releasing her grip. Before Cody Joe could even utter a mild protest, she was off to find her parents.

Jennifer turned to Cody Joe and declared, "Well, Cody Joe, you aren't much of a talker, but you climbed to a new level with Veronica tonight. I didn't know you had it in you."

The bewildered Carter just stared at Jennifer, thinking, "I don't have a clue as to what you are talking about. I didn't do anything. Veronica was the one in charge."

Still, the perception among his friends was that the shy Cody Joe Carter was on the move. He had now gained a greater status just by following Veronica's lead. Certainly, Veronica Slade had gained greater status in the eyes of Cody Joe.

Rue Carter had agreed to take Cody Joe's gang to the Dairy Queen after the game for the Friday night ritual of banana splits. The Carters had come to the game in two cars so Jack could take Kate and Chip home while Rue chaperoned her Blue Devils for some sweet treats.

The Dairy Queen was the social hub of Snyder. Everyone went to the Dairy Queen whether you were young or old. You always could run into someone you knew at the Dairy Queen. It was said that all business transactions in Snyder were ultimately finalized at the Dairy Queen. It was also the place to find a girlfriend, propose marriage or eat a great hamburger. To say that the Dairy Queen was functional in all regards would simply be an understatement. In fact, it's proper to say that the city of Snyder would not be functional without the Dairy Queen, a Texas staple in small towns all across the state.

Butch Cassidy was an expert when it came to banana splits. He asked for double scoops of vanilla, strawberry and chocolate while adding a pile of nuts scattered over the top before a liberal dose of whip cream. Also, he asked for his banana to be split precisely down the middle so his "split" wouldn't be lopsided.

The rest just ordered regular "splits" because all the Dairy Queen staff knew exactly how each of them wanted it. This wasn't the first banana split foray for this group. After all, they were growing boys and Dairy Queen regulars.

The place was packed, but the boys found a booth that would hold all five, if one sat in a chair at the end of the booth. Rue was fortunate because her friend Madelyn Ross was there with her husband, Frank, and they asked her to join them. This was just fine with Rue because she didn't want to be extra baggage for the boys. This was a time they needed their freedom.

It didn't take long for the gang's conversation to turn to Cody Joe and Veronica. Of course, it was Cassidy that got straight to the point. He relished turning the conversational knife and he always loved getting a rise out of his best friend.

"Hey, Cody Joe, have you gotten to second base with Veronica yet?" Cassidy probed.

Cody Joe was taken aback with the bold question from Cassidy. He honestly didn't know how to answer that question.

First, his mom had always told him to be respectful of the girls he was with and he also didn't think Cassidy had any right to know secrets like that between Cody Joe and Veronica.

And there was the one other matter – he didn't really know what constituted getting to second base. Cody Joe didn't even know if holding hands was good enough to stand on first base. If holding hands didn't count, he wasn't on any base at all.

He wondered what it took to get on base, but this wasn't a time to declare his ignorance. Everyone here already thought he was naïve in the ways of love. Cody Joe thought he knew what it meant to hit a homerun, but the process between first and third left him secluded in a dark cloud and he almost had a foreboding about his future dealings of rounding the bases with a girl.

Right now, all Cody Joe wanted with Veronica was to be able to speak in complete sentences – and another chance for sitting close and holding hands on a chilly night. He would have to deal with what base he was on at a later date. Somehow, Butch's question seemed out of place, disrespectful and inappropriate.

"I don't think that's any of your business," Cody Joe finally answered. "Why would you put me on the spot like that in front of these guys, Butch?"

The eyes of everyone at the table suddenly cast wild-looking eyes in Butch's direction with the anticipation that this conversation was going to get interesting in a hurry.

"Oh, c'mon Cody Joe. Don't be like that. We just want to know how things are going with you and Veronica. We all saw you holding hands and we naturally wondered if a little more was going on. You can tell us. We're your friends."

Butch's response shed no light for Cody Joe on whether or not holding hands was a first base event. He thought that maybe holding hands was like running to first base. Maybe kissing got you on first base, but if that was the truth, Butch had no right to talk about second base. Second base had to be way out of Cody Joe's tactical skills and he wanted this conversation stopped now.

"Butch, leave it alone. I'm not going to discuss Veronica with you on any level now or in the future. So, don't ask me again."

Pug picked up on the rising anger in Cody Joe and helped to defuse the situation, saying, "Butch, drop it. We don't need to let this thing get out of hand here. We're all friends and I would like to keep it that way."

However, the mischievous Cassidy just had to interject one more barb before letting go.

"Well, Pug, then tell us if you've gotten to second base with Alexi."

Everyone at the table, including Cody Joe, erupted with laughter and the night ended with the gang still showing a united front.

Still, Cody Joe went to bed that Friday night wondering what constituted second base. It would be the least of his worries come Monday when he would find out what it was like to play for a team that had lost a game. It was officially time to grow up because Coach Tom Nix went to bed Friday night still stewing over the loss to Runnels. That unhappy truth was going to be a seventh grade game changer come Monday afternoon.

Chapter 15

MAN IN THE RING

C ody Joe woke up to a frosty Monday morning. His chin hurt, his forearm was still deeply bruised and he was actually sore from the Sunday afternoon tag football game the boys played on the grass of Snyder High School.

The high school had a sloping berm that ran down to the street, but was flat like a plateau on top. Cody Joe went sailing off the berm on one pass reception and the resulting crash on the lower sidewalk had shaken him up, but left no lasting injuries other than soreness, which he was now learning to live with nearly on a daily basis.

Carter forced his aching body to step off the bus as it arrived at school. He walked to home room with Stacy Trout as usual, but ran into Tracks as he reached the school entrance.

"Hey, Cody Joe, I went to the field house before school and I heard Coach Nix talking with Coach Heart. I'm not sure what's going on, but something different is happening at practice today. I hope y'all are ready for whatever it is."

Cody Joe grabbed Tracks by the shoulder before he walked away and said, "Whaddaya mean, Tracks, what did they say?"

"I'm late. I have to go now. Just be ready for a tough day. I really don't know what's going on. I do know they aren't very happy about the way the game went last Thursday in Big Spring.

As Tracks walked away, he yelled back, "I'll make sure your chin is padded. I read up on how to do it."

Tracks disappeared around the corner while Cody Joe and Stacy looked at each other in bewilderment before heading to home room.

Cody Joe did eat lunch with Veronica and Jennifer in the cafeteria. Veronica was still worried about Cody Joe going to practice with his raw looking chin and the deep bruise on his forearm. Her point wasn't lost on Cody Joe because he was concerned about it too. Both his chin and arm still hurt at the touch and he had some major doubts that Tracks could fix him up good enough to avoid a long day at the practice field.

By the time the team had begun its daily march down Ave. M to the practice field after school, word had spread that something was up for practice. No one, however, had the slightest clue of what to expect. Everyone had a different thought on the subject.

"They're going to run us until the sun goes down and our tongues draggin' the ground," said Mac Cone.

Dirk Bolger offered, "Betcha they're going to make us push that rusty, ole blocking sled over a hundred acres of land."

"Yeah," chimed in Stoney Wall, "And I bet we'll hold our blocking drills in that sticker patch over by the south fence. Won't that be fun?"

Good to his word, Tracks met Carter at the door of the field house with an arm full of stuff that Cody Joe couldn't quite piece together.

Tracks said, "Take all this to your locker and I'll be there by the time you get dressed. I'm going to fix you up."

Cody Joe did as instructed and was fully ready for practice when Tracks appeared again. Tracks placed some rubber pads on Cody Joe's chin and expertly taped the pieces together with ankle tape. If nothing else, it gave Carter a feeling of extra protection and he could even touch the bandage without feeling any sense of pain.

Also, Tracks brought a rubberized padding for his fore-arm. That was by far the most pleasing of the protective measures taken by Tracks. It gave Carter a good padding and it didn't even hurt much when he threw his arm up against the wooden post of his locker.

Carter felt he was ready for whatever was about to come until Coach Nix entered the room and yelled, "All of you on the practice field now. This is the day you grow into men – or die tryin'."

* * *

Nix was the only coach on the field. No one knew where Coach Heart or Coach Hixler were. No one had seen them. Nix led the team in a brief round of calisthenics and then marched his charges to an area around the north goal line.

"OK, guys, form a big circle with about two steps between each of you and do it now," Nix said with his sternest voice.

The team jumped at his orders like a well-drilled army platoon. The circle wasn't perfect at first, but another command from Nix sent the troops into perfect formation.

"Since you can't seem to match up with a tough team, I'm going to make you tougher. By the end of practice, I promise that most of you will be tougher than you were yesterday.

"It works like this. I'm going to place one player in the middle of the ring. He's the man in the ring. Cody Joe, you were the captain in our loss, so you are the first man in the ring."

Cody Joe didn't have to be told. He walked quickly to the center of the ring.

Nix continued, "I will point to one of you in the ring and you will run to the center of the ring to throw your best block at Cody Joe. Cody Joe, you will ward off the attacker by meeting him head on. That means you will have to keep your feet moving because you won't know from where the next attacker will come. Do you understand that?"

"Yes sir. I got it."

"Then we can continue. Anyone who tries to soften a block will do laps and then will be the next man in the ring. It's a simple game, but we're going to find out who's tough and who isn't.

"OK, now, you ready, Cody Joe?"

Nix then pointed to the team's most devastating blocker to start off the drill by pointing to Butch Cassidy, which also happened to be one of Cody Joe's best friends. The symbolism wasn't lost on the team as they instantly knew Coach Nix meant business today.

Cassidy unrelentingly charged at the awaiting man in the ring. He was intent on landing a superb blow at his friend because Cassidy hated running laps worse than he did putting Cody Joe on the ground.

Cody Joe, however, held his own as Cassidy delivered his blow. He kept his feet and had no sense of pain from either the chin or the arm as adrenalin began to kick in. But Nix had already sent Mac Cone into the fray before Cody Joe could recover from Cassidy's best blow. Cone was just about to make a blind side block when Cody Joe swung around to meet Cone head-on, avoiding being torn in half.

Nix sent two other players at Carter and Cody Joe began to tire. His legs were moving slower and he was having trouble keeping pace with Coach Nix' pointing finger that kept sending attackers in motion.

Finally, Cody Joe half-heartedly met a tough block from Dirk Bolger and he went to his knees for the first time. Before he could get up, Nate Christian landed a blow square in Cody Joe's back, sending him flying across the ring like a puppet without strings.

Cody Joe crashed face forward into the five-yard line. As he was climbing to his feet, he was trying to flush the grass and dirt out of his mouth and nostrils. Blood was streaming from underneath Tracks' chin bandage. He looked at Christian only to see Nate break into a wide grin.

Nate said, "I've been waiting for this drill with you all my life."

Cody Joe raced at Christian and hit him with a vicious full-formed tackle and drove him into the turf with a force rarely seen on the seventh grade level.

Coach Nix was quick to intervene, but he had a sly smile on his face as he said, "I guess you two are getting the idea of how to play this game. I just want you to put all this aggression toward the other team."

The drill continued. Tiny Marc Sanchez was the next man in the ring. Nix let him endure three blockers before removing him because he was getting run over by the bigger guys. Kirby Tanner and Pug Preston also got a taste of the ring.

While Pug was in the ring, Coach Nix sent Joseph Moore in for the block. Moore tentatively hit Pug, but it was easy to see he didn't have his heart in it.

"That'll cost you laps, Moore. Get out of here," Coach Nix commanded.

Moore did two laps and then was inserted into the ring. Nix had no compassion, sometimes sending two at a time against Moore. The backup quarterback was bleeding from his nose and shin when his time finally ended.

The drill was beginning to take its toll as the practice wore on, but Coach Nix continued to point his finger.

Those that had been in the ring were beginning to fade. Their movements weren't half-hearted, but they were slowing down. Most stood around the ring with hands on their knees. Nearly all were tending to scrapes and bruises the best they could.

Cody Joe wondered why Coach Nix didn't stop. The team had gotten the idea that they had played poorly. Carter felt he had entered a dream, inexorably tied to football, defeat and the ring. There was no escape or relief from the nightmare. He wished Coach Heart and Coach Bear were here. He wished his father was here. But he couldn't be saved in this dream. His reality now was to survive. He would not let Coach Nix defeat him, no matter what.

Cody Joe was launched from his pity party when Nix pointed his finger at Carter. Cody Joe once again raced into the ring to meet T-Quay head on. Cody Joe delivered a big blow that held consequences for both participants. T-Quay fell to his back while Cody Joe fell in the opposite direction like tall timber falling in a forest. Both had trouble getting up while Robert Lieberman, the next sent into the ring by Nix, couldn't decide who he was supposed to block. He sure wasn't going to hit a man that was down.

His indecision cost him. He was sent for two laps and then inserted into the ring. He also got the two-on-one treatment from Coach Nix.

Eventually, everyone on the team, even starting quarterback Lee Line, had experienced the ring at least once. Practice ran 30 minutes longer than usual and it was almost dark when Coach Nix gave it up.

"OK, that's it," he said. No sprints today. Get a good shower and have the managers look at your wounds. You should wear those wounds with pride after today because you have now become true brothers of the ring."

With that, Coach Nix walked off the practice field while most of the seventh grade Blue Devils collapsed in place, wondering if they would ever get up.

Pug turned to Cody Joe and said, "Do you feel like we are brothers of the ring?"

Cody Joe answered, "I just think Coach Nix is out of his mind. I don't know about the brother thing, but I promise you, I'm not going to let Coach Nix or the ring beat me. I'm going to be here when this thing is over. I guarantee you that."

* * *

Cody Joe didn't say anything to his parents about practice. Jack Carter, however, heard about it from Ernest Cassidy. Butch apparently gave his father a blow-by-blow description even down to the fact that Cody Joe and Nate Christian were mixed up in another run in.

Jack wanted to confront his son about all the details he had heard from Ernest, but he refrained, thinking Cody Joe would tell him if it was important or if he couldn't handle the situation. He didn't know why, but it was obvious that Cody Joe didn't want to talk about it. What Jack did know, however, was that Nate Christian was still a problem. Jack didn't know how much longer he could put up with that situation.

The next two days of practice were normal. There was no man in the ring drill. Coaches Heart and Hixler were back. Nix never even mentioned anything about man in the ring. It was as if it hadn't happened.

In fact, the focus had switched to Sweetwater. The seventh grade Blue Devils would next play their first football game against arch-rival Sweetwater. It didn't matter the grade, Sweetwater was the enemy. Lose a game to Sweetwater and your year was pretty much shot. Snyder High only had to play Sweetwater once a year, but the Blue Devils would meet the baby Mustangs on Thursday and again on Nov. 13 to end the season.

While this was a first introduction into the rivalry, few of the Blue Devils were oblivious to what was at stake. Most had heard from their parents about the flame-throwing dragon monster that is Sweetwater football. The mantra of Snyder was officially, "Beat Sweetwater."

The man in the ring was now a hidden past. The reality now for Cody Joe Carter and the seventh grade Blue Devils was to beat Sweetwater. On this they all stood united.

Chapter 16

PLAYING SWEETWATER

As far as Cody Joe Carter was concerned, it was forever before Thursday arrived, the day the seventh grade Blue Devils would meet the Sweetwater Mustangs for the very first time.

Of course, the morning kicked off with a pep rally in the gymnasium. Due to Sweetwater being on the schedule, the gym was bursting at the seams with parents, grandparents and siblings.

Cody Joe was learning quickly that beating Sweetwater was important in Snyder, Texas.

Carter looked for Veronica and Jennifer, but didn't see them. He did spy his parents along with Kate and Chip. Rue had decided to bring Chip and Kate to one pep rally this year and she naturally picked the Sweetwater week. She would take them to school an hour late on this special day. Rue would also pick up the kids a half-hour early from school so the entire family could make the 30-mile trek to Sweetwater for the game.

This alone was enough for Cody Joe to get the message that this wasn't any ordinary game. If Rue Carter would let any of her kids miss school for a football game, it was a big game. Cody Joe knew that, in his mother's mind, missing school was right up there with missing church. It didn't happen that often.

Cody Joe also saw Grandma and Grandpa Taggert in the stands. Rue had mentioned to Cody Joe at breakfast that Grandma and Grandpa were coming to the game in Sweetwater.

After some rousing music from the band and performances from both the cheerleaders and twirlers, Coach Jimmy Lee Heart gave a rousing speech on how his team would beat Sweetwater and represent Snyder to the fullest.

Then it was time to name the two game captains.

"It gives me great pleasure to name our two captains for this great game. They are two of our team leaders and these are the two we will follow into battle today," said Coach Heart. "Butch Cassidy and Thomas Quay. We just simply call him T-Quay."

Cassidy was horrified by the announcement. He now knew he was going to have to give a speech. Butch feared no man in uniform, but he was terrified over the prospect of speaking to a large crowd.

Of course, everyone in school knew of the likable Cassidy, so it was a popular pick for the crowd. A huge roar blasted through the gym as the audience gave its undeniable approval.

T-Quay was the first to speak, saying, "All my life I've been waiting for this game. We actually get to play Sweetwater and I can't wait."

Once again the crowd went berserk. T-Quay was now an instant hit.

Then Cassidy timidly walked up to the mic, and with head down, limply said, "I think we will beat Sweetwater."

This time the cheers weren't quite as loud and you could even hear a few snickers along the way. For Butch Cassidy, this was as bad as he had imagined. He was hoping he would never be game captain again.

Butch meekly walked back to his teammates and dropped

in place by Cody Joe. He looked at Carter and mumbled, "Well, I just couldn't think of anything to say."

After being badgered by Butch about rounding the bases just this past weekend, Cody Joe didn't have it in his heart to let his friend off the hook.

Cody Joe brought out his widest grin and said, "Butch, why didn't you just ask the crowd about how many of them had ever reached second base?"

Pug Preston and Kirby Tanner broke out in a gale of laughter. In another second, all four were bent over howling as the band played in hysterical support.

* * *

On the way out of the gym, Cody Joe stopped long enough to say hello to his parents and to his grandma and grandpa. He thanked them for coming, and asked, "Y'all coming to the game today?"

Grandpa Taggert answered, "Why sure, Cody Joe, we're playing Sweetwater today, ain't we? We wouldn't miss it. Somehow we're going to fit your grandma and me into your car with your parents and Chip and Kate. It's going to be a cozy family trip. It's a good thing you're riding the team bus because this family has gotten too big for one car."

When Cody Joe finally got outside the gym, he found himself facing a panicked Veronica Slade.

In near tears, Veronica said, "Cody Joe, I don't know if I will be at the game today. I just found out that Jennifer called in sick today. Her parents were going to take us to the game and that's now off. What am I going to do?"

Here was a time Cody Joe could actually be Veronica's saving hero, but all he could come up with was, "You could go with my family, but they already have a car full of people since my grandma and grandpa are going with them."

"Well, I may not be at the game. I don't have a ride and there's no way my parents are going to take a road trip for a football game."

This news threw Cody Joe for a loop. He was going to play the most important football game of his young life today and his girlfriend wouldn't be there. They had planned for two weeks on how to get her to the game and Jennifer Axel's parents had stepped up to the plate.

This was a fine time for Jennifer to get sick. Why couldn't she be sick next week when the Blue Devils were scheduled to play Goliad in Big Spring? No one ever gets sick on the week when you play Sweetwater.

* * *

Cody Joe didn't see Veronica again during school hours because the team was allowed to leave classes after the noon bell. They made their daily walk down Ave. M with a solid purpose. This was a team walk except for team bully Nate Christian, who walked to the practice field alone and far behind the gaggle of team members that led the way.

"This is the day we get our first win over Sweetwater," Adam Quay told the walkers. "And there will be a lot more to come before we are through."

"You can count on that," chimed in quarterback Lee Line. "I can see it now – undefeated for all time against the Sweetwater Mustangs. We'll be legendary when it comes to Snyder football. People will be talking about us from now on."

Cody Joe grounded the confidence train by saying, "Let's just get ready for this game today and let the future take care of itself. We've got a big game to play today. We can't win all those other games against Sweetwater until we at least win this first one."

Eric Blade said, "Cody Joe's right. Coach says to take 'em one at a time. Well, it's time to take this one."

When the guys reached the field house, Coach Heart was there to greet them. He gathered them around the center of the locker room and told them to get comfortable. Some of the players sat on their locker bench while others laid on the floor, using shoulder pads as a pillow.

Cody Joe moved from his regular locker spot to the floor down a ways between Pug Preston and Butch Cassidy to avoid sitting by Nate Christian. The honor of being next to Nate now belonged to Pug.

"Thanks a lot, Cody Joe. I don't think Christian even bothered to take a shower this week. At least, those Sweetwater guys won't want to block him. If they do, they'll get more than they bargained for, I guarantee you that."

The boys were literally giggling over Pug's predicament when Coach Heart interrupted.

"If you haven't figured it out, we play Sweetwater today. We don't lose to Sweetwater. I want you to think about that man in the ring drill we had on Monday. I want the same effort. Give us everything you have when you are on that field.

"I'm not going to tell you this is the most important game of the year because it's not. We play Sweetwater again on Nov. 13 here at our place. So, you might say this is the second most important game we play this year.

"I want to say again, Snyder teams don't lose to Sweetwater. It's not an option. I hope you guys understand that. Just remember the ring. To get out of the ring, you had to survive. Let's get out of that ring today."

"OK, let's start by going over what is going to happen today."

With that, Coach Heart pulled out his chalk and started

drawing plays on the board. He went over every blocking assignment for more than an hour. No one said a word other than Coach Heart. It would be hard to say if the seventh grade Blue Devils were honed in on every word Coach Heart was saying, or if they were just trying to get out of that ring in one piece.

And, of course, there was Nate Christian. He slept through the whole thing.

* * *

It was around 2:30 p.m. when bus driver Thomas Mann drove his yellow hound bus to the front of the field house doors. Coach Heart instructed his players to get on the bus quietly. Not a word was spoken, but Pug and Cody Joe boarded together so they could grab a seat together.

It was a bit crowded since the team was traveling in full football attire. Each player had pulled their jersey over the shoulder pads and held them on their laps for the short 45-minute ride to Sweetwater.

Mann would drive his Blue Devils through the small towns of Hermleigh and Roscoe before gaining access to Highway 84 that led to Sweetwater and Mustang Bowl.

The Sweetwater stadium was a West Texas icon in 1958 and was a popular playoff site for high school teams, not only for its unique bowl concept, but also for its central West Texas location that allowed for popular neutral site playoff games.

When the bus arrived, Coach Heart told the kids to drop the shoulder pads in the shade next to the bus. He then ordered them into the stadium for his pre-game walk-around to shake off some of the cobwebs.

For many of the Blue Devils, this was the first time to lay eyes on Mustang Bowl. Most were unimpressed at first sight simply because there wasn't much to see. Most of the stadium was below ground, in a bowl, just as the name would suggest.

A few jaws dropped, however, when they entered the stadium. When entered from ground level, fans gained access to their seats by walking down the bleachers instead of up. The press box, on the home side, jutted above ground level, but most of the seats were at ground level or below. It was a cozy environment for a stadium. And all the bleacher seats, the goal posts, the scoreboard and the press box were all brightly painted in red, supporting the Mustangs.

Mustang Bowl was the home of Sweetwater's high school team, the junior varsity team and the junior high squads, not to mention many playoff games at the end of the season. Naturally, the playing surface was less than desirable with chewed up grass and portions of the field that were hard as concrete.

"Hey, Pug, their scoreboard lights are in red, which is the same as their uniforms. This place is awesome," Cody Joe said, as they surveyed the stadium's makeup.

"I agree, but don't get too carried away by the surroundings. These guys are wanting to beat us as bad as we want to beat them," Pug answered.

Butch Cassidy broke in, saying, "I think it's a shame that someone would waste all this money on a team like Sweetwater. I mean somebody must have money to burn. Wonder if we could get them to move to Snyder?"

It was then that the guys heard a scream from the stands, "Cody Joe."

It was Veronica Slade and Alexi Taggert waving wildly. The whole gang, Cody Joe, Pug, Butch, Tracks and Kirby, walked over to the railing that separated the bleachers from the field.

"How did you get over here?" Cody Joe asked Veronica.

"Well, Jennifer is sick, so I found out that Alexi's parents were bringing her to the game and she said there was plenty of room for me."

"Thanks, Alexi," Cody Joe said. "I owe you one. You might turn out to be a good cousin after all. And I'm glad you are here Veronica. This is going to be the best game ever. I promise you that."

Veronica had the biggest smile that Cody Joe had ever seen, but only Veronica knew the real reason for the smile. This was the biggest fuss Cody Joe had ever put forth about his girlfriend in public, and she was thoroughly pleased that he wanted her at the game. It made the hectic effort all worth it to be in Sweetwater.

It was then that Cody Joe caught in the corner of his eye Chip running down the bleachers as fast as he could navigate the steep incline. Trailing far behind was Kate, but she too was coming as fast as she could.

Cody Joe flinched at the sight because he never knew how Chip was going to act around his friends.

Even though Chip was out of breath from his run down the stadium steps, he blurted out, "Hey, Cody Joe, is that your new girlfriend over yonder with Alexi? Man, she's top drawer like you said. I didn't really expect her to be that pretty because you exaggerate all the time."

Cody Joe wanted to climb in a hole and hide. He was wondering why he had a brother like Chip and a friend like Cassidy.

Sure enough, Cassidy answered Chip, "Your brother's got a good one, but he doesn't know what to do with her."

Everyone laughed except Cody Joe and Veronica.

"Get out of here Chip," Cody Joe bellowed. "I've got a game to play."

Kate arrived and was quick to say before this contingent

departed, "Mother wants to know when you are going to introduce your girlfriend to her and Dad. They're right over there."

"Well, I've got a game to play right now and the coaches will be calling us in a few minutes," Cody Joe said, trying to avoid this introduction. He knew it had to happen someday, but why did it have to be on the day when Snyder plays Sweetwater?

Carter was beginning to wish that none of his family had even come to the game. He was ready for the game to begin because he was ready to hit someone – and any Sweetwater Mustang would fill the bill at this particular moment. He guessed that would be better than turning his brother and sister into scrambled eggs right in front of all his friends.

* * *

The ball rose high toward the Sweetwater goal line as Henry Styles put his toe to the pig hide and the game between Snyder and Sweetwater was officially underway. Marc Sanchez and Jack King were the first to arrive on the scene and brought the Sweetwater runner down at the 28-yard line after the short kick.

Pug was double-teamed on the very first play from scrimmage, but Cody Joe was quick to fill the hole, allowing a meager three-yard gain. This was pretty much how this game was going to be played. Neither team could generate much yardage, or any consistency. It was a battle of wills and both teams played as if this was the most important game of their lives.

Snyder finally had halfback Lester Jarvis back after missing a couple of weeks with injury, but he wasn't his old self yet. He couldn't get outside. Leaving Snyder with an attack that featured Butch Cassidy up the middle and Cassidy off tackle.

Even Coach Heart was wondering which team would blink first. The two teams muddled their way to the half and remained tied at 0-0 in a game featuring four bloody noses and a roll of tape worth of scrapes and bruises. Neither team, however, had suffered any game-ending injuries.

During this whole time, Cody Joe had not given one thought to Veronica, Chip, Kate or his visiting members of his extended family. He was totally absorbed in his game, which was his best performance of the year on defense. He was disappointed, however, with his lackluster effort on offense. The line just couldn't seem to crack a hole for the running backs.

Snyder would receive to open the second half and started play at its own 32-yard line. This is when Coach Heart brought out his surprise for Sweetwater. He had noticed that the two Sweetwater safeties were strictly playing the run. And the more Snyder ran the ball, the more Sweetwater's safeties began to cheat towards the line of scrimmage.

West Texas junior high football teams rarely threw the ball deep. First, seventh-grade quarterbacks didn't usually have strong arms and Lee Line was no exception. He was, however, smart and talented enough to get the job done if the right circumstance presented itself. Also, Coach Heart worked with his quarterbacks every day in the passing game.

Heart reasoned that the time was right. It was now or never. So, on the first play of the second half, he called for Adam Quay to go on a deep route that was to split the two Sweetwater safeties. End Mac Cone was sent on a pattern in the flat while halfback Hank Cline was sent on a short sideline pattern to the opposite side of the field.

Lee Line, head down, took the ball from center Robert Lieberman and made a perfect fake to fullback Butch Cassidy as Quay streaked to the middle of the field. By the time Line had completed his fake and planted his feet for the pass, he could easily see that everything was in perfect order. The Sweetwater safeties bit on the fake and went straight for Cassidy. Adam Quay was free and clear before anyone on the Sweetwater defense could react. All Line had to do was hit his target.

Line let loose, praying that Quay wasn't already out of his reach, but the ball arched on a path that looked to be over the intended target. Coach Heart's heart almost stopped. He felt like his quarterback had overthrown the ball with a rush of adrenalin.

Adam Quay was thinking differently than everyone else on his team. Somehow, he was going to catch this ball. He reached as far as he could and managed to hold on to the slippery projectile as it hit the tip of his fingers. He had to extend so far that he almost fell, but he retained his balance, got his feet under him and ran unmolested for a Blue Devil touchdown.

Cody Joe pulled his face mask out of the Mustang Bowl dirt just in time to see Quay make his catch and just stayed on the ground as he watched the big end run goalward. It was only then that he thought of looking into the stands and it may have been the happiest moment in his life to see Alexi and Veronica jumping, clapping, yelling and hugging each other. Even Rue Carter was standing and clapping while Jack Carter was beating Ernest Cassidy on the back. Chip was waving his coat in the air while Kate looked as if she was still trying to figure out what had happened.

Styles easily kicked the extra point and Snyder led 7-0 with 7:31 still left in the third quarter.

After that, the game returned to its predictable course until the four-minute mark of the fourth period. That's when defensive guard Stoney Wall met the massive Sweetwater fullback head-on at the Sweetwater 15-yard line, forcing the game's first fumble.

Cody Joe was quick to pounce on the ball before a mass of bodies covered him like flowing lava. But this ball belonged to Carter. When the pile cleared, Cody Joe rose from the bottom of the pile with the ball held high above his head. His family and girlfriend were once again thrown into a state of hysteria. Only this time it was Ernest Cassidy beating Jack Carter on the back in celebratory acknowledgement.

Three plays later, Lee Line scored on a 10-yard quarterback option as he pushed the football just inside the goal marker with over three minutes left to play in the game. Styles was once again true on the extra point. At that point, it was clear that Snyder had beaten the Sweetwater Mustangs. The Mustangs never generated a serious scoring moment in the contest.

Cody Joe was hugging every teammate he could find. He walked over to where Veronica was waiting at the bottom of the bleachers.

"You were great, Cody Joe," Veronica said with tears in her eyes. "That's the best game I've ever seen and I almost died when you recovered that ball."

"Thanks. We could have played much better, but we did play good on defense."

Jack Carter interrupted as he came up behind Veronica, "Son, that's how it's done. I'm awfully proud of you. Even Chip was telling everyone around him that you were his brother. I'd say that's pretty high praise in this family."

Cody Joe then heard a coach's whistle, so he started toward the exit where the team bus awaited. As he walked under the south goal post, a disheartened Sweetwater player said to him, "Just remember, stud, that we will play again and it's going to be different next time."

Cody Joe kept walking, but replied, "Come on over. We'll be seeing each other a lot over the next few years. It's doubtful that Snyder and Sweetwater will ever quit playing each other."

Thomas Mann drove his bus out of the stadium parking lot and back onto the road leading to Snyder.

Butch Cassidy didn't miss the moment. "Nothing's better than seeing Sweetwater in your tail lights."

Chapter 17

THE LOST BLANKET

The seventh grade Blue Devils were basking in the glory of beating Sweetwater and the team was out in full force for the game on Friday night between the Snyder Tigers and the Midland High Bulldogs at Tiger Stadium.

This was a chance for the Blue Devils to be seen in public and all wanted to be seen. Also, Snyder was playing a team from Midland that was in a higher classification and this game offered the Tigers an opportunity to play and beat the big boys.

The Tigers had already beaten Big Spring earlier in the year, 25-20, and Big Spring was also a rung up in classification over Snyder. Big Spring and Midland High were in the same district together.

But for Cody Joe Carter, this game was a lot more than Snyder bragging rights and the lofty prospects of big time football. This was the last home game for the Tigers before they began a three-week span of road trips.

So, Cody Joe knew this would probably be his last dating opportunity with the lovely Veronica Slade for a long period of time. Cody Joe was more than aware that he and Veronica had never been on a date other than a Snyder football game.

And Carter's memory still lingered on the last two weeks when Veronica brought a blanket to ward off the cold and had shared it with Cody Joe. He remembered how nice it was to be holding hands with her while covered in secrecy from the world by the warm blanket. He was very much looking forward to another night of bliss while being cozy with his girl.

But the early October weather had played a prickly trick on Cody Joe Carter. It had turned warm. There was no need for a blanket and Veronica Slade was carrying no blanket when she arrived at the stadium and crawled over the legs of Pug Preston and Alexi Taggert to take her seat by Cody Joe.

Carter was almost at a loss for words. This turn of events would ruin this great opportunity to be close to Veronica. How would he cope? What would he have to do to maintain at least an appearance of being on a date? He knew he could never hold her hand out in full public view. It was like having a leg injury, but with no crutch on which to rely.

However, the night turned out not to be as horrible as Cody Joe immediately imagined. Veronica sat down and started talking so fast that she sounded a bit like the constant clicking of a typewriter.

Veronica filled in her attentive boyfriend on the status of Jennifer Axel, who was feeling better but was still unable to attend tonight's game. Veronica's parents had just purchased a new car, but she hadn't seen it yet. All she knew was that it was an Oldsmobile. She didn't even know the color.

Veronica then turned to Alexi and again thanked her for the trip to Sweetwater on Thursday and then both girls began to tell Pug and Cody Joe of their adventures on that trip and how excited they were on the trip home after beating Sweetwater. Of course, these were words that greatly pleased both Pug and Cody Joe.

Veronica had opened a floodgate of conversation. The two boys were eager to fill in the girls on what it was like playing in the biggest game of their lives. They also talked about the game at hand before the first kickoff as Pug declared that

Snyder had a real chance of winning this game.

All in all, Cody Joe held his own with conversational football. He had never felt so comfortable being with Veronica, but he was nowhere being close to showing any kind of outward display of affection. At least, he didn't feel like a bump on a log and Veronica made it extremely easy for him with a constant string of chatter that littered the air with excitement and joy. In Cody Joe's way of thinking, Veronica Slade was at least glad to be in this place, on this night, sitting with him. For Cody Joe, that was as good as the blanket.

Snyder quickly took control of the game and easily disposed of Midland High, 34-12. The Tigers would now head into District 3-3A play with a 4-2 record and they owned wins against the two largest schools on their schedule.

Cody Joe would not remember the details of this game as he marched life's highway, but he would always remember the night. As far as being in the seventh grade, this night was the highpoint of existence. This was a night to remember.

As Alexi, Pug, Veronica and Cody Joe stood to begin their trek out of the stadium, Veronica and Alexi performed a planned maneuver that would shock both boys. They had planned this unexpected move while sitting together during the Sweetwater game.

Alexi and Veronica, in a single motion, turned, leaned toward their boyfriends and simultaneously gave them a light kiss on the cheek.

Butch Cassidy didn't miss any of it. "Hey, did you guys see that? They're kissin' now. Right out here in public, they're kissin'."

Veronica gave Cody Joe a little wink, turned with Alexi and they departed without saying another word.

Pug and Cody Joe looked at each other and said nothing, but the message was clear, "Did what happened really happen?"

Cody Joe was in a fog, but he was left with a myriad of questions. Is that to be considered our first kiss? Was it even a kiss? He really had no part in it. Maybe he was nothing more than a recipient of a kiss. And was he expected to come up with some kind of response, or thank you?

Should he have kissed her back on her cheek? What brought all this on? It was proof that she liked him, wasn't it? What were the guys behind him thinking? And what would be the price he was going to have to pay for this outward display of kissing when the guys had a chance to unleash their jealous fury?

But most important in Cody Joe's mind was the wondering if he was now officially on first base. He thought, "This is the best night of my life!"

* * *

Once again Rue Carter took the boys, Cody Joe, Pug,

Butch, Tracks and Tanner to the Dairy Queen after the game. Cody Joe never mentioned to his mom about the kiss encounter with Veronica, but he knew in his heart that the news would never escape her with this motley crew as backup.

In fact, no sooner had Butch bounded into the back seat, he blurted out, "Mrs. Carter, did you know that Cody Joe and Veronica were kissin' at the game tonight? So were Pug and Alexi."

Rue answered, "Oh, is that so?" while looking squarely at Cody Joe, who was sitting right beside his mother in the front seat. She caught a glimpse of Pug in her rear view mirror with his head down and twiddling his thumbs as if this conversation didn't include him.

"Mom, Butch is blowing it all out of proportion and he's trying to make it out like we had a big make-out session.

"Butch, I'm going to tear your head off and feed it to the hogs if you don't button it."

"You and whose army?" Butch squealed with a wave of laughter.

Butch added, "Mrs. Carter. You better keep a closer eye on these boys. They're growing up way too quick."

Another wave of laughter gushed forth as Rue smiled and continued the short trek toward the Dairy Queen.

She did silently think, "My boy really is growing up so fast. He's not a baby anymore."

* * *

Jennifer Axel, bright and perky as ever, was already in her home room seat on Monday morning as Cody Joe walked into the classroom. Her eyes followed him all the way from the door to his seat, salivating for the moment he would finally speak.

"Well, if it isn't the sickly girl from the wrong side of the tracks," Cody Joe teased. "You feeling better these days?"

"Oh, Cody Joe, don't make small talk with me. You know what I want. Tell me everything. And start from the beginning," Jennifer said as she cupped her face in her hands while resting her elbows on the front of Carter's desk.

"What are you talking about, Jennifer? Tell you what?"

"You're the dumbest boy I've ever met. Tell me about the kiss. Everyone at school is talking about the kiss. Butch tells me he's never seen anything like it. What did you think?"

"Jennifer, I didn't do nuthin'. Veronica just gave me peck on the cheek after the game on Friday night. Alexi also gave Pug a little kiss. We didn't do nuthin'."

"Well, it don't sound like nothing to me," Jennifer said as if disappointed in Cody Joe's obvious downplay of the most significant event of the school year. "I swear, Cody Joe, you wouldn't know a big moment if it smacked you right between the lips."

Little did Jennifer know that Cody Joe was well aware of this huge moment in his life, but he wasn't going to share it with Jennifer Axel, who was well known for getting the school's news skinny first hand and spreading the delicious facts to everyone she talked with in her large circle of friends.

Cody Joe was thinking that telling Jennifer of his thoughts was like writing a newspaper account of the event, complete with printing and circulation.

"So, you're not going to tell me about it? How did it feel? Did you like it? Were you embarrassed? Would you want her to do it again? Tell me."

Cody Joe ended it by saying, "Jennifer, I'm not telling you anything. If you want to be in the know, come to the games and quit playing at being sick. And you were also supposed to be in Sweetwater to see us beat the Mustangs."

This had the desired effect as Jennifer turned toward the front of the class at the same moment as Mr. Perry walked into the classroom.

But it didn't stop the late arriving Mandy Mayor from reaching over and pinching Cody Joe on the arm.

"Heard you had a big weekend, stud," she whispered.

Cody Joe closed his eyes thinking, "I'm never going to get away from all this."

* * *

There was a definite swagger in the collective walk of the seventh grade Blue Devils as they made the trek down Ave. M toward the practice field on Monday afternoon.

After all, they had beaten Snyder's most hated rival Sweetwater and bloated chests were pretty much poppin' shirt buttons.

"I guess we showed those plowboys a thing or two last Thursday," chimed in Dirk Bolger. "I bet they don't want no more of us."

Butch Cassidy agreed, "Well, if they do, they know where to find us. We'll kick their behinds again when they come callin'."

The team was feeling a little cocky, but it also meant they were quickly forming a bond that they could depend on. They now trusted each other and were learning what fraternity and brotherhood meant in real terms. If that left the scars of swagger and cockiness, so be it. The team was now a team. Lost, however, was the idea of vulnerability. No one could take them now and they had no fear.

They entered the field house laughin' and slappin' like a bunch of seventh graders. Life was good and they were more than ready to take the next big step.

There was one big difference, however, on this Monday afternoon. The door to Coach Heart's office was closed and his red tag on the door knob meant to stay out.

Nobody thought much about it and the innocent horse play continued as they dressed and headed for calisthenics, which began every practice session.

The coaches arrive shortly thereafter and put the team through the regular exercise routine with side straddle hops, pushups, sit ups and a few selected isometric routines.

Then the day – and the mood – changed in the time it took for Coach Heart to say, "OK guys, form up in the ring."

A dread swept through the team. Their once unshakable confidence drained into the very ground where they stood. They were once again vulnerable as Coach Nix called out, "Mac Cone, in the ring son."

Cone went to the middle of the ring as instructed and it was only seconds later that Nix began sending waves of attackers in his direction.

It didn't escape the Blue Devils that both Coach Heart and Coach Bear were present for this session of man in the ring, but they did not participate as Coach Nix continued his brutal barrage on each man that took his turn in the ring.

Cody Joe was never called into the ring on this particular exercise, but he was called on to go after Nate Christian. Unlike their last meeting in the ring, no one went to the ground as the two met head-on. There was a definite pop of leather as the two collided in center court.

But instead of the two breaking on contact, Christian grabbed Carter by the jersey and tried to throw him to the ground. The tactic didn't work. Carter turned and head-butted Christian helmet on helmet. And the melee was on.

Coach Nix was quick to intervene, but it was like unlocking the horns of two bulls in heat. This was an unholy war where the rules of society lay dormant among the civilized.

"Whoa boys," Nix yelled, "We ain't got time for this. Both of you take a lap, but Cody Joe you start your lap up here on the north end and Christian you start down there on the south end. I don't want you two close to each other."

The drill continued unabated, but unlike Nix's first foray into the ring experience, this one didn't last the entire practice. It mercifully ended in about 45 minutes, still long enough to leave even the strongest among them drained and deflated.

The swagger was gone and vulnerability had returned. Coach Heart made sure it stayed that way.

"It was easy to see that you guys were beginning to think you were a pretty special group. But I think you were forgetting that we still have five games left. This season is only half over. We haven't accomplished our goals yet. We already have a loss on our record.

"If any of you here are not up to the challenge that lays ahead of us, get up and leave now. I don't need your cocky attitude and if you one day aspire to play for the Snyder Tigers, you need to learn today that every week requires your full attention and that you have to take every opponent seriously. Now, let's get ready to play Goliad."

For the rest of the season, there was not one Blue Devil – with maybe the exception of Christian – who didn't approach each day of practice with a little fear and trepidation.

The dreaded ring increased the team bond overall, but now cockiness had given way to respect. That is except for Cody Joe Carter and Nate Christian where the bonds of hatred grew like red coals in a hot fire.

Cody Joe told Pug, "One of these days, Nate's gonna' go too far and I'm gonna' bust him in the nose. I swear I am."

* * *

By Thursday, the Blue Devils were more than ready to take on Goliad, the Big Spring team they had beaten 22-0 in their first meeting to open the season. This game marked Round II of the junior high league in which Snyder was involved. Every team met every other team twice in a virtual round robin format.

The Blue Devils just wanted to take care of business. While still confident in the team sense, they had dropped the cocky flair, replacing it with a workman-like sense of duty and mission. Coach Heart said they should be proud to be allowed to wear the uniform representing the community of Snyder. He said they should treat it as an honor. They were beginning to understand what he was saying.

And to prove the point, the Blue Devils started the game on foreign soil by recovering a fumble on the opening kickoff to set up a 15-yard touchdown run by halfback Lester Jarvis, who was now back to 100 percent.

Goliad was really no match for the onslaught of the Blue Devil machine. Butch Cassidy seldom was given the ball in this game after being the team's leading rusher through five games, but his blocking opened up huge holes for Jarvis and Hank Cline. The return of Jarvis to the lineup once again limited the playing time of Kirby Tanner.

Pug and Cody Joe had never before worked so well as a team on defense. Pug plugged the line like a stopper in a drain while Cody Joe was given the blitz opportunity often, recording four sacks and a blocked pass. Carter had never had so much fun playing football. Everything went as expected. There were no curve balls in this matchup, giving the Blue Devils a chance to play everyone on the roster in a 38-0 romp.

Snyder's seventh graders left the field with a respectable 5-1 record. Colorado City was next on the slate, a team Snyder had beaten 20-0 in the second game of the year.

Only Ernest Cassidy and Jack Carter had made this trip to Big Spring among the regulars. The cheerleaders didn't even show up due to other school functions back home. But the Blue Devils were glad to take the win and to move on up to the next rung in the season's ladder.

On the bus trip home, Pug reminded Cody Joe that this was the weekend of the trip to Lubbock to see the Red Raiders of Texas Tech play the TCU Horned Frogs.

"We'll pick you up Saturday morning around 9:30. My Dad wants to get there before noon so we can take my grandmother to eat at Underwood's. So bring money to eat for noon and for tickets and food at the game. I think we can get tickets for about $6 each if we can find someone trying to sell their extras. I do it all the time when we go to see my grandmother. We'll have a blast."

Chapter 18

GOING TO COLLEGE

C ody Joe spent Friday night with his family because Rue Carter told him, "You're spending Friday night with the family."

The message couldn't have been clearer. When Rue Carter made such pronouncements, there was no getting around it. But it still rankled Cody Joe because all the guys, including Pug, were going to meet up at the Palace Theater, in downtown Snyder, for a movie.

Pug was also going to Lubbock on Saturday and he was allowed to go to the movie. It simply wasn't fair in Cody Joe's way of thinking.

So, the Carter family, as ordered by Rue Carter, spent a family night at home. Instead of attending the movie, Cody Joe was stuck playing Monopoly with Chip, Kate and his parents. Cody Joe didn't really mind playing Monopoly, but Chip didn't know how to count money very well and he insisted on being the banker for the night. This definitely slowed the whole process down in a game that was a marathon under the best of circumstances.

The family also listened to the Snyder Tigers on the radio as Pete Brock's booming voice produced an enticing play-by-play. Brock was a local legend in the community. He had done Tiger play-by-play for over 20 seasons. He sold his own advertisement, so that's how he got to do the broadcasts for the local KSNY radio station, 1450 on your dial.

It had helped his business and Brock was one of the most successful businessmen in Snyder. He was also passionate about his Tigers. His voice cackled in delight every time he said, "And that, my friends, is another Tiger touchdown."

But Brock, and his listeners, were to be somewhat disappointed on this night as the Tigers tied the C-City Wolves in a 12-12 defensive battle. Snyder had been a huge favorite to take this game, but had to settle with a sour kiss. This was the start of District 3-3A play, so neither team was overly excited with the final outcome.

Brock ended his broadcast with, "We came to the biggest game of the year and ended up kissing each other at mid-field. And Colorado City, my friends, isn't all that pretty."

It was at that point when the Carter family gave up on the never-ending Monopoly game much to the horror of Kate, who had a pile of cash and a solid stash of property. But the others had lost heart and interest after listening to the game.

Meanwhile, Pug, Tracks, Tumbler, Trout, Tanner and Butch enjoyed a movie at the Palace, clueless that the Tigers were kissing their opponent.

* * *

As promised, Pete Preston, and his son Pug arrived at the Carter household at 9:30 a.m. on Saturday. Mr. Preston gave Jack Carter a brief trip itinerary before departing. Jack gave Cody Joe a $20 bill in hopes that would be plenty for an overnighter in Lubbock that would include three meals and a game ticket.

Jack was thinking that it was expensive to go to a college game, but he really wanted Cody Joe to see a college campus and get the feel for the college life. No one in the Carter family had ever been to college and Jack hoped Cody Joe would be the educational trailblazer for his family.

In that spirit, Jack was more than grateful to Pete for taking the boys along on his trip to see his mother.

When Pete tied up all the loose ends, he turned to his son and said, "OK James, you guys get in the car and we'll head out."

Pug hated it when his dad called him James, especially in front of friends. None of his friends ever called him James. In fact, Pug sometimes didn't even realize his dad was talking to him when he used James in a conversation. Pete had admonished his son several times for not paying attention when, in fact, Pug didn't even realize his dad was talking to him.

But Pug had a good relationship with his father. He guessed everyone could bring up some fault with every parent. It was just one of those quirks James had to live with. But he was sure he wanted to be Pug for the rest of his life.

It took Pete one hour and 15 minutes to cover the 84 miles from Cody Joe's house to Mrs. Preston's home. She lived on 22nd street just three blocks from the southern edge of the sprawling Texas Tech campus.

The Tech campus was fronted by 19th street, running east to west. University Avenue ran the length of the Tech campus from south to north and intersected 19th street on Tech's southern border. It was here where the college life began and ended. It was also the spot where game day traffic began in earnest.

Even though it was hours away from the 7 p.m. kickoff, Cody Joe and Pug could feel the excitement being generated by the hordes of people walking and driving up and down University Avenue. People were honking their horns and pretty girls were riding in convertibles like parade queens.

Pete Preston added to the excitement as he took the boys on a brief excursion of the Tech campus so they could see the layout and get a glimpse of Jones Stadium on the far north end of the campus.

Pug was excitedly telling Cody Joe where they would walk that night in order to get to the game. He pointed out certain landmarks like the band hall, student union building, Knapp Hall, the Tech circle and the famous statue of Will Rogers and his horse Soapsuds.

Jones Stadium was huge in the eyes of Cody Joe. The stadium sat 35,000 people and was the second largest stadium in all of West Texas. Only the Sun Bowl in El Paso was larger.

To Cody Joe, everything seemed bigger and larger in Lubbock and he couldn't wait to go to the game.

But first things first. Pete said they had to head to his mother's house because she liked to eat at regular meal times, which meant lunch was at noon. Pete had planned to take her and the boys out to eat, adding to their Lubbock weekend experience.

Of course, when the Preston family ate out in Lubbock, there was only one choice ever considered. That would be at Underwood's on Lubbock's southeast side of town. This was Texas barbeque at its best and Pete wasn't the only Snyderite to think so. People from Snyder and other small communities in the region often made special trips to Lubbock just to feast at Underwood's.

But first, the three guys needed to pick up one Mrs. Emma Preston. Emma was waiting on her wooden floored porch as the Preston car turned into a driveway that had two cement runway looking strips to guide the car's tires.

Pug was first to jump from the car and quickly called out even before Cody Joe had time to get out of the car, "Grandma, I've brought a friend with me today. His name is Cody Joe

Carter and we're going to the game tonight."

"Well, Pug, it's good to see you too," Emma answered, "And your friends are always welcome at my house. But your father had already called me to say that you were bringing a friend.

"Hey, Pete. Good to see you, son. I'm hungrier than a bear. I didn't think you would ever get here."

Seeing Cody Joe up close for the first time, Mrs. Preston said, "I can't believe you two would keep this fine young man from eating for so long. Pete, we better get going before we all collapse. Cody Joe, I just want you to know that we don't always treat our guests this way."

"Oh, I don't mind, Mrs. Preston," Cody Joe offered. "They took me by to see the Tech campus and I guess I just forgot about lunch myself."

For Pete Preston, the cherry cobbler was to die for. Cody Joe had never seen so much food and Pug piled on the free ice cream after the meal. Cody Joe had never eaten at Underwood's so he didn't know how to pace himself. He had to forego the ice cream.

In the afternoon, Pug and Cody Joe walked over to a small park close to Mrs. Preston's house. Pug had brought a football with him and the two played some pass and catch for about 20 minutes before a group of four other boys asked them if they wanted to play some tag football. Before the afternoon was over, the group had grown to 16 and a serious game of tag had ensued. For Cody Joe, the day had already been perfect and they hadn't even gotten to the game yet.

* * *

Cody Joe couldn't help but feel an excitement in the air as the afternoon progressed. Finally, at 5 p.m., two hours before

226

game time, Pete allowed the boys to begin their trek to the stadium. They snaked their way across the dangerous 19th street and walked across a well-manicured lawn until they passed the band hall where the Goin' Band from Raiderland was already gathering for their ritual game day march to the stadium.

But Pug and Cody Joe didn't wait for the band to march like hundreds of other fans because they needed to get to Jones Stadium and buy some tickets.

Pug pointed out Knapp Hall, a girl's dorm, as they passed by. Boys, dressed in their best Sunday suits, were already beginning to pick up their dates. The girls were all dressed in pretty finery and Cody Joe took notice.

"Pug, I've never seen so many good looking girls in my life. I didn't know there were this many girls on the whole planet."

Pug answered, "Well, that's what you get from growing up in Snyder. This is why you need to get out of that town every once in a while and see the real world."

"Gosh, this is more than I ever dreamed of. Going to college must be the greatest experience ever."

Pug had gone to a couple of Tech games before, so this wasn't his first trip to this rodeo. He just let Cody Joe revel in the moment because he didn't want to ruin one more surprise Cody Joe was bound to encounter later on in the night.

The two weaved their way across the Tech campus moving mostly from south to north, stopping to admire and soak in all the Tech traditions like the victory bell tower at the school's Administration Building, and of course, to admire the statue of Will Rogers and Soapsuds, which was covered from head to hoof in red streamers for game day.

Tech legend has it that the horse and Will were turned 23 degrees to the east so the horse's posterior was facing the direction of Texas A&M, the school's most prevalent rival.

Eventually, the two walked down the science quadrangle and made their way to Jones Stadium. The game with TCU was not a sellout, but Pug didn't want to walk up to the window and buy tickets.

He explained, "If we find some guy in front of the stadium trying to sell his tickets, we'll get them cheaper because he wants to at least get something back on his purchase."

Sure enough, Cody Joe and Pug quickly found a guy with two tickets and got them for five bucks each. They saved a dollar each on two of the best seats in the house.

Instead of using the seats, however, they got past some weak security efforts to land seats in the student section. Pug thought this was where the action was anyway. Each bought a hot dog and a soft drink for another buck and considered it highway robbery.

"At those prices, we could go to five movies back in Snyder," Pug complained.

Then Cody Joe got his first taste of Tech's Masked Rider and its coal black horse. A blast from a cannon was the signal for the masked man and his horse to bolt from the player entrance on the southwest side of the stadium.

The satin black colt bounded out of the ramp and raced in front of the home crowd toward the north knoll where a giant Double-T sat on the grassy embankment. Cody Joe got a surprise, however, when the Tech mascot raced up the knoll and did a Lone Ranger imitation of hoofs in the air at the top of the Double-T circle. The horse then sprinted down the knoll and headed north to the visiting team's entrance ramp. The Masked Rider passed the student section in a blur as Pug and Cody Joe yelled as loud as they could. Cody Joe simply had never seen anything like that and he couldn't wait to tell everyone he knew about it.

Unfortunately, the Texas Tech Red Raiders didn't have much of a team in 1958, winning just three games the entire season. On this night, Tech fell to TCU, 26-0, in a lackluster performance.

"Well, I guess we don't get to hear the victory bells tonight. Tech loses again," Pug complained as the game came to an end.

However, Cody Joe thought he was in heaven. He had never seen football played on a stage like this. Besides, there was plenty to look at other than football. There were horses, twirlers, cheerleaders, bands and college girls everywhere. How could it get any better than this? But it would.

* * *

The two quickly started their trek back to Mrs Preson's house because they had promised Pete they wouldn't tarry after the game. It was late and the boys were mindful of Pete's instructions – until they passed Knapp Hall.

It was here that Cody Joe noticed several cars with the

windows all steamed up. With a street light right overhead, Cody Joe got a shock when another car had its driver's side window rolled down and he could easily see inside. There in full lamplight a couple was engaged in a very long kiss. In fact, Cody Joe wondered if they were ever going to come up for air.

"Hey, Pug, look at those two going at it. How can they even breathe like that?"

Pug laughed, "I told you there is a big world out there."

"Is this what happens when you bring your date home after a ball game?" asked Cody Joe, who was beginning to believe he indeed had led a sheltered life.

Cody Joe was left pondering what base this couple was on, but at least he now knew the meaning of making out.

Suddenly, the night's calm was shattered when the guy, in the car, stuck his head out of the window and shouted, "Scram you little pests or I'll tear your heads off."

Cody Joe and Pug took one horrified look at each other, like they had been caught with their hand in a cookie jar, and started sprinting toward 19th Street as fast as they could. They collapsed on the grassy lawn on the south side of Knapp Hall and laughed uncontrollably once they were certain that the guy was not in pursuit.

"Man, what a night," Cody Joe said. "Thanks Pug for inviting me along. I've never had so much fun."

"Me either," Pug agreed as both went into another laughing spasm.

On the rest of the way to Mrs. Preston's place, Cody Joe got lost in deep thought. He had no idea what he wanted to be when he grew up. He wondered if he would go into business with his father or blaze a new trail made just for him.

But now he knew where he wanted to go to college. That was for sure. And he couldn't help wondering if he would ever get to take Veronica Slade to Knapp Hall after a Texas Tech game. Or was that just too much to ask for in one night?

Chapter 19

A CHRISTIAN DEMISE

T he week following Cody Joe's introduction to college proved to be a tough one for Carter, starting with practice on Monday afternoon.

Cody Joe and Nate Christian were at each other's throat every day of practice. It started on Monday, in the fieldhouse, when Cody Joe moved some of Nate's equipment off of Carter's dressing bench seat so he could start getting dressed for practice. Nate took exception and verbally blasted Carter with a full barrage of language that few seventh graders of the time had ever witnessed.

The effect was not one of peacemaking. Cody Joe didn't forgive or forget this challenge. During practice, Cody Joe met every confrontation from Nate as a duel under the sun. No longer would he back away where Nate was involved.

During a team scrimmage session on Monday with Carter and Christian playing on defense, Cody Joe tripped over Nate while meeting a running back at the line of scrimmage. A big pile-up ensued with Carter and Christian locked in all out combat at the bottom of the pile. The coaches had to pull the two apart, but words continued to be thrown like darts between the two combatants.

There were pushing and shoving matches on all three days of practice. Coach Heart noticed, but had hoped the clashes wouldn't escalate any further than the usual squabbles that formed from the very activity of full contact work.

Coach Heart knew the two didn't get along in the best of conditions, so he tried to keep them separated as much as possible during drills, but inevitably the two would find a way to get at each other.

Finally, Heart had a heart-to-heart with the two boys in his office after Tuesday's practice.

"Boys, I can't have any more of this fighting between you two. It's beginning to disrupt the team and I don't want people taking sides in this feud you two have going on. I won't put up with it.

"Now drop this squabbling and let's get back to work tomorrow on beating Colorado City. Get out of here and don't make me call you two in here again."

During the whole lecture, Nate and Cody Joe sat with a wicked scowl entrenched in each face while staring at each other straight in the eye. Coach Heart knew his words had not been heard in the real sense, but he hoped it would at least slow down the escalation process.

Unfortunately, Coach Heart's hopes were dashed in the most unexpected fashion.

* * *

On Thursday, The Blue Devils were eager to face Colorado City for the second time this season. They had beaten C-City, 20-0, in Colorado City during the second week of the season and expected a good result this time around.

Cody Joe was equally thrilled to see Veronica Slade and Jennifer Axel in their usual seats near midfield. His parents were also in attendance, but Chip and Kate were nowhere to be seen. They would show up a little later with Grandpa and Grandma Taggert. They had stopped at the grocery store to pick up some snacks for the game. That would never have happened with Jack and Rue Carter, but the snack rules were a little different when traveling with Grandpa and Grandma.

The Blue Devils struck for a 7-0 lead on the first drive of the game, using the bull-like rushes of Butch Cassidy as the workable catalyst. Carter was able to block his man effectively, opening up some huge holes for his thunder-footed friend.

The Blue Devils were on top of the world, but the view at the top would change radically over the next three quarters. C-City was far from dead and the game turned into a grass chewing battle between the two 30-yard line markers. Defense ruled as the two offenses were mired in midfield burnouts.

In the third quarter with the score unmoving at 7-0, the season's defining moment took place much to the horror of three unbelieving coaches.

Colorado City owned the ball at its own 41-yard line and tried a simple counter up the middle, which was fiercely met by both Nate Christian and Dirk Bolger. The runner gamely pushed for extra yardage until Blue Devil help arrived. Carter unintentionally burrowed his helmet in the small of Christian's back as the heap was finally toppled by the extra weight that Cody Joe supplied.

However, Christian bounded from the pile and angrily shoved Carter to the ground. Without thinking where he was or what was going on around him, Carter jumped up and slammed his body into Christian with full force. The two then started slugging it out with little chance of either landing a meaningful blow in full gear.

The umpire looked at Coach Heart and shrugged, "Coach, I've never seen anything like this. We've had a lot of fights in games before, but your own teammates are fighting each other. I'm going to toss them both."

Coach Heart didn't even argue the call. He, too, had never seen anything approaching this on the field of play in a real game.

"We can't even tackle that big running back, but we can sure kill each other," Heart stammered. "What is going on here?"

Coach Bear turned to Heart and said, "Coach, we're fighting with each other. Did we forget to point out the bad guys?"

Heart then turned on Cody Joe as he came off the sideline, saying, "Cody Joe, what are you doing out there? We are in the middle of a game. I'm really disappointed in you, because of anyone on the team, I thought you would do the right thing in a situation like this."

Unabashedly, Cody Joe answered, "Coach, I can't take anymore from Nate. I've reached my limit. I won't back down from him any longer no matter what anyone says. I'm not the one at fault here, but everyone acts like it's me that's wrong. I don't see how backing down every time is right. Why do I have to be the one to back down?"

Coach Heart didn't have time here and now to work this out with the distraught youngster, so he just sent him to the fieldhouse. Christian was kept on the sideline to avoid the two busting heads in the locker room.

Jack Carter met Cody Joe on the way to the fieldhouse. "Son, what possessed you to strike back like that?"

"See, Dad, you even think I'm wrong. I've just had enough. I can't take his bullying any longer. I've never started anything with Nate, but he uses every little thing to get at me. Well, if he wants some of me, let him come and get it. I'm no longer living in fear of him. He's not going to control my life."

"This isn't the way to handle your problems. You need to come to me or Coach Heart if you are facing issues like this,"

Jack instructed. "I've asked you to let me know if there were things going on between you two, but you said nothing."

"Dad, I have to handle my own problems. Nate is Coach Heart's special project, so he isn't going to do anything. And I'm just not about being a tattle-tale."

"Well, go get dressed and we'll talk more about this when we get home. I'll have a talk with Coach Heart after the game.

In the stands, Kate started crying when she saw her older brother headed for the fieldhouse.

"Mom, is Cody Joe hurt again? Can I go see how he is?"

Rue tried to calm her daughter by saying, "No, Kate, Cody Joe will be just fine. Your father is with him."

But Rue Carter felt sick in her stomach. She was horrified by what she saw and she feared for the safety of her son. It was the first time she had gone to a game where the fear off the field was greater than the dangers presented by the game of football.

Veronica Slade was also in tears as was Jennifer Axel. They had little understanding of what had just taken place, but they knew that it was bad whatever it was. They had never seen two players kicked out of a game before.

Veronica asked Jennifer, "Will they kick Cody Joe off the team for this? If they do, he will be devastated."

"I don't know Veronica, but we haven't seen the last of this mess. You can bet that both Cody Joe and Nate are in big trouble."

Soon after the dismissal of Cody Joe and Nate, Colorado City mounted a scoring drive to cut the lead to 7-6, but C-City missed the extra point as the Blue Devils maintained the lead. In the fourth quarter, Snyder scored when Kirby Tanner broke free on a swing pass out of the backfield from quarterback Lee Line for a 43-yard touchdown and a 14-6 victory.

Despite the turmoil, the Blue Devils were 6-1 on the season. But the seventh graders left the field with plenty of questions about the future with no answers.

* * *

Veronica and Jennifer were left in a confused state after the game. Veronica wanted to go see Cody Joe to find out if he was alright. She knew she couldn't go into the fieldhouse and she had no idea how long Cody Joe would be in there since she saw his dad go into the fieldhouse after the game. She reasonably figured that it might take some time before any of them came out.

She decided she would call Cody Joe later that evening. Kate answered the phone and told Veronica that Cody Joe still hadn't come home. That, at least, made Veronica feel much better since she could never have waited that long to see him even if she had stayed.

Meanwhile, immediately after the game and without knocking, Jack Carter barged into Coach Heart's office unannounced. He was upset and had no intention of hiding his current state of mind.

"Coach, we have a problem here and I want it solved," Jack said with a red face. "We've talked about this before and I warned you that this problem wasn't going away. Evidently, the two have been sparring for a while now without me knowing, but you should have noticed. You promised me you would take care of this."

"Listen, Mr. Carter, Cody Joe has been as much to blame as Nate recently. I expected more out of him. I can't believe he let the team down like he did out there today. Look, Cody Joe is a great kid and a pretty darn good football player. I don't want to lose him. The kids like him and seem to follow his lead. I need him to be that leader and to stay strong.

Right now, he may be losing some of those qualities with his actions."

"Stop right there, Coach," Jack intervened. "You knew that Nate was pushing Cody Joe into a corner. I wanted you to get rid of that kid long ago, but you didn't listen."

"Look, I'm just trying to save a kid's life here," Coach Heart said with a hanging head. "Nate hasn't got a chance. His dad is dead drunk most of the time. His mom is working three jobs to take care of the family and she doesn't have time for him. Heck, Nate wouldn't even be in school if it weren't for football. We've got to help kids like this."

"Coach, it's hard to help people who don't want to be helped. Nate doesn't seem to be responding to the chance you've given him. I admire you for what you are trying to do with this team and these kids, but this isn't working out. I choose to protect my son. Get rid of Nate or I'm going over your head on this one to the school board."

"I hope you don't do that Mr. Carter. That would be bad for everyone. I'm not sure your son would come out of something like that totally unscathed.

"We aren't having practice Friday, so at least give me the weekend to find a good solution for both kids."

"I trusted you once before Coach to take care of this and I'll not let it slide by again. I promise you that. I'll give you the weekend, but I better like your solution on Monday morning or I'll move forward on getting this matter solved."

Jack took his son to get a hamburger at the Dairy Queen before returning home while Rue, Kate and Chip were driven home by the Taggerts. When Cody Joe and Jack arrived at the house, Kate greeted Cody Joe at the door with, "Cody Joe are you OK? Why did those mean people take you out of the game? I saw Nate push you first."

"It's a long story Kate. I'll tell you all about it later," Cody

Joe said, delaying a long explanation to his inquisitive sister.

"Well, Veronica wants to know all about it, too. She called and wants to talk to you."

Little could brighten Cody Joe's day, but the words that "Veronica called" was an elixir of happiness. His spirits were immediately lifted as he quickly called the number Kate had for him.

"Hello," Veronica answered, praying it was Cody Joe.

"Hi Veronica. This is Cody Joe. Kate said you called and I'm really glad you did."

"Cody Joe, are you OK? They didn't kick you off the team did they?"

"No, not yet anyway. Dad says some decisions will be made this weekend," Cody Joe said before adding, "Veronica, I just let everything get away from me. I hope you are not disappointed in me. I should have held back, but Nate keeps pushing and pushing. I can't take that any longer. I can't back down any more when it comes to him."

"Oh, Cody Joe, I would never blame you. Nate pushed you down. We all saw it. I just want you to be OK."

"Well, we'll see how it all plays out on Monday. Dad tells me that Coach will have a decision by then. Who knows? I may have played my last football game."

"Oh, not that. Don't think that way, Cody Joe. Let's stay positive until we hear the decision. Surely, Nate won't get away with this."

"Well, thanks for calling, Veronica. I saw you at the game. I appreciate that. To tell you the truth, I just needed to hear your voice tonight. That helps more than anything because I'm feeling a bit low tonight.

"I couldn't wait to hear from you," Veronica countered. "Now that I know you are OK, I'll sleep better tonight. Nite, Cody Joe."

"Goodbye, Veronica."

Cody Joe had never talked to Veronica in such depth. And he was thrilled that she was genuinely on his side through this whole mess. He had never felt closer to Veronica Slade than he did at this very moment.

* * *

Cody Joe had to field questions about his ejection from both fellow students and teachers throughout the school day on Friday, but Veronica tried to be close to him at every break. She was always quick to defend Cody Joe's actions during the game.

Cody Joe was relieved when the final school bell rang for class dismissal. He went straight to the bus and home after school.

The Snyder Tigers had drawn an open date in the schedule for this particular Friday, so the gang of Cody Joe, Pug, Tracks, Cassidy, Tanner, Kevin Tumbler and Stacy Trout all had agreed to meet at 7 p.m. at the Palace Theater in downtown Snyder to see Alfred Hitchcock's popular movie "Vertigo" with James Stewart and Kim Novak.

Cody Joe thought it was never a good idea to miss a movie starring Kim Novak. That alone was enough to make the experience worthwhile.

The boys arrived at the Palace one by one, bought their tickets and singly entered into the flickering darkness of the theater in search of the group. They had all arrived and were seated together by 7:15 p.m. The movie had started, but it was the habit of Snyderites in those days to enter the movie house upon arrival and watch the movie to the end. You would then sit through the start of the film on the next showing and leave when the film advanced to the part you had already seen.

On this showing, however, the latest arriving kid, Trout, had missed only 15 minutes of the picture.

The entire group sat through the first 15 minutes again on the next showing so Trout could see the whole movie before leaving. They exited the theater together into the ticket booth portico where the neon lights of the Palace beckoned customers with its red flashing brilliance.

While waiting for their parents to pick them up, they strolled around the entrance looking at the posters of coming features at the Palace. Every poster made every movie look like a must-see flick. Cody Joe was mentally making a list of movies that fit his must-see agenda. Of course, most of them were westerns.

Tumbler and Trout were the first to leave. Tanner quickly followed, leaving Cassidy, Carter, Preston and Tracks as yet without a ride, waiting on Pug's dad to pick them up.

It was then that Nate Christian came sauntering alone into the theater's neon portico. Nate was as surprised to see Cody Joe and his friends as they were surprised to see him.

"Well, it's a bad sign when they let the likes of you into this theater," Christian scowled while looking directly at Carter.

"You don't have to worry, Nate, we've already seen the movie. We're leaving," Carter replied.

"That's too bad," Christian whined. "You could stick around until I at least beat your face in. But I'm sure you're too chicken for that. I just want you to know that I'm still going to get you for that cowardly hit you gave me in the game."

"I'm here right now," yelled Cody Joe. "If you think you can get me, c'mon and do it now. I'm tired of your constant harassment and bellyachin'."

Christian ignited in a full toothy grin. "OK, Cody Joe, just keep your friends out of this and be a man."

Cody Joe started toward Christian with an angry determination, but was met with a Christian fist to the mouth. Carter was staggered by the quick sucker punch. Pug, Tracks and Cassidy yelled encouragement for the staggering Cody Joe.

Carter might have been a little dazed from his bloody nose, but he was not backing down. He delivered his own connecting blow that landed hard on Christian's jaw. This blow also slowed Christian's advance, giving the onlookers a chance to cheer even harder for Carter.

But the game changed, at that very moment, as Christian ripped out his switchblade while getting up off the ground. He grinned and lunged hard at Carter with the blade gleaming under the neon lights.

Cody Joe only had time to throw his right arm in front of the blade to ward off that first stabbing motion. That last-second movement might have literally saved his life, but it did not keep the knife from slashing his right forearm.

Blood gushed from a rather deep wound where the knife had cut through Cody Joe's light jacket to find naked flesh. Christian raised his arm for another forward thrust, but the stunned Cody Joe was quick to respond and caught his arm on the downward swing while entangling his body with Nate like a pretzel.

The three witnesses to this fight moved quickly to aid Cody Joe at the first sign of the knife, but it was too late to keep Cody Joe from being wounded. Still, the three landed simultaneously on Cody Joe and Nate. Cassidy delivered a blow straight into the face of Christian. Pug pulled the knife from Nate's hand while Tracks kicked the knife out to the sidewalk in front of the theater.

Christian was strong enough, however, to escape the clutches of his enemies and raced out of the light into the darkness of a downtown side street, disappearing from the scene almost as fast as he had arrived.

It was at this point that theater security showed up in the form of Mo Burcher, better known to the boys as the official bouncer of the Palace Theater. It was Mo who ejected trouble-makers from the theater when disputes arose on the grounds.

While he didn't see many stabbings in his theater, it was not uncommon to break up a fight or two just about every week. He was sorry he didn't arrive in time to catch the one with the knife, but he could at least offer aid to the kid who had spilled a good amount of blood on the floor of his portico.

"I'm sorry guys that I didn't get out here any quicker," Mo told the boys, "but I have Eve calling the cops and an ambulance.

"I've had trouble with Nate before. I'm on a first name basis with him. He's trouble."

Pete Preston arrived only seconds later and was shocked to see Cody Joe holding his arm and a lot of blood on his jacket and on the floor.

"What happened?" Pete yelled as he left his car in the theater's no parking zone.

Cassidy started ripping off the events of the night in machine gun fashion. But Butch's words hardly surprised Pete. In his heart, he knew what had happened before he even asked the question.

Pete then entered the theater to place a call to Jack Carter, who was on the scene even before the ambulance departed for the hospital.

Before Cody Joe was taken to the hospital, however, Tad Dixon, a member of Snyder's police force answered the call and he interviewed both Cody Joe and Jack about the incident. He took Nate's knife as evidence. But it was Jack who ended up doing most of the talking as he filled in the whole story of Nate and Cody Joe.

"I want Nate caught and we want to press charges. We

have three witnesses who saw the whole thing and Mr. Burcher saw part of the incident.

"And don't worry, I'll see to it that the school knows about this tonight."

Jack didn't say it, but he thought that Coach Heart was going to know about this as soon as the doctors took care of Cody Joe's arm no matter how late it was. In fact, he secretly hoped he would have to wake him up with this news.

Cody Joe was given six stitches to close his wound. The doctor told Jack it could have been much worse, but the jacket had helped to deflect some of the blow.

Mr. Cassidy had dropped by with Butch to see how Cody Joe was doing, but he and his dad had not come home before that visit. This was where the rest of the Carter family had learned most of the story. It was 11 p.m. before the Carters arrived at home. Rue was understandably upset. She had inicially learned of the incident from a call by her husband at the hospital.

Chip, still awake, said, "Wish I could have seen it, Cody Joe. I miss all the good stuff. Did you hit him good? Butch said you hit him good."

Mr. Cassidy had dropped by with Butch to see how Cody Joe was doing, but he and his dad had not come home before that visit. This was where the rest of the Carter family had learned most of the story.

Jack called Coach Heart as soon as he could, quickly telling him the events of the night before adding, "Coach, I want Nate off the team. It's now beyond bickering, even fighting. It's now life and death. After what happened tonight, I have no doubt that Nate Christian would kill my son without blinking an eye.

"I'm pressing charges. I don't just want him off the team, I want him put away in a juvenile center of some kind. He's a

244

dangerous threat to this community."

Stunned, Coach Heart simply said without argument, "After this, I have no choice but to take this matter to the school board. I'm sure Nate will be handled appropriately, Mr. Carter."

"Oh, Coach, I know he will. Believe me when I tell you that I'll see to it."

On Saturday evening, Officer Tad Dixon paid the Carters a visit. It was not encouraging news.

"Mr. Carter," Dixon began, "We haven't been able to find Nate Christian.

"I went by his house late last night. Both his dad and mom were drunk and didn't know where their son was. I don't even think they knew where they were. They did manage to say that Nate had some relatives among the migrant workers. So, we are speculating he has run away to join them. He knows he's in a lot of trouble."

Jack Carter asked, "Well, where do we go from here?"

"That's a good question because we are pretty much at a standstill here. You see, I spent all day looking for him and I ran into a guy that Nate worked for last summer choppin' cotton. He told me that he might have left town in an old truck loaded with some cotton pickers. They're most likely wetbacks from Mexico, but there is no way of really knowing that.

"If that's true, it's possible that we will never see Nate Christian again. Heck, he may already be in Mexico or at another farm here in West Texas or eastern New Mexico. It's hard to say, but we've had problems tracking the whereabouts of some of these illegals for years. They're just like nomads roaming from one farm to another. I assure you Mr. Carter that we will continue to look for him. We've put the word out on him and he may turn up, but don't count on it."

"That's disappointing news," Jack lamented. "I don't like the fact that he still could be hanging around. At least, he won't be anywhere near the school and he will have a tough time showing his face in these parts."

Cody Joe chimed in, "And you still have his knife. He won't be doing much to anyone without his switchblade."

Chapter 20

CELEBRITY

By Monday morning, Cody Joe Carter was a Snyder celebrity. At least, he was as close as you can get to celebrity status in Snyder. He could even be classified as famous in the halls of Snyder Junior High School.

Everyone seemed to know about Cody Joe's encounter with Nate Christian at the Palace Theater. In fact, Butch Cassidy had taken it upon himself to describe the event as "legendary."

There had been a small story in the Snyder Daily News in Sunday's edition and word of mouth had presented several versions that all contained a morsel of the truth. One version said that Cody Joe had been shot with a handgun while another said Cody Joe single-handedly beat Nate to a pulp.

Those versions were being carefully compared by the students on Monday morning as Cody Joe's bus arrived on campus from its trek across town.

The bus landing was full of students waiting on one Cody Joe Carter. As soon as the swinging door of the bus opened, there arose a clatter of yelling and clapping. This was before Cody Joe had ever reached the bus exit. When he first showed his face to the crowd, another wave of excitement filled the chilly air.

It was as if the conquering hero was finally returning home to present his spoils of victory. Cody Joe, of course, was caught completely off guard by the monumental gathering and really had no idea what was happening. He kept looking around to find out what all the commotion was about.

But to his added surprise, he was greeted by a surge of shouts that included, "Attaboy, Cody Joe, attaboy." "Cody Joe are you OK?" "You really showed him, Cody Joe." "You're the man, Cody Joe."

Cody Joe quickly realized they were cheering for him because of his tussle with Nate Christian. He had gotten a similar, but somewhat more subdued, reaction at church on Sunday. Even some adults were giving him a pat on the back.

He really didn't know what to do, but as he stepped off the bus, the kids quickly surrounded him, asking him a myriad of questions. As soon as he tried to answer one question, dozens of others flew at him like a windmill that had lost its brake.

Fortunately, Cody Joe heard two familiar voices calling in the midst of the crowd, "Cody Joe! Cody Joe!"

It was Veronica and Jennifer. They pushed their way through the crowd and each grabbed one of Cody Joe's arms, while falling in pace toward his home room class. Veronica was careful not to touch Cody Joe's right forearm in fear she would cause him great anguish.

Veronica knew exactly where he was hurt because she had called him on Saturday after she found out about the incident. They had talked for over two hours on the phone. Rue Carter thought that had to be Cody Joe's phone record because she didn't think Cody Joe had ever been on the phone for two hours in his whole life.

Veronica knew all the details from start to finish because she left no stone unturned in her quest to find out what had really happened. Cody Joe felt a real comfort in talking to Veronica. After that phone call, he was thinking that only last week that he was more comfortable talking to Jennifer Axel than to his own girlfriend. But that had all changed now.

Veronica seemed to understand him and she supported him thoroughly through the upsetting events of the past week.

Cody Joe was now glad to have both Veronica and Jennifer accompanying him to class because, quite frankly, he didn't have the slightest idea of how to handle this situation. The mob continued to follow in step, but now it was as if he had a force shield protecting his flanks.

Some of the girls in the crowd were a bit put out by the fact that Veronica and Jennifer had such close access to Cody Joe while they had to merely follow along without any interaction with the school's new hero. After all, just about everyone wanted to offer Cody Joe their sympathy or their praise.

Yes, Cody Joe Carter was now Snyder royalty and his SJHS kingdom was at his beck and call.

* * *

Celebrity status lasted for Cody Joe all the way to his fifth period math class where he promptly received his score from the last test, which had been taken last week during all the troubles with Nate Christian. He was credited with a 76 on the test, far below the expectations of a student that made all A's and B's in his course work.

Cody Joe knew that Rue Carter would not be impressed and he dreaded presenting this grade to her. At this moment, he didn't feel like a hero because he knew that hero status at home meant bringing home good grades.

After math class, Cody Joe and his band of Blue Devils hit Ave. M for the daily trek to practice. It was upon arrival at the fieldhouse where Cody Joe received another huge setback. Coach Bear called Cody Joe into Coach Heart's office.

"OK, Cody Joe, let's take a look at your arm," Coach

Heart commanded. "Let's see how serious this cut of yours is."

Coach Bear removed Cody Joe's bandage. There was still some swelling and a blue bruising appeared on both sides of the wound. Still, the wound was clean and well-stitched.

"Well, Doc Rivers did a good job with this wound. I think it will heal quickly," Coach Heart said.

"Does that mean I can play on Thursday against Lamesa," Cody Joe quickly asked.

"I don't doubt for a minute that you want to play, but we have a lot of things to consider here," Coach Heart reasoned. "Under normal circumstances, we might be able to get you ready to play by Thursday. We probably could rig up some kind of protective shield for your arm that would cause little discomfort for you and would protect the stitches.

"But to be quite honest, I really don't want to take that chance, Cody Joe. This stabbing has drawn a lot of attention to you and our program. If you were to somehow re-injure that arm, we would catch a lot of flak, and deservedly so. I'm keeping you out this week for sure. I'll talk to Doc Rivers the first of next week and see what he thinks. He tells me you'll get these stitches out on Tuesday or Wednesday of next week. We'll make our decision then.

"But, Cody Joe, there's another problem with letting you play. I'm still not happy with the way you handled this problem on the field. If I let you play, others will think I'm showing favoritism for you. I do think you could have been a better example, even though you probably would win a team vote if it was up to them."

Cody Joe felt like he had been punched in the stomach. He wanted to play. He was confident, in coming to practice today, that Tracks would somehow rig up an arm guard for him to use. Now he got this news. He secretly wondered if his father had put Coach Heart up to this. Even Coach Heart admitted that it probably could be worked out where he could play.

Cody Joe, however, lost some of his anger when he rushed out of Coach Heart's office and accidently slammed his right forearm up against the door facing. It was a brutal reminder that he was in no real shape to be playing football. The blow brought tears to his eyes.

* * *

Cody Joe maintained his celebrity status through the rest of the week, while at school. He got a lot of attention. Virtually everyone he talked with wanted to know how his encounter with Nate Christian went down.

Also, Veronica went everywhere with him. She told him she couldn't bear being apart. She inspected his wound daily and attentively listened to every word that came out of his mouth. In this respect, Cody Joe was on top of the world.

But he didn't feel like much of a hero anywhere else. His mother was angry at him for letting his school work slide. And he was basically ignored at practice as the team prepared for the road game in Lamesa.

He couldn't believe how lonely it felt not being a part of the team. He felt like a man without a country despite owning his campus kingdom. He held a kind of kingly status, but had no power to participate in the activities of his fiefdom.

Cody Joe spent his time at practice in sweat gear, running laps and sprints to keep in shape. He did exercises that didn't involve his arm, but mostly he sat on blocking dummies, watching the team practice with sad puppy dog eyes and a slight scowl on his face.

On Wednesday, Coach Heart told Cody Joe he could travel with the team on the bus if he wanted, but he was not allowed to bring his game gear. Cody Joe told Coach Heart that his father planned on taking him to the game and he would be there on the sideline. Jack Carter was not planning to go to this game because of business commitments, but he now felt that he owed Cody Joe an escort to the game.

On game day, Cody Joe at least got one perk for being a de-facto member of the team. He got out of school early and traveled with his teammates to the fieldhouse. It was here that Jack Carter promised to pick up his son in time to get to the game. Cody Joe was alone at the fieldhouse about 45 minutes before his father hailed him from the curb. Cody Joe had fallen asleep while waiting on his ride.

The trip to Lamesa was about an hour's drive west of Snyder. The only town in between was Gail, where the road climbed the Caprock escarpment to the table flat cotton land for which it was famous. In fact, it was this table flat resemblance that had given Lamesa its name, even though the Spanish version would have been La Mesa (the tableland).

While going through Gail, Jack pointed out that Gail possessed one of the few high schools in the state that played eight-man football. Ira, just to the south of Snyder, played the more popular six-man version of football.

Jack said, "Some of these rural schools don't have enough students to play 11-man football, so they choose to play either six-man or eight-man, depending on student enrollment. I really like the eight-man game, and here in Borden County, is the only place close to Snyder that plays the eight-man game."

Cody Joe acted like he was interested in what his dad was saying, but his mind was lost in a maze of befuddled thoughts that made him extremely depressed.

He couldn't imagine what it was going to feel like when his team raced onto the field of battle without him. He couldn't imagine not taking part, in not playing or being an integral

252

part of the team.

He wondered why Nate Christian had become such a hated enemy. What had he done to make Nate dislike him so much? It was not that Cody Joe was a far superior football player. In fact, Cody Joe thought Nate had a lot of raw ability, but he didn't necessarily channel his talent to its best advantage. In Cody Joe's way of thinking, Nate Christian could have been one of the best players on the team.

Instead, Nate was a seventh grader running from the law, harboring a hate that would allow him to kill Cody Joe Carter on sight. Actually, Nate should have been in the ninth grade, but his irregular attendance in school made it hard for him to pass his course work.

If this fact had been known, Jack would have blown a gasket. That would mean Nate was ineligible to play seventh grade football. All of this could have been easily avoided if Heart had done his due diligence on Christian's eligibility status. If anyone reported this news, the Blue Devils could be made to forfeit all the games in which Nate participated. Now, it was just as well nobody knew Nate was ineligible, especially Jack Carter.

Cody Joe secretly wondered if he would ever have to have another showdown with Nate Christian again. It was a thought that troubled his soul, but a subject he never brought up to anyone in his life. In Cody Joe's way of thinking, this was his cross to bear.

* * *

Coach Heart had thought long and hard on how to replace Cody Joe in the lineup. Cody Joe had been a two-way starter since the first week of play. He decided Stoney Wall could start at Cody Joe's right guard slot on offense and still remain as an interior lineman on defense. However, it was much harder to replace Cody Joe on defense. His linebacker post was critical and Coach Heart knew few on the team had Cody Joe's instincts and savvy to play that position on a full-time basis.

But there was one thought that Coach Heart couldn't escape. Before he had moved Butch Cassidy to fullback, he had been the best defensive player on the whole team. Coach Heart decided he would move Cassidy back to linebacker even though that would force moving the lightweight Hank Cline to fullback. In addition, Heart once again brought Kirby Tanner off the bench and put him in Cline's halfback slot.

To replace Nate Christian at defensive tackle, Coach Heart went with the versatile Eric Blade, who had a lot of playing time this season as a reliable sub in both the offensive and defensive lines.

These were moves that Coach Heart felt would give his team a reasonable shot at winning. After all, the Blue Devils had scorched Lamesa, 46-0, back in late September.

Pug Preston mourned the loss of Cody Joe. He sat by Stoney Wall on the trip to Lamesa, hoping to help Wall with his new offensive assignments. Wall was thankful for the help, but Pug felt a bit lost. He had never sat with anyone other than Cody Joe on a road trip and this felt really weird. For some inexplicable reason, Pug felt guilty for being able to play while Cody Joe had been sidelined.

Pug couldn't help but feel partially at fault for the whole thing. He felt he should have taken a bigger role in the confrontation with Nate Christian. He was sure he should have never let Cody Joe take Nate on alone. He would never put his buddy on an island alone again.

Pug's demeanor brightened somewhat when he saw Cody Joe enter the southeast gate of the Lamesa Stadium with his father. At least, his friend would be on the sideline during the game.

The team huddled at midfield just minutes before the game. Quarterback Lee Line said, "Guys, listen up. I haven't talked this over with any of you, but I think we should play this game for Cody Joe. He's going to be with us today, but not on the field. We all know what he has gone through, and if we dedicate this game to him, it will be our statement to one and all that we are in his corner. What do you say?"

The team erupted in wild glee as Line ended, "OK then, let's break with Cody Joe. One, Two, Three, Cody Joe!"

The response was not lost on the coaches or Cody Joe Carter. Carter was deeply touched and his depression vanished as if he had taken some secret elixir. Coach Heart smiled, knowing his team was still unified and sticking together through thick and thin.

* * *

The game started on a good note for the Blue Devils as Lester Jarvis broke loose on a 46-yard touchdown run early in the first quarter. That run set the tone for the rest of the game, as the Blue Devils continued its offensive rampage throughout the cold, late October afternoon.

Cody Joe talked often with Pug Preston during breaks in the action or during times when Coach Bear would bring Pug out of the game. Like Cody Joe, Pug was rarely out of the game since he played on both sides of the ball.

Cody Joe was a bit surprised, however, how little he could see what was happening on the field while standing on the sideline. Most of the time the action just looked like a jumbled maze of bodies.

At one point in the game, Adam Quay made a tackle

along the sideline, which also managed to take out teammate Jack King and Cody Joe. Carter's forearm took a pretty good hit and pain shot up Cody Joe's right arm, but he tried to dismiss it, hopping up as fast as he could and acting as if the blow hadn't even happened. It still ached through the last two quarters of play.

Coach Heart was extremely happy with the play of his team, but the biggest impression of the day was made by Butch Cassidy. Heart had forgotten just how good Cassidy was on defense. Butch had not practiced on defense since the second week of the season, but he played as if he had been at the linebacker post all season long.

Cassidy had a natural instinct for finding the ball and the brute strength to overpower the big linemen on his way to the tackle. But it was the tackling that had everyone talking. When Butch hit a runner, the runner went down. For seventh grade, some of the blows Butch delivered were sledge hammers coming out of nowhere. Before the game was over, the Lamesa runners wanted no part of the man in the middle of the Blue Devil defense.

In fact, Lamesa never crossed midfield except for one possession when Lee Line threw an interception. It was the only pass of the day attempted by Snyder.

Coach Heart couldn't help but wonder what his defense would be like if he could play both Cody Joe and Butch as the inside linebackers at the same time. He thought it was a plan worth nurturing as the season was headed for an interesting ending.

At the end of the day, Snyder pummeled Lamesa, 36-0. Kirby Tanner had a touchdown. Eric Blade came up with six tackles as Christian's replacement. And Stoney Wall proved, without doubt, that he could play on both sides of the ball.

This was the last road trip of the year for the 1958 seventh grade Blue Devils. They now owned a 7-1 record for the season with two games left to play on the home field. Big Spring Runnels and Sweetwater were all that remained. By far, these were the toughest two teams Snyder had faced all season. It was time for the Blue Devils to face the brutal schedule they had been dealt.

And for Cody Joe, his mind was made up. He wouldn't miss these last two games for any reason. He was going to play no matter what.

Chapter 21

HALLOWEEN

It turned clear and cold on Halloween night, as the Snyder Tigers prepared to meet District 3-3A rival Sweetwater. Of course, this seemed perfect conditions for a rivalry that was destined to be decided under an over-sized celestial orb that appeared to be made of solid gold.

For Cody Joe Carter, it was a chance to sit under that magnificent moon with Veronica Slade. Such was the life of romance when you were in the seventh grade in Snyder, Texas, on the night of ghosts and goblins. Even on such a night, football was front and center. Halloween could never really compete with Snyder vs. Sweetwater, big moon or not.

But as of late, Veronica Slade had clouded Cody Joe's mind on such issues. The game was in second place while Halloween was a distant third to the opportunity to sit with Veronica under her blanket on a cold and crisp night. He desperately hoped Veronica wouldn't forget the blanket.

He got his wish. Veronica entered the stadium with a blanket in tow. She quickly climbed the steps in the stands to find Cody Joe and his band of friends. She promptly crossed over Cody Joe's legs in order to sit on his left side. She had always sat on Cody Joe's right side at other games, but she had designed this maneuver entering the stadium so that she could hold Cody Joe's left hand in order not to cause him pain with his injured right arm, which still carried stitches.

She quickly spread the blanket over their legs and grabbed Cody Joe's left hand, pulling it close to her stomach. She did it without flinching and Cody Joe was surprised at how natural it felt. And he was ecstatic that Veronica did all of this without his encouragement. He readily knew that these matters seemed to work best when Veronica took charge.

Cody Joe was beginning to feel much more comfortable around Veronica, but he was still shy in showing outward affection. In his way of thinking, just being able to carry on a regular conversation with her was a vast improvement. His tongue now actually cooperated with him when he spoke to her. He guessed all that time recently spent on the phone with her opened up his vocal cords.

Butch Cassidy, sitting one row back of the cuddling couple, asked, "Hey, Veronica, why don't you come up here and share that blanket with some guys that might appreciate it more than Cody Joe?"

Veronica slightly turned, put on her best smile and looked at Cassidy straight in the face. "Well, Butch, that's a mighty fine offer, but I think you would be better off if you found your own girlfriend, preferably one with her own blanket.

"She got you there, Butch," said Kirby Tanner, "but I really doubt if you are going to find a girlfriend that's willing to sit next to that stinking body of yours."

Tracks, Cody Joe, Tumbler and Trout all joined Kirby in a fit of laughter. Veronica was now officially considered one of the gang.

It was at that point that Pug, Alexi Taggert and Jennifer Axel arrived. Pug sat on Cody Joe's right side. There was no danger there of hurting Cody Joe's injured arm because there would be no hand holding between those two. Alexi sat next to Pug while Jennifer crossed over the entire group to sit by Veronica. Veronica immediately offered Jennifer a corner of the blanket she was sharing with Cody Joe. Jennifer couldn't get the blanket to stretch quite far enough to cover her entire lap, but it did help knock off the chilly wind that swept through the stands.

Then an event happened that no one saw coming. In fact, jaws dropped and even Butch Cassidy was left speechless. Kirby Tanner dropped down from the row above and slid in beside Jennifer Axel. The two started talking like they had known each other forever. The truth was that Tanner had never spoken to Jennifer before. Of course, he had seen her with Veronica and Cody Joe many times, but this was the first time he had ever busted a move.

All of Tanner's friends were swept up in a swirl of emotions. On the one hand, they couldn't believe one in their group could make such a bold move right in front of them. On the other hand, every one of them felt pangs of guilt over the fact that they hadn't been the one to make the move. After all, Jennifer was available and she wasn't that hard on the eyes either.

Well, it was a huge move in the eyes of Kirby's friends. They couldn't believe what they were seeing. After all, Kirby had never given any of them an idea that he was a lady's man, but he was proving to be the man of mystery in this group. Cassidy finally got over his surprise and started elbowing Tracks and Tumbler on each side of him.

"Hey, Kirby, ask Jennifer why she didn't bring a blanket," Butch roared as his cohorts chuckled in the background.

Kirby turned red in the face, but Jennifer didn't even flinch. "Don't worry, Butch, I'll bring it next time."

This was all the encouragement Tanner needed and he was hooked at her side for the rest of the game.

But as far as the game was concerned, Snyder lost in the last 1:07 of the game when Sweetwater scored a touchdown after a long fourth quarter drive, handing the Snyder Tigers a 27-20 defeat. The loss pretty much ensured that Snyder would

260

not be in the 1958 state playoffs. Losing to the district favorite was usually football's death knell in District 3-3A. That's one of the main reasons why the Snyder-Sweetwater rivalry was taken so seriously in this little corner of a big state.

Cody Joe and Pug each got another goodbye peck from their gals, making the night another huge success for the two dating novices. Tanner, however, simply told Jennifer he enjoyed sitting with her and walked out of the stadium with the guys as usual.

Of course, he was being bombarded with questions along the way by his jealous friends. Snyder had just fallen to Sweetwater, but the talk after the game was of Tanner and Axel pairing. Some would say this was a mark of growing up, but some would say, in this part of the world, that you simply had lost your entire sense of priorities.

The mood in the community was as somber as the fading harvest moon that was now shrinking in the sky with each fleeting hour. No blanket could ever cover the woe of Snyder losing to Sweetwater on Halloween. This was nature's supreme trick.

* * *

Since Halloween fell on a football Friday this particular year, the boys decided to have a sleepover at Tracks' house on Saturday night. And just because Halloween was in the rear view mirror, the thoughts of Halloween pranks were not forgotten. That could never happen when you counted Butch Cassidy as one of your gang members.

Around 8:30 p.m., Cassidy said, "Hey guys, I stashed some toilet paper rolls under a bush this afternoon near Coach Nix' house. I think we need to paper his house tonight. It'll be our way of getting back at him for his man in the ring game."

Tracks, being the nervous host and one who never had even been in the ring, asked, "What if he catches us? He'll probably shoot us with a shotgun."

"Oh, he can't do nuthin' but make us run laps," said Cassidy. "And he can't do that any longer than a week from Thursday because the season will be over. This is our time to get him and get him good."

The guys finally agreed, but not without some deep soul searching and feelings of trepidation. In Cody Joe's heart, he was sure this venture was not going to end well. But rarely could the guys stand up to Cassidy when he had his mind set. After all, Butch had done the logistics work already and this was just too good an opportunity to stick it to Coach Nix. It might even be worth getting caught.

Tracks made some lame excuse to his parents to get the boys outside and they quickly headed to Coach Nix's house, which was only a couple of blocks away. Cassidy had stashed a whole carton of toilet paper rolls under a thick bush across the street from the targeted home. The big box had been left unmolested and was waiting for the Halloween driven agitators to arrive.

Each boy armed themselves with several rolls before creeping onto the Nix property. Cody Joe and Kirby Tanner teamed together with Carter on one side of the house and Tanner on the other. Quickly they began tossing the rolls of paper streamers over the top of the house. Then they would pick up a completed toss and hurl it over the house again until the rolls were empty. It only took a few minutes before the roof looked as if it had been perfectly wrapped.

Butch took care of the tree in front, using a similar tactic of throwing the rolls between the limbs. Sometimes the rolls stuck in the tree, but it didn't deter Butch from covering the branches with white streamers from top to bottom.

Tracks and Trout stretched streamers over the bushes around the house while Pug decorated the front porch and swing set in the latest Halloween décor.

The task was almost complete, but the clean getaway was doomed as the boys saw flashing lights roaring toward the house from two directions. Carter and Tanner climbed behind a hedge that ran along one side of the house. Pug hid behind a chair on the porch while Tracks and Trout climbed the fence that separated the front yard from the back and then climbed the back fence adjoining the alley.

Tracks and Trout had the best chance of escaping capture, but actually were the first offenders caught as Officer Pete Loney arrived a block from the house, swerved down a side street and entered the alley, snaring the two boys in the middle of the alley road like two deer caught in throbbing headlights. They gave the battle up quickly without any attempt at further flight.

Meanwhile, Officer Tad Dixon pulled up in front of the house and left his vehicle with police lights pulsating with its red, blue and white theme. Dixon pulled out his flashlight and began a sweep of the Nix property. It was at that time when Coach Nix exited his front door and signaled Dixon by finger-pointing toward the chair on the porch.

"C'mon out from behind the chair," Dixon commanded. "Your party is over for the night."

Pug gave it up without a fuss and Dixon recognized him instantly.

"Pug Preston isn't it?" Dixon asked. "Fighting at the theater and now mischief in the neighborhood. You keep this up, we're goin' to become good friends."

"Pug, what are you guys up to out here?" Nix interjected. "Did you think I wouldn't hear all the ruckus takin' place? I called the cops on you."

It was at this point when Officer Loney brought his two captives around to the front yard and Dixon knew Tracks from the theater fight. This was his first meeting with Trout.

Cody Joe knew the gig was up, so he tapped Tanner on the arm and they voluntarily walked into the open as Dixon re-started the sweep of the area.

"Is that you Cody Joe?" Dixon asked. "I can't believe you are a part of this. Isn't fighting with Nate Christian enough excitement for one month? You still have your arm in a sling for goodness sake.

"OK, guys, who else is involved here?"

The boys didn't know how to respond to the question because they didn't know if Cassidy had gotten away or was still hiding on the property. They didn't want to rat him out if he was already gone, so they just kept quiet. As far as Officer Dixon was concerned, this was a full admission of guilt.

"Keep looking Pete. I think there are more out there somewhere."

Officer Loney moved to the center of the yard and directly under the branches of a big mulberry tree. A six-inch slice of bark came tumbling down out of the tree and landed on Loney's shoulder. He looked up, pointing his flashlight into the leafy limbs.

His light immediately lit up Cassidy's big eyes, but before Loney could utter any kind of command, Butch uttered a hearty, "Chirp, chirp."

Even though the boys knew they were in big trouble, they couldn't help breaking out in a fit of laughter.

Loney said, "Hey Tad, I think I've cornered my first 180-pound canary."

Cassidy joined the post-Halloween cast of criminals as they stood in a single line before the three men, ever bit resembling a full-fledged police lineup.

"Well, gentlemen," Officer Dixon began, "I'm going to start by calling Cody Joe's dad because I know him best. Then we'll decide where to go from there."

Coach Nix stepped forward and offered, "Guys, I'm going to leave you for now and go back into the house, but I look forward to seeing you on my field on Monday afternoon."

Nix then looked at every one of the boys square in the eye, leaving each and every one of them literally quaking in their boots.

Officer Dixon quickly made his call to Jack Carter from inside the Nix home. He didn't even have to ask Cody Joe for a number since he still had his number in his shirt pocket from last week. The talk was short as Jack promised to be there in a few minutes. Before leaving the house, however, he called all the parents of the kids involved except for the Trouts because he didn't know them and there were six sets of Trouts in the phone book.

As fast as Jack arrived at the scene, Pete Preston was already there and Taylor Tracks was driving up just as Jack was about to talk with Dixon. Ernest Cassidy would arrive a good 15 minutes later since he lived outside the Snyder city limits. Officer Pete Loney had already left the scene before any of the dads arrived to continue his patrolling duties.

"Well, gentlemen," Dixon began again outside of ear shot of the offending gang. "It looks like your boys have been into a little mischief this evening. As far as I can tell, nothing has been hurt and Coach Nix doesn't want to press charges. I'm OK with all of this as long as this place is cleaned up tonight. And that's probably going to take a couple of hours at least."

"Officer Dixon," Jack Carter said, "I'll take full responsibility for the clean-up. I guarantee you this place will be top drawer before the sun comes up."

The other dads nodded in agreement and promised to remain on site until the work was completed.

Jack then walked over to the boys and said, "The good news is that you guys aren't going to jail tonight. The bad news is that you are going to spend the night with your fathers as we conduct a clean the neighborhood party.

"I want every scrap of toilet paper picked up until this property looks like it did before you started this escapade. OK, get started, and I don't want to hear one complaint from any of you the rest of the night."

Mr. Carter caught his son by the arm as he walked past saying, "Cody Joe, I don't know about the other boys, but you are going to be spending a lot of Saturday nights with the family. I've never liked the word grounded, but you are so grounded for the foreseeable future."

Cody Joe got the message and was really sorry he had let his father down again.

Mr. Carter then went to talk with Coach Nix while the

266

other fathers started the boys on the task at hand.

"Coach, I know it's already late, but we'll have this cleaned up tonight. I'll be here with the guys to see that it's done," Jack promised. "I can't talk for everyone involved, but I'm so sorry that my son was in on this caper. We really expect more out of him than this,"

Nix answered, "I appreciate your attitude, but don't be too hard on them. They're all good kids. I did much worse when I was a kid. In fact, I wish you could have been here when we caught Butch in the tree making bird sounds. It was the funniest thing I've ever seen. We couldn't keep from laughing. That alone was worth this entire experience.

"And, oh yes, I wanted to tell you that I tried to put the fear of God in the boys before leaving them by saying I looked forward to seeing them on Monday at practice. I think it worked, but I want to promise you that there will be no child abuse involved because we only have Runnels and Sweetwater left. We need to spend our time getting ready for those games. We need them to focus and I'm going to use this to obtain their attention."

Before Officer Tad Dixon left, he pulled Jack aside and said confidentially, "I didn't expect to see you tonight, but I was going to get with you tomorrow anyway. We got a report this afternoon from the Texas Rangers that they have reason to believe that Nate Christian is now in Mexico.

"That's really about all we know right now. I don't know what 'credible evidence' means, but they really think he is out of the country. We do know he was seen in Del Rio on Thursday and the Rangers think he may be traveling with some cotton pickers. The rest is all a guess, but I thought you should know. I don't think you are going to have to worry about Mr. Christian for a long time."

"You might be right," Carter pondered, "but I would feel

much better if he was in your custody. At least, I would know where he was on any given day."

The long night got longer as the clean-up progressed, but the job was finished long before dawn. Still, Jack Carter had Cody Joe in his church pew on Sunday morning with strict orders that he better not fall asleep. That turned out to be a more difficult proposition than the clean-up itself.

Chapter 22

THE
CONUNDRUM

C ody Joe was grateful to see Monday morning roll
around. It was his get out of jail free card. Except
for church, he had spent the entire Sunday afternoon in the house, trying to avoid his parents, who had been
particularly curt to him for his late-night activities.

After all, it was only so long that Cody Joe could put up
with Chip, while cornered in the shared bedroom. Chip wasn't
under house arrest like his older brother, but there was nothing he loved better than getting under Cody Joe's skin. Therefore, Chip spent every moment in the bedroom with Cody
Joe. It was like a double dose of punishment.

School was the saving grace. Cody Joe actually hoped the
school day would never end. He was out of forced confine-
ment and ready to take back his place in proper society.

Cody Joe met with Butch, Pug, Tracks and Kirby at the
bus landing before the start of school. All had varying stories
of how their Sunday had gone, but only Butch had escaped
any real punishment. It seems Ernest Cassidy had drawn a job
on Sunday, so Butch glided through the day pretty much as
usual. He even slept until 11 a.m. on Sunday morning.

"I'm coming to live with you Butch for the next six
weeks," Cody Joe exclaimed. "Maybe longer than that if my
Dad doesn't come around."

"You guys are welcome at my house anytime you want,"

Butch answered before adding, "and I've got a few more houses lined up for us to paper."

Before Butch could say another word, the four boys pounced on him, slapping at him like a worn out punching bag.

"OK, OK! I get it," Butch said. "It was just a suggestion."

Cody Joe headed for home room to start the school day, arriving at an empty room. It was only seconds, however, before his classmates were filing in behind him.

Arriving late, as usual, was Jennifer Axel, but she was buzzing like a bee as she saw Cody Joe. She was asking Cody Joe rapid fire questions as she deposited her books and put her coat on the back of her chair.

"Cody Joe, what did he say?" Jennifer coaxed. "Does he like me? Did he ask you about me? What did you tell him? Is he ever going to sit by me again?"

"Whoa, Jennifer," Cody Joe teased. "Who are you talking about? Do you have a new boyfriend that I don't know about?"

This snarky reply deflated Axel. She didn't like Cody Joe teasing her at a moment of such importance. She never treated him this way when it came to Veronica. She quickly turned in her chair, folded her arms in front of her and performed her best sulking routine.

"Oh, c'mon Jennifer," Cody Joe offered. "Don't be such a baby. Kirby never said anything to me after the game. That's something between you two. That's something us guys don't talk about a lot. Butch teased him some, but we let it go at that."

"You guys are just a bunch of duds. And, Cody Joe, I thought you would take care of my interests in a matter like this. After all, I had your back when you and Veronica were starting out. But now you just make fun of me. You don't care how I feel."

"Look Jennifer, I'll talk with Kirby and try to find out how he feels about you, but I can't promise anything. Kirby's a private kind of guy and he might not be up to talking about how he feels about girls.

"Besides, I don't think you are stupid Jennifer. You and I both know he's interested in you or he would never have sat down beside you. It's clear to me, why isn't it clear to you?"

"I just want to know if he really likes me a lot. Is that too much to ask? I don't think so."

Elmer Perry walked into the room as the home room bell rang, ending the conversation and starting a new school day.

At lunch, Cody Joe did ask Kirby Tanner how he felt about his friend Jennifer.

"I think she's really cute," Kirby said honestly. "I don't know if she likes me or not, but I'd like to get to know her better."

"Oh, she's interested alright," Cody Joe said. "She couldn't keep from asking questions about you and your intentions to-day in home room. I'm sure I could arrange another meeting."

"Well, I really would rather do this on my own, Cody Joe," Kirby said emphatically. "I like to take things slow. But if she asks again, tell her I said I thought she was great."

"Kirby, we'll do it your way, but I can't help but laugh when you say you like to take things slow. That move you put on her Friday, at the game, came out of the blue and we all had drop jaw."

"I saw the reaction, but at least it was my way. I wasn't pressured into anything. And I was a little scared that I might scare her off."

"You couldn't scare Jennifer with a howitzer," Cody Joe laughed. "Besides, I think girls like that unexpected stuff. You may be the school's best Romeo."

* * *

Cody Joe had to miss Monday's practice in order to get the stitches out of his injured arm. Carter almost waited until the doctor had finished his task before popping the real question of the day.

"Doc, can I play on Thursday," Cody Joe gushed out.

"Well, I really wish you would wait another week and give this wound some more time to fully heal."

"But we play Runnels on Thursday, and we have only two games left in the season, and I feel good. I really do."

Doc answered, "I know all that, Cody Joe, but it would serve you better to wait another week. Remember, this is a significant injury. You were basically cut open with a knife. And even though you now have the stitches out, this wound is still pretty tender. You would have a lot of discomfort if you played with this arm now."

Jack Carter interrupted, "Doc, could Cody Joe further injure the arm if he played Thursday."

"Well, I really doubt he could hurt it any worse, but he would have to play with pain. You do understand that don't you, Jack? The worst thing that he could do is rip this cut open again, but I don't think that's going to happen.

"His main worry is keeping the wound protected and I'm really not aware of any equipment out there that will do the job."

Cody Joe once again chimed in at that point, saying, "Doc, you know Rick Tracks. He's one of our trainers. He's great at rigging up pads for guys who are injured. He's done it for me before. I hardly felt any pain when he fixed me up earlier in the season. I'll bet he can do it again. In fact, if I know Tracks, he's already working on something for me."

Doc had given his best professional advice and had other patients to visit, so he ended the conversation with, "Jack, Cody Joe could play, but I don't think he should. There seems to be no reason good enough for me to put your son through that kind of pain. But that decision will have to be a family decision, not mine."

Of course, Cody Joe talked of nothing else the rest of the day. He badgered his father and mother continuously to let him play.

"Mom, there are only two games left in the season. I can't miss this one. And if my arm hurts too bad, I'll take myself out of the game."

"Dad, I can play. I can take it. They say on TV all the time that guys play with pain. It's only pain. It's not like I'm going to hurt myself any worse."

Finally, fed up with the pleas emanating from the Cody Joe Carter front, Jack Carter said, "I don't want to hear any more about this. You aren't getting a clearance from me until I see what they can do to protect that arm. Son, is that clear?"

"Do you mean I can play if I can protect the arm? That's a deal, Dad. I'm calling Tracks right now."

Cody Joe was on the phone before thinking. Tracks was still at practice and there would be no way to reach him. It seemed like forever to Cody Joe before enough time had passed for Tracks to make it home. He quickly made another call and this time Tracks answered.

"I was just about to call you, Cody Joe. Coach Heart told me you were getting the stitches out today. Are you going to play Thursday?"

"Well, I don't know if I'm going to play or not. It's kind of up to you, Tracks."

"Up to me? How do you figure that?"

"My dad says I can't play unless he is satisfied with the

arm protection that the team can provide. I figure you're my ticket to the game. You think you can come up with something that will work?"

That was just what Tracks was waiting to hear, exploding with, "Cody Joe, that's why I was fixing to call you. I think I've already come up with a pad that you're going to love. You won't feel a thing when you play. It'll be ready for practice tomorrow."

Cody Joe said, "Well, it won't really matter if I like the pad or not. It's all up to Dad. He better love it."

"Cody Joe, let me come over tonight and show your dad. I've got all the stuff right here. I was going to try it out on Mama, but now I'll have the real thing.

"That's great, Tracks. C'mon over."

Tracks was banging on the door in less than 30 minutes. He didn't even pause long enough to eat any supper. He grabbed two cookies, rounded up all his gear and headed out the door for his four-block walk to the Carter house.

The Carters were in the midst of their evening meal when Tracks rang the doorbell. Cody Joe was so excited to see Tracks that he tripped over a chair trying to get to the door. Unfortunately, he grimaced when he caught his injured arm on the corner of the table. He didn't need to be showing any signs of outward pain to the Carter family while a forearm pad rescue was underway.

Rue Carter noticed and almost put a stop to the experiment before it was even presented. She wasn't on board with this crazy idea anyway. She thought it was ridiculous to even be entertaining the thought.

But Tracks was prepared. He laid out his equipment and started to work.

"Mr. and Mrs. Carter, I've had a whole week to think about this and I think it's going to work. Of course, we won't really know until Cody Joe goes through a full practice, but I think you will be able to see he's going to be well protected."

Tracks had Cody Joe hold out his injured arm. He placed a strip of foam rubber on the top, over the scar, and a matching strip on the bottom of the forearm. He then secured the two strips with several rings of adhesive tape until the top strip literally married with the bottom strip, forming a complete foam rubber cocoon.

"You can see this will absorb blows from both sides of the arm lessening any blow, no matter where it comes from," Tracks explained.

Then Tracks took two pads covered in harder rubber sleeves and attached them in like fashion over the foam rubber strips.

"This gives a hard casing around his arm to absorb any really hard shots to the arm," Tracks said.

Tracks then slapped Cody Joe's arm with a medium blow without any warning. Cody Joe said he felt the strike, but didn't feel any pain.

But Tracks wasn't through. He took some knee and arm bandages and completely wrapped the arm before tightly wrapping adhesive tape around the whole project. Cody Joe began slapping hard on his own arm and proudly announced himself fit for combat.

Tracks' invention was definitely serious padding, but it was bulky. Jack Carter didn't have much confidence that Cody Joe could catch a pass or even hold a ball in his right hand, but he had to admit the padding looked to be substantial.

He said, "Rick, I can tell you put a lot of thought into this, but it is still unproven. Cody Joe, if your mother agrees, we will let you practice tomorrow with the pad. I'll go to practice with you so the coaches don't take advantage of you being out there. I'll allow only so many hitting drills just to test the pad.

But that's all I'll promise you right now. We still have a lot of decisions left."

Rue said, "I'll go with your dad's best judgment for tomorrow, but you are not playing if I think this isn't going to work."

* * *

Cody Joe literally ran to practice after school on Tuesday, leaving his teammates in the dust. He wanted to get started dressing his arm for its first test of real contact. Cody Joe almost ran over Coach Heart as he raced through the fieldhouse door.

"Whoa there, Cody Joe! Where are you goin' in such a hurry?"

"Coach, Dad said I could try out Tracks' new arm pad today in practice. If he likes it, I might get to play on Thursday. I've got to get ready."

"Well, I've already talked with your father. You can go ahead and go in there and get dressed out for practice, and Tracks can put on the pad. But here's the deal, Cody Joe. You can take your time getting dressed out because you aren't going to participate in a full practice. You will briefly participate in only one drill to see if you can handle contact. You can learn the new blocking schemes we have for Runnels from Coach Bear. He will help you with that."

Coach continued, "I really hope you can play because we need you, but you can't help us if you aren't ready to play your best. We will make a decision that is best for you and the team."

Getting the pad on took longer than he ever imagined. Tracks was leaving nothing to chance and was excruciatingly meticulous in his every move. Every piece of tape had to be perfect. Every fold in the bandage had to allow for flexibility.

However, when finished, Tracks proudly announced, "Cody Joe, This is your Thursday ticket."

"Thanks Tracks. If this works, I'll owe you for the rest of my life. Even if it doesn't work, it means a lot to me that you would put in this kind of time for me."

"Oh, quit patting yourself on the back," Tracks said with a small tear in the corner of his eye. "This ain't just for you. The team needs you out there. So, go make this work."

Cody Joe didn't make it to the practice field until the team had already finished calisthenics. Cody Joe went through his own set of exercise maneuvers to get limber, and just as he was satisfied that he was ready, his moment of truth arrived.

"Cody Joe! Are you ready to go?" asked Coach Heart. "This is it. Let's find out where you stand. Your dad is here. I see him coming through the gate now.

"Mr. Carter, we're going to do a little one-on-one blocking drill with Cody Joe. This should give us a good indication of what he will see and feel in the game. I'm going to put him up against Dirk Bolger because the kid from Runnels is about Dirk's size and ability. Even under the best of circumstances, Cody Joe will have a long afternoon with that No. 68."

Jack never said a word in reply. He simply nodded because he was ready to see what this test offered.

Coach Heart then turned to Bolger, saying, "Dirk, I know everyone on the team is sorry for what Cody Joe has gone through, but I need you to go full tilt in this drill. Holding back won't help Cody Joe or the team. We need to know if he can play. Do you understand that?"

"Yes sir," Dirk said before turning to Cody Joe, "OK, this is just you and me all out."

"You bring what you got, Dirk. I've never been so ready for this drill in my entire life."

But Cody Joe wasn't ready. He never dreamed that with just one lousy week off, he would be so rusty. Dirk solidly beat him in Round 1 as he sent Cody Joe to his knees. Cody Joe was embarrassed, never realizing that there was no pain coming from his arm. In fact, he jumped to his feet and called for another try.

Round 2 went a little better, but if scores were to be given, Bolger had won again. Cody Joe was not pleased and called for another try.

"OK guys, one more time," Coach Heart allowed.

This time Cody Joe exploded on the sound of Coach Heart's whistle, placing his helmet up under Dirk's chin, standing Bolger straight up. Carter's legs then began to relentlessly churn forward as Dirk began to topple over backwards. Carter not only won this battle, but had destroyed his opponent right at the point of contact."

"Man, Jack, that's how we draw it up on the board," Coach Heart bubbled. "You won't see a block at the line of scrimmage better than that. Now, that's blocking."

But Jack was more interested in the arm, asking, "Son, how's the arm?"

The question jolted Cody Joe back into the real world.

He said, "Dad, I just now realized that I never felt a thing. My ego was hurt a lot more than my arm on those first two tries. Dirk's not an easy one to block. He has me by a good 20 pounds."

Jack couldn't help but smile, offering, "Why is it that I knew all along what you were going to say."

Before Jack left, he obtained a promise from Coach Heart that he would keep Cody Joe away from contact drills at least until Thursday so the family could make a final decision. He told Coach Heart, flat out, that the family would make the decision. This decision would not be left up to Coach Heart.

But in Jack's heart, as he left the practice field, he saw no way that he could keep his son from playing. He knew how important this was to Cody Joe. He remembered back to the Little League disappointment and how bad that was for Cody Joe and the family. He thought keeping Cody Joe out of this game might be even worse.

He also knew, in his heart, that one Rue Carter was not going to be on board with what he was thinking. Jack couldn't help but think that no matter what decision was reached there was going to be hell to pay.

"What we have here is a real conundrum," thought Jack as he started the car and headed back to work. It was far too early in the day to face Rue Carter one-on-one.

Chapter 23

RUNNELS II

No sooner had Jack Carter arrived home from work when the battle erupted.

"Now, Rue, listen to me before you go off the deep end here," Jack started, "I think we should let him play..."

But Rue was not having any of it, quickly interrupting her husband with, "Jack Carter, I can't believe you are even entertaining the notion of letting Cody Joe play with that arm. There is no reason in the world that justifies him playing. I think you two have gone crazy."

"Relax a little, honey. All you have to do is to go back to that Little League experience we had just a few years ago. That devastated Cody Joe to the extent I think he is just beginning to shake that rejection. His importance to this team has boosted his self-confidence to new levels.

"Heck, he even has a girlfriend – in the seventh grade. Was that on your radar this year? I didn't think he'd ever speak to a girl.

"He needs this. In fact, I'm going to say this right now. Cody Joe needs this to happen far worse than any other consequence he might suffer. The doctor says the worst case scenario is that he pulls the newly stitched skin apart. That can be fixed, but I'm not sure if we can ever fix a situation where he misses the last two games in a year he seems to have found himself. And the pad works great. I saw it in practice today. He didn't flinch, even in full contact.

"Now you want to push him back into a coma that could carry on for months, years, even a lifetime? Rue, we have to let him play. That's all there is to it."

"Jack, I'm not onboard with this at all. I don't want him to risk his health when there is no purpose to it that I can see. There is no pad in the world that will protect him if he isn't fully healed. The doctor is against it. You know that. And I'm against it if the doctor is against it."

Jack Carter paused for a long while before acquiescing to his wife's call, "OK, Rue, I give up. I think you are wrong on this call, but I'll back you if this is your final decision. But you are going to tell him. I just can't do it. I'd rather see him in blissful pain than to see that face when he's told he's not going to play."

It wasn't long after the rare confrontation between Jack and Rue when Cody Joe came bouncing through the door, arriving home from practice. It was as if his feet barely touched the floor as he skipped across the room headed directly for his mother.

"Mom, the pad was terrific. I didn't even think about the arm out there. Dad saw it all and he said if the pad worked, I'd get to play. I've never been so happy in all my life. Mom, can I play? Dad did say you had to agree. Can I play? C'mon Mom, let me play?"

Rue Carter burst into tears and quickly headed to the bedroom with a final lamentation, "Oh, you two boys. I don't know what I'm going to do with either one of you. Just go out there and kill yourself, and see if I care."

Cody Joe rarely saw his mother cry. He saw her cry once at Aunt Julie's funeral and maybe once again when she got her first ever traffic ticket a couple of years ago. He remembered her saying, "It's just like throwing good money down the drain."

But now he was baffled. He turned toward his father, after Rue Carter had left the room, and asked, "Dad, what did I do wrong?"

"I'm not really sure, son, but I think you are going to play on Thursday."

* * *

Cody Joe was so excited that he had to tell someone. He even got up the nerve to call Veronica at home. Of course, her dad answered the phone, crashing his once-soaring confidence level.

"Oh, Mr. Slade. This is Cody Joe Carter. Could I please speak to Veronica?"

Fortunately, Mr. Slade didn't draw out the process. Carter heard him call for Veronica before laying down the phone.

"Hello," Veronica answered.

"Hi, this is Cody Joe. I just called to tell you that I'm going to play on Thursday against Runnels. Isn't that great?"

"Well, do you really think that is a good idea? It's awfully soon after the fight if you ask me."

"I'll be fine," Cody Joe said. "My mom isn't thrilled about me playing, but I showed them I could do it."

Cody Joe then told her of the week's events at the doctor and at practice before asking, "Are you going to be at the game?"

Veronica said, "I think so. Right now it looks OK."

"Well bye," Cody Joe said, not knowing where else to take the conversation.

"Bye," Veronica said before hanging up the phone.

Cody Joe was a little puzzled. Veronica didn't seem too fired up about him playing. In fact, she didn't seem to be all that interested and she was a bit non-committable to even going to the game. Well, it was just another thing to worry about as two of the three women in his life had thrown him curves on the happiest day of his life.

At least little sister Kate was readable. She was oblivious to everything going on and didn't care if Cody Joe played or not. Her world would be untouched no matter what happened. After all, Thursday was a whole day away, a lifetime in her little world.

Her reaction was simply, "Cody Joe, will you listen to my new piano piece."

"Sure, Kate, I'd love to."

* * *

Cody Joe's Thursday game day started badly. At the morning pep rally, he couldn't find Veronica in the crowd. He saw Jennifer Axel sitting with Alexi Taggert in the bleachers, but there was no Veronica to be found. Usually, Jennifer and Veronica were tied at the hip. He couldn't remember a pep rally this year when they hadn't been together.

To make matters worse, Veronica was not waiting for him outside the door of the gym as was her usual custom. In fact, Jennifer was also a no-show, leaving Cody Joe to wonder what was going on. Alexi, of course, was front and center to greet Pug, at least giving Cody Joe the opportunity to ask about Veronica.

"Alexi, where's Veronica and Jennifer?"

"Well, I don't think Veronica made it to the pep rally today. I didn't see her. Jennifer said she had to go all the way to the front of the school to her locker before her next class."

Alexi and Pug happily strolled away content in each other's company. That left Cody Joe plowing alone to class like an old farm mule tilling a cotton furrow.

Cody Joe knew something wasn't right, but he didn't have any real answers. Cody Joe didn't see Veronica all day at school. He now even wondered if she would be at the game. He didn't see Jennifer either. They were in the same home room class to start the day, but there was no home room on the day of a pep rally. He could always depend on Jennifer to tell him what was going on, but he was without his chief informant on the day he needed her most.

The school day seemed long to Cody Joe. He couldn't stop thinking about Veronica. Her unexplained absence was driving him crazy. He tried to tell himself that he was over thinking this whole scenario, but his mind was telling him something was amiss. He didn't like the feelings that loose ends tend to amplify.

This was just the beginning of the worst Thursday in Cody Joe's young life. Friday wouldn't be any better.

* * *

Cody Joe received permission to leave school at 2 p.m., 30 minutes prior to the rest of the team, to get his arm padded for the game with Big Spring Runnels, which carried a 4 p.m. starting time.

That meant he had to walk alone to the fieldhouse, giving him no opportunity to ask some of his teammates if they had seen Veronica.

Tracks was already waiting for Cody Joe to walk through the door. He had all his taping tools at the ready and couldn't wait to get his hands on that arm.

"Cody Joe, I'm going to fix you up like never before. When I get through, you won't feel a sledge hammer hitting you."

Tracks got straight to his task, creating an arm cocoon that any self-respecting caterpillar would love.

Cody Joe felt good about his arm protection. He didn't fear any physical pain that might come, but his heart was heavy, his stomach churning and couldn't seem to control his thoughts. Rue Carter would simply say he was out of sorts.

It wasn't until Cody Joe saw Veronica, Jennifer and Alexi all sitting together in the stands that he felt a little better. At least Veronica was at the game. She even waved at him from a distance. This small token of acknowledgement allowed him to place his focus back on the game. He entered the game with his mind at peace. But for Cody Joe Carter it was a shallow peace as he was about to discover.

* * *

The first game between Snyder and Runnels had been played in a virtual rain storm in Big Spring. Runnels won that meeting by a sloppy 6-2 margin, handing the Blue Devils their only loss of the season. Both teams entered this contest with identical 7-1 season records, since Runnels had already finished a two-game split with Sweetwater.

This particular afternoon didn't offer a single cloud in the West Texas sky to mar the second meeting between two squads trying to win the seventh grade title. There was, however, a November nip in the air that would cause any self-respecting Texan to pull his coat collar up around his neck. But as they say in Texas, "It's perfect weather for a football game." In Texas, it's always good weather for football.

Even though this was a seventh grade game, it had generated a lot of interest in Snyder, giving the local team its largest home crowd of the season with around 400 showing up on this chilly day. Title aspirations always run deep in the Lone Star State. Championships are coveted on every level of play.

The significance of this game was not lost on Cody Joe. As much as he loved baseball, football was the path to respect and honor in the community. If you played football, you were idolized by young and old alike. But if you won a championship, you would be remembered forever. At least, that was Cody Joe's take on it. After all, the eighth grade was undefeated last season and seventh graders and people were still talking about them. That may not ring the definition bell for the term being remembered "forever," but in Cody Joe's eyes, the eighth grade team, which was also undefeated this year, was a wonder of the known world, or at least Snyder, Texas, which was pretty much the same thing in Cody Joe's thinking.

So, this game represented a chance for this band of seventh graders to carve out a unique respect of their own. It was, also, a chance to exact a little revenge for that earlier loss to Runnels. What was not even considered in Cody Joe's thinking was that the team on the other side of the field carried the same dreams and aspirations as his Blue Devils. They had come to Snyder to set themselves up for a championship.

By the time the refs opened play with the blast of a whistle, both teams were begging to get at each other. It didn't take long to prove the point. The Blue Devils took a big hit early when end Mac Cone twisted his right ankle on the opening kickoff and was out for the game. Later, in the first quarter, big Butch Cassidy was sidelined when a Runnels player stepped on his arm, driving a nylon spike through the skin and into muscle.

Cassidy was in great pain. However, he pleaded with Coach Heart to put him back in. He badgered Tracks to make a pad for him like he had done for Cody Joe. Instead, he was sent to the hospital for stitches, screaming in protest at the top of his lungs the whole way.

This left Coach Heart in a real bind. He had no true fullback other than Cassidy. He was in his own ring, without a good counter move, against a team that was physical and fast. Runnels could stop the sweep, as it had proved in the first game. Snyder's best success had always been running up Runnels' gut. Now the ability to do that had been drained like pulling the plug on a dam.

Coach Heart had a good idea that this game was over even though it was still a scoreless tie in the first quarter. He moved Hank Cline to fullback and put Kirby Tanner in at Cline's halfback slot. It was the best shot he could take even though it had limited possibilities. At least, Cline knew the plays as a fullback even though he had very little game or practice experience. Coach Heart had used him at fullback in a couple of blowouts against Lamesa and Goliad just as a hedge against a Cassidy injury. But now, his worst fears had come to fruition and Cline was no Cassidy against the enormous Runnels defensive line.

Meanwhile, Cody Joe was having the game of his life. He was doing a fair job of single-handedly keeping Runnels' bevy of large backs under wraps. It seemed like every time Runnels ran the ball, Cody Joe hit the right gap and laid the wood to an unsuspecting runner. Runnels didn't have the speed in its backfield to run wide, so they tried to bludgeon the Blue Devils to death with their powerful running backs.

Cody Joe felt no pain from his arm and even seemed emboldened to take on the big backs with his new pad. Tracks was right about not feeling a sledge hammer hit. In fact, he was using the pad like his own personal sledge hammer. And Runnels was paying the price.

With Runnels mired deep in its own territory, a Runnels back broke the line of scrimmage and looked to be off to the races. However, Cody Joe outstretched his padded arm as far as he could and found a direct hit on the ball. The pigskin fell to the dead grass, bringing a redirection of focus to the game. Cody Joe was falling forward as the ball came free. He did get his good hand on the ball, but it squirted back toward the Runnels goal. Stony Wall and Pug Preston both had a shot at the ball, but it also eluded them. Two Runnels players took their turn in trying to corral the wayward prize, but this show more resembled an old-fashioned Keystone Cops episode than a championship football game.

Finally, as fate would rightly reward, Cody Joe fell on the greased pig at the Runnels 6-yard line, setting up the best scoring opportunity by either team in the game just minutes before the half.

Quarterback Lee Line called four plays that netted only two total yards as Runnels somehow held. Coach Heart let each of his running backs have a try, but nothing worked. Line's quarterback keeper off tackle was the fourth down killer as he was sacked for a yard loss. In fact, Tanner's sweep right was the best play of the short-lived drive, good for three yards, but no touchdown.

Heart was disgusted with himself. He knew his team was short-handed on offense with Cone and Cassidy out. He now reasoned that he should have let Henry Styles try a short field goal. At this point in the game, three points would have looked awfully good.

At the half, Coach Heart tried to put a good spin on the game. He praised his defense and urged them to keep fighting. He challenged his offense by saying this was the time to step up and be in position to win a championship. In his heart, he didn't possess much hope. His team looked tired. He was hoping Runnels felt the same way.

The fans in the stands were awe-struck by how physical these seventh grade teams were. There were the usual grandstand quarterbacking calls, but Jack Carter was proud of Cody

Joe. He had never seen him play with such intensity. Rue was miserable. She just knew that the next play would be the one to send Cody Joe back to the hospital. Cassidy's injury made her even more apprehensive. In her mind, this was turning out to be one of the longest games in history.

The second half was more of the same with neither team able to gain any real foothold on the situation. Then, near the end of the third quarter, Runnels got a break. Snyder's Jay Coy, a defensive back, got into a skirmish with a Big Spring player, and received a 15-yard penalty, giving Runnels the ball at the Snyder 24-yard line. That was Runnels' deepest penetration of the game thus far.

Runnels' big fullback then rumbled to the 10-yard line. The visitors cracked into the scoring column on the next play with a little swing pass that covered the needed distance. Runnels missed the extra point, but the bleeding had started. Even seventh graders were smart enough to figure out that this was a damaging blow, considering how the game had gone up to this point.

Snyder could never mount a serious offensive threat. Runnels, on the other hand, mounted a 67-yard, fourth quarter drive for another score and ended up a 12-0 winner.

It was over. The championship hopes of the Blue Devils were pretty much destroyed. It was the first time to lose at home. There was nothing about this loss that felt good. Even the sterling play of Cody Joe was not enough for him to gain consolation. Tears fell from his eyes. Other teammates were also openly crying. To a man, they felt like they had let down their coaches, fans and themselves. It was worse than a nightmare because this was real.

* * *

But Cody Joe was dealing with more than just a loss. He had to find Veronica. He wiped the tears from his face and headed for the stands on the west side of the stadium. Meeting him on the way were Alexi and Jennifer, who were headed toward Pug. Of course, Jennifer was hoping that Kirby Tanner would be close by.

Cody Joe asked Jennifer, "Where's Veronica?"

"Oh, she had to leave. Her mother was here to pick her up. She told me she would see you tomorrow."

Jennifer quickly left Cody Joe standing alone as she raced to catch up with Alexi. Cody Joe didn't know what to think, but he did catch a glimpse of Veronica leaving the game through the stadium gate on the north end of the field.

It was then that Rue Carter hugged her son, asking, "Cody Joe, are you OK?"

Cody Joe gave her an answer that she didn't want to hear, "No, Mom, I'm not OK."

But his woeful answer had absolutely nothing to do with his arm.

Chapter 24

A SECRET
REVEALED

R ue was fully aware that this was not the right time to confront Cody Joe. She knew he was upset about losing the game, but she couldn't help but think that there was something more involved.

Still, she somehow managed to keep her mouth closed, hoping that her son would eventually reveal what he was so obviously upset about. She did tend to his arm and was vastly relieved to see that she could find no further harm was done. In fact, she couldn't detect any difference than when she last inspected the arm Thursday morning.

As for Cody Joe, he spent most of Thursday night moping around the house, feeling sorry for himself. He thought about the game, reliving every agonizing moment. He thought of a dozen moments in the game where he could have done something different to help change the outcome.

He failed to realize that he had actually played a solid game under bad circumstances. His arm had come through the battle seemingly none the worse for wear. He should actually be happy.

But of course, Veronica Slade also weighed heavily on his mind. It was tough enough losing, but the quick disappearance of his girlfriend after the game, coupled with a no-show at the pep rally, did more than anything to send Cody Joe Carter into a tailspin of misery and uncertainty.

He just knew he had done something wrong to offend Veronica. But what?

"What could she be mad at me about?" Cody Joe wondered over and over. He knew he had a lot of faults as far as boyfriends go, but he couldn't think of a single thing he had done to cause the light-hearted Veronica Slade to shun him so.

He wanted to call her, but he hated the thought of discussing this matter on the phone. Also, he was afraid her father might answer the phone again. He might even ask Cody Joe to stop calling Veronica at home.

The perils of calling seemed to be too great at this point in time, so Cody Joe continued to sulk while waiting for the time to pass, hoping he could see Veronica face-to-face on Friday morning.

* * *

The next morning Cody Joe was surprised to see Jennifer Axel waiting for him at the bus platform. She heartedly waved at him as he stepped off the bus.

Cody Joe walked straight for her, saying, "What's up, Jennifer?"

"Cody Joe, Veronica wants to see you before school if possible. She told me she could meet you at her locker if you agree. Will you do it?"

"Sure I'll do it. I want to see her too, but Jennifer, what is this all about? Why has she been avoiding me?"

"I would prefer that you talk with Veronica about this, Cody Joe. I'll always be your friend, but this is something she should tell you."

"But I don't understand any of this, Jennifer, and I know you know what this is all about. Give me a heads up before I go see her at least."

"I promised Veronica to give you the message. She asked me not to say anything else. So, I have to keep that promise," Jennifer said as she turned to walk away. But she made a half turn and looked back at Cody Joe, "After all, she's my friend too."

Cody Joe set a torrid pace toward Veronica's locker, but part of him wanted to avoid the meeting altogether. Everything Jennifer said seemed to be so ominous. He knew in his heart that the outcome of this meeting was not going to produce a good result.

As he made his turn down the hallway toward Veronica's locker, he could see her standing there waiting for him just as Jennifer had promised.

"Here goes nothing," Cody Joe muttered to himself as he approached what he thought was the most beautiful girl in the world. Even through the pain of the moment, she took his breath away when he laid eyes on her. He couldn't deal with the thought that he might lose this precious jewel in his life.

He braced himself for the worst and managed to blurt out, "Hi, Veronica. Jennifer told me to meet you here."

Veronica looked him straight in the eye, boring a hole into his very soul, "Cody Joe, thanks for coming. I have something to tell you that's going to be very hard for me to say. I want you to listen and let me get through it. I just don't know how you are going to take this, but it's going to break my heart."

Cody Joe said, "I really want to know what is on your mind. I know I've done something wrong, but I'm willing to correct it, no matter what it is. I've never intended to hurt you, ever."

"Oh, Cody Joe, you just don't know. You haven't done anything. Believe me none of this is about you except for the fact that you've been caught in the middle of something neither of us can control."

At this point, the first tears began to roll down Veronica's face. It was as if she was being tortured into a disturbing confession.

"The truth is, Cody Joe, that my Dad has been given a new job in San Antonio. My whole family is moving there next Friday. We're moving from Snyder and we are never coming back."

This unexpected news was like a spike being driven through his heart. Cody Joe's whole body went numb. He could barely stand on his own two feet. He had never experienced a blow like this in his entire life. Even the disappointment of Little League paled in comparison. He wanted to say something, but two things prevented him from saying anything. First, his body shut down on him and he literally couldn't talk. Second, he really didn't know what to say. Everything he thought of sounded stupid.

What could he say? "It'll be OK," "Don't worry, it'll all work out," "I'm sorry you're going to be gone," or "I guess it was meant to be."

No, nothing sounded right at a time like this. In fact, Cody Joe wanted to crawl in a corner and cry. He felt like he had been kicked in the stomach.

Veronica, however, took up the slack and continued to talk even though her mutterings were coming through woeful sobbing.

"Cody Joe, I promise I didn't want this to happen, but Dad says we must go. I'll miss you more than you will ever imagine, but I know you will find another girlfriend. You are one of the most popular boys in school. I was just lucky to have been your girlfriend even if it was for a short time.

"Here, I want you to have your bracelet back. I thank you for letting me wear it. It always made me feel special."

Finally, Cody Joe broke in, saying, "No, no, I want you to

keep the bracelet. At least. I'll know it is with you.

"I can't believe you are leaving so soon. We never really got to know each other. I wish I had talked to you more. I wasted all our time together."

"Oh, Cody Joe, I didn't want it to end like this."

With that Veronica flung her arms around Cody Joe and gave him a big kiss full on the mouth. She then turned and fled down the hallway sobbing and without looking back, leaving Cody Joe standing alone in his misery. As he watched her flee, he failed to even notice several snickering students, who had seen the unexpected all-out kiss in the middle of the Snyder Junior High School hallway.

Chapter 25

THE PLAN

Cody Joe was completely dazed by Veronica's unexpected news. He thought she was mad at him for something he had done. Instead, this news was even worse than that. She was going to be out of his life in a week. This was not something for which he could offer an apology. He was stuck with an awful result and he had to live with it, like it or not.

He felt empty, alone and discarded. Within the passing of the last three minutes, his life had crumbled into a lifeless mass of protoplasm. He had no girlfriend, no future with one Veronica Slade, and he felt he couldn't bear the consequence.

Cody Joe had a hard time moving on. He was just standing in the middle of the hall staring in the direction of Veronica's disappearance. Other students were passing by him on the way to homeroom, staring at him all the while. Cody Joe never noticed, as if he were in a vacuum. He longed to be somewhere else, anywhere else, but he couldn't seem to move. He wished he was at home. This grown-up seventh grader wouldn't even mind if his mother would take him in her arms like she used to do when things went all wrong in his life. But he thought he was far too old for that luxury now, even though he desperately wanted her to simply hold him without saying a word.

Finally, he began a slow shuffle toward class, as his mind swirled with questions that had no answers. There was no way to change the direction of this situation short of Veronica's father getting fired before next Friday.

Still, Cody Joe had a week before Veronica would walk out of his life. He didn't want to waste it. He thought about seeing her at the Tigers' game tonight, but suddenly realized Snyder was on the road against Lamesa. Then an idea hit him.

This gave him the impetus to move toward class where he planned to have a meeting with Jennifer. She could help him set his plan in motion.

* * *

"Jennifer, you have to help me," Cody Joe pleaded, as he raced to explain his plan before the home room bell started ringing. "I have to be with Veronica one more time. Can you get her to come with you to the movies at the Palace tonight?

"I need to pull this off. If you will do this, I'll make sure that Kirby Tanner is there. I know Kirby would enjoy sitting by you."

Cody Joe knew this promise would be extremely appealing to Jennifer, but he had no idea if Kirby was even available tonight. He was pretty sure Tanner would like a "date" with Jennifer, but he had not even approached Kirby about such a clandestine meeting.

"Well, Cody Joe, I'll try everything I can to pull this off, but have you even talked to Veronica about going to the movies?"

"Oh no, she doesn't know anything about it, but I bet her parents would let her go if she went with you."

"I'll try, but I don't even know if my parents will allow me to go."

"Tell them the whole gang is going. I'll get Pug and Alexi. I'll bet they will go. And I bet we can count on Tracks and Butch to come. Tumbler might even come. We'll have everybody there."

It was at that point when the school's first bell rang in the day with a shrill clanging that brought the class to total silence. Well, it would have been total silence except for the lone loud voice of Jennifer Axel, who loudly proclaimed for the entire class to hear, "Yeah Cody Joe, but how are you going to be there? Don't you know you are grounded?"

* * *

Cody Joe was sent into a panic attack by Jennifer's astute proclamation. He had forgotten that he had been grounded "forever" by his father after an unwise choice to paper his coach's house on Halloween night.

Jack Carter was not one to lift his stiff ban after less than a full week. Cody Joe was sure his plan was being engulfed by flames even as he thought about it. Besides, he wasn't the only one grounded. Pug and Tracks had also been sidelined. However, Cassidy and Tanner were still free as were Alexi, Jennifer and Veronica. They just had to have permission, which had to be a lot easier to accomplish than breaking a "grounded" ruling.

As hopeless as it all seemed, Cody Joe decided to press forward with his idea. He talked with all the guys. Pug was doubtful even though he thought he could be included if Mr. Carter allowed Cody Joe to go. Otherwise, he was going to be sitting at home. Kirby jumped at the idea and told Cody Joe he would be glad to be there even if Cody Joe didn't come.

So, when Cody Joe arrived at home, after school on Friday, he correctly discerned that his best course of action was to take the matter up with his mother first. He quickly found Rue in the kitchen and told her the whole story. It was unusual for him to gush forth like this to his mother, but he left out no detail. He told her of the tearful confession by Veronica, of his plan to see her one more time and his predicament of being grounded at a time when he desperately needed mercy.

Cody Joe, unapologetically, told her for the first time how he felt about Veronica and how he was devastated to hear she was leaving town. Rue's heart broke for him because of the news, but she was also extremely proud of him for the way he came to her and opened his heart. He was growing up, she thought.

Rue put her arms around her son, in a loving manner, while telling him, "Cody Joe, you have to tell your father the same thing you've told me. I agreed with him when he grounded you for what you did on Halloween. You must learn to respect the property of others. It will be up to your father on whether or not the grounding holds for tonight."

Cody Joe's heart sank at hearing her pronouncement. "Dad will never let me go," he thought.

* * *

Jack arrived home about an hour later and Cody Joe went to him quickly because there wasn't much time to wrap up all the details of this proposed date night.

The meeting with his father didn't go as well as Cody Joe had hoped. Jack Carter didn't hand out punishment lightly and he was not quick to divert, shorten or lessen the penalty of such severity. He remained firm on his demands.

"Son, I'm truly sorry for your current situation, but you should have thought about these kinds of things before you went off on a reckless and unprofitable adventure that carried no merit or honor with it. You must know that I am disappointed in you for your actions and you must pay the price. You're not leaving this house."

"But Dad, I'll do whatever you want for the rest of the year. Just give me this one night with Veronica. I promise, you won't hear another word out of me."

"No, son, I told you the punishment. I'm a little surprised that you even have the nerve to ask me to break the grounding rule. You deserve much worse than that. To tell the truth, I thought I was going easy on you."

Cody Joe raced to his room, threw himself on his bed and started crying.

Chip asked, "Hey, Cody Joe, you upset or something?"

"Get out of here Chip," Cody Joe screamed, throwing a football at him just as Chip's behind disappeared through the bedroom door.

Rue couldn't help but hear what Jack had told her son. She was not happy with Jack.

"Jack, I want to talk with you right now in the bedroom," she said as she stomped away.

Jack knew what this meant even before going to the bedroom. He knew Rue was mad and that his decision on Cody Joe was going to be changed, as biblically put, "in the twinkling of an eye."

In the bedroom, Rue said, "Jack, we've made decisions together in all the years of our marriage. I absolutely supported you when you grounded Cody Joe after Halloween. It was the right thing to do. But don't you go and confuse punishment with what that kid is going through right now. His world has crumbled, and you won't even let him breathe. He needs to see that girl tonight and she needs to see him. I don't support you on this and I never will. You need to let that boy go. He has poured out his little heart to the both of us and you need to acknowledge that."

With that, Rue walked out of the bedroom and marched straight to the kitchen. Jack called in Cody Joe and said, "Your

Momma says you are going to the movie tonight. I hope you have a great time."

Chapter 26

THE DATE

C ody Joe arrived at the Palace early. He felt he was responsible for this "date" night since it was his idea, and everyone had to jump through a lot of hoops in order to satisfy Cody Joe's plan to be with Veronica Slade one more time.

The Palace theater lights were still on, prior to the first showing of the night's double feature. It was western fare of "Buchanan Rides Again" with Randolph Scott and "Gunman's Walk," starring Van Heflin.

Cody Joe had staked out a row close to the middle of the theater. He expected a large movie crowd tonight, so he wanted to make sure everyone had a seat together. It wasn't that the two movies slated for screening demanded a large following, but all Friday nights at the Palace were crowded, if the Tigers weren't playing at home, no matter what was showing.

The first to come prancing down the aisle was Kirby Tanner. He was excited to be meeting Jennifer Axel. Cody Joe quickly showed him where to sit, leaving two seats in between the two boys.

"Jennifer and Veronica always sit together, so I need you to be on the end," Cody Joe told Tanner. "The others should be here soon."

It was just then that Pug and Alexi walked in together, so Cody Joe elected to sit by his cousin and let Pug sit on the far end.

Butch Cassidy and Kevin Tumbler both showed up and

sat on the far side of Pug. It looked like most of the gang had escaped the "grounded" sentence except Tracks, who was still banned from society despite the pleas on his behalf.

Since Tracks didn't have a girlfriend, his parents saw little reason why he should even be at this event whether he was grounded or not. In other words, Tracks had no real bargaining chips with which to offer a feasible case.

Veronica and Jennifer were not far behind and took their pre-arranged seating, just as the lights went down for the cartoon feature. Cody Joe thought Veronica was the most beautiful girl he had ever seen. He felt bad when the lights went down, and he couldn't see her very well.

Then panic set in. Cody Joe instantly realized that he had prepared for this entire evening together with Veronica but had failed to plan out what they could talk about. Everything he thought about saying seemed wrong.

Possible conversation starters raced through his head like, "Was it cold outside?" He knew the answer to that because he had just come in himself.

"I'm so glad you could come; we may never get to do this again." No, he couldn't say that. It might make her feel awful.

"I wish you weren't leaving." "I wish you could stay here." "I wish your Dad would die." These were all topics Cody Joe felt he should avoid.

This "date" idea had come to Cody Joe in a rapid succession of events. He had admirably put the plan in motion, with great success, only to leave out any substance for the date. How could he possibly tell her the things he wanted to say without making her cry again, like when he met her in front of the lockers this morning?

He surprised even himself when the first words out of his mouth to Veronica were, "You want some popcorn?"

* * *

It wasn't long before Mandy Mayor, and some of her loyal minions, came down the aisle, assessing the crowd as they looked for seating. Of course, she spotted Veronica and Cody Joe as her group found seats two rows in front of the woeful couple.

"Oh, Veronica, I'm so sorry to hear that you are leaving town. You must be devastated to be leaving Cody Joe," Mandy blurted out above the sound coming from the theater's speakers. "We're going to miss you, but don't worry one little bit. We're going to take real good care of Cody Joe."

Cody Joe went limp in his seat after Mandy's unwelcome greeting. He couldn't read Veronica's reaction. On the surface, she seemed unfazed, but Cody Joe was almost certain Veronica would love to stand up and slap Mandy's face. And if Veronica didn't have that feeling, Cody Joe sure did. Mandy Mayor may be the best looking and most popular girl in school, but she loved making other people feel small.

Cody Joe did have enough gumption to turn to Veronica and declare, "Don't pay any attention to her. She's always that way. She's just trying to get under your skin."

Veronica replied, "She doesn't bother me. She hardly knows who I am. In fact, she wouldn't know me at all if it wasn't for you. And she's probably right. She has a lot of friends, who would probably love to go out with you after I'm gone.

"I just want you to know that I don't want to tie you down after I leave. You'll find another girlfriend soon. I'm sure of that, but I sure hope you will keep me as your girlfriend at least until next Friday."

"Oh. I will," Cody Joe proudly proclaimed. "I don't want another girlfriend. I just want you to stay."

As predicted, Cody Joe had said the wrong thing. Veronica was crying once again. He wanted to avoid making her cry, yet he opened the door for a flood of tears. He didn't know what to say, so he said nothing and continued to hold her hand.

Veronica sobbed mournfully, for the better part of the next four or five minutes, before reaching in her purse for a handkerchief to dry her tears. Of course, Cody Joe was terribly afraid of saying another word to her because it might produce another crying outbreak. Cody Joe simply couldn't stand to see Veronica trying to float the ark anew.

Veronica eased the tension after composing herself. She understood that her crying had upset her boyfriend, and that was not her intention, even though her emotions had gotten the better of her. She turned, looked at him right in the eye and declared, "Cody Joe, I think I would like that popcorn now."

* * *

The rest of the night went without a hitch, except for the fact that little of importance was said between the two heartbroken souls. Those around Cody Joe and Veronica hardly noticed their presence. Kirby and Jennifer were laughing and giggling throughout the two movies. They were becoming much closer and Kirby was beginning to think that Jennifer was just the right girl for him. Pug and Alexi were always comfortable around each other while Butch and Kevin spent most of the night tossing popcorn at Mandy's entourage two rows in front of them. The girls acted like they were disgusted with their tormentors, but nothing was done to stop the junior high flirtation ritual.

Cody Joe, however, felt like the entire night had been a failure, and he powerfully sensed it was totally his fault. He should have planned better. He should have told Veronica how he feels about her. But he didn't know how to do that, and he couldn't cope with those dreaded tears pouring from those beautiful eyes. In Cody Joe Carter's way of thinking, the night had been an utter disaster. He felt worse now than ever before.

The truth was that Veronica Slade would be leaving town in a week, and nothing under heaven's sun would change that.

Chapter 27

SWEETWATER WEEK

On Sunday morning, after the ill-fated date with Veronica Slade, Cody Joe Carter found himself in the next to last row at Colonial Hill Baptist Church with his head resting on the pew in front of him, offering a somewhat confused, but honest, prayer to God.

"Dear Lord, I know you don't want to talk with me right now because you are angry with me. I know you are mightily displeased with me because you are taking away my girlfriend and I'm grounded, probably for the rest of my childhood.

"I know I've done some bad things, but I really don't understand why the punishment is so severe. Now, the papering of Coach's house was plain wrong. I get that. But I've tried my best to be good with Veronica. I know I have problems opening up with her. I have a hard time talking to her and explaining how I feel, but I've never set out to outright hurt her. I know that I've made her cry, but not intentionally. I don't understand why she has to go away. Why am I no good for her? Please let me know.

"My Dad is always saying that you are all-powerful, so I know that you could make it where her family could stay so we could be together. But I also know you aren't going to do that. Her dad has to be at his new job a week from tomorrow, so the decision has already been made by him and you. I feel like I've got no chance in this matter. What am I supposed to do, Dear Lord?" In his seventh grade mind, he was still trying to figure out the workings of the Lord, but at least he knew where he needed to turn.

* * *

Cody Joe woke up on Monday morning only to find Snyder enveloped in a thick, white fog that covered not only the West Texas landscape, but Cody Joe's soul as well. The weekend of "Date Night" had not given the grieving seventh grader one bit of closure or comfort for the future that awaited him. He was drowning in his sorrow and the fog only added to the gloom he felt in his heart.

When Cody Joe pulled open the drapes to his window, he couldn't even see the row of houses across the street. He felt the same way about his future. He couldn't grasp in his young brain any picture that showed him a path to the future without Veronica.

The fog persisted throughout the morning as Cody Joe walked to his homeroom class from the bus. He gave Jennifer Axel the expected, "Hi," salutation, but said little else to her. The truth of the matter is that neither one really knew how to respond to each other. Not only was Cody Joe losing his girlfriend, but Jennifer was losing her best friend. Both were virtually inconsolable.

It was that way most of the week. Cody Joe and Jennifer rarely talked and that was about as rare as the sun setting in the east. Cody Joe did walk Veronica to class on occasion when the schedule allowed, and he ate lunch with her daily, but little was said. Neither one could even muster enough courage to cast a glance in each other's direction for fear that tears would fall. All in all, it was a miserable week.

It was also a miserable week at football practice for Carter. On Monday afternoon for the week's first practice, the fog broke, leaving bright skies with a hint of early November nip in the air. As far as practice was concerned, it couldn't have been a better day. But for Cody Joe, it proved to be one more example of how the world had turned against him.

* * *

When the offensive drills began, Coach Heart wanted to work on a simple dive play off tackle where he thought Sweetwater was most vulnerable in personnel, based on film from the previous meeting between the two teams. Carter was supposed to perform a rather simple cross-block with tackle Dirk Bolger to his left. When the play was run, Bolger took on the defensive player to his right in good execution, but Carter didn't reach the defender on his left in time to make his block and the play was dead in the water.

"Run it again," Coach Heart screamed. "We have to be able to run this play to perfection on Thursday, and Cody Joe, that wasn't perfection."

The team ran the play again...and again...and again, but couldn't get it right. And, yes, it was Cody Joe's fault each and every time.

Without knowing it, Coach Heart actually hit the nail on the head when he said, "Cody Joe, we've run this play a thousand times this year and you've probably gotten it right 900 times. Today, you're acting like your girlfriend has left you or something. Quit moping around out there and do your job."

Coach Heart may not have known the full meaning of his piercing arrow of words, but the kids sure did. Some giggled while others, like Pug, felt bad for Cody Joe and remained silent. For Cody Joe, it was a devastating blow to his pride and left him in an even deeper depression if that was even possible.

When the team ran the play again, Cody Joe drove the defender into the ground with a vicious block. The savage blow came from a pent-up rage that was rarely seen coming forth from the mostly mild-mannered Carter. He had not displayed this kind of reaction to anyone except for Nate Christian early in the season.

"Now that's more like it, Cody Joe," Heart said. "You haven't completely quit on us. There's still a light shining in there somewhere."

The comment didn't make Cody Joe feel any better. His heart was still racing. His soul was still empty. His anger was now all-consuming. And anyone who crossed ways with Cody Joe for the rest of the day would feel his wrath, either through words or action. He was in no mood to consider the feelings for, or criticism from, his teammates.

The coaches loved the new Cody Joe. He was showing them a new, upgraded brand of the old Carter. It worked well for football, but not so much for the devastated psyche of a young pre-teen. Cody Joe felt like he was lost. He didn't even know if he wanted to play football anymore. He didn't even know if he wanted a chance to play against Sweetwater. That in itself was a serious thought crossing the brain of a young male who lived in Snyder, Texas.

* * *

On Tuesday morning, on the way to homeroom from the bus, Cody Joe ran into Butch Cassidy and a gaggle of his friends. Of course, Butch was out of sorts since learning that he couldn't play Thursday in the season's last game because of his injured arm.

"Hey, Cody Joe, I heard you didn't have a great practice

yesterday. Is that girl getting you down? Most of us would give a leg to play in that game. I guess playing Sweetwater doesn't mean much to you."

Cody Joe bristled at the comment and took a step toward Butch, facing him eye-to-eye, saying, "Don't push me Butch. I can't help it if you are injured, but don't take it out on me."

"Oh, you want to get a bit uppity, huh," Butch said between clenched lips. "You take me on and you'll get something you'll never forget."

It was at this same moment, while Pug Preston was walking Alexi Taggert to class, that he heard this confrontation in the beginning stages of escalation. Pug literally threw down his books and raced to the side of his two friends, leaving Alexi in his proverbial dust.

"Hey guys, stop this right now, both of you. We're all friends here and we don't need this kind of bull out here in public. Just back off from each other. I'm not going to ask you two to shake hands right now, but, Butch, you go on now, and, Cody Joe, you get on to class. Hopefully, we can get this all sorted out later. It just makes no sense to destroy friendships over some badly chosen words. Now get going, both of you."

Neither Cody Joe or Butch were in the mood to apologize, but both did as Pug commanded, reluctantly passing each other with heavy scowls etched on their faces.

For the rest of the week, up to game time on Thursday, no one dared confront Cody Joe or Butch with any smart remarks. Everyone instinctively knew that these were two powder kegs ready to blow. No one in their right mind would ever want to pick a fight with the heavy-set Butch because he could probably take on anyone in the school and come out on top. And while Cody Joe was not known for his fighting prowess, he had lived through a knife fight and his eyes now showed an anger that might come unhinged even with the slightest off-target remark. So, the best course of action would be to avoid both of them.

However, Veronica Slade didn't avoid Cody Joe even though it might have been easier if she had. Cody Joe wasn't himself. The confrontation with Butch didn't help, but he was losing his girlfriend, his coach was ragging on him, he was grounded and God had left him all alone. He also made a 76 on his recent math test and he was somehow going to have to explain that to his mother and father.

Regardless, he stayed at Veronica's side throughout this ordeal even though he was totally incapable of giving her any comforting counsel. However, Veronica cherished her time with Cody Joe. She was miserable when he was away from her. She was grasping to keep every second she could have with him. Of course, it was an ill-fated clinging that existed between the two, but first love offers both enlightenment and tragedy in a neatly wrapped package of discovery. Cody Joe and Veronica were now in the midst of learning that hard-taught lesson.

Chapter 28

FINALES

On Wednesday, the night before the big game with Sweetwater, Snyder got what is called by West Texans, a gully-washer.

A gully-washer is a heavy rain that comes down in a short period of time, flooding all low-lying areas, roads and creeks. Deep Creek had run over its banks, flooding much of the downtown area. Many intersections were deemed too risky to cross.

However, school was not canceled, even though many students wouldn't be able to find a way to school. Cody Joe caught a bus at West Elementary that was able to cross the rivers of water to SJHS. But the bus had problems maneuvering through the maze of streets because of flooding and had to take some streets that were not on the scheduled route. The bus, also, had to go very slow.

Why was this important? This was the morning of the weekly pep rally in the gym. They delayed the start of the Sweetwater pep rally by 15 minutes, but had already started when Cody Joe finally arrived. He quickly looked to see if Veronica and Jennifer were in their regular seats. They were, so Cody Joe quietly joined his teammates on the gym floor.

With 15 minutes cut off of the 40-minute rally, things went quickly. Coach Heart was called on to present his game captains. He picked Pug Preston and Lester Jarvis. This sent waves of excitement through the portion of stands where Alexi Taggert resided.

"Oh, my gosh. Did you hear that, Sally?"

Sally Hall, Alexi's best friend, replied, "You are so lucky to be going with him. Just think about it, he's the game captain for the most important game of the year. He must be really good."

Jarvis was picked by design by Coach Heart. He knew the running back would have to have a big day with Butch Cassidy on the sideline. After all, Butch had been such a big part in the previous win against Sweetwater.

But then the announcement came, "We really don't know if the games will be played today or canceled. Our field is muddy but it's not flooded. The question is, can Sweetwater make the trip? We will just have to wait and see."

This news crushed the seventh grade Blue Devils just thinking about the biggest game of the year not being merely postponed, but canceled altogether. The boys started gathering around Coach Heart for some more definitive information.

Heart said, "Now, wait a minute. We don't know what is going to happen right now. We are in touch with them hourly on this situation. They want to play, the same as us, but there are parents and both school boards talking about this matter. We'll just wait and see.

Cody Joe was greatly impacted by this news. This could mean that Veronica wouldn't be able to see him play the final game of the season and she would be gone on Friday. He was distraught.

Thursday proved to be the longest day of the year for the young Blue Devils. Few were paying attention in class and this was clearly seen in both the seventh and eighth grades. The smart teachers just decided to review some things, but took on nothing new. Besides, there were many absentees on this day.

Cody Joe did spend some time with Veronica. He walked

her to her homeroom class, ate lunch with her in the cafeteria (avoiding the chili sandwich at the Snack Shack) and they walked out under the trees by the swollen creek bed that was usually dry. It was somewhat muddy, but neither seemed to mind. They were together, and that was all that mattered.

Still, it was awkward. Neither could bring themselves to talk about the looming departure of one Veronica Slade. It was just too painful. Instead, they talked about the game and how it might not even be played. Both felt terrible that the game might not be on. It had quit raining. However, more rain was still in the forecast.

It was 1:30 p.m. before the announcement came on the classroom speakers.

"Both eighth grade and seventh grade games with Sweetwater will be played today, beginning at 4 p.m. Much of the flood waters have receded significantly. So, go Blue Devils. Beat Sweetwater."

There was a huge eruption of joy, especially among the two football teams. Teachers basically lost control for the rest of the afternoon. At least, the football boys were released at 2 p.m. to make their trek to the fieldhouse. Sweetwater was on its way to Snyder.

* * *

Coach Heart didn't give his team an emotional speech before the game. With a controlled voice, he offered, "Guys this is it, your last game in the seventh grade. You have worked hard and you have done everything we have asked of you. Now, how do you want to be remembered? You have to understand, even though you are only in the seventh grade, that there are expectations in Snyder, Texas, when it comes to beating Sweetwater. We've had a wonderful season, so let's go out there and end it right."

The team exploded in a frenzy of back slapping, head butting and general seventh grade celebratory behavior. It was time to play some ball.

The crowd was pretty small, but not bad for the weather, which was not looking good for the game. Heavy, water-soaked clouds hung low in the sky, threatening to drop its load once again on Snyder. And it started to rain again.

"It never rains here and this is the second time it has rained on us this season," said Pug Preston. "I just don't get it."

Cody Joe's parents were in the stands, but Grandpa and Grandma Taggert decided not to come. Chip and Kate were left at home with Aunt Wanda, screaming their heads off because they wanted to see Cody Joe play. Rue was afraid they would catch their death of colds in the damp and heavy air.

Jennifer and Veronica were in their usual spot. They were both covered in rain gear, prepared for whatever would come. However, it made talking hard, but neither could talk anyway without crying.

* * *

The whistle finally blew and the game with Sweetwater was finally being played. The ball headed skyward, but the moderate rain greatly slowed its trajectory, only getting as far as the 20-yard line, where Hank Cline had difficulty in corralling the loose, slippery pig hide. The ball squirted through his arms and ended up on the 15-yard line where Jack King saved the Blue Devils with the recovery.

Coach Heart noticed, right off the bat, that the Blue Devil offense was going to have trouble moving the football against the larger Sweetwater team without Butch Cassidy at fullback. Lester Jarvis was held to no gain on the first play from scrimmage and got two yards off tackle on the next. Kirby Tanner squeezed out five on third down, bringing up a punting situation.

Hank Cline had been given the punting chores, but his punt went for only 22 yards, setting up the Sweetwater offense at the Blue Devil 44-yard line. Sweetwater had already turned the field over on Snyder.

Sweetwater's bruising fullback, Pete Drexel, got the first call. Cody Joe and Joey Taylor met him head on at the 46, but the burly back surged through the two linebackers like butter and gained eight yards. From the 38-yard line, Sweetwater began a slow, but methodical push goalward, converting two fourth down carries. Finally, the Mustangs broke the goal line, kicked the extra point in a driving rain and took a 7-0 lead with only two minutes left in the first quarter.

That was pretty much how the game was played the rest of the afternoon. It was tough to score because of bad footing on a muddy field that already had its grass waylaid by games and practice. The passing game simply wasn't an option for either team. However, Snyder's defense gave the Devils a big break right before the half as Tony Carrillo recovered a fumble, following a great hit by Marc Sanchez at the Sweetwater 20-yard line. Snyder scored in only one play. Quarterback Lee Line covered the distance in an option play to the wide side of the field. But the Devils missed the extra point and were still trailing 7-6 at the half.

The relentless rain continued into the third quarter, leaving the playing field in no better shape than a pig's slop pen. Sweetwater was basically dominating Snyder, leading in first downs, 12-4, yards rushing, 136-58, and held the scoreboard, 7-6, heading into the fourth quarter.

Sweetwater boldly started a promising drive in the fourth quarter, eating up over four minutes of play and finishing a

56-yard drive with another TD by Drexel, who was Snyder's nemesis of the day. The Mustangs got the extra point again for a 14-6 lead.

Snyder showed some signs of life after the Sweetwater score. Taking the ball at the 36-yard line, the Blue Devils marched into Mustang territory with time quickly running out. That's when Jarvis finally cut loose with a long run to the Mustang eight-yard line with only 24 seconds left on the clock. However, Jarvis fumbled the ball after being caught from behind by the Sweetwater safety, Bryce Jennings.

Jarvis and Jennings were fighting for possession of the wet and loose ball. Neither could gain possession as the ball squirted this way and then that until a horde of players descended into a rugby scrum. Cody Joe and Pug had been trailing the play, but arrived in time to get in the fight. A huge pile-up resulted with some heated in-fighting on the bottom of the pile. When the referees finally pulled all the contenders off the heap, Cody Joe and Pug equally held a share of the ball, giving Snyder a chance to tie the game. Kissing at this point was by far preferable to losing to Sweetwater.

With six seconds left in the game, Heart called his last timeout to set up the last play. The rain had subsided somewhat, but was still a factor. Heart took a gamble. He announced his strange call and his Devils took to the field intent on following orders without question or one word of protest. Lee Line took the snap from center and went into a drop-back passing stance. But instead of throwing for the endzone, he threw a safe out to Kirby Tanner, who went unmolested into the endzone. Sweetwater 14, Snyder 12.

Sweetwater had been caught flat-footed with the play since Snyder had not thrown a pass all day. Jennifer Axel almost fell down the row of bleachers, tripping over her rain gear. Her Tanner had scored and her friends, Cody Joe and

Pug, had recovered a fumble to make it possible. She now felt like the Blue Devils could tie the game up with a two-point conversion. Veronica Slade was happy for Jennifer, but was so sick with dread of the final meeting with Cody Joe that she barely noticed how the game was going. Alexi Taggert, Pug's girlfriend, also got a lot of attention for his part in the fumble melee.

Coach Heart now had another decision to make. He decided not to push his luck with another pass so he sent fullback Hank Cline up the middle, just off the left shoulder of offensive guard T-Quay. The play went nowhere. Sweetwater had held, 14-12. At that very moment, it stopped raining.

* * *

The Blue Devils were devastated. T-Quay just laid on the ground, knowing he had missed his block at the line of scrimmage. Adam Quay tried to console his twin brother, but was caught up in the emotional quagmire himself and he started crying while on one knee next to T-Quay. Many of the players were left crying, while walking to the fieldhouse.

Cody Joe was left numb because he knew the moment had come that would change his life forever. He saw Veronica coming his way and he shuttered at the thought of meeting with her. What would he say to her at a time like this?

As it turns out, Cody Joe never said a word. Veronica came up to her boyfriend, and said, "Cody Joe, I want you to know that being your girlfriend was the best thing in my life.

"I'm sorry that I'm leaving town. I apologize. It's all my fault, so don't blame yourself. I'm proudly wearing your bracelet, but I want you to eventually find another girlfriend because you deserve that and, whoever she is, she will be the lucky one."

Unsurprisingly, Cody Joe didn't know how to reply to all that and it was as if Veronica instinctively knew of his limitations. She drew close to his dirty, smelly body, getting mud on herself from toe to head. She kissed him full on the lips for a full five seconds. Cody Joe was stunned.

He thought about trying to place his arm around her, but he was filthy. Once again Veronica saved him. She quickly turned away from the kiss and started running for the exit at the northwest corner of the stadium.

Cody Joe tried desperately to call her name, but any word to his lost love stuck in his throat. He was helpless.

He watched her run through the exit, turning westward to cross to the far side of Ave. M. From there, she headed down Ave. M, eventually being swallowed up by the parked cars along the street. Cody Joe Carter never saw Veronica Slade again.

* * *

Rue Carter didn't see the tearful departure of Veronica. She was looking for her defeated warrior, but was more focused on avoiding the puddles of water that blocked her path from the bleachers to the field. After negotiating through friends and puddles, she caught a glimpse of her son. His helmet was on the ground and he had his head bowed as if he were in great distress. These are things a mother knows when she sees it.

She walked up to him, and offered, "Cody Joe, are you OK?"

Cody Joe replied with tears rolling down his eyes, "No, Mom, I'm not OK."

Even with his repugnant body odor and mud covered uniform, he grabbed his mother and unabashedly cried into the nape of her neck. Rue knew better than to talk to her son in this moment of crisis, but she secretly wondered why he was so upset over losing a football game. It just didn't seem like him.

But Cody Joe knew he had lost so much more than a football game. This was much worse than the Little League crisis. He felt like he had lost his soul. He felt like he accounted for nothing. And all he had to remember was one long kiss from one Veronica Slade, who now could only be a lost memory in time.

Chapter 29

LATER

Three days before Christmas, Pug and Cody Joe were tossing the football around in the Carter's backyard with the only light coming from a porch light bulb. They were waiting on Rue Carter to ring the dinner bell.

Pug was spending the night with the Carters to celebrate the beginning of the Christmas break from school. Of course, both boys felt like they had a weight lifted off their shoulders and looked forward to some down time with each other.

But no matter the joy they were feeling, it was difficult catching a football with one dim light to work with. Pug had already hit Cody Joe in the face with one toss. Finally, the two gave up on the game and sprawled out on the dead winter grass. Each boy looked skyward at the massive show of stars brilliantly displayed on this West Texas evening.

Pug asked, "What is your mother cooking for us tonight?"

Cody Joe said, "I think she's doing tacos just for us. I love her tacos."

"Me too. Her tacos are world famous. I'm already glad I came tonight," Pug said while licking his proverbial chops.

Cody Joe quickly turned the conversation around, asking, "Pug, do you realize that we have finished our first semester of junior high and now have a full football season under our belts?"

"Yeah. It seems like a hundred years ago when we put on those pads for the first time. I can't wait for next season. I know one thing; we're going to beat Sweetwater. By the way, do you ever think Nate Christian will come back to town? If he does, that can't be good for you."

"You know, I haven't even thought about Nate in a long time, but now that you mention it, I can smell him right now. Remember when he would wear the same underwear that he used to practice in for days on end? I doubt he's coming back though. He would have already done it if he had any bad intentions for me. The police are keeping my dad informed about once a month, but there has been little information coming from them."

"Well, I would be worried all the same. He tried to rip you open. And I want to apologize to you for not jumping right in to help you. I've been bothered about that since it happened."

Cody Joe sat up to get some circulation going in his arms. "Oh, don't think about that. I know you got my back. It never crossed my mind that you weren't behind me all the way.

"But I will say this, Pug. What I really miss is spending time with you at school. You're always busy with Alexi. We used to always be together. I want us to always be friends."

Pug was a little taken aback by this unexpected declaration by his friend, saying, "We'll always be friends, Cody Joe. I can guarantee you that. I guess I thought we were together at practice and rode together on road trips. We sat with our girlfriends at all the Tiger football games. We've spent a lot of time together."

"I know, but it's not the same as it was. You've left me to have lunch alone with Tracks and Butch. Now don't get me wrong, I like Butch a lot and consider him a friend, but there are only so many of his jokes that I can take."

"I get your pain on that account. Alexi has certainly saved me from some of that torture. But hey, I'm willing to make a small compromise. I'll have lunch with you at the Snack

Shack two times a week. I don't think Alexi will mind when I explain the situation. After all, she's your cousin."

Cody Joe replied, "You don't know women very good, do you? She's going to be all over your case if you try that."

"Oh, and you know women? Who's the one right now without a girl on his arm?

"By the way, have you ever heard from Veronica?"

Cody Joe replied, "Oh sure. We write back and forth ever so often, but I know now that she is never coming back. I think the Lord wants me to move on. I can't live like this forever."

Carter rolled over on his side, propping up his head with his left arm, and offered, "I think junior high is great, but in many ways, it has been a really tough year for me. Losing Veronica was a real bummer and that still hurts some. And you still have Alexi. I have to admit, Pug, that I'm jealous of you."

"Don't be jealous, Cody Joe. Do something about it. You could have a girlfriend tomorrow if you really wanted one. Alexi is always telling me that Anne Archer has eyes for you. There are probably a dozen girls out there who would want to go out with one of the linebackers on the football team."

"Who is this Anne Archer?" Cody Joe asked.

"You know Anne Archer. She's that cute twirler in the band and she is a real knockout if you ask me. She's had eyes on you since the Nate Christian thing. I think a lot of girls fell for you after that, but you were taken then and you are free now."

Cody Joe pondered those words and then said, "I don't know if I'm ready for that. I couldn't even talk to Veronica in complete sentences. I just nodded a lot."

"Well, you better get over that – and fast. You'll be left with Butch and Tracks for the rest of your life. Do you ever see them getting a girlfriend in the next millennium?"

Both boys rolled in laughter as Rue Carter called, "Tacos anyone?"

MAY, 1970
Chui Lai, South Vietnam

It was 12:30 a.m. when Spec. 4 Cody Joe Carter started the process of waking his good friend Pfc. Noah "Cue Ball" Brantley from a deep sleep. And it was a process with Cue. Once asleep, you had to shake him until he fitfully responded.

Cody Joe had just finished his two-hour watch on the perimeter of Company B's jungle camp site. Carter had done Brantley a favor, letting him sleep an extra half hour, but the favor didn't sink in completely with Cue.

"Cody Joe, leave me alone. It can't be two hours yet," Cue said while trying to roll over on his jungle air mattress for a more comfortable position.

"Cue, it's time for you to pull guard duty; get yourself up now. I've already pulled a half-hour of your guard, so don't give me any problems."

Cue reluctantly crawled out of his temporary sack and started the other process of shaking off the cobwebs. When Cody Joe thought Cue had been awake long enough to perform his task, he said to Cue, "You're on until 0200. Wake Neil when your shift is over. He's just about 30 feet over to your right. You got that, Cue?"

"Yeah, I got that. Neil at 0200."

Cody Joe laid down on his portable air mattress and was out like a light the moment he closed his eyes.

So, a frustrated Cue Ball began the third process of pulling night guard. He started by doing all the right things. He checked the M60 machine gun in front of him to make sure a new belt of ammunition had been locked in. He checked his own M16 rifle to make sure it also was fully loaded with a fresh magazine. He discovered his magazine was not at full capacity, so he put three new rounds into the clip he was currently using. Cue then checked his two Claymore detonators to make sure they were attached to the two mines pre-set in front of his position before nightfall. Claymore mines are shaped charges that will only send its blast forward. That makes it perfect to place anywhere from 50 to 100 feet in front of your position. When you squeeze the hand-held detonator, it sets off a blasting cap attached to the mine and causes the C4 explosive to explode, sending not only a powerful blast forward, but also hundreds of small steel balls flying into whatever it is pointed at. It is a deadly deterrent to any enemy approaching your position.

He then began the monotonous task of "pulling guard," noticing that it was extremely dark on this particular night. There was no moon to provide light. The brush and trees in front of him were swallowed up by the night. It made Cue uncomfortable, and this light-hearted soul was rarely put off by the changes presented to him by nature.

It was well into the first hour of Cue's guard when he heard the crackle of a dead tree limb in front of him. Already somewhat jumpy, Cue tried the best he could to see through the blackness that was beyond him, but it was a futile effort. Cue didn't want to bother Cody Joe because he was deep in slumber, but Brantley was now in a state of deep alert with all his senses and adrenaline pumping through his body. If only he could see in front of him better. He thought about using his flashlight in the direction of the sound, but correctly reasoned that any bright light would only serve to worsen his already limited night vision.

Just then, Cue actually caught sight of something moving about 25 yards out. Instinctively, Cue raised his M16 to firing position, disengaged the safety and waited for one more confirmation of movement. Confirmation came quickly with another movement detected only 20 yards away. Cue fired his rifle at the sound without really seeing his target. However, when he fired, he heard a low, almost silent, guttural sound that came across to Cue like a blaring sound system at a movie theater.

With Cue's shot, Cody Joe sprang to alert, automatically taking position behind the M60.

Now, Cue completely ignored the silence protocol and yelled, "Cody Joe, I hit something out there and I don't think it's an iguana. We might be under attack."

Cody Joe didn't take Cue's warning lightly, but like Cue, he couldn't see much beyond 10 feet in front of him. Because of Cue's shot, the whole perimeter of Company B was now awake and battle ready.

Cody Joe had one finger on the trigger of the M60 and one hand on the Claymore detonator. It was only seconds later when Neil Albright jumped to the side of Cody Joe and Cue. Spec. 4 Albright was the operator of the M60. It was his job to tote the heavy weapon and take care of it. However, he saw that Cody Joe was already behind his M60, so he grabbed Cody Joe's M16 and made it operational by taking off the safety. In the fourth platoon, everyone had been trained to use every weapon in the platoon, so it didn't matter much who was behind what weapon. Pfc. Jim Baker soon followed with his grenade launcher.

"Jim, put a couple of grenade rounds just over that tree line out there," Cody Joe suggested.

Baker was good at his job, but he could barely see the tree

line through the darkness. However, he had helped Cody Joe set out the Claymores before dark, so he had a pretty good idea of the distance. In his best estimation, he lobbed two of his grenade canisters in front of their position, hoping to get some definitive result.

There was one loud cry, and all four instantly knew it was human. Further confirmation came when full out fire was heard from down the line of the perimeter. Company B was under attack, probably by a North Vietnamese Army unit. The Viet Cong rarely produced all out attacks on company size elements.

Cody Joe said, "Save your ammunition until they come at us. I don't want to waste the ammo we have."

Company B commander, Capt. Jim Stillwell, had ordered flares to the north of the perimeter where Cody Joe and his crew had taken position for the night.

Second Lieutenant Craig Smith, an ROTC grad, was in charge of Cody Joe's platoon. He was moving up and down his perimeter line, giving instruction.

"All you guys alright?" He asked. "Hold this position. I've gotten confirmation that a full attack is already taking place down the line. They'll be coming here soon, so be ready."

Lt. Smith then moved on down the line as Albright exclaimed, "As if we didn't know to be ready. That was really useful information."

At least, the foursome could now see the tree line as Capt. Stillwell kept the flares coming. They were grateful they saw no attack underway at their position while significant action was clearly taking place at various points on the perimeter circle.

Then it came. Rushing out of the tree line toward Cody Joe and his platoon mates were NVA regulars, about 50 in all. Cody Joe squeezed the detonator trigger, causing a deadly blast to rake through the oncoming onslaught. There weren't 50 anymore, but some survived and continued the attack. Cody Joe started raking the area with M60 rounds, getting good results. Cue and Albright were firing short three round bursts from their M16s while Baker was dumping grenade canisters into the thick of the charging NVA troops. Cody Joe set off the last of his Claymores, adding to the NVA death toll.

There was enough fire power from the foursome to quell the attack on their position, but there remained some heavy action down the line. It was then that artillery rounds from LZ Stinson began to fall with full force. Stinson was the base for the heavy artillery company and it could hit just about every target in the operational area of the 198th Infantry Brigade. Capt. Stillwell had called in for the strike and it was obviously doing some damage as the assault seemed to be losing steam.

Cue stood up to see if he could see any more movement

while the flare was giving off its light. A shot rang out from one of the wounded NVA soldiers, lying in front of the foursome's position, hitting Cue in the chest. Cue buckled and fell to the ground. Cody Joe didn't think his heart could beat any faster, but when he saw his friend go down, he raced to his rescue without a moment's hesitation. Cody Joe drew fire to himself during his flight, but was not hit. He could see that Cue was still alive before the flare expired.

He grabbed Cue in a low crawl approach and said, "Cue, I'm here. I'm going to get you outta here. Just relax."

"Cody Joe, I'm hit bad. I don't think I'm going to make it. It hurts bad. Cody Joe are you here?"

"I'm here, Cue. Just hang on," Cody Joe answered as he gazed upon Cue's sucking chest wound for the first time."

Cody Joe emptied his stomach at the horrible sight, but Cue didn't even notice as he went in and out of consciousness.

Cody Joe tore a piece of Cue's T-shirt and made a makeshift bandage, tying it over the wound. He knew it wouldn't do much good since Cue was bleeding profusely. But it was the best he could do.

He then heard the rotors of several choppers to his rear. Capt. Stillwell had a landing zone cleared out on the south of the perimeter and medivacs and ammunition resupply were already taking place. Cody Joe pulled Cue behind their position and then literally carried him to one of the rescue choppers. Albright and Baker manned the position.

A medic from one of the helicopters met Cody Joe, who was struggling to just keep moving on his feet with Brantley's dead weight.

"We've got him now. We'll get him out of here," the medic said.

"Tend to that wound quick. I really didn't have much to use to stop the bleeding. He's lost a lot of blood," Cody Joe told Cue's new lifeline.

Cue was now unconscious, but still alive. Cody Joe couldn't even say a proper goodbye to his companion, but he knew enough that it would be a miracle from heaven if he lived.

On the way back to his position, Cody Joe grabbed four new belts of M60 rounds and four boxes of M16 rounds. He didn't see any grenade canisters. If Baker ran out of ammo, he would just have to use Cue's M16.

Cody Joe, Jim and Neil kept the attack on their position at bay for the next two hours, as Apache attack helicopters arrived and started raking the tree line with rockets, grenade canisters and 50 caliber machine gun rounds. The Navy was also doing their part as fighter jets gave a napalm run on the far side of the trees where it had been decided where the NVA's staging area was operating.

Those two factors literally halted the NVA advance and the quietness of the jungle descended once again on Company B. Cody Joe took assessment of the ammo that was left and decided to send Baker to the rear to pick up anything he could get his hands on. After all, Baker was out of grenade canisters and needed resupply the most. And Cody Joe had no more Claymores to work with and couldn't set anymore out even if he had them because that would mean going out near the tree line.

Capt. Stillwell was making his own sweep of the perimeter, and when he reached Cody Joe's position, he told the threesome, "I think we have really hurt them, but they are still out there. Expect another attack. We've lost some good men ourselves, but we can't let down. We have to protect this ring or everything is lost."

Cody Joe thought, "Protect this ring? I've been in the ring my whole life. I'll never get out of the ring, but I'm not going down."

After Stillwell left, Cody Joe literally canceled the silence protocol by yelling at the tree line, "Coach Nix, are you out there? Well, keep sending them. Bring it on. Bring them all. I won't quit. We won't quit. You haven't beaten us yet."

And then the attack resumed.

* * *

Four years later, Cody Joe was sitting in his new born baby's bedroom, slowly swaying to the creak of the old rocking chair. He thought his son had to be the most perfect baby in the world. He also wondered if his son would ever have to be in the ring.

Cody Joe was still haunted by those dark days in Vietnam. Every time he sat alone in down time, his thoughts drifted back to that horrible night when he almost lost his life. His Purple Heart medal was proof of that.

But mostly, Cody Joe thought about Noah "Cue Ball" Brantley. He always wondered if he could have done more for his friend. Cue died three days after being shot on that fateful night in 1970. Cody Joe never saw Cue again after placing him on the medivac chopper. It was closure that Cody Joe wanted, and that was a commodity that would never be offered to this new father.

Carter, however, knew now that he must live for this new baby boy. He was convinced that he had to spend his life directing this child toward a rich heritage. He prayed that this perfect child would never have to see the horrors of war. He wanted a better life for his son – one without the tragedy that came with the ring.

The ring would always be a part of Cody Joe Carter. He would never be able to escape how he was perpetually tied to that symbol. Nate Christian had tried to kill him after animosity developed from the ring. Cue, his best friend, was killed by the ring and Cody Joe had received a shoulder wound. He never left the battlefield until the fighting stopped.

Cody Joe had survived. He wondered why. All he knew was his whole life had placed him as the man in the ring.

Made in the USA
Middletown, DE
21 April 2023